"WHY DO YOU KEEP DOING THIS TO ME, Mc-BRIDE?" SHE ASKED SOFTLY. "WHAT IS IT YOU WANT FROM ME?"

"I already told you," he answered, his thumb brushing lightly over the whispered question. "A kiss."

"A kiss?" She said the word as if she had never heard it before, knowing she was in the arms of a man who had already proved he could not be trusted with any manner of compromises. "You've already kissed me. More times than you should have."

He shook his head slowly, the moonlight tarnishing the thick waves of his hair. "Not nearly enough, by my reckoning."

Marsha Canham

UNDER THE DESERT MOON

A DELL BOOK

Published by
Dell Publishing
a division of
Bantam Doubleday Dell Publishing Group, Inc.
1540 Broadway
New York, New York 10036

ISBN: 0-440-20612-X

Printed in the United States of America

Published simultaneously in Canada

October 1992

10 9 8 7 6 5 4 3 2

RAD

This one is for The Chief,
who passed his love of westerns on to me;
and for The Mother,
who tolerated the pair of us
whooping and hollering in front of
the old black-and-white TV.

Prologue

"Don't let her get away!"

Aubrey ducked low and scrambled deeper into the thickets, heedless of the sharp thorns that tore and stabbed at her bare arms like a thousand fiery lances. She prayed the shadows were dark enough to hide her. Her heart was pounding wildly, her breath was drawn in labored gasps that were more like sobs as she grasped for the air that might save her legs from crumbling to chalk beneath her. The voices were all around her: right, left, front, rear. She was trapped. She would not even have the darkness to protect her much longer, for already there was a faint smudge of purple light on the horizon. With the coming of dawn, she would be naked and vulnerable in the sparse vegetation that grew along the arroyo.

Aubrey sobbed again as her cotton nightdress snagged on a thornbush. The resultant tear sounded like a scream on the night air and she huddled closer to the ground, crawling on hands and knees over the rough terrain.

"Over there!" someone cried, the voice coming from thirty yards behind her and moving in the opposite direction.

Aubrey swallowed at the lump of terror that had lodged in her throat and leaned her forehead against the cool bark of a tree, grateful for a moment's respite. She had to clench her teeth hard to keep them from chattering out loud, frightened that the slightest sound would betray her presence in the arroyo.

They had come an hour ago; six of them. As stealthily as death in the night. They were efficient, practiced. Two set off for the bunkhouse, two stood guard in the yard while the final pair of killers crept soundlessly up to the second-story bedrooms. They were holding guns over Jonathan and Luisa Granger's bed before the frightened couple had blinked fully awake.

Making no attempt to conceal their features or their deadly intentions, one of the intruders lit a lamp and placed it on the sideboard beside the bed.

"Evenin', Granger. Pleased to catch you to home." The words were hissed through stained and broken teeth. His red-veined, bulbous nose looked grotesque in the flickering light, as did the badly pockmarked skin that underscored a thickly scarred half-closed eye.

"What the hell do you want, Holwell?" Jonathan demanded. "What do you mean by breaking in here like this?"

"We got a message for you from Mr. Fleming. Seems he offered you a reasonable settlement for this land of yours. Offered you double what most of the other dirt farmers got. Seems you insulted the man by refusing. Embarrassed him by trying to get the others to stand up against him. Mr. Fleming don't like to be embarrassed."

Aubrey, wakened by the harsh, foreign voice, emerged from her room and stood in the dim wash of light that spilled into the hallway. One eye was blinded by the fist she was using to knuckle away the sleep; the other took a moment to realize the scene unfolding at the end of the hallway was not part of any nightmare, but very real. The man her father had once brusquely identified to her as Scud Holwell was standing over her parents, pointing a gun. A second gunman, similarly recognized by his shock of white hair and almost totally colorless features, was standing with his back to the hall, but with the stock of a shotgun protruding from under one arm.

"Mr. Fleming wants the deed, Granger," Holwell said slickly. "And he wants it tonight."

Jonathan tightened the arm he held around his wife's shoulders. He was bare to the waist; the reddish-blond mat of hair on his chest made it appear as if his torso were on fire.

"I already gave Fleming my answer, Holwell. The ranch is not for sale. Even if the deed was here—which it isn't—you'd never get me to sign it over."

"No?" Holwell grinned and glanced casually at the personal items that cluttered the top of the sideboard. "Funny thing, you sayin' that. Some of your other greaser-lovin' friends said the same thing . . . before Whitey 'n' me convinced them otherwise."

Without warning he reached out a hand and swept the jumble of small stoppered bottles and painstakingly acquired treasures into a shattered heap on the floor. Equally carelessly, he yanked open the top drawer and rifled through the contents, tossing some onto the floor, tucking others—a delicately worked silk handkerchief among them—beneath his sweat- and grease-stained shirt.

"I told you, the deed isn't here!" Jonathan said, his voice raised to cover his wife's sudden cry.

Holwell looked from Jonathan, to Luisa, to the delicately carved sandalwood box he had taken from the drawer. It was locked—a trifling nuisance as he struck the brass filigree with the butt of his pistol. A flick of a stubby thumbnail opened the lid, and a long, low whistle gave the contents a nod of approval.

"Well, well now, ain't this purdy," he said, lifting a gleaming emerald broach out of its bed of crushed velvet.

"Please," Luisa whispered, ignoring the warning squeeze in her husband's arm. "The broach belonged to my mother, and to her mother before that. It is all I have to remember them by, all I shall have of my heritage to pass on to my daughter."

"All you have, eh?" Scud Holwell's mouth stretched into a leer. "I wouldn't exactly say that, señora."

Luisa Granger's classic beauty reflected her proud, Castilian blood. Olive skin framed vivid, wide-set blue eyes; her hair fell long and thick in lustrous raven curls to her waist. Bringing three children into the world had not altered her slim, graceful figure, nor did the cheap flannel nightdress she wore conceal it.

Aubrey, flattened breathlessly against a wall out in the hallway, pressed icy cold fingers against her lips to stifle a cry as she saw Holwell walk slowly around to her mother's side of the bed.

"Maybe you can tell me where your husband keeps the deed, señora," Holwell murmured. "Maybe it's worth this here trinket for you to do so?"

Luisa stiffened, trying not to shrink away from the foul odor of his body and breath as he leaned closer.

"No," she stammered. "I . . . I do not know where it is."

"I think you do."

"Leave her alone, Holwell," Jonathan warned, his muscles tensing as he gauged the distance from the bed to a rifle half-hidden behind a panel of curtain beside the bed. "She doesn't know anything."

"Maybe she don't. Then again, maybe she can help us persuade you to cooperate."

Jonathan stiffened, a move countered with oily swiftness by the albino, who was only a beat slower in thrusting the barrel of the shotgun up against Granger's throat.

"The deed is in town," Jonathan said again. "I keep it in the bank."

Holwell sighed and ran his stubby fingers over the shiny blue-black length of Luisa's hair.

"I tell you, it isn't here!" Jonathan snarled, but his words were choked short as Whitey drove the double barrels deeper into the soft flesh under his chin.

"Maybe I think you're lying," Holwell said casually. "Maybe I don't think a greaser-lover would have the savvy to lock a deed up safe and sound in a bank . . . especially since Mr. Fleming owns the only bank in Santa Fe." He grinned as the shock registered on Jonathan's face. "Has since this afternoon. And didn't he just have to read through some of the records to find out who his most valued customers were? Danged if your name weren't one of the first to crop up."

"All this . . . for one section of land?" Jonathan asked.

Holwell shrugged impassively and stroked Luisa's hair again. She flinched out of his reach and pressed closer to her husband.

"Not just one, Granger, and you know it. You're at the center of all Mr. Fleming's troubles. Once you sign over, they'll all sign. All those bloody peons and scratch farmers will be out of our hair once and for all. As for your land—hell, it controls the water rights for most of the valley."

"I've already told Fleming, I'll do nothing to cut off or divert the flow!"

"That ain't the point. Mr. Fleming wants to be the one to make the decisions. How long do you think them dumb farmers will stand by for cattle grazing on the best

land? How long before they string barbed wire and
build dams to block off the water routes? Cattle gotta
feed. Cattle gotta water. These damned Mex *campesinos*
already give us enough headaches with their damned
sheep; we don't need a flock o' wide-eyed corn growers
givin' us more aggravation over a few trampled crops."

"The Mexicans were here first," Jonathan pointed out
angrily. "So were their *damned sheep!*"

"Yeah, but we'll be here last. And I ain't here to argue with you, Granger, so if you'll jest give over what we
came for maybe you and your missus here will live to
see daylight."

"You aren't stupid enough to kill us, Holwell," Jonathan grated. "The valley is a keg of dynamite now—kill
us, and it could blow into a full-scale range war. Not
even a pimp like Fleming wants to see that happen."

Holwell took a slow, deep breath. In a move too sudden to anticipate, he swung his pistol up, cracking the
barrel against Jonathan's temple, hard enough to daze
him, easy enough for him to be aware of Luisa being
dragged out of the protective circle of his arm. Jonathan
lurched drunkenly across the bed after her, but was
brought up short by a second blow from the stock of
Whitey's shotgun, a blow that opened his cheek to the
bone and sent a torrent of blood streaming down his
face. Stunned, he sprawled half on the bed, half on the
floor, his wound staining the stark white sheets crimson
beneath him.

"Get the bastard on his feet," Holwell hissed. "Make
sure his eyes stay open. We'll see how long it takes him
to start talking."

Holwell holstered his gun and, grasping two fistfuls of
Luisa's nightgown, tore the garment open from throat
to hem. She screamed and tried to twist out of his grip,
but his hand clawed around a skein of long black hair
and jerked her head in a painful arch backward, slam-

ming it against the wall. His body pressed lewdly against hers, and he laughed as her hands flayed ineffectually against his chest and throat.

"Looks like we got us a real fire-cat here, Whitey. Damnation—" The scarred and misshapen eyelid opened wider as one hairy paw closed around the firm swell of her breast. "Ain't she a sight fer sore eyes!"

Whitey Martin's colorless eyes glazed over as he watched Holwell lower his mouth to the writhing woman. "Boss ain't gonna like you messin' around too much," he rasped. His voice, damaged in a failed attempt to hang him, perfectly complemented the skeletally thin body and chalk-white complexion.

"The boss ain't here," Holwell grunted. "How's he gonna know what happened unless you tell him?"

"There's kids, ain't there? They got eyes and ears, don't they?"

"No!" Luisa cried, her efforts to dislodge Holwell's slippery, grasping mouth coming to an abrupt, horrified halt. "No, please! Leave them be! They have done nothing! They are no part of this!"

Holwell grinned. "I hear one of 'em is a she-bitch. If she's anything like her mama—" A calloused hand was thrust roughly between Luisa's thighs and the rest of what he said was drowned by a scream of pain.

Aubrey flinched from the wall boards as if they were suddenly red hot. At thirteen years of age, she was old enough to know what a man like Holwell wanted from women, and how he went about getting it. Her stomach knotted with fear and she searched around frantically in the gloom. Where could she run? Where could she hide?

The twins! She had to get them to safety first; it was what Mama and Papa would expect her to do.

Jeremy and Jason's room faced the front of the house, their window overlooked the neat patch of green grass Luisa had so lovingly coaxed out of the brown plain. Aubrey's room faced east toward the river and the looming magnificence of the Sangre de Cristo mountains. Between the house and foothills, a pair of five-year-old boys who made a regular game out of burrowing into coyote's lairs could find a thousand places to hide, but to get them out of the house, she would first have to bring them from their room to hers.

Aubrey inched her foot along the wooden floor, her nightgown making her feel as bright as a beacon in the light that throbbed from the bedroom door. As quickly as the fear had flushed through her, anger replaced it, rising in a heated wave to flood her cheeks and make her clear blue eyes spark defiantly. How dare these animals force their way into her father's home! How dare they hold a gun on him and threaten him under his own roof! If she had a gun of her own . . . if she could just fetch one of the rifles from Papa's study . . . !

Jonathan Granger was justifiably proud of the ranch house he had built with his own two hands; meticulous about its upkeep. When Aubrey gingerly turned the brass latch and opened the door to the twins' room, the well-oiled hinges moved without a squeak.

It was the sound of scraping wood just over her shoulder that made Aubrey jump and gasp out loud.

Five-year-old Jason Granger was standing behind the door, his brother shadowing him to the left, the two of them straining mightily to hold aloft a thick wooden beam.

"We could have killed you," Jason announced quite calmly. He glanced at Jeremy, who nodded in vigorous agreement before they set the beam aside. "We heard shouting and we were going to have a look, but then we thought it must be robbers, so we thought we better stay here so Papa didn't have to worry about shooting us. Have they gone? Has Papa chased them away?"

"No, *queridos*," Aubrey whispered, touching a finger to her lips to quiet them. "The robbers have not gone yet. You are going to have to be brave a little while longer."

"I want to go to Mama," Jeremy wailed.

"Me too," said Jason, visibly fighting the urge to cry.

"No. No, the *yanquis* are very bad and Papa is very angry. He would be even angrier if we put ourselves in the way. Instead, we must run from the house and bring help."

As she spoke, Aubrey hustled them to the door, silencing the beginnings of a tearful mutiny with a warning pinch on each of their arms. They had to move quickly; they would not have much more time before the men came in search of them.

"Hurry now," she hissed and sped them across the hallway and into her own room. It was a warm night and she had left the shutters of her window open. The moon at once seemed too bright, but there was nothing to be done about it. The branches of a sturdy alder leaned against the wall, and Jason was out the window, shimmying along the fattest limb even as Aubrey lifted Jeremy to the sill and gave him a quick hug and kiss for luck.

"Remember: run as fast as you can to the Taylors. I'll be right behind you, and we can make it a race to see who reaches the adobe first."

"We'll win," Jeremy declared, brightening. "We always win when we race you."

"Then you had better be especially good tonight, for I shall be running with the wind on my feet."

Accepting the challenge, Jeremy launched himself out the window and scrambled nimbly down the gnarled joints of the tree. Aubrey watched until they had cleared the corrals, and were halfway to the belt of thick brush and cactus that lined the banks of the arroyo.

Luisa moaned, startling Aubrey's attention away from the moonlit yard. It was a low, plaintive sound, much like the groan a dying animal might make. It continued on and on, causing the hairs across the nape of Aubrey's neck to prickle and stand on end. She glanced once, longingly, after the twins, but something made her walk to the door, made her step out into the hall and stare into the garish light coming from her parents' room.

Luisa Granger lay spread-eagled on the bed, pinned there by the massive, heaving bulk of Scud Holwell. Blood from a split lip and a cut over her eye was splattered on her hair, her skin. Her cries punctuated each of Holwell's savage thrusts, her voice echoing with unimaginable pain and shame.

Aubrey pressed her hands over her mouth, stifling her own scream of terror as she saw Jonathan Granger shove the distracted Whitey Martin to one side and dive for Holwell. He clawed his hands into the bullish neck, his rage giving him the strength to drag the gunman off his wife's body and smash the ugly face once, twice with fists as hard and unyielding as granite. His nose crushed to a bloody pulp, Holwell was flung back against the wooden footboard of the bed, cracking the seasoned mahogany under his weight. Whitey Martin recovered enough of his senses to leap on Jonathan from behind, but the rancher's fury was at its peak and a hammered blow to Whitey's gut lifted the albino and sent him hurling against the wall. Jonathan lunged for his rifle, raising it and cocking it in one smooth motion.

The sound of two gunshots fired simultaneously reverberated in the small room like an explosion. Jonathan stood by the side of the bed, his eyes blazing, his rifle barrel sending a thin finger of smoke curling into the yellow lamplight. Scud Holwell crouched by the foot of the bed, his pistol held steady in a hand spattered red with his own blood.

For a long moment, it seemed as though both men had missed, but in the next, Aubrey saw her father's chest collapse into itself in a tangle of flesh and blood. His mouth gaped and his hands clutched at fistfuls of empty air as he fell backward, the life gone out of him before he struck the floor.

Holwell stared at the shredded flesh of his upper arm and had barely cursed his surprise when Luisa was flinging herself at him, her nails raking a bleeding path from his hairline to the edge of his jaw. Roaring in agony, he struck out blindly with the hand that still held the gun. The barrel caught Luisa on the temple and struck her head sideways, snapping her neck with such force it sounded like another gunshot.

Someone else was screaming.

It took several long moments for Aubrey to realize the scream was coming from her own throat, a strange and terrifying sound that shocked both men into turning and gaping out into the hallway.

Aubrey backed away from the light, still screaming, still seeing her father's crumpled body and her mother's wide, sightless eyes. And then, suddenly, she was running. She was somehow out in the open courtyard, running toward the sanctuary of the arroyo and the protective shield of brush and cactus. Her feet were flying across the sand as if the devil himself were snapping at her heels, yet the ground passed beneath her like molasses, sucking at her ankles, slowing her to a frantic crawl with the brush still a hundred yards away.

There was an explosion from somewhere behind her and she felt a whistle of hot air sting her hair and scalp. Another shot and another shattered the moonlit silence, augmented by the shouts and pounding fury of footsteps chasing after her.

She veered for the corral and dove beneath the lowest post, scraping the skin off her knees and the palms of her hands. The horses scattered as she ran past them, their screams and snorts of outrage following her out the other side and into the shadows alongside the bunkhouse.

"Don't let her get away!"

Men were running across the yard toward the arroyo, hoping to cut her off. Scud Holwell was the last to enter the chase, but the one most determined to catch her.

"Get the little bitch!" he shouted. "Don't let her get away!"

Aubrey plunged into the stiff scrub brush and burrowed into the deepest shadows for cover. The voices were everywhere: right, left, front, rear. She was trapped! She had to get away, had to ignore the pain of the stones and sharp pebbles that pierced her flesh, the thorns and brambles that scratched her face and arms, and snagged repeatedly on her nightdress.

"Over there!"

The voice was thirty yards behind her and moving in the opposite direction. Aubrey swallowed hard to dislodge the lump of terror that had swelled her throat shut, and leaned her forehead against the cool bark of a tree. The bark moved, the tree shifted, and the shadows took on the human form of Scud Holwell. He laughed when he saw the look of horror on her face. The great bellowing howl of triumph overpowered Aubrey's screams as she saw the bloodied hands reaching down for her.

She was dragged, kicking and fighting, out of the scrub and thrown into a circle of grinning, leering faces. The albino was the only one who studied her without expression; the others were looking on avidly as Holwell stood forward and brushed the tumble of black hair away from her face.

"Well now, what do we have here, boys?"

At thirteen, Aubrey's breasts had already blossomed

with the promise of womanhood. Her waist was narrow, her legs long and lithe as a young colt's. She had her mother's hair, the gleaming black waves framing a face that trembled on the brink of great beauty. She had her mother's eyes as well, deep startling violet blue that flashed and smoldered with emotions too vivid and headstrong to ever be governed by caution. They glowered almost black with the hatred she felt that moment, hatred Holwell seemed to relish and feed off to fuel his own malevolent lusts.

"Jest like her mama, boys," he said thickly. He wiped the back of his hand across his mouth to smear the slick of blood and mucus draining from his mashed nose, and grinned. "Only this one ain't gonna cheat us out of a little fun."

One of the other gunmen hitched his trousers impatiently. "Quit wastin' time, Holwell. Someone's bound to see the fire soon and come to have a look-see."

Aubrey turned and saw the reason why she could see their faces so clearly. The windows on the main floor of the ranch house glowed brightly; orange and yellow flames were lapping up curtains, leaping from chair to chair inside. They were burning her home to cover their tracks and make it easier for the sheriff to dismiss the death of her parents as accidental. They obviously did not plan to leave any witnesses to dispute the "accident," a certainty Aubrey accepted with a calmness far beyond her youthful years.

"Lookee them claws gettin' ready to take us on," Scud growled. "By God, I'm gonna enjoy this."

Aubrey cried out in pain as Holwell snatched a fistful of her hair and jerked her around to face him. His mouth, wet and slimy, crushed down over hers, gagging her with the sour taste of rotten teeth and blood. His free hand fumbled at her breast, his fingers pinching her nipple until it swelled and stiffened from sheer agony.

Aubrey kicked and fought, ignoring her own pain as she scratched for his eyes, his ears, the bleeding runnels her mother had already torn into his skin. But she hadn't a tenth of his bulbous strength, and it was with a grunt of contempt he struck her across the cheek with the flat of his hand and sent her sprawling into the dust at his feet.

Dazed, she rolled weakly onto her knees and started to crawl blindly away from the brilliant glow of the fire. Hands grabbed her roughly around the ankles and hauled her back, flipping her over so that still more hands could stretch her arms high above her head and pin them flat on the ground. She heard the sound of tearing cloth and felt the cool night air on her bared flesh. She managed to wrench a leg free and knew a moment's satisfaction as she felt her heel sink into Holwell's bulging groin, but the victory was short-lived. Two more vicious slaps knocked her half-senseless. A third brutal blow to her stomach all but crippled her under waves of pain and nausea.

Greedy hands spread her limbs wide apart.

Coarse, hurtful fingers poked and prodded and hinted at the forthcoming horror as Holwell slowly unbuttoned his trousers and pushed them down below his hips.

"The game is over, sweet thing," he muttered thickly. "You can keep on fighting if you like it better that way, but the game is over."

"Scud! *Over there!*"

Whitey Martin was thrusting a yellowed finger toward the shadows beside the bunkhouse. Six saddled horses— their own—were thundering off into the darkness, driven by two screeching dervishes who pelted their rumps with sticks and stones.

"Christ almighty!" Holwell shouted, flinging himself away from Aubrey. "Get them bloody horses! And get them damned kids!"

Four of the six men surrounding Aubrey raced after the bolting horses. Holwell hitched his trousers with a curse as he stalked toward the barn, his gun drawn and searching out two small targets. The man left to stand guard over Aubrey suddenly found his eyes, nose, and mouth filled with a stinging hail of dirt and pebbles. Staggering back, he gave Aubrey the opening she needed to reach up, pull the gun out of his holster, cock and fire it.

The exploding recoil of the heavy pistol and the roar of surprised agony from the gunman were more than enough to give her legs new strength. She tripped once, losing hold of the gun, but scrambled to her feet again and ran, scarcely aware of the popping sounds of gunfire behind her. Something small, hot, and stingingly sharp pierced her arm, but she kept running. She tumbled down the bank of the arroyo and tore the soles of her feet on the glasslike shards of shale and stone, but she kept running.

Desperation pumped speed and stamina into her legs and, her arm awash with blood, her lungs screaming for air, she headed for the one place she knew the twins were sure to go. It was their secret place; a fissure in the lava rock that led to a deep cavern the size and shape of a giant's maw. She knew, as surely as she knew the sun rose over the rim of the Sangre de Cristo mountains each morning, the twins would be inside waiting for her.

By moonlight she saw the rocks and the latticework of crevices that split the boulders like lightning forks. The cave was there, in the darkest heart of the shadows, and she was almost at the entrance when a form detached itself from the rocks and moved to block her path.

It was Holwell!

He was grinning and the blood from his wounds had drenched the front of his shirt red, had slicked the hooked talons that were his fingers, splashing her skin as he reached out to grab her. Aubrey opened her mouth to scream, but no sound came forth. She screamed again . . . and again . . .

•

Aubrey sat bolt upright in bed, drowning in her own sweat, chilled to the bone and shivering as if the window had burst open to an icy gust of wind. Her cheeks were streaked with tears, her hands were clenched tightly into fists. The air trapped in her lungs was expelled in a rush and it took several frantic moments for her to identify the familiar, nonthreatening shadows of her hotel room.

The Dream again.

It was the second time she had wakened from it in as many weeks. The second time she had wakened numbed and shaken by horrors she had thought she had successfully banished to the hidden recesses of her mind.

As suddenly as the chill had overtaken her, a dry smothering heat now closed her throat and constricted the walls of her chest until she could not breathe. Aubrey pushed herself out of the bed and staggered to the window, fighting a moment with the ugly gingham curtains until she could push them aside and pry the warped sash higher than the few scant inches she had managed earlier.

Dawn was beginning to light the avalanche of gold and purple clouds rolling across the sky, and, as Aubrey sank to her knees, she gulped the crisp, dewy air as if her very life depended upon it.

The Dream again. The nightmare. In the beginning, almost a daily occurrence, along with the fever and delirium that had come from her infected wounds. As the weeks, months, years had passed, the occurrences had come less frequently, but when they did . . . when they did, dear God, it was like living through the fear and pain and horror of that night all over again.

Aubrey leaned on the chipped windowsill and rested her forehead on her arm. She squeezed her eyes tightly shut to force away the memories and images that always lingered in the aftermath of the Dream, but it was no use. She had to see them all, acknowledge them all singly and together before she would be able to push them away to that place where all black things crept away to hide.

Her brothers had not been waiting for her at the cave, nor had they appeared any time over the next three days. By then Aubrey had been burning with fever and had wandered out onto the plains, where she had been found nearly a week later by a traveling merchant. Lucius Beebee had carried the huddled, unconscious girl to his wagon and, with reasons of his own hastening his departure from Santa Fe, nursed her as far as Taos. He had fully intended to leave her there in the care of the local authorities, but when he learned that a runaway matching Aubrey's description was being sought for questioning in the fiery deaths of her mother, father, and two little brothers, he knew she would not be safe anywhere in New Mexico.

Lucius had sat through several nights and days of Aubrey's fevered rantings and deduced quite correctly that it would be her word against Maxwell Fleming's as to who had set the fire and why. And, since his own brush with the law had resulted from a misunderstanding with Fleming, Lucius had no reason to believe either one of them would live long enough to utter a single accusation.

He took her east, declaring his intention to leave her off at each town and army post they passed through, but there were always reasons to delay the decision. Fort Union was too barren, Upper Springs was hardly more than a watering hole. In Dodge City, the only other women were whores. There were budding settlements along the Cimarron, but there were Indians as well, and Lucius could not justify removing her from one horror only to place her at the mercy of another. Moreover, the farther east they traveled, the fonder Lucius became of her company. She never whined or complained when a day or two lapsed between meals. She even proved adept at winning the tears and sympathies of customers who might otherwise have scattered his merchandise at the end of a broom.

Aubrey had not minded playing the part of a waif, nor had she minded the days and nights when the leaky wagon had been their only shelter against the elements. Lucius Beebee was kind and concerned for her welfare. He did not grudge sharing what little he had and, over the years, assumed the role of parent and teacher with an ease that suited them both. He would never take the place of Jonathan or Luisa Granger, and to his credit, he never tried. But Aubrey could look back and say with perfect honesty that he probably taught her more about adapting to the hard realities of life than she would have learned on a sprawling rancho on the plains of New Mexico.

Her early years had hardened her to death and violence, and it was always a little unsettling to Lucius to know that she could view the aftermath of a bloody gunfight or watch a hanging without flinching or being reintroduced to her last meal. Over the years, after the pain faded, she was even able to look back over the death of her parents with a certain degree of calm detachment. The West was a wild and savage place, a place where only the strongest survived and the weak became like the dust that simply blew away, forgotten.

Aubrey could accept the wildness and the savagery, and the danger. What became increasingly difficult to accept was the possibility of Jonathan Granger's murder being forgotten, or worse—the man who had ordered it,

Maxwell Fleming, growing rich and powerful on the blood of others.

Aubrey raised her head off her forearm, mildly surprised to see the sky outside her window had turned a clear pale blue. There were men on horseback in the street below; store owners were whistling and shouting hails of greeting as they unhinged doors and windows for business.

Aubrey pushed herself upright, her bones feeling as if they belonged to a ninety-year-old woman. She walked slowly over to the scarred, dusty dresser that crowded the narrow bed against the wall, and her gaze fell to the yellowed newspaper clipping that sat where she had left it last night. Reading it over and over by lamplight had probably been what had triggered the Dream, and she picked it up again, rereading it as if she had not already memorized the content of the two-inch column word for word.

The article was two months old, cut from the pages of the *Wichita Gazette.* Maxwell Fleming's name had leaped off the printed page when she had first read it, slamming into her gut like a fist. He had come east to arrange the sale of cattle and to attend a much-publicized auction of jewels and artwork, the proceeds of which were to aid a European monarchy embroiled in a civil war.

Against Lucius's better judgment, Aubrey had persuaded him to travel to Wichita. The thought of her enemy being so close seared her mind like a brand, but as luck would have it, they arrived a day late and Fleming had already set out on the return journey to New Mexico. A few prudent questions had determined the route he was taking, and they might have had a chance to overtake him had Lucius not suffered a bad fall and dislocated his shoulder.

Aubrey laid the clipping back on the dresser and stared into the mottled reflection in the mirror.

Exactly when she had made the conscious decision to return to Santa Fe, she could not have said. There had probably never been any question but that she would return one day. At any rate, Lucius had not seemed the least surprised to hear her calm announcement.

"And what will you do when you get there?" he had asked. "Challenge him to a duel?"

Aubrey had set her jaw stubbornly. "I have to go. I have to see him face to face."

"Yes, well, I know you well enough to predict you will not be content just to see him. You will want to walk right up to him, stand nose to nose, and spit in his eye!"

"Are you saying I should just shoot him?" she asked dryly.

"Hah! You think he would let you get close enough to try? The whole of New Mexico is embroiled in cattle wars and land wars; the man would as soon shoot you out of hand as bother to give you the time of day. And if you think you can simply walk into the sheriff's office and accuse Maxwell Fleming of a ten-year-old murder, you had best arrange your own funeral plans ahead of time. Ten years ago, Fleming all but owned Santa Fe, and I doubt his powers have slipped any as the town has grown in size and wealth. Go if you want to. Kill yourself if you want to, but I'll have no part of it."

"I wasn't even asking you to come with me," she said quietly.

"Just as well, too, because I wouldn't go. I'm too old to start rumbling across plains and deserts in a stagecoach. Too old and too fond of my scalp, thank you very much."

The echo of the argument faded and Aubrey leaned forward, studying herself critically in the mirror. There were dark smudges ringing her eyes and shadows dulling the clear blue spheres to a metallic gray. The smooth skin across her cheeks seemed to be stretched taut over the bones, and her lips were a bloodless pink, drawn into a thin, unyielding line.

This past week in Great Bend had been the first time she had been on her own in ten years. The four walls of the hotel room had become like a prison and she was looking forward to leaving them far behind.

With a slight grimace, she took up her hairbrush and endeavored to tame the thick, damp tangles of hair that spilled like a black waterfall over her shoulders and halfway down her back. Intent upon catching every wisp and tendril, she twisted it into a severe, painfully prim chignon at the nape of her neck, trapping it there with a tightly woven snood. She scrubbed her face in the tepid water left overnight on the washstand, then dressed without haste, without expression, in her traveling suit of sturdy brown worsted. Her feet protested, but were crammed into high buttoned boots that were a size too small and forced her to take small, ducklike steps. A drab, feckless bonnet was planted squarely on her head, its lone bit of feather trim drooping sadly over her ear. Wire-rimmed spectacles were perched on the delicate bridge of her nose to complete the picture, and as she stood back to study herself once again in the mirror, she was satisfied that she could not envision a less appealing, less noteworthy creature than the one glaring owlishly back at her.

Still without expression, Aubrey packed the last of her belongings into the carpetbag and, glancing one last time around the hotel room, she walked out into the hallway and locked the door behind her.

Part One

Oh, what a tangled web we weave,
When first we practice to deceive.
—Sir Walter Scott

1

In the niche that passed for a lobby, Aubrey paid her bill and relinquished her key to the clerk, who neither spoke nor looked up from the pages of the penny dreadful he was reading. Once outside, she paused a moment on the stoop to let her eyes adjust to the harsher sunlight and to cleanse away the last of the inner chills.

Great Bend, Kansas, was the last major collection point along the Santa Fe Trail, and the last real glimpse of civilization the settlers had before starting off across the plains. Merchants and traders did a thriving business; prices soared each spring and summer, and for six weeks out of every year, the streets were congested daily with massive Conestoga wagons and plodding oxen. Having already traveled the easiest two hundred miles of the Trail from where it originated in Independence, Missouri, there were another six hundred unfriendly, inhospitable miles to go before it ended in dusty, sunscorched New Mexico.

Over the last three days, an enormous train of wagons had been gathering outside the city limits, due to leave Great Bend before the end of the week. Men were lured west by the rumors of gold in the mountain ranges, and families were drawn to the prospect of free land, sweet rivers, and the vast wealth to be made on the ranches spreading northward from Texas. The Atchison, Topeka railway was already making plans to expand west to Santa Fe to accommodate the exodus, but in the meantime, there was only the wagon train or the stagecoach available to eager entrepreneurs. California, Colorado, and New Mexico were the new lands for building dreams, and very few dreamers were discouraged into turning back.

From Great Bend, the wagon trains took upward of twelve weeks to travel the Santa Fe Trail. Burdened by heavily laden Conestogas, they were forced to take the less hazardous fork of the Trail where it divided at the Cimarron Crossing. Moving only as fast as the slowest team of oxen, they followed the Arkansas River to Bent's Fort and farther into the mountain ranges, through the carved swath of the Raton Pass, and down onto the grasslands where it rejoined the main trail at Wagon Mound, New Mexico.

Stagecoaches took a much more direct route, shaving off some one hundred miles by crossing through stretches of grassland, desert, and Indian territories made far less risky by virtue of their speed. Along this southern fork, the Trail had always been a prime target for raiding Apache and Comanche, but in the twelve years since the end of the Civil War, the Union Army had been concentrating its efforts on clearing the plains and confining the Indians to reservations. There were army posts every hundred miles, and regular patrols between the way stations. It was nonetheless a daunting proposition: eight days and nights of high-speed travel along a scarred ribbon of a road rutted three feet deep in places, with no guarantee of safe arrival at the other end.

"Hey, lady! Watch where the hell you're going!"

Aubrey jumped back as a covered wagon came within inches of foiling all of her carefully laid plans. She had not even been aware of walking onto the road, or that the streets had become an obstacle course of horses, men, wagons . . . all in a raging hurry to be somewhere else.

Coughing away the dust, Aubrey maneuvered her way across the rest of the street, taking care to lift the hem of her skirt out of the furrows of dirt and animal dung. The Kansas Stage Company office was at the far end of the boardwalk, and, as she hurried toward it, she kept one eye on the uneven planks, another on the faces of the people she passed. Not one gave her a second glance. They were too absorbed in haggling and bickering with store owners, shouting at passing wagoners, or ogling the upper balconies of the saloons where the early rising working girls were sunning against the railings, displaying their ample wares.

Aubrey ignored the lewd hooting and hollering and jostled her way toward the door of the stage office.

Her footsteps slowed again as she drew abreast of the gleaming new Abbot-Downing Concord stagecoach drawn up in front of the stage office. Painted the recognizable shiny red with enormous yellow wheels, the Concord had its door open and the canvas raised over the triangular luggage boot at the rear. One of the best and most modern conveyances, the Concord could seat six comfortably inside and another four on the roof behind the driver's box. It boasted thorough brace suspension—the body being slung on straps of tough steerhide, which absorbed the worst of the jolts and bumps along a rough road and caused the coach to roll and sway like the motion of a ship. Six matched bays waited patiently in their traces; a young, clean-shaven hostler lounged nearby, his hat pulled low over his forehead, his eyes half-closed with the heat and boredom.

The stagecoach line would have a relay station with a fresh team ready and waiting every fifteen to twenty miles along the route. The run to Santa Fe allowed for only two overnight rests at way stations. The majority of the traveling would be done day and night, with the seats folding down to provide sleeping arrangements for the passengers on an alternating schedule.

Aubrey felt a small measure of relief in seeing several round hatboxes piled on the boardwalk waiting to be loaded into the boot. She had not relished the prospect of journeying eight days and nights in all-male company. While she was not eager to strike up any friendships or encourage any particular camaraderie, another woman on board would hopefully create a greater measure of distraction for the other passengers.

She was actually still savoring this thought when she was stopped cold in her tracks again, not by any threat to her physical well-being this time, but by a distinct and shocking affront to her senses.

Advancing toward the stagecoach office from the other end of the boardwalk was a woman dressed head to toe in vibrant, garish shades of purple. Yards and yards of dyed velvet had gone into the making of a cloak that created its own minor dust storm as it swept along the walk. Splashes of fuchsia-colored silk frothed at each footstep; a towering spire of plumage bobbed and danced over curls as yellow as pirate's gold and fashioned into ornate, stiffly turned curlicues and corkscrews. A lace parasol twirled in one purple-gloved hand. High-heeled satin slippers *tap tap tapped* her arrival on the boards, and in the event there was still a pair of eyes ignorant of her presence, a laugh much like the sound of breaking crystal parted the painted red lips and wrought a serious strain against the already alarmingly low décolletage of her gown.

In her wake, had anyone cared to notice, was a lean,

dark-eyed man dressed completely in black broadcloth. He did not follow the woman into the stage office, but lingered a moment by the door, his gaze approving the effect his companion had had on the openmouthed bullwhackers and stunned pedestrians.

Aubrey was directly in front of him as his visual sweep came to a halt. For a full minute they just stared at one another, but then his eyes—as black as the expensive clothing he wore—raked casually down the unflattering lines of her traveling suit and came to rest on the carpetbag.

"Are you by chance planning on taking the stage this morning?"

She managed a nod.

"Then permit me to introduce myself as one of your fellow travelers. Darby Greaves," he said, bowing with a flourish. "Agent and manager to the incomparable Magenta Royale, Jewel of New Orleans."

He said the name and the title loud enough for passing wagoners to hear him over the rumble of their huge iron-clad wheels. Moreover, he again cast his eyes around the curious crowd as if expecting them all to recognize the name and drop dead from the privilege of having seen her. From Aubrey, most especially, he expected the usual leading questions, full of enthusiasm and awe, so that he might expound in true showmanlike fashion upon his songbird's fame and talents.

"I am pleased to make your acquaintance, Mr. Greaves," Aubrey said dryly. "Now, if you will excuse me, I must finalize my travel arrangements."

For a moment the smile remained fixed and dazzling on the handsome face. In the next, when the first snickers from the onlooking crowd reached his ears, the smile dissolved and a sudden hardness focused his attention more sharply on the bespectacled spinster.

"Excuse me," Aubrey said again, raising an eyebrow

to indicate he was blocking her path to the door. But instead of moving aside, he leaned closer and propped his hand against the wall.

"I'm sorry, I didn't catch your name."

Aubrey recoiled slightly from the strong scent of whiskey on his breath. She debated simply pushing past him and ignoring his rudeness, but a man who needed whiskey this early in the day could be, at best, unpredictable.

"Blue," she said tersely. "Aubrey Blue."

"Aubrey Blue," he murmured slowly. "It has an intriguing ring to it, much like Magenta Royale . . . but then . . . hers is only a stage name. One I made up myself, truth be known. And yours?"

The heat of his breath, so near, sent a chill down Aubrey's spine. "Mine?"

"Aubrey—an unusual name; I can't quite imagine the origin. The Blue is, on the other hand, remarkably suited to the amazing color of your eyes. I couldn't have chosen better myself."

The objects of his admiration darkened considerably as she stared at the arm he had stretched out across the door. They rose slowly, as did Greaves's, as Magenta Royale stepped forward out of the shadows.

"If you have quite finished with the theatrics," she said archly, "we have another small problem to contend with."

"Theatrics?" Greaves dropped his arm and smiled. "Since when is spreading your good name and enhancing your vaunted reputation *theatrics*? Is it not my job?"

"You call hustling a silly piece of baggage enhancing my reputation? I call it trying to add a few notches to your own."

"Really, my love." Greaves stifled a yawn. "We're allowing our breeding to show."

"My breeding is right where I put it this morning, Darby dear. Yours is the one that needs tucking back into your pants." She cast a cool, scathing glance in Aubrey's direction. "You can run along now, sweetheart. Mr. Greaves is all finished with you."

Aubrey blushed furiously. As she hurried past them, she overheard their parting comments, as she was expected to.

"Really, Darby. Surely even you can do better than a knock-kneed old maid who probably wears a vest and woolly drawers to bed."

"I've seen worse," he drawled in return.

"You've bedded worse," she countered succinctly. "But they have all just said *b-a-a-a* and gone quietly back into the pen in the morning."

Aubrey approached the shoulder-high wicket and managed to calm herself during the few moments it took for the clerk to notice her.

"Ticket?"

"I already have one," she said. "For Santa Fe. Is the stage on time?"

"Your ticket paid for?"

"Last Wednesday."

"Eh?" The clerk lifted his head and peered through his pince-nez. "Ohhh yeah, I remember you now. The schoolmarm. You jest missed the other coach and bought your ticket then to beat the rush." He paused and snorted derisively. "Welcome to the rush. Just you and her ladyship so far . . . that is, if'n she can make up her mind one way or t'other. Seems she wants a coach all to herself. Fancy that."

Aubrey looked around the small office, puzzled by the empty benches along the walls. The previous week, the seats had been full of impatient travelers, with more waiting in line, clamoring for passage on any coaches heading west.

"Comanche," the clerk explained. "Rumor has it they're out on the warpath again, jest the kind of news what gives folks a hankerin' to stay to home. You might want to share some of that wisdom yourself, Missy, and wait until the army has a chance to cool them down some."

"I . . . can't wait. I have to be in Santa Fe as soon as possible. Is the stage not running?"

"Oh, it's runnin'," the clerk assured her. "Jest can't say for certain when. Seems the driver had some trouble comin' in from Little River."

"What? What's that you say?" Aubrey was unceremoniously elbowed aside as a short, round-faced gentleman pressed up to the wicket. "Excuse me, my good man, but did I hear you say the coach may not be leaving today?"

The clerk tilted his head to see over the rim of his pince-nez. The newcomer had a florid complexion, caused as much by the heat out-of-doors as the rotund size of his girth. A ring of graying hair wisped out from under the brim of the derby he wore, while his mouth was all but hidden beneath an impressive bush of a moustache, the ends of which had been waxed and groomed into perfect little circles at each end.

"You got good ears, mister. I said what I said."

"But good gracious . . . why are we being delayed?"

"Can't rightly say for certain, but I heard the driver lost his gun. Ain't *nobody* fool enough to head into Injun territory without a shotgun, not even Stink Finger Jim Brody."

This seemed too much for the little man to absorb. He doffed his derby and swabbed an enormous white handkerchief across the bald dome of his head.

"A gun? We are being forced to rearrange our schedules because one of your drivers lost his *gun*? Can he not purchase another at the hardware store?"

The clerk's eyes narrowed. Moving with exaggerated care, he removed his pince-nez and polished the lenses slowly on his shirtfront. When they were smeared into a cleaner state, he replaced them on the bridge of his nose and peered belligerently at his customer.

"Mister . . . where are you from?"

"Pennsylvania. Pittsburgh, Pennsylvania."

"And jest what might you be carrying in them tinker's cases you got with you?"

"I . . . er, have a quality line of products which have met with great success throughout the Eastern states."

"You ever been west of the Mississippi?"

"Why, er, no. No, I haven't had the pleasure until now."

"Never would have guessed it," the clerk snorted.

The salesman stiffened. "See here, my good man, if this is an attempt to extort more money—"

The ticket agent sighed and shook his head. "I said the driver lost his shotgun, mister. Every stage that leaves this here depot leaves with two men ridin' up top in the driver's box, or it don't leave at all. One does the drivin', the other rides *shotgun.* Man loses his *shotgun,* he ain't about to give a hang one way or t'other about schedules, quality products, or"—he glared pointedly at Aubrey—"a bunch of snot-nosed Mex kids missin' out on their ABC's. You savvy what I'm sayin', mister?"

"Oh. Yes. Yes, I see." The square of linen swept across the shiny pate again. "But I simply must get to Santa Fe before the month's end. I simply must."

"Nothin' I can do about it, mister. Not till I hear one way or t'other from Jim Brody. Why hell, he might be over to the hardware store right now tryin' to find himself another gun." The clerk chuckled at his own joke. "On the other hand, he's more'n likely over to the Silver Dollar Saloon sippin' his way through a pint of good whiskey."

Darby Greaves, seeming to have ignored the exchange until then, straightened from where he lounged against the wall. "A commendable idea, all things considered. Magenta, my love, what do you say we step over to the Silver Dollar ourselves and see if we cannot work on finding you an engagement closer to civilization."

Magenta's expression did not change and no one else overheard the response that came through her almost motionless lips. "Take one step toward that saloon, Darby Greaves, and I will personally shoot out both your kneecaps," she hissed. "They are paying me *five thousand dollars* to sing in the new opera hall in Santa Fe and you are not—I repeat, you are *not* going to piss away an opportunity like this from the bottom of a whiskey bottle!"

"The opportunity, as I see it," he replied nonplussed, "is to get yourself scalped . . . or worse. Didn't you hear him say the Comanche are on the warpath?"

"Good God, this is 1877. There are no more Comanche; they're all either dead or confined to reservations, and I'll be damned if a few unfounded rumors ruin my one big chance at success."

With a practiced toss of her bouncing gold curls, Magenta swept across the cramped room, her voluminous skirts raising a small cloud of dust in her wake. At the wicket, she leaned forward, allowing the startled clerk an unimpeded view down the dusky cleft of her cleavage.

"Now then, Mr.—?"

"Gibbon," the clerk croaked. "Sidney Gibbon."

"Mr. Gibbon . . . surely there must be something we can do to clear up this unfortunate situation."

Aubrey sighed and retreated to one of the long wooden benches. She set her carpetbag on the floor and tried not to think of what another delay would do to her plans or her nerves. She blocked out the squabble of voices behind her and stared out the fly-spotted window, but there wasn't much to see through the thick film, and after a few moments, she found her eyes wandering to the notice board hung on the wall beside her. A mosaic of scraps of paper was pasted and nailed up for display, including one for a miracle tonic that claimed to grow hair, cure warts, and prevent personal discomforts in warm weather. A gunsmith named Bullet had printed his handbills on paper cutouts of pistols, complete with an artistic puff of smoke. Warnings were posted to be on the alert for a pair of con artists who had been seen last in the great state of Louisiana; below that were neat rows of wanted posters, some with crudely sketched caricatures of faces, some with the ominous DEAD OR ALIVE stamped across the top.

"A fascinating overview of our society, don't you agree?"

"I beg your pardon?" Aubrey glanced beside her and was greeted by an effusive smile beamed out from beneath a handlebar moustache.

"The notices." The portly salesman pointed to the board. "Small pieces of life displayed for all to see."

"Yes," she murmured. "Quite fascinating."

"I could not help but overhear the clerk mention you were a teacher. An admirable profession, Miss—?"

"Blue."

"Miss Blue." He tipped his bowler and offered a curt bow. "Armbruster P. Shillingsworth, at your service." He opened his mouth to say more, but a further disturbance behind them changed his intent somewhat abruptly. "Oh! Oh my!"

Two new arrivals were standing in the doorway of the stage office, their presence causing a sudden and absolute silence both inside and outside on the boardwalk. The first of the pair was tall enough and broad enough for his silhouette to block most of the flaring sunlight. He was dressed in an open-necked buckskin shirt and cord pants, neither of them too new or too clean. Brass-colored hair fell long and shaggy to his collar, the unruly waves framing a face that was weathered by sun and open air to the shade of warm teak. The eyes gazing out from beneath the wide brim of his hat were slate gray and moved casually around the airless little room, observing, assessing, dismissing his surroundings with a wry twist of his lips.

Not quite so easy for the occupants of the stage office to dismiss was the sight of the second man, a Plains Indian. He was nearly as tall as the white man and every bit as formidable, judging by the bulge of muscles that swelled beneath his buckskins. His starkly chiseled features could have been hewn from granite, for all the expression he betrayed. Straight, gleaming black hair hung to mid-chest, with several thin strands plaited into a braid that originated at his temple. His eyes were bottomless brown pools, threatening in their intensity, and not the least reluctant to challenge each stare that greeted him.

The white man crossed over to the wicket and nodded perfunctorily at the clerk. "When does the next stage leave?"

"I . . . well, uh—" The clerk's nervous gaze flicked to the Indian and back again. "I was jest tellin' these here good folks that I wasn't too sure at all when the next coach would be headin' out."

"There is a scheduled departure at ten, is there not?"

"Well, ah . . . yes."

"And that is a stagecoach pulled up out front, is it not?"

"I . . . uh, yes. Yes, it shore is."

"Am I wrong in assuming it is still the custom of the stage line to sell seats on board their coaches?"

"Well now—"

"Fine. How much for two seats to Fort Union?"

The clerk hesitated again, his eyes flickering now be-

tween the silent Indian and the bulging leather pouch
the plainsman withdrew from his pocket. The solid
chink of coin caused him to lick his lips and rub a finger
nervously along the starched edge of his collar.

"Will, ah . . . will these seats be for you and your,
ah, friend?"

The stranger's smile was easy. His voice was decep-
tively soft as well, tinged with the friendly slur of the
plains, but his eyes were hooded with a distinct and
growing animosity, as if he knew full well the cause of
the agent's reluctance and was not about to make the
going any easier for him.

He pushed back the brim of his hat with a tip of a
finger and leaned his elbow on the counter. "I suppose
you have a clever reason for asking, considering there
are only the two of us standing here."

"In that case"—the clerk swallowed hard—"the fact
of it is, I can't sell you two seats to nowheres."

"Is the stage full?"

"No . . . ah, I mean . . . *yes.*"

The gray eyes fixed him with a shriveling stare.
"Which is it . . . no, or yes?"

"Fact of it is, mister, the Kansas Stage Company plain
don't allow Injuns on board their coaches."

"Sorry?" The plainsman leaned farther over the
counter, a motion which triggered the instant appearance of fine beads of sweat across the ticket agent's upper lip. "I don't think I quite heard you."

The clerk cleared his throat and adjusted his pince-
nez. "It ain't my rule, mister. It's the policy of the Kansas Stage Company, and I ain't about to get fired for
breakin' company policy rules."

"Come now, Mr.—?"

"Gibbon," Magenta supplied smoothly. She had
moved up behind the plainsman and was enjoying not
only the clerk's squirming discomfort, but the extremely

interesting view of hard, rippling muscles where they
strained the seams of the buckskin shirt. "His name is
Sidney Gibbon."

The plainsman acknowledged the inviting smile with
an obliging grin of his own before he turned back to the
clerk.

"Well, Mr. Sidney Gibbon, with business as poor as it
is these days, shouldn't you be thankful you have customers who are willing to pay? A less accommodating
fellow might simply stop the coach outside of town and
insist that *you* pay *him*. Me? I could care less where I get
on board—here, or ten miles down the road—but my
friend there, why he might take it in his head that you
insulted him deeply. You ever insulted an Ute warrior
before, Mr. Gibbon?"

The clerk shook his head. "C-Can't say that I have,
mister, and can't say that I particularily want to, but
policy is policy. Besides . . . I got other passengers to
consider. I doubt they'd be all that partial on the idea of
havin' an Injun ride on the coach with them."

The plainsman's mouth curved thoughtfully. He
turned toward the profusion of purple silk and dyed
ostrich feathers and waited for Magenta's eyes to drag
themselves upward from the gaping neckline of his shirt.
"Ma'am. You have any objections to me or my friend
joining you on the stage? I know it's a long trip at close
quarters, but I can assure you that both Sun Shadow
and myself are housebroken. We can act civilized when
the occasion warrants it."

Magenta smiled. "And when it doesn't?"

It was his turn to take a slow, leisurely inspection of
the bountiful flesh testing the constraints of the purple
bodice. Two good handfuls apiece, he judged, enough to
keep a man busy for a few hundred miles.

Magenta read the interest in his eyes and moistened
her lips. "I have no objections whatsoever to your com-

pany, sir. On the contrary, I'm sure we would all feel so much safer with you on board . . . wouldn't we, Darby dear?"

Greaves was staring at the Indian, as he had been since the pair had appeared in the doorway. He made no effort to conceal his contempt or his distrust for a race he considered inferior even to slaves.

"Darby dear?" Magenta said again.

"No," he said quietly. "I have no objection."

"There"—the plainsman spread his hands easily as he addressed Sidney Gibbon again—"you heard it yourself: no objections."

"They ain't the only customers," the clerk said tightly, grasping at his last avenue of escape. "The schoolmarm and the salesman over yonder; they both paid full fares."

The gray eyes cast around again and found the dapper little man in the derby. Before he could pose his question, the salesman bustled forward, his moustache quivering around his assurances. "No indeed, sir. I have no objections whatsoever. And the name is Shillingsworth. Armbruster P. Shillingsworth. A household name for corsets and trusses, braces and splints for all areas of the body . . . er . . . not that either you or your friend look as if you require any further bracing. No indeed."

The plainsman sought the final vote, his gaze turning toward the window. Aubrey's brown worsted suit and brown hat blended perfectly with the dull brown walls of the office, a blandness not aided by the fact that a haze of sunlit dust hung suspended in a cloud around her, obscuring all but a faint impression of a pale face and glinting spectacles.

Conversely, Aubrey's view was not hampered in the least. The eyes that had narrowed slightly in an effort to see who was passing the final judgment were as cool and unperturbed as a winter sky. His hair was very thick and cut by an impatient hand so that the ends curled in ragged lengths over his collar; the shoulders beneath the buckskin were broad and powerful and barely contained by the limits of mere cloth. His mouth was immodestly sensual, shamelessly curved with the devil's own arrogance, no doubt the result of being too many years the recipient of the kind of response shining in Magenta Royale's eyes. In fact, there was a general look of casual debauchery about him—as if he had spent the past few days energetically entangled in a tumble of warm bedsheets, and would not have been the least dismayed by the prospect of returning.

Aubrey's guess was closer to the truth than she might have wanted to know, for the plainsman had indeed been spending the better part of the last ten days and nights heartily enjoying the fleshy bounty of Great Bend's finest whorehouses. He had innocently lost track of the numbers of long, white limbs that had eagerly locked themselves around his waist, nor could he have identified any one prominent feature of the many blurred faces, bodies, and breasts he had worshiped with such fanatical devotion.

He was, however, reasonably certain none of them had worn bottle-bottom spectacles or presented themselves for his pleasure in tweed armor—the only two distinctive qualities of the faded, dusty schoolmarm who stood before him now. That sobering reality, had it not been counterbalanced by the swish of purple satin at his side, might have done more to send him right back into the arms of Madame Pearl's beauties than all the irritating company policies the clerk could splutter.

"Ma'am? Excuse me, but I didn't see you standing there."

Aubrey felt more than one pair of eyes turn toward

her and she lowered her lashes quickly to avoid contact with any of them.

"No need to apologize, sir, and I have no objections to you or your companion traveling with us."

"Much obliged." The plainsman turned back to the clerk and tapped a long, calloused finger on the countertop. "Two tickets to Fort Union, if you don't mind."

"I tell you I don't make the rules," Gibbon declared, his complexion flooding a sullen red. "Stage company says no Injuns, it means no Injuns. You want to take it up with Mr. H. P. Nanglinger at the head office, you be my guest. Telegraph is right up the street. If'n he says *he* has no objections, then hell, I'll sell you two tickets to China, you want 'em."

What might or might not have happened next was forestalled by a furious burst of energy that exploded through the rear door, bringing with him a fresh cloud of dust and the echo of a raucous oath. A small, wiry grunt of a man, he reeked of cheap hair pomade and even cheaper whiskey, both of which caused Magenta to reach for a perfumed handkerchief and flinch away from the wicket as he approached. His pants and shirt were soiled stiff with sweat and grime, his face was partially hidden behind the fuzz of a coarsely maintained beard that might have been any color beneath the layers of dust and expelled tobacco juice. A much abused Hardee hat was crammed low over his forehead, the crumpled rim level with the slits that were his eyes.

"Well, Gibby?" A bullet-shot of tobacco juice *poing*-ed against the lip of the spittoon as he wiped the cuff of his sleeve across his mouth. "You find me a gun yet?"

Gibbon's shoulders squared for battle. "No. No, I ain't. Strange as it sounds, I been busy with my own job and—"

"I ain't a goin' nowheres without a gun. Man cain't be expected ter ride six hunnerd mile with no gun an' no relief. That there coach'll jest set there where she be till I gits me one, takes a week o' Sundays to do it!"

"Now you listen here, Jim Brody," Gibbon said, relieved to be able to turn his back on the plainsman. "You were hired to drive the coach to Santa Fe—"

"I know'd my job, boy. Been doin' it five years now."

"Then you should also know that if you lost your outrider on the last run, it is your responsibility to go out and find a replacement!"

"Been lookin', ye danged syrup-ass! Ain't no one willin' to git hisself shot at ner scalped jest ter git yer blamed coach to Santy Fay." He shifted his cud into an enormous bulge in his cheek and grimaced. "I ain't neither, fer that matter. Not fer the handful o' cow chips I'm paid."

"Perhaps my friend and I can be of some assistance," the plainsman said.

"Ho!" Jim Brody raised his head and squinted along his nose as if seeing the formidable pair for the first time. "Travelin' ter Santy Fay, are ye?"

"Fort Union, actually . . . that is, if we can manage to overcome a slight problem with company policy."

Stink Finger Jim Brody looked at the Ute and snorted. "Policy, eh? Policy be damned. What be yer name, young fella?"

"McBride," said the plainsman. "Christian McBride."

"McBride." Brody rolled the name around on his tongue as if he were tasting day-old bread. "I know'd that name from somewheres." He peered up at the sun-bronzed face again and worked his cud with a vengeance. "Yep. I know'd that name . . . but the why of it 'scapes me fer the time being. You wanted fer anything, McBride?"

"Not that I am aware of."

"Mmmm." He tilted his scrawny head toward the Indian. "Either one of yus shoot worth half a damn?"

"Fair to middling," was the casual reply.

"And this y'ere Injun . . . he Comanche?"

"Ute."

"Ute! Cain't say as I've ever seen one this fer east afore. Cain't say it makes no never mind anyhows. My ma always told me: never trust an Injun ner a whore, they'd both as soon take a knife to yer balls the minute yer back was turned. Right then—" He crooked his head and spat juice out of the corner of his mouth. "You and yer Injun can come along so fer as one of yus is willin' to ride topside with me, and I don't rightly care which one. The other'n had best pay up to ol' Gibby there afore he ruptures a natural vessel. By the by—" He hooked a stubby thumb in Sun Shadow's direction. "He savvy English?"

"Some," McBride nodded.

"Best tell him in his own lingo anyways, so's there's no misunderstandin': he so much as blinks funny I'll plug a hole in 'im so wide the shit'll fly fer three counties. Think he'll catch my meaning?"

"I'm sure he will."

"Fair an' good." Brody scratched savagely at an armpit and bellowed over the spluttering protests of the company clerk: "Best shrink yer bladders whilst you have the chance, folks. We roll in ten minutes!"

2

"All aboard! Keep yer danged feet off'n the seats!"

Brody took the reins from the hostler and in three nimble steps was in his seat in the driver's box. He fixed the Indian with a beady stare, reiterating the main thrust of his threat, then gave a cursory glance to the excess luggage and express strapped to the rails of the roof. A large green box marked Wells, Fargo, and Co. was in the smaller boot beneath his seat, and he rattled the lock to ensure it was properly sealed. A double-barreled ten-gauge sawed-off shotgun was propped on the seat beside him, ignored by the Ute, who preferred to cradle his own sixteen-shot Henry repeating rifle.

Brody cast a rheumy eye around the crowd of onlookers, some of them more than mildly alarmed by the sight of an armed Indian atop a Concord coach.

"All right, you varmint-eared, rag-tailed, sow-bellied excuses fer horseflesh—" Three of the six-up team's ears flattened at the growled address. "I don't 'spect to see a one of yus go side-steppin' around folk too blamed stupid to git out o' the way. Plow 'em under, goddammit, an' the next one's'll think twice as hard on movin' out'n the way."

The throaty admonition directed at the team of horses was effective in scattering the men and women who loitered in front of the coach. A further incentive was marked with exasperated curses as he puckered his lips and projected a spurt of tobacco juice over the heads of the lead span. A booted foot released the brake as he uncurled his whip and took up the slack on the reins. The horses strained against their collars in anticipation, the traces snapping taut, the metal fastenings jingling like a ring of keys.

"G-along! Ho-hup, there!"

The whip snaked out over the top of the horses' heads, the foot-long lengths of corded silk at the end popping loudly in the air.

Inside the coach, Aubrey braced herself as the coach pitched gently back and rolled forward, swaying into motion as the huge wheels churned the dusty road beneath them. She and Magenta had been accorded the best seats, those facing forward. Normally adequate for three, with the volume of ruffles and petticoats that augmented the songstress's skirts, there might as well have been four of them crammed onto the padded leather seats.

Shillingsworth, Greaves, and McBride occupied the seats opposite them, but because of the natural tendency of the coach to tilt toward the rear while it was moving, their legs were stretched forward to maintain their balance. The peddler had the greatest difficulty, being in possession of the shortest legs, and although it gave Aubrey the benefit of more room in front of her, he was twice propelled clear off the seat to land in a heap at her feet. He tried to compensate by clutching both hands around the windowsill, but that only caused him to swing suddenly and violently into a crush against the door. To his credit, he never lost his grip or his smile, and each time the action of the coach steadied to a predictable roll, he pried his fingers loose long enough to offer around a small tin of bitter lemon drops.

He had a wife and eight children, he confided ten minutes into the journey, and expected to be a father again by the time he completed his circuit and returned to Pennsylvania. It was the reason why he had been so anxious to reach Santa Fe before the month's end. With luck, he would be able to conclude his business and be back by his wife's side in time for the birth.

Darby Greaves swallowed this and every other personal bit of information with a healthy mouthful of the whiskey he carried in a silver pocket flask. He had used the ten minutes before the coach's departure from Great Bend to purchase several large bottles of the raw liquor, and despite Magenta's killing stares, indulged openly and often.

Magenta was equally unhappy with Jim Brody's driving. Her squeals and giggles of modest dismay were all very well and good the first few times she found herself rocketed into the plainsman's lap, but even the pleasure of feeling his big hands setting her aright began to wear thin. Her squeals degenerated rapidly into muttered oaths, earning more than just a vague suspicion from Aubrey that the dainty chanteuse had had her beginnings in the back rooms of a saloon somewhere.

As for the plainsman, under different circumstances Aubrey might have approved of what she saw, or at least, felt more reassured by his presence. He wore twin Peacemaker Colt .45's strapped to his lean hips, the barrels measuring an uncommonly long nine inches apiece. Moreover, something about him—the way he stood, the way he commanded attention with his eyes—said army loud and clear. Whether it was a past or present influence, she had no way of determining without asking outright, and to ask him a question would have drawn more attention to herself than she wanted or needed from the slate gray eyes.

They had unsettled her enough in the few seconds it had taken him to politely assist her on board. Hat in hand, the sunlight had streamed down over the burnished waves that framed his face, and she had actually caught herself holding her breath. Without the shadow of the wide brim, his eyes were disturbingly direct. She had felt self-conscious then, and she had felt self-conscious every time thereafter when he caught her looking at him, regardless of the reason. Thankfully, the clerk at the stage office had assumed she was schoolteacher, an impression everyone had accepted without Aubrey's confirmation or denial. The plainsman had evidently not seen anything to offer argument, only a young, dry spinster who sought to improve her lot by heading out west. He had been quite content to catch Magenta whenever she flew into his lap, and to humor himself by seeing exactly how bold his hands could become before the amber tiger-eyes demurred.

In spite of Brody's whip and shouted threats, it took nearly an hour to maneuver half a mile, and when they finally broke free of the town traffic and rolled onto open road, the wiry little driver was irritated enough to want to make up for lost time. With no sympathy to spare on his passengers, he curled his whip into the air, plunging the team down the scarred brown road that joined up with the continuation of the Santa Fe Trail.

Clear of the city, the Trail followed the gleaming blue ribbon of the Arkansas River. The plains on either side were a lush green, covered with wild wheat and grasses that rippled in the warm breeze like waves on the ocean. Huge flocks of crows rose in screaming black clouds as the coach thundered by, and in the distance, a group of riders raised their hats and sent the Concord on its way before they carried on toward their destination.

Constant traffic in all weather had gouged deep ruts in the Trail, no welcome source of comfort to passengers. Many novice adventurers had, over the years, lost their meals, their teeth, and their dignity while leaning out of a coach window watching the ground rush past at breakneck speed beneath them. Most drivers were polite and conscientious, aware that the paying customers contributed to their handsome salaries. They would go slowly over the worst stretches of the road, sparing their passengers bruises to their hips, rumps, and heads.

Stink Finger Jim Brody was not only among the least tolerant of drivers, he was also the proud holder of the record for the shortest haul between Great Bend and Santa Fe—a record he generally thought could be improved upon if people were not so hell bent on eating and sleeping. He was generally well liked by anyone who had never had the privilege of riding with him, and as a result, it seemed that every mile they passed brought a new rider galloping across the plains to challenge Brody to a farewell race. He accepted each and every one with a whoop of glee—a sound that everyone inside soon recognized as the signal to brace themselves against whatever or whoever was convenient.

Long before Brody's need to make up for lost time was mollified, they heard the loud blast of his trumpet alerting the relay station up ahead that they were less than a mile away. The fresh team was already in harness and waiting when they rolled to a dusty halt, and in less than ten minutes, the jaded, lathered horses were backed out of their traces and led away, and a new six-up team was champing impatiently in their spans.

Jim took the second leg at a more reasonable pace, covering the distance to the next relay station in a little over two hours. This time the passengers were encouraged to stretch their legs, eat their lunch if they had brought one, or purchase a boxed lunch from the relay manager if they had not.

Magenta, her curls askew and her cape dragging on the ground, was left swaying in the shade of the coach while the others disembarked behind her. When the shock of straightening her bruised limbs passed, she began a slow, horrified inspection of her outward appearance, finishing in such a state of outraged disbelief, that Jim, chuckling to himself a few feet away, rewarded himself with a fresh plug of tobacco.

"Ruined," she gasped, pointing to a tear in the seam of her cape. The smudge of dirt that came away on her fingers earned another cry and another protest. "My God, look at this. It's ruined! Ruined, I tell you."

Aubrey, next out of the coach was also the first to come in contact with the blazing amber eyes. "A stiff brushing will take out most of the dust, I'm sure. As for the tear, it's hardly noticeable. A few stitches will put it right."

"Put it right?" Magenta snapped. "I suppose you know this from experience, do you? I suppose you are a seamstress in your spare time?"

"No," Aubrey replied calmly. "But I have lifted a needle and thread on occasion."

"Not very well and not on too many occasions if the charming outfit you are wearing now is anything to go by."

Aubrey opened her mouth, then closed it again without responding to the sarcasm. She saw Armbruster Shillingsworth plump down on a nearby boulder and used the excuse to walk away from the smug challenge in Magenta's eyes.

"Are you all right, Mr. Shillingsworth?"

He swabbed and reswabbed his dripping brow and sucked noisily on a lemon drop.

"Oh yes. Yes, I shall be fine in a minute or two—when my stomach decides where it wants to be. I assure you I am more than passingly familiar with the vile conditions of traveling by coach. It just seems to take longer each time for my inner workings to adjust." He belched softly and dabbed at his temples. "Not quite as young as I used to be, y'know."

"Try a few sips of water," said a deep baritone from over Aubrey's shoulder. An arm clad in buckskin reached forward, offering a dipperful of water he had just fetched from the station well.

"Why, thank you, Mr. McBride. You are very kind." Shillingsworth accepted the dipper and breathed a sigh of relief as the cool water eased some of the burning in his throat. The relief was only temporary, however, for in the next moment, McBride was lighting a thin black cheroot and smoke was drifting straight into the peddler's face, turning his skin from rosy pink to cobweb gray. Clamping a hand over his mouth, Shillingsworth lurched to his feet and staggered around behind a thick copse of bushes.

"How very considerate of you indeed," Aubrey said, turning around to glare at the plainsman.

McBride shrugged his shoulders indifferently. "Better it happened now than later, inside the coach."

Aubrey would have retorted, but a second drifting cloud of smoke caught her full in the face and she felt her own stomach flop unsteadily end over end.

"Maybe you'd best sit down yourself, Miss . . . er, Blue, is it?"

"Thank you," she said tautly, "but I am perfectly able to tend to myself, Mr. McBride."

"So I see." He tossed aside the cheroot and caught her by the elbow just as it looked as if she would teeter head-first into the bushes. He held her, steadying her until she was able to steer herself down onto the boulder the peddler had vacated. Picking up the dipper Shillingsworth had cast aside, McBride returned to the well and refilled it.

Aubrey accepted the ladle grudgingly. Equally as irritating as his manner was the fact that the plainsman looked hardly affected by the stifling heat, dust, or motion sickness. His jacket and shirt were open in a carelessly deep vee, exposing more smooth, hard flesh to the cooling air than was acceptable in mixed company. His hat shaded his face, but she had the feeling that even without it, he would not have had the civility to sweat.

Aubrey, conversely, could feel the heat trapped beneath the layers of worsted wool and linen she wore. She could feel each whalebone rib of her corset digging into her flesh, directing the channels of moisture to where the skin was most susceptible to prickling with the heat. Miserably, she fanned her cheeks with the folded square of her handkerchief and wished she could be alone long enough for a hearty scratch or two.

"You should have something to eat," McBride advised, stooping to retrieve his cheroot. "Give your stomach something to think about other than being where it isn't wanted."

Aubrey glanced up at him, scowling at his easy grin. "I presume you plan to take your own advice?"

"I do."

"Then by all means, do not let me detain you, sir."

McBride's hand paused, the cheroot halfway to his lips. She was pinched and rumpled-looking in the ill-fitting tweed. Her small concession to fashion—the drooping bit of feather in her hat—had given its last gasp a few miles back when a bump had sent her head into an abrupt meeting with the coach wall. Now the quill was broken and the crown of the hat indented. The spectacles she wore kept slipping down the bridge of her nose and the gloved finger she used to push them back had left a trail of smudges on her skin.

She hadn't made as much noise as a mouse since leaving Great Bend, and now here she was telling him to go and amuse himself elsewhere.

Not a gracious recipient of orders, however innocuous the order or the person giving it might seem, McBride stretched and planted a booted foot on the rock beside her. He leaned his weight casually forward on his arm and looked down at her, his head tilted to one side, his mouth settling on an expression that was somewhere between humor and irony.

Aubrey suffered under the discomfort of his stare for as long as she could without giving him the satisfaction of a response. Every scrap of instinct and feminine intuition cautioned her against an overt challenge to his male vanity, yet her own pride was somewhat at stake here. It was obvious he did not think much of women. He probably did not think of them at all unless it was to consider their attributes from the neck down. It was equally obvious that he was far more accustomed to having women trip over themselves to win his attention than he was having them shoo him away like a pestering fly.

"You are staring, Mr. McBride. Was there something else you wanted?"

His eyes were on a level with hers, gray and steady. It was the kind of slow, considering look that usually sent men's hands to their gunbelts and women's hands to their throats in terror, but this one barely flinched. She returned his studied appraisal, not the least intimidated by his closeness or his masculinity.

His smile thinned and took on a sardonic twist.

"You'll have to excuse me, ma'am. I guess my manners have become a trifle rusty over the past few years—

not that there was any great call for social niceties at Leavenworth."

"Leavenworth? You were posted at Leavenworth?"

A brow arched lazily. "Posted? Now there's a genteel way of saying it."

Aubrey fanned herself with her handkerchief. "Leavenworth is an army post, is it not?"

"Yes, ma'am." He drew on his cigar, finally, and exhaled a fine stream of bluish smoke. "It's also a prison."

The handkerchief stopped fluttering and she looked up, her eyes magnified hugely by the thick lenses. "Prison? You were . . . in prison there?"

The gray eyes gleamed and the set line of his jaw grew harder, deepening the cynicism and the contempt as he watched the changes in her expression. Leavenworth was where the worst, most dangerous criminals were sent—those who were only spared the hangman's noose in exchange for long years at hard labor. He had offered up the information to shock her, and in that he had succeeded. A faint blush of soft pink had crept up her throat and into her cheeks, warming her complexion to the point where he would have liked to reach over and remove the spectacles to see the overall effect. And her hair. Why did all schoolmarms assume they had to make themselves look as flinty and shrewish as possible?

"What made you think I was army?" he asked, his eyes still intrigued by the thick black knot of hair at her nape.

Aubrey ran the tip of her tongue across her lips to moisten them. She could feel the heat in her cheeks as his inspection continued. She hadn't invited this conversation; she certainly did not want to prolong it any longer than necessary with small talk. *She wanted him to go away.*

"I . . . don't know. You just looked . . . disciplined."

A slash of strong white teeth appeared as he laughed out loud. "Discipline. Yes, ma'am, I suppose you could say five years of cracking rock instills a man with a certain amount of discipline."

Aubrey folded her hands tightly together in her lap. Her sense of unease was deepening and there was nothing she could do to stop it, or to stop him from slaking his warped sense of humor at her expense. She glanced around, but the others had gone inside the relay station —all except the peddler, who was still behind the bushes, retching and praying for mercy with equal gusto.

The logical thing to do, she supposed, was just to stand up and walk away, but the heat and sun had frayed her logic, and the plainsman's belligerence pricked her like the sting of a rash.

"Five years is a long time, Mr. McBride," she said evenly. "I assume your crime was more serious than failed etiquette."

He clamped the cheroot between his teeth and leaned even closer, his voice lowering to a conspiratorial murmur. "They said I murdered a man. Fortunately, my lawyer was able to convince the judge I only killed him by accident."

"You're telling me you accidentally killed a man and they put you in prison for five years?"

Her voice dripped sarcasm and McBride grinned.

"No, ma'am. It was more like I accidentally killed the wrong man after the one I was aiming for moved out of the way."

Aubrey took a deep breath and stood up. She was above average in height for a woman, yet the plainsman still towered over her by a full head. His shoulders were massive—the muscles no doubt built up over the years of breaking and hauling rock—and his arms were as thick around as branches on a tree. She felt very small and very vulnerable in his shadow—feelings she did not particularly relish at the best of times.

"I'm afraid you have me at a disadvantage, Mr. Mc-Bride. While I am indeed overwhelmed that you would choose me to share this small confidence, I am more at a loss to know why you would think I would care."

She started to brush past him, but his hand shot out and caught hold of her upper arm. His grip, gentle but firm, forced her to stop and look up into a face that was cold and hard and impassive.

"Maybe I was just trying to give you a friendly warning, Miss Blue."

"A warning? About what?"

"About how everything may not be exactly what it seems on the outside." He paused and his grip eased. "Did I hear the clerk at the stage office say you were a schoolmarm?"

Aubrey straightened her sleeve and brushed at an imagined wrinkle with greater care than the worsted warranted. "You heard him correctly."

"And you're planning to teach school in Santa Fe?"

She stiffened imperceptibly and hoped she looked more annoyed than cornered. "Why yes, at the . . . at the parochial school at San Miguel."

Now why had she said that? Why embellish a lie with more lies—not that he would know if there was a school at San Miguel or not. And why did she feel the need for embellishment at all? It wasn't as if McBride needed to know or cared what she was going to be doing in Santa Fe.

"San Miguel?" he mused. "The mission? You're a missionary?"

She glared at him. "I am a teacher. Missions need teachers too, you know."

He grimaced. "Yes, but no one needs a job that badly. What was wrong with going somewhere civilized like

Washington or Boston? For that matter, there must
have been a thousand other places you could have chosen."

"I chose Santa Fe," she said evenly, bristling at the
sarcasm in his voice.

"Ahh. The lure of the West. Soft music, rich cattlemen, streets paved with gold? I hope you won't be too
disillusioned when you wake up each morning and find
you've been bedmates with a family of cockroaches. It's
not an easy life, Miss Blue."

"I am not afraid of a challenge, Mr. McBride."

"In that case—if it's a challenge you want, you won't
be disappointed. In fact, if I know Padre Sebastian, he'll
have you wearing horsehair smocks and grubbing with
the local *campesinos* before your head has stopped spinning. Padre Sebastian . . . he is still in charge of the
mission, is he not?"

Good God! This was going from bad to worse. "I
. . . gather you have been to Santa Fe before?"

"A time or two." He grinned faintly. "The good padre
used to stop in at the saloons frequently to try to reform
his flock. You might say hello to him for me; he'll remember me as being one of his bigger failures."

"I'm sure he will be pleased to offer a novena for
your soul, Mr. McBride," she said tartly.

"Get him to say one for yours, while he's at it, although frankly, horsehair robes notwithstanding, I can't
see you lasting much past the first month—and that's
only assuming you get there at all."

"And why would I not get there?" she asked angrily.

"Well, for one thing, in a day or so from now, we'll be
heading into desert. You think it's hot and uncomfortable now . . . it's going to get a whole lot worse before
it gets any better. This"—he plucked the heavy wool of
her jacket between a thumb and forefinger—"will have
you sweating away more moisture than you can afford

to lose. You won't get ten miles wrapped up in twenty layers of propriety."

Two hot splashes of color flared in Aubrey's cheeks and she deliberately kept her eyes lowered, shielding her growing fury from his further amusement.

"Obviously, sir, the knowledge you lack in social refinements over the past five years does not include an ignorance of fashion. Once again, I am astounded to find myself in your debt, for I am sure I *never* would have thought to adjust my clothing to the climate without your expert guidance."

His grin returned with a predatory vengeance. "In that case, Miss Blue, if I can ever be of any assistance in helping you decide which garments to remove, feel free to call on my guidance any time."

Aubrey's cheeks glowed a dull red. She could hear the blood rushing past her ears and the anger pounding in her temples. A tinkle of gay laughter sent her gaze flicking to the doorway of the relay station, where Magenta Royale was emerging into the sunlight in a swath of purple satin.

"I would suggest you try making your offer elsewhere, Mr. McBride. No doubt you would have much better luck."

"Better luck," he agreed dryly. "And better results."

Aubrey made small fists out of her hands and spoke through the grate of her teeth. "If you will excuse me, I should see if Mr. Shillingsworth requires any aid."

McBride lifted his hand and touched a finger mockingly to the brim of his hat. She turned, and with as much dignity as she could rouse, stormed away in her crushed hat, her drooping feather, and a worsted skirt that snagged and caught on a needle-sharp thistle. A kick and a vehement curse freed it, both reflexes so violently out of keeping with the stiff-backed indignation of a proper schoolmarm that Christian McBride stopped mid-stride and was startled yet again into staring after her.

He kept staring, his grin widening until he became aware of another presence by his side. The Ute had moved with his customary stealth, not even stirring the air to forewarn his arrival.

He was bareheaded under the glare of sunlight, his hair gleaming blue-black against his bronzed skin. Gleaming elsewhere was an ornately wrought thunderbird fashioned from silver, inlaid with beads of fine turquoise. It hung from a thong around his neck, jostled free of the chamois by the bouncing ride topside with Jim Brody.

"Your years away have caused your tongue to grow loose, McBride," Sun Shadow remarked in lilting Shoshonean. "Or is it your intention the wind should carry news of your parole back to Santa Fe before the stage arrives?"

"I have no doubt my early departure from prison is news there already."

"Still, you were never one to part with more words than were necessary, and rarely any words at all when all you wanted was a skirt lifted."

"Those particular skirts would not lift to anything less than a blast of gunpowder," McBride snorted derisively. "And the rewards would be as sweet as bile and vinegar."

"I have seen you take vinegar before instead of wine. And yet, perhaps the Songbird is indeed more to your liking?"

Knowing the faint tremor in the Ute's voice was the closest he came to laughing out loud, McBride responded with a scowl. "Perhaps she is. Or perhaps I should tell her that the mighty Ute chieftan is searching for somewhere to poke more than his nose. She seems fit for the challenge, and I have no doubt your wife would thank me for delivering you home with a few of your feathers trimmed."

Only the Ute's brown eyes registered a trace of alarm as the plainsman stalked away, and they found no further assurance in seeing that Aubrey had emerged unobserved from behind the bushes and could not have helped but overhear their entire exchange. Neither her eyes nor her expression gave any indication she had understood a word they had said. Nonetheless, it was a source of further annoyance to see her gaze drop to where the thunderbird glittered against his deerhide shirt.

"Stolen," he said in crisp Shoshonean. "From between the breasts of a white whore."

The blue eyes lifted calmly to his and she offered a politely hesitant smile. "I'm afraid I don't understand . . . is Mr. Brody ready to leave again?"

The darker eyes narrowed. "You would do better to join the others inside," he advised, still in his own language. "Those bushes are a favored resting place for rattlesnakes."

"I beg your pardon? Forgive me, Mr.—?"

But he was no longer listening. With a scornful nod, Sun Shadow turned abruptly away and was walking back to the coach.

Aubrey closed her mouth slowly, pressing her lips together until they were a thin, tight line.

"Touchy creatures, these savages," said Shillingsworth as he came up beside her. He was pale and his hand trembled as he pressed his handkerchief to his brow, but his stomach no longer rumbled like a volcano and the earth had stopped shifting beneath his feet. "But didn't Mr. McBride say he understood English?"

"He understood," Aubrey said quietly. "He was just checking to see if I did."

"You? Understand gibberish? Rather a farfetched suspicion, isn't it?"

Not so farfetched, she mused, if he'd known her father had had many peaceful dealings with Utes and Navajos, and had believed the way to friendly coexistence was through communication. But she only smiled and said, "They're a suspicious lot, I suppose. And not without a sense of humor. If one of us were to suffer, say, a bite from a rattlesnake, he could claim, quite truthfully, that he had warned us away from the nest."

"Rattlesnakes!" Shillingsworth exclaimed. He flinched away from the copse of stubby trees as if they had suddenly erupted in flame. "Oh my. You don't suppose that's what he was doing, do you?"

"No," Aubrey murmured, her gaze wandering to where McBride stood in the shade with Magenta Royale. "The only rattlesnakes in these parts are right out in the open."

3

 At the end of their first full forty-eight hours of travel, Aubrey's neck was stiff with agony. Her legs were cramped and bruised from the constant need to compensate for the motion of the coach, her spine refused to unbend without making major compromises and made disembarking an unspeakable misery.

The way station outside of Fort Dodge looked like a palace, even though it was a plain pine-board construction with a packed earth floor and narrow cubicles partitioned off the main room for sleeping quarters. It sat within twenty yards of the Arkansas River, the building, stables, and corals well within sight of the army outpost less than a mile away across the dry plain.

Directed to one of the cubicles, Aubrey stretched out gratefully on the hard cot, fearing she might never be able to rise again. As monotonous and wearying as it was to travel by day, it was nothing compared to the bouncing discomfort of trying to catch a few hours' sleep while the coach rumbled on through the darkness. The men had gallantly spent most of the night in the open air on the roof of the coach, allowing Aubrey and Magenta to fold the seats down inside and convert them to beds. But there was nothing to hold onto, nothing but a hard rim of wood to prevent them from rolling head-first onto the floor in any sudden plunge.

Jim Brody, she was sure, would have had no qualms about pushing forward this second night and traveling straight through, had it not been for the fact that the next sixty miles between the Arkansas and the Cimarron rivers were barren desert. A driver short on sleep or shy of visibility could easily lose his way, spelling certain doom for animals and passengers in the heat and end-less miles of sand.

In preparation for the crossing, the Concord had been driven into the shallow waters of the river, there to spend the night so the wheels would soak up the needed moisture. Extra water barrels would be strapped to the boot, and the horses would be replaced with sturdier mules who worked harder and better under adverse conditions. There was a relay station midway across the desert, where they would change mules and take on more water if necessary, but it was also located in the heart of Indian Territory and more often than not, Co-manche and Kiowa raiders carried off the extra mule teams and fouled the water to express their displeasure at the white man's presence on their land.

Less than half an hour was spent prone on the cot before Aubrey's fears of paralysis were proved false. A mouth-watering aroma drifted through the cracks in the thin plank walls, indicating the first hot meal anyone had had since boarding the Concord in Great Bend. One by one the bleary, grimy travelers who had stag-gered blank-eyed into the way station appeared around the scrubbed wood trestle table, as eager and giddy as children awaiting a feast.

Magenta Royale, to no one's surprise, commanded the center of attention. She had changed gowns, replac-ing the purple satin with a bustled frock of deep green brocade. There was not a yellow curl tumbled out of place, and her rouge had been restored to its full glowing strength.

Aubrey's sturdy brown suit, having withstood rigorous conditions out of sheer, iron obstinancy, was showing equal zeal in keeping the dust scratching at her flesh and the stifling effects of the long departed sun trapped against her skin. The bridge of her nose was red and irritated where the wire-rimmed spectacles constantly rubbed against it, and where her hat had formerly been perched on the crown of her head, there was now a darker circle of jet black hair that had been shielded from the layers of dirt and dust.

She took a seat at the end of the table, as far from the others as was discreetly possible. The peddler eased his bulk into a chair diagonally opposite her, leaving Greaves, Magenta Royale, and the plainsman to share the other end.

Jim Brody had declared himself ravenous enough to eat the jaded team of horses, and indeed, had helped himself to monstrous portions of fried venison steak, mesquite beans, and corn bread before the stationmaster's wife had finished loading the serving platters. Sun Shadow, looking as agile and rested as he had from the outset of the journey, had come inside with the others, but only long enough to accept a plate from their hostess and help himself to a cup of steaming coffee. Seeing that the Indian had elected to eat his meal out-of-doors, Jim Brody followed suit, scraping the first plateful of food into his mouth before refilling it and prowling outside after the Ute.

In their two days and a night together, the unlikely pair had formed a working alliance of sorts. Brody, by nature, had little or nothing to do with any of the other passengers and felt quite comfortable with the silent companionship of the Ute. He fidgeted and worked his

tobacco cud ferociously each time McBride took a spell
on the rooftop, and by mutual consent, the spells became shorter and shorter. Jim claimed a touch of nervous disorder whenever Sun Shadow was out of his sight
for very long, as if he were waiting for the moment when
the savagery would explode and the calm, placid Indian
would leap to his feet with a bloodcurdling howl and
dive for the nearest scalp.

For Sun Shadow's part, he appeared to tolerate
Brody's suspicions with a wry eye. Moreover, he was
rigidly uncomfortable on the few occasions he had ridden inside the coach, due in no small part to Magenta's
tactless insistence that he sit on the floor, or Darby
Greaves's constant stare and even more constant shifting to give ample view of the ivory-handled Smith and
Wessons he wore in a gambler's rig—suspender-like
holsters that cradled the guns next to his ribs.

McBride would have made it a trio dining under the
stars if not for Magenta Royale's insistence that the
more "cultured" members of the party should dine together, ostensibly to get to know each other better, but
more likely to regale her captive audience with her long
list of accomplishments on stage—the full recital of
which had been sorely hampered by the inability to con-
verse inside the coach in anything less than a shout.

Pots of coffee, as black as coal and viscid enough to
float the crystals of sugar on its surface, accompanied
the meal. It had the same revitalizing effect on hearts
and pulse beats as the half-quart of whiskey Darby
Greaves consumed with his food. Magenta, disdaining
the coffee after the first scalding mouthful, insisted he
share the other half of the bottle. Despite her repeated
insistence that hard liquor had rarely passed her lips,
she finished her first glassful and was well on her way
through the second before she stopped talking long

enough to eat. Armbruster Shillingsworth was more than happy to take up the slack.

"Mr. Brody tells me we are making excellent time."

Aubrey looked up from her venison. "Did he indeed, Mr. Shillingsworth. I must say, I am not surprised."

"Bruster, please," he smiled. "Please, everyone"—he glanced around the table—"call me Bruster; it is so much less taxing on the tongue. And since we still have a fair distance to travel together—"

"Yes, well, as I was saying," Greaves interrupted, "distance is no object when it comes to an appreciation of the arts. Miss Royale and I are traveling to Santa Fe at the request of a very influential patron; hopefully for what will become an extremely long, extremely lucrative engagement at the Golden Eagle Emporium."

"A saloon?" Bruster asked guilelessly.

"An opera house," Magenta snapped. "With an impressive theater stage and the most modern facilities in the Western territories."

Greaves took a satisfying swallow of whiskey. "It seems the owner happened to be present at one of Miss Royale's recent performances. He offered an exorbitant sum for the privilege of having Magenta grace his stage, and simply would not take no for an answer."

"A man with impeccable taste, to be sure," Bruster said quickly.

"Maxwell Fleming is not noted for his lack thereof."

Aubrey was not expecting it and was therefore caught off guard at the mention of Fleming's name. She dropped her knife with a clatter and stared, along with everyone else, at the thin red weal of blood swelling on the pad of her thumb.

"H-how clumsy of me," she stammered. "Please, I'm sorry. Go on with what you were saying."

"I hardly remember," Greaves murmured dryly.

"You were discussing the merits of Maxwell Fleming," came the low, lazy drawl of Christian McBride. His remark was directed at Darby Greaves, but the smoky gray eyes were fastened curiously on the sudden and total absence of color in Aubrey's cheeks.

"Mr. Fleming, I am told, is one of the most influential men in New Mexico," Magenta interjected. "I believe he is very good friends with the new governor . . . Axtail, Oxtail . . ."

"Axtell," McBride said with a faint grin. "The governor's name is Axtell."

"Whatever." Magenta dismissed the error with a flicker of painted fingernails. "At any rate, from what we have been able to ascertain, Mr. Fleming owns nearly everything of importance in Santa Fe."

"Not to mention every*one.*"

"I beg your pardon?" McBride's voice had been so low, Magenta was able to take advantage of the opportunity to lean forward, not only to intimate the comment had been for her ears only, but to give him an unimpaired view of the ample white flesh swelling over the edge of her bodice. "Did you say you know him?"

McBride enjoyed the view, as intended, then delayed his answer a moment longer to spare a glance in Aubrey's direction. "Our paths have crossed a time or two," he admitted.

"Then you have been to Santa Fe before?"

"I was born and raised in New Mexico, ma'am."

"Really! How intriguing. Darby, dear, isn't that intriguing?"

"Profoundly."

Magenta shot Greaves a black look, then smiled and fluttered for the benefit of the plainsman again. "But I am crushed, Mr. McBride. You have not booked passage all the way to Santa Fe."

"The name is Christian. And I'm afraid I have some business to tend to first."

"First? Does that mean . . . Christian . . . that you might find time to come and see me perform at the Golden Eagle? I shall be there at least a month, hopefully longer if the reception is as warm as the climate."

"I don't think you'll have much to worry about there, Miss Royale. I wouldn't be a bit surprised if you sing to a full house every night."

"Really," she purred again, managing to stretch the word to a dozen syllables. "And here I was, concerned that Santa Fe would be full of peasants and farmers who would not be willing to part with a few pennies just to hear me sing."

"On the contrary. These are boom times for Santa Fe. I would expect the town is full of nothing but rich *yanquis* who are only too happy to be separated from their double eagles and gold nuggets . . . even more so if done in the company of a smile and a beautiful woman. Ranchers, businessmen, merchants—not to mention traders and miners—are always starved for a few genteel remembrances from home. And then there are those of us who haven't had the benefit of life's simple pleasures for quite some time"—Aubrey kept her eyes deliberately averted, but she could sense another glance cast her way—"and speaking for myself, I don't see that you'll have any problem at all."

"Why, you're absolutely right. I hadn't quite thought of it that way . . . men yearning for the sights and sounds they left behind; sweethearts torn asunder in the pursuit of a greater dream . . . a dream that can only be bought for the price of great loneliness." Magenta's eyes misted over for full, dramatic impact as she rose slowly to her feet, her hands clasped before her and pressed to her bosom. "Lost loves. Absent sweethearts. Yes . . . yes, I do believe you have given me the very inspiration I need. Why, I have several positively heart-wrenching ballads in my repertoire that should do perfectly."

She sighed, envisioning the cheers and rousing applause, then sank back down onto her chair and brought her large, golden eyes to bear on the plainsman's bemused face.

"Thank you, Mr. McBride," she whispered.

"Christian."

"Thank you . . . Christian. But tell me, do they have any real musicians, or must I be content with a simple guitarist?"

McBride rolled an unlit cheroot between his thumb and forefinger and stared at Magenta. "Those 'simple' guitarists play some of the most beautiful music in the world, ma'am. I'm sure you'll find them more than adequate accompaniment for your singing. And now, if you'll excuse me—" His chair scraped away from the table. "It's been a long day and morning comes early. I think I'll have me a last smoke and catch as much sleep as I can."

He nodded and unhooked his hat from the railback of the chair, seating it firmly on his head again as he walked to the door. Magenta's tiger-eyes measured the long-legged stride and when he was gone, she dipped the painted tip of her finger into her whiskey glass and thoughtfully licked it clean.

"He certainly makes Santa Fe sound appealing, doesn't he?"

"I have a feeling it isn't Santa Fe you find so suddenly appealing," Greaves muttered thickly.

Magenta drew a brusque breath and turned to him. "And just what is that supposed to mean?"

"It means if you made your invitation any clearer, the man would have more than his nose stuck down your corset by now."

She arched a finely shaped eyebrow and smiled

tightly. "Why, Darby dear, do I detect a note of jealousy?"

"Jealousy over what?" he scoffed. "A cowboy who travels with his own pretty Indian boy? Or the daunting possibility I might lose my place in your bed for a turn or two?"

A dull red seeped up beneath Magenta's face powder. Her eyes narrowed to brittle amber slits and her knuckles turned pink where her hand grasped her glass.

"I suppose I should have grown used to the fact by now that your vulgarity increases in direct proportion to the amount of whiskey you consume."

Greaves smiled crookedly. "You've never complained before. The more vulgarity the better, I thought."

"You're drunk," she said coldly.

"Not quite," he declared, lifting his glass in a mocking salute. "But trying hard."

"Then by all means, take your bottle and try elsewhere. You are beginning to bore me."

"Whoa, now, I wouldn't want to do that," Greaves insisted, pulling himself to his feet. He snatched the bottle off the table and, without a further word to anyone, followed McBride out into the darkness.

"A hopeless drunkard," Magenta hissed while he was still within earshot. Conscious of the others still in the room, she snapped open her fan and agitated it so vigorously the few crumbs left on Bruster's plate jumped off onto his lap. "I only humor him because he was once a dear and sweet friend. Alas, I suppose we all have our crosses to bear, and Darby Greaves is mine."

"He seems nice enough, er, to a point," Bruster offered solicitously. The corresponding glare he received from Magenta by way of a response prompted him to gulp down the last mouthful of his coffee and hastily excuse himself into his assigned cubicle.

"Men," Magenta snorted. "I swear I don't know what

I see in them sometime. Which isn't to say we could get along without them, now could we?"

Aubrey looked up, aware suddenly that she was the last one seated at the table with Magenta Royale. Moreover, she was being stared at, the kohled eyes waiting for either corroboration or argument.

"I . . . I wouldn't know."

"No. I don't suppose you would. Well, take my word for it, most of them are all bluster and ass wind. Once in a rare while you come across a *real* man, one with guts enough to stand up to life, guts enough to take what he wants and to hell with asking first. McBride, for instance. I'll bet he doesn't ask anyone's permission to do anything."

"I . . . I wouldn't know that either," Aubrey said, and started to rise.

"Come now, dearie," Magenta laughed. "Don't give me that cow-eyed innocence, it just won't wash. I've seen the way you look at him sometimes, and don't misunderstand me—there's nothing wrong with a good look now and then. Hell, if you *didn't* look, it wouldn't be healthy. All the same, clamping your knees together and going beet red in the face every time a man looks back isn't going to get you anywhere fast. Relax a little. Try not to act as if you'd sooner carve a man up for fish bait as give him the time of day. Once we get to Santa Fe, there will be plenty of men just hopping up and down looking for a warm place to put it. As long as you're alive and breathing, you'll do all right."

Aubrey heard a creaking floorboard and glanced at Bruster's closed door.

"Thank you," she said tautly. "I'll consider your advice carefully. If you'll excuse me now, however, I think I would like a little fresh air before retiring."

Magenta's wave of dismissal sent a rush of heat into Aubrey's cheeks and she hurried out into the cooling night air. The angry crunch of her footsteps carried her rapidly away from the way station, away from the moon-washed stables and corrals, and down to the riverbank. She descended the steep embankment and walked a short distance along the sandy shoreline until she was certain she was well out of sight of any eyes that might have been watching from a window or the yard. For all of the hasty exits made from the station over the past few minutes, there was no sign of anyone else on the plain or by the river.

The station had been built where the Arkansas was its narrowest and shallowest to make for an easy crossing. Where Aubrey walked, the water rushed alongside her, skimming over a ledge formed from gravel and shale, gleaming like molten pewter under the moonlight. The breeze chased small whorls of sand up from the river's edge, swirling it past Aubrey's skirts and salting the slender boughs of the trees that grew nearby.

She kicked savagely at the first loose object she spied on the coarse sand—a broken piece of driftwood—then paced in an angry circle, her hands on her hips, her lips moving in a silent litany of all the things she would have liked to say aloud to the incomparable Magenta Royale, Jewel of New Orleans. There were limits to what she could endure, and both Magenta and McBride were sorely testing them.

Six more days.

Aubrey removed the owlish spectacles and rubbed the bridge of her nose. There were six more days to go until the coach arrived in Santa Fe, only one more overnight stop scheduled at Taylor Springs. She could do it. She had tolerated far worse over the years, and undoubtedly had far worse ahead of her when she reached her destination.

She felt the gooseflesh rise in a cool spray along her arms and she found herself unconsciously tracing the area on her upper arm where a pale crescent-shaped scar marked where the bullet from Scud Holwell's gun had creased her flesh. She was going back to Santa Fe. After all of these years, she was going back. Wasn't that something in itself?

The tight-fitting shoes she wore pinched her feet and made her hobble to a halt. In a last surge of rebellion, she kicked out again, this time startling a pair of frogs into flight.

"Well, well, well. Can this mean the schoolmarm has a spark of fire in her after all?"

Aubrey whirled around, searching for the owner of the voice, and was rewarded by the sight of Darby Greaves detaching himself from the dark overhang of the embankment. When he stepped into the full moonlight, something sparkled in his right hand—the whiskey bottle, a good deal lighter in content than when he had left the station.

"Got to you too, did she?" he grinned. "That's my Clara. Never leaves a rock unturned if she can help it."

"I'm sure I don't know what you are talking about, Mr. Greaves. I just came out for some fresh air."

"Sure you did. Well, you came to the right place—" He swayed slightly as he waved a hand across the span of the horizon. "There's one hell of a lot of fresh air here, and not much more."

Aubrey inched casually back out of arm's reach, deciding the air was considerably fresher away from the alcoholic fumes of his breath.

"I'm a city boy myself. Born and raised in New Orleans. Closest I came to living in nature was when my daddy and I rode the riverboats."

Aubrey edged closer to the river. "He was a captain?"

"Hell no," Greaves chuckled. "Jefferson Beauregard Greaves was the best damned poker player east or west of the Mississippi. He could sit down at a table with a dollar and walk away with a few thousand more to keep it company. He used to take me with him sometimes— to teach me the ropes, you know? But my hands were never as quick as his, and it used to get him madder than hell when I missed an easy play."

He stared at the rushing water for a long, silent moment, then lifted the bottle and sucked the last two mouthfuls dry. The bottle arced away with a flick of his wrist and shattered against rocks somewhere out in the darkness.

"I met Clara out on a riverboat," he continued matter-of-factly. "Four years ago, to be precise. Clara Nobody from Nowhere. She was finding more work to do on her back than she was on any stage. But I saw the potential. I showed her how to dress, and walk, and talk. She already had talent and plenty of it, any fool could see that . . . and if nothing else, I was no fool. At least I wasn't back then."

"Are you certain you ought to be telling me this?" Aubrey asked, glancing over her shoulder to see how far she was from the edge of the water.

"My dear Miss Blue. I am a man of infinite wisdom and piercing insight. The very nature of your character assures me that whatever we might say . . . or do tonight will go no farther."

"Yes, well, as much as I should like to stay and chat, Mr. Greaves, it has been a very long day and—"

"Are you afraid of me, Miss Blue?"

She stopped and met his gaze with a directness that took him by surprise. "No, Mr. Greaves, I am not afraid of you. I am merely extremely tired. It has been a long and aggravating day, which you are causing to be even longer and more aggravating. Now, if you don't mind—"

"My, my." His eyes narrowed and his mouth curved

up at the corners. "I do believe that was the longest
single speech I have heard you deliver."

"Good *night*, Mr. Greaves."

She started to walk briskly toward the embankment,
but no sooner had she passed Darby Greaves than he
was in front of her again, grinning and blocking her
path. When she tried to dodge, he moved with her, and
when she opened her mouth to demand he stand aside,
his hand came up to clamp roughly over her lips, while
his free arm circled her waist and jerked her forward in
a crush against his body.

"Now, we don't want to make a scene, do we, schoolteacher? We both have a pretty good idea why you followed me out here tonight, and frankly, while I can't say
you're exactly the kind of woman to make a man break
out in a sweat, I will admit to there being *some*thing
about you that makes the blood flow a little warmer. I
can't quite put my finger on what it is that just doesn't
add up about you, but I know it's there. Like an itch you
can't quite scratch."

Aubrey twisted and tried to free her hands to claw at
his face, but her arms were pinned tight to his body. She
lashed out with her feet and managed to kick him
smartly on the shin, but her triumph was short-lived. He
lifted her and dragged her into the deeper shadows of
the embankment, slamming her sharply against the
rough bark of a tree. Her head struck the trunk and for
the moment it took her to regain her dazed senses,
Greaves had insinuated his hand beneath the wool of
her jacket and had discovered the unexpected bounty
hidden there.

"Hey now, looks like you've been keeping secrets
from us, schoolteacher. Why on earth would you want
to keep lovely little things like these all wrapped up in
worsted?"

Aubrey cursed as he squeezed a hand around her

breast and she kicked out again, striking nothing more than air for the most part. She wriggled her hands free and bunched them into fists, pushing and beating against his chest, but the liquor Greaves had consumed made him immune to her struggles as well as her muffled cries of outrage.

"Like that, do you? Well, you'll like this more." He pushed forward, pressing the heat of his body against her. He sank his lips and teeth into the arched curve of her throat and ran his tongue up to her ear, thrusting it wetly in and around the delicate pink curls of flesh.

Aubrey strained to break out from under the hand that was now clamped over both her mouth and nose. She could not breathe. She could not see anything in the black heart of the shadows. She could only feel the slimy wetness in her ear and hear his rasping breath, and she was horribly aware of his hand kneading and fondling her breasts.

Something darker than the shadows moved up behind them. Greaves made a choking sound against her throat and in the next instant, she was free. He was flung to one side, landing hard enough to slide several feet in the coarse sand.

Aubrey stumbled clear, her arms stretched out in front of her, groping for the clearer sanity of the moonlight. She gasped for deep mouthfuls of air and scrubbed the cuff of her sleeve over her ear and neck to blot up the disgusting wetness.

"You all right, ma'am?"

It was the plainsman. Where he had come from and how much he had seen and overheard, Aubrey did not know, and did not care. He had followed her out of the shadows and his broad shoulders and wide-brimmed hat were a welcomed silhouette against the moonlight.

Before Aubrey could answer, a curse and the sound of pounding feet brought Darby Greaves up off the ground at a run. He went straight for McBride, but the plainsman was ready for him, pivoting easily and lightly around, stepping to one side so that Greaves ran smack into the powerful swing of his fist.

The impact doubled the agent over, folding him in half as every last scrap of air was slammed out of his lungs. He hung there a moment, his eyes bulging and his mouth agape before he crumpled heavily to his knees, then to an unconscious sprawl on his back.

McBride straightened slowly. He flexed his fist and shook it once to release the tension in his arm.

"Hell of a waste of good whiskey when a man can't hold it," he mused. He looked at Aubrey and pushed back the brim of his hat so that his face was bathed in moonlight.

"You all right, Miss Blue?" he asked again.

"I . . . I think so." She fumbled with her jacket to settle it properly, and ran a trembling hand up to her hair, attempting to recapture the long wisps that had been torn loose from the chignon. The knot itself had been worked askew, with pins and curls straggling over her shoulders, threatening to come completely unwound in the next turn or two of her head.

McBride watched her efforts in silence, wondering if it was the ethereal light playing tricks with his eyes, or if there really was more substance and shape to the schoolmarm than her bulky clothing and bottle-glass stares let on. With her arms raised, the wool of her jacket was drawn tight around an amazingly slim waistline, while at the same time, emphasizing a generous fullness elsewhere.

"I expect I should thank you for coming along when you did, Mr. McBride."

"What?" His gaze snapped up to her face.

"I honestly don't know what happened. He was just talking one minute, and the next—"

"You shouldn't come out for walks in the moonlight with men you hardly know. Drunken men at that."

"I did not come out for a walk with him," she protested archly. "I thought I was quite alone, in fact, until he came out of the shadows."

"Didn't your mother ever teach you to watch out behind you?"

Aubrey stopped fumbling with pins and curls and looked up at the plainsman's starkly handsome features. While the remark had not been blatantly rude, it had not been delivered in the kindest of tones either, and not without the increasingly annoying presence of an insolent smile curled on his lips. Locks of his hair were ruffled forward by the breeze, the tarnished blond rendered almost silver in the moonlight. Compounding her distraction, that same breeze brought her the fresh, raw scent of tobacco and faint proof that he did indeed sweat like mortal men.

McBride's eyes narrowed. The strands of long black hair that had been torn loose of the spinsterish bun trailed over her shoulder and fell in a dark ripple almost to her waist. The moonlight revealed a smooth-as-ivory complexion, and without the ungainly spectacles to divert attention, he could see that her brows were as delicately arched as angels' wings. Her eyes were cornflower blue, he remembered, and up until now, he had assumed they had been distorted out of all proportion by the thick lenses she wore. But that wasn't the case. The only thing the glasses had distorted was the shape, and he could see now that they were large and disconcertingly direct, surrounded by absurdly long lashes.

The unveiling of her beauty blew every other thought right out of his mind. The brown worsted shapelessness of her skirt vanished in a blink of his eye, replaced by an image of long, lithe limbs and hips gently flared to complement the trimness of her waist. A second blink restored the barrier of wool, but the damage was done. He was not normally so thick in the head where women were concerned—and he blamed his years in prison for his present shortfall—but this one had managed to fool him. Moreover, he suspected she was well aware of her beauty and had deliberately set out to conceal it.

A groan from Darby Greaves drew their attention to the huddled form on the shale. He was still out cold, but his bruised stomach was reacting to the combined effects of too much alcohol and a too-violent meeting with McBride's fist. The plainsman heard a sluggish gurgle and, with a snort of contempt, he went over to the agent and rolled him onto his side so he would not choke on his own vomit.

He caught a sparkle of glass in the sand nearby and retrieved Aubrey's fallen spectacles, but after fingering them thoughtfully for a moment, he slipped them into his pocket unseen.

"You might want to take this as another lesson, Miss Blue," he remarked casually as he returned to her side. "Frontier men are not all patience and good manners."

"Like yourself," she added dryly.

He hooked a thumb over his shoulder and smiled in Greaves's direction. "Didn't you just thank me a minute ago for pulling him off you?"

"He was drunk. I could have handled him. And since you questioned my mother's teaching, Mr. McBride, did yours never teach you it was highly impolite to lurk about in the shadows spying on people without making your presence known?"

His eyes glittered faintly. "If I'd wanted to be *real* impolite, I could have offered to hold you down for him. I only interfered because your squawkings were keeping me from a good night's sleep."

"In that case, I do apologize," she said stiffly. "The

next time I am accosted, I shall try to have it done in some place that will not inconvenience you."

"I'd be obliged, ma'am," he grinned, offering a mock salute.

Aubrey spun on her heels and covered the distance back to the way station with angry, striding steps. McBride followed at a bemused distance, intending to return the spectacles the first time she tripped and fell flat on her face. But she did not fall. She did not even stumble over any of the treacherously half-buried roots that crisscrossed the top of the embankment.

The only crash came at the door of the station house where Aubrey ran headlong into Magenta Royale.

"Well! I was beginning to think there was a party going on out there," the songstress declared.

"If there isn't, I'm sure you'll know how to start one," Aubrey snapped, pushing past the woman without another word.

Magenta's eyebrows lifted gently. She watched the door to Aubrey's cubicle slam shut behind a sworl of brown worsted, then turned and gazed curiously out over the moonlit landscape. McBride's formidable silhouette was easily identifiable against the backdrop of the river and the star-studded sky, and Magenta smiled wryly.

"Silly chit. That's what comes of trying to hand out good advice."

She made a casual adjustment to the front of her bodice, slipping several more buttons from their loops so that it looked like one good breath would set everything springing free. She had a sudden vision of McBride's hands on her flesh and she shivered in anticipation, but when she looked back toward the river, he was gone. She looked to the left and to the right; she craned her neck and stood on tiptoes, but there was no sign of him.

Assuming he couldn't have gone far, Magenta started

across the compound. Halfway across, her steps slowed, and at the corral, she stopped completely.

Darby would be furious if she threw herself at the plainsman. He was furious anyway with the way she was flirting, but instead of doing anything about it, he had gone off somewhere to nurse his pout with a bottle of whiskey. And Magenta . . . well, Magenta hadn't gone to all the trouble of washing and primping and preening for nothing. If Darby couldn't take a little healthy teasing, there were others who could—and probably do a better job of it. Judging by the look and size of McBride, he could more than likely reach places Darby could only dream about, and do it with the coarse lack of finesse she often found herself craving from her earlier days on the riverboats. Then, she liked them big and ugly and rough. Darby had supposedly "saved" her from all of that, and in the beginning he had been an adequate lover as well as a clever manager. Lately, however, the whiskey he consumed left him flaccid and of little use to her between the sheets. A few quick stabs here and there and he was bleating like a stuck pig, proud of himself for even managing that much.

This wouldn't be the first time Magenta had encouraged him to drink himself into oblivion. She'd had her eye on McBride since the depot at Great Bend and had played enough visual games with him all blessed day long to know he was primed and ready. Hell, if he had sent the schoolmarm fleeing back to the station in a state of near-panic, he was more than ready—desperate, in fact, and obviously not too discriminating.

Magenta started to smile, then stopped.

That wouldn't do either, would it? She had never played second choice to anyone, not as far back as she could remember, and certainly not to a knock-kneed spinster with a shrewish tongue and not enough gumption to know how to put it to better use.

Maybe, just maybe, she was going to have to let Christian McBride stew a while longer in his own juices. Maybe she should wait until *he* came to *her;* when he found his pants too tight and his situation too painful to sustain a fascination for dry virgins.

Fine . . . in theory. But what was she supposed to do in the meantime to work out her own travel tensions?

She released a small gust of frustration and turned to go back to the station. A lantern was burning inside the stables and the door was opened just enough to throw a weak streamer of light against the boards outside. The mule-handler stood there relieving himself, a big brute of a man with massive, apelike arms that hung down from shoulders as wide and thick as a bull's. As he turned, startled by the sound her skirts made scuffing over the dry earth, Magenta saw an even thicker, trunk-like appendage slung halfway down his thigh, dripping its last few steamy drops against the wall.

Magenta stared and felt herself grow weak in the knees.

The hostler stared back, his eyes fixed on the straining mounds of firm white flesh that seemed to swell harder and firmer with each stilted breath. Aware of the instant and uncomfortable effect the view was having on him, he moved one hairy paw to cover himself, and was doubly surprised to feel Magenta's hands there to stop him.

"Sumpthin' I kin . . . help you with, ma'am?"

Magenta moistened her lips.

"As a matter of fact," she rasped. "There is."

4

 They were gone.

Aubrey searched high and low, shook out the folds of her skirt and turned the pockets of the jacket inside out, but they were gone.

A small thing, those damned spectacles, but a large contributing factor in making her feel as if she was succeeding in hiding within herself. She had deliberately purchased the thickest, ugliest pair she could find, knowing how unattractive they would make her appear, how plain and uninteresting—not to mention clumsy when she stumbled and bumped into misjudged objects.

Frustrated and close to tears, Aubrey slumped down on the edge of the hard cot. She had slept very little—if at all—during the night, and was tired enough to wish she *could* cry. She had allowed for a certain amount of unexpected surprises along the way. After all, when did anything ever go exactly as planned? But McBride was proving to be a nuisance—an increasingly annoying one, and Greaves would probably cause more trouble if he could. So far Magenta was more amused by the schoolmarm's presence than threatened by it, but that was only because she had no reason to regard Aubrey as a rival.

Aubrey held up a small silver-backed mirror and frowned at her reflection. Lucius had always said her eyes were her most striking feature as well as her greatest asset. Large and expressive when she wanted them to be, capable of projecting an array of emotions at will. She had learned to use them to good effect, changing frowns to smiles, anger to sympathy, mistrust to tears. She had even manipulated Lucius a time or two, leaving him to wonder if he had been told the truth or just a clever variation.

Aubrey lowered the mirror and turned to look out the window. The frayed piece of cheesecloth serving as a curtain wafted gently in the perpetual breeze that blew off the Kansas plains. The sky beyond was still dark, with only the faintest, quivering suggestion of paler light along the horizon to indicate dawn was a breath away.

She must have lost the accursed spectacles somewhere out on the riverbank last night, which meant she would either have to go and look for them, or resign herself to going on without them.

Such a small, stupid thing.

She consulted the mirror again and mouthed a soft oath. Even with her hair skinned back into a severe knot and her complexion insulted by the dull brown wool, it was not enough. Magenta's eyes were too sharp and her feline instincts too ingrained. It would be like waving raw meat before a vulture. McBride's vanity had already been pricked; he would amuse himself to no end, stalking her like a cat stalks a mouse, watching for any other small slip to pounce upon. Greaves had already said he *thought* something about her was not quite right, but McBride would *know*. He was nobody's fool.

Aubrey dropped her mirror and brush back into her carpetbag and stared at her feet. She wriggled toes that were aching and blistered from being squeezed into too-tight shoes, and she thought of how wonderful it would

feel to run barefoot to the river and wade knee-deep
into the cold rushing water.

Sighing an apology to her toes, she pulled on the mur-
derously thick black wool stockings and reached for her
shoes. Forcing her feet into them and hooking the row
of buttons was agony, but she succeeded, and cracking
the door half an inch to ensure there was no one else
about yet, she tiptoed out of the station and into the
open yard.

The air was still blessedly cool, damp with the moisture that had collected overnight on the grasses and
scrub. The rim of light along the horizon was glowing
pink now, promising another clear, dry, hot day under
the sun. A scruffy ball of sagebrush tumbled by, and a
fine layer of sand, almost like fog, skimmed along the
packed earth of the yard and spilled over the bank to
the river. A curious horse nickered softly in the corral,
but as Aubrey moved past, he lowered his head and
returned to the more important business of scratching
against a post.

She picked her way carefully down the embankment
and followed the river to the spot where Greaves had
attacked her. The agent was nowhere in sight, but the
sand was well scuffed and indented where he had lain.
She started her search in the general area where she
had been pacing, and, finding nothing but shiny stones
and broken sticks, widened her search to the dark copse
of trees.

The light improved with every minute that passed, but
there were still shadows hugging the embankment—
shadows deep enough and dark enough to raise the
prickle of an alarm across the nape of her neck. Her
back was to the trees but her every sense was tuned to
whoever was there watching her. And if it was Greaves,
she had no intention of allowing a repetition of last
night.

Shielding the movement with her body, she slipped her hand inside the pocket of her skirt and closed it around the reassuring comfort of the .22 derringer she'd had the foresight to remove from her carpetbag. She eased her finger around the trigger and waited, knowing that the watcher knew she had sensed his presence.

"Looking for something?"

Aubrey closed her eyes. Her fingers uncurled from the mother-of-pearl handle and were withdrawn from the pocket as she turned to confront the plainsman.

"Don't you ever sleep, McBride?"

"Never more than one eye at a time. It's a habit I've had to acquire over the years." He moved out of the shadows, looking much the same as he had under the moonlight, except that his head was bare and his shirt hung open to his waist. She had evidently interrupted him while he had been washing in the river, for the skin on his face and neck was damp, and tiny rivulets of water glistened on the boldly sculpted muscles of his chest. Most men, cowboys or city slickers, were rarely caught out in the sun without their shirts buttoned to their throats, with the result, they were burned bronze from the neck up, but milky white elsewhere. The dress codes at Leavenworth had obviously not been so strict, for his tan extended down to his waist. The only hint of paleness was over a welt of scar tissue that ran from just below his left nipple, cutting on a diagonal down across the flat belly. It was an ugly scar, and one that would have been caused by a horrendous wound—from a knife, or a saber blade . . . or an axe? Nor was it the only mark on the weathered torso. Finer scars scored the flesh here and there, suggesting a relatively normal, if violent frontier life.

Until this very moment, she had not troubled herself to wonder at his age or background. He said he had been born and raised in New Mexico—a common link she had deliberately avoided thinking about—but that was all he had said. His age? It could have been anything from the mid-twenties to mid-thirties, the confusion courtesy of any combination of factors beginning with a harsh youth spent on the arid plains and ending with five years of forced labor at Leavenworth. Moreover, he wore his guns slung low on his hips, suggesting they were not casual accessories. The commanding stance she had initially attributed to army training could as easily be applied to a man who had made his living with a gun.

Who the devil *was* Christian McBride, and what was he doing on a stagecoach bound for Santa Fe?

"I suppose I could ask you the same thing," he murmured.

"What?" Her eyes snapped up from where they had become lost on the hard planes of his chest.

"About your sleeping habits. I would have thought you'd have slept until the coach was rolling out of the yard."

"Oh. Yes, well . . . I dropped something out here last night. And since I wasn't sure what time Mr. Brody would want to get underway, I thought I should come and look as soon as possible."

"Ah." He stepped even closer and took something from his pocket. "And would these be what you've come looking for?"

Her spectacles were cradled in the calloused palm, the wire arms folded in a neat crisscross over the lenses.

"I found them last night when I was saving Greaves from himself," he admitted. "I figured you might come back for them . . . although, from the way you hightailed back to the station, it didn't look to me like you had all that much use for them in the first place."

Aubrey ignored one implication and focused on another. "Are you saying you found them *before* I went back to the station?"

"Greaves practically landed on them."

"Why didn't you give them to me then?"

He grinned easily. "I thought I'd wait and see how much you *wanted* them back."

"So you waited here all night?" she asked incredulously.

"One place is as good as another to sleep. Mind you, Greaves was a pain in the ass, but he seemed to sober up quick enough after I rolled him into the river."

"Why?"

His grin broadened. "I already told you, I don't like my privacy disturbed."

Aubrey laced her fingers tightly together. "I mean, why did you keep my glasses? Why did you wait here all night, and what possible business is it of yours if I want, or indeed, need them?"

McBride's eyes flicked over to the eastern horizon, to the spreading fingers of red and gold light that stretched across the sky.

"Let's just say I'm a curious kind of fellow."

"Curious? Curious about what?"

His eyes narrowed as they approved of the effects of the dawn light on her profile. She had come without the upper armor of brown worsted and the stark whiteness of her high-necked blouse was doing nothing to deter the breeze from drawing attention to the flattering curves beneath. In another few minutes he would know if the moon had been playing tricks with his mind, although he could see enough already to feel a smug measure of satisfaction.

"Greaves said it last night: there's something about you that doesn't sit right."

"Last night Greaves was drunk. A spiny cactus

wouldn't have sat right with him. Now, if you don't mind, I'll just take my property and—"

McBride's fingers curled over the spectacles and he drew them back, out of reach. He had attributed the soft pink stain on her cheeks to the dawn light, but as the light grew bolder, he could see it was anger, not nature, governing her color. It still galled him to think he had missed it. She was very good, and that was some consolation, but why was she out here on the plains east of hell, and why was she doing her best to look like yesterday's news?

The ice blue spheres of her eyes fixed him with a hard stare. "May I ask what game you are playing at, Mc-Bride?"

"Not Virginia," he mused. "And not the Carolinas either."

"I beg your pardon?"

"The accent. It isn't North and it isn't South. You've got the spunk of an outraged Southern belle, yet the frosty glow is pure Yankee."

Aubrey continued to stare at him. She was sorely torn between two urges: one, to simply turn and walk away, and two, to stamp her foot and scream her frustration, *then* walk away.

Instead, she released a slow, exasperated breath. "Mr. McBride—"

"Christian."

"*Mister* McBride . . . I would very much like to go back to the way station and finish packing up my belongings. *All* of my belongings, including my spectacles."

"You still haven't told me how badly you want them."

Aubrey turned and looked at the river, drawing on its calming effects before she gazed back at McBride, a wry and disdainful smile thinning her lips. "And just how badly do you want me to want them, McBride—as if I didn't know."

"Don't flatter yourself, schoolmarm," he said seriously. "You haven't got anything I want, or anything I couldn't take if I did."

"I wouldn't bet on that, McBride," she said. "Better men than you have tried and come up empty-handed. Keep the damned glasses. You need them more than I do, if only to see past your own arrogance."

She started walking away, but only managed to cover a few steps before a curse brought the plainsman after her. He reached out to grasp her arm, but before he could do so, she spun around, the derringer in her hand, cocked and primed to fire.

McBride stopped, the shock flaring in his eyes when he saw the gun. A more deadly response rippled through his arms and he had to curb the ingrained reflex to reach for his own gun. He stared at the derringer—a wickedly inventive weapon boasting four loaded chambers—then at the slender white hand that held it without a waver or tremor of hesitation.

"An interesting addition to a schoolteacher's equipment; right handy alongside a slate and chalk."

"Don't make the mistake of thinking I can't or won't use this," she said evenly.

He spread his arms wide and took a slow, easy step back. "The hand is yours, ma'am. You win the pot."

Aubrey's eyes glittered. "Thank you. I'll take back what's mine now, if you have no further objections."

He glanced at the spectacles, still folded in his hand, and with a smile of capitulation, brought them forward. He held them over Aubrey's outstretched hand for a moment, but at the last second, moved slightly so that they missed her palm and dropped onto the sand. Still smiling, he stepped forward, crushing the glass and wire beneath the heel of his boot.

Aubrey gasped . . . then gasped again as she felt his fist close around hers and wrench the derringer free.

She was quick to swing her other hand up, her nails hooked and ready to claw his face, but he was ready for that as well, catching her wrist with laughable ease and twisting it around to join its mate, already pinned at the small of her back.

"Now then," he grated, "let's deal the deck again and see who comes up aces."

He transferred both of her wrists into one steely hand and held her trapped against the heat of his body while his free hand plucked and pulled at the pins binding her hair at the nape of her neck. Aubrey wriggled and cursed, but he only adjusted the angle at which he held her arms behind her, so that the pain caused her to suck in her breath and endure his torment in outraged silence.

Her hair sprang free, spilling in thick, glossy waves halfway down her back. She twisted sharply in his arms, scattering the curls across her shoulders and sending them lashing across his face.

"Let me go, you son of a bitch!"

"Interesting language too," he mused. "They teach you that at Miss Prim's Academy for budding educators?"

Aubrey stopped struggling for all of ten seconds—long enough for their eyes to meet and lock and an unspoken understanding to pass between them.

"Go to hell, McBride," she spat.

"Thanks, but I've already spent five years there and have no intentions of going back just yet."

His fingers, like an iron vise around her wrists, were under no compunction to spare her any discomfort. He was holding her so close she could smell the musky heat of his skin and the earthy taint of buckskin. She could see the fine beads of water silvering the ends of his hair, slicking the bulge of his muscles, strengthening the impression that there could have been steam rising off his hard flesh. He was too close, and she vented a final, futile surge of energy before falling breathlessly still against him, her breasts heaving from the exertion, her face flushed and her teeth clenched in fury.

"Finished?" he inquired solicitously.

"Let go of me."

"Not just yet. We haven't played out the hand."

"This isn't a game, McBride, and you're *hurting* me."

"If it isn't a game, then why the play-acting?"

"What?"

"Come now. The virginal missionary schoolteacher? It's a pretty good performance, I grant you, but you should have done your homework a little better."

"I'm sure I don't know what you mean," she replied frostily.

"Whereas I'm sure you do."

"I am a teacher. At least, I will be when we reach Santa Fe. For the parochial school at—"

"At San Miguel. Yes, I know. You told me."

"Then I don't—"

"For one thing, Miss Blue, there is no parochial school at San Miguel. It burned down back in '67. And the only Padre Sebastian I knew was a shriveled old Mexican half-wit who claimed to have wandered onto the *llano estacado* and lived off the sage wisdom of Jesus Christ for forty days and forty nights."

Aubrey's mouth opened, then closed again. He had called her bluff with the oldest trick in the book and she could almost see Lucius groaning and shaking his head in disgust. She shook off the image and met his gaze defiantly.

"You have also been away in prison for five years, Mr. McBride. Schools can be rebuilt in that length of time, and new priests can be sent out from the seminary to take charge."

It was a petty comeback, and one which neither of them thought sounded very convincing.

The gray eyes turned molten as they drifted down to the luscious fullness of her lips. As he surveyed the full effect of the growing light on her skin and hair, he knew beyond a doubt it wasn't just the years he'd spent deprived of female company that were causing his blood to slow to a sluggish pounding in his veins. She might not be beautiful in the Eastern sense of appreciation for milk-white complexions and flaxen hair, but the combination of startling blue eyes and jet black hair was stunning. She had a straight nose and a firm little mouth that was portioned for better things than scowling, and he tried to envision it not taut with indignation, but soft and moist and trembling with passion.

"For brevity," he mused, "and the sake of my temper, let us assume that I accept the part about you being a teacher. What other reason is taking you to Santa Fe?"

"Other reason?" she asked on a quick breath—quickened further by the perceptible tightening of his arm around her waist.

"I'm not a stupid man, Miss Blue."

"You give a good imitation of one, McBride."

His eyes narrowed and sharpened. "Excuse me?"

"Think about it, McBride. Why would you suppose a woman like myself would go west? A single woman, with no prospects, no family, no skills other than what were taught at . . . at Miss Prim's Academy for budding educators?"

It was McBride's turn to stare. "You're heading west to hook yourself a husband?"

Aubrey closed her eyes and hoped she looked sufficiently mortified, even swooning a little against the support of his arm for effect.

"You don't have to put it quite so bluntly," she whispered.

He watched the thick black lashes grow shiny with trapped tears and the lushness of her lower lip quiver involuntarily until it was caught and forcibly restrained by the fine white teeth. She was suddenly all innocence and pained vulnerability, and a better man than Christian McBride might have felt chagrined, or at the very least, repulsed by the knowledge that she was just out to trap a man . . . if he believed for one snap of a moment that that was what she was up to.

"You're very good," he murmured. "Really. *Very* good."

The sooty lashes lifted fractionally and she saw the mocking half-smile curve slowly across his handsome face. She also felt a not so subtle change in the tension of his body—he was holding her close enough she would have had to have been numb from the waist down not to have felt it.

"Please . . . let go of me."

"Please?" A sandy-brown eyebrow arched. "A new tact to go along with the tearful confession?"

"Mr. McBride—"

"Christian."

"*Mr. McBride* . . . I don't know what else you want from me."

The smallest hint of a tremor was in her voice, and the echo of it shivered along McBride's spine and triggered a response he was not expecting. The hardness in his body surprised him not at all; these past two weeks since his release from Leavenworth, anything in skirts had had the potential of winning his utmost attention in that area. But this was something else. Something he couldn't quite put his finger on.

Something that definitely needed further investigation.

Aubrey saw the answer to her question in his eyes and tried to push away again, but his hand was suddenly cupping her chin, forcing her to tilt her face up to his. He drew her even closer, pausing when their mouths were only a breath away and the deep, drowning blue of her eyes was all he saw.

"No . . . !"

McBride's mouth smothered the protest, capturing it and stifling it with an ease that left Aubrey without any air or any sense of how to go about replenishing it. She tried to gasp another plea, but that only provided him the opportunity to breach the taut barrier of her lips, to thrust his tongue where it was wanted least and shocked her the most. Aubrey fought the unwanted intrusion, renewing her attempts to wriggle free, but that only provoked him further, as she should have known it would, and his hand moved from her chin to bury itself in the rippling mass of her hair.

Aubrey's struggles grew weaker. McBride's kiss was as cynical and uncompromising as the man himself, but what it lacked in anything vaguely resembling emotion, it made up for in sheer, mind-reeling skill. He knew just how to plunder her mouth so that other areas of her body grew heated with envy. He knew just how to use his lips and tongue so that they became the entire focus of her being; until the languid, liquid waves of light-headedness threatened to leave her sagging in his arms without strength or substance.

Somewhere along the way she discovered he had released her wrists, but the fiercely balled fists she raised against him somehow went limp when they met the iron-hard bulge of muscles in his arms. Even worse, as she clutched at handfuls of buckskin, the cloth shifted and bared his flesh to the shoulders, and her hands betrayed her again by grasping at this sinfully masculine bounty.

McBride's mouth slanted more forcefully over hers and his arms tightened around her, nearly lifting her off the ground in his eagerness to grind himself into the soft valley between her thighs. His breath was harsh and dry in his throat and the blood started to pound through his temples; his tongue lashed at her sweetness and his heart hammered against his chest; his body strained against a long, leggy litheness that made the breath jam somewhere deep in his throat.

Aubrey regained her senses on a flush of pure panic. She burned where he touched her, burned where the bruising pleasure of his body crushed against her. Never in all of her twenty-three years, had she been kissed like this, and if the shameless, urgent hunger that drenched her belly and loins was proof of the power a man could have over such things, she did not want to ever be kissed like this again! Not by anyone. Most definitely not by Christian McBride!

She forced her hands into fists again and finally won McBride's attention. The kiss ended as it had begun, with his fingers cupped roughly under her chin and his eyes blazing intently at her face. But for the briefest of unguarded moments, there was none of the arrogance that had been there previously, none of the bold smugness, and certainly none of the clinical curiosity.

He hadn't expected to enjoy the taste and feel of her half so much. Nor had he expected to end up wanting so much more.

Aubrey stumbled back out of his embrace, retreating two full steps on an energetic thrust that found no resistance this time. Still trembling from the sensations he'd unleashed within her, she wiped the back of her hand across her mouth, as if that could have removed the scalding imprint of his lips.

"You and Greaves have more in common than you realize, McBride," she said raggedly. "You are both bastards."

"I never said I wasn't," he countered evenly.

Aubrey took another step back. And another. He did nothing to try to stop her this time, and only when she had turned completely away and was running back along the riverbank, did he release his breath on a muttered oath and flex his hands to rid them of the memory of her softness.

Unfortunately, there was no such easy remedy for the throbbing tightness in his loins and he mouthed another halfhearted curse to all of womankind as he flung his shirt aside and walked into the swift flow of icy water. When he was thigh-deep, he dove head-first into the current, staying there until his flesh was shocked out of any lingering carnal thoughts.

5

"No mistakes," said Jim Brody. "I knew I smelt trouble a mile or so back, and there it be: straight ahead."

He had halted the coach a mile from the relay station. There was pitch darkness all around them, it being the eerie hour before the moon deigned to appear and the stars were still too shy to spare much light. The desert panned out like a pale sheet of velvet, with no discernible formations or shapes to break the monotony. Nothing moved. No lights shone in the shallow dip of the valley where the relay station was supposed to be.

The passengers had fallen deathly silent at the casual pronounciation of "trouble" up ahead. Throughout the incredibly long, unbelievably jinxed day, they had met with nothing but trouble, starting with a sandstorm that had blown up out of nowhere, and ending with one of the mules pulling up lame.

The storm had struck without warning—none except from Stink Finger Jim Brody who "felt a prickle in his parts" and searched the horizon behind them until he saw the rolling black mass hurling toward them. He had ordered the blinds on the coach windows lowered and fastened tight, then had driven hell bent for leather to a

shelter in the lee of some rocks. With the help of Mc-
Bride and Sun Shadow, he had unhitched the team and
hobbled them separately to a large boulder, thereby
avoiding the danger of having them panic and bolt with
the coach in tow. As it was, one of the mules had ob-
jected to the canvas sacks Jim had started to tie around
its eyes and nose, and had bucked into a rock, tearing
open a wound that would later cripple him too badly to
work his spot in the traces.

The squall itself had been brief, but savage. A maelstrom of boiling, swirling sand had descended upon
them, driving stinging needles of glasslike particles into
mouths, noses, and eyes despite the protective shields of
handkerchiefs and leather blinds. Coughing and choking, the passengers had huddled together out of necessity, with Magenta wailing the loudest and longest at
each gust that shook the coach in its steerhide braces.

When it was over, the seats and floor were covered in
a thick layer of sand. The canvas boot had sprung open
and there was luggage scattered in a semicircle on the
ground. One of Magenta's cases had come to a violent
parting at the seams and there were petticoats, corsets,
and chemises carried away to adorn cactus belles for a
mile in the wake of the departing cloud of sand and
wind.

Inches of fresh, soft sand had been dumped on the
road as well, and once the mules had been calmed and
hitched, and the Concord on its way again, they made
no better than a few miles per hour. The huge yellow
wheels slid and mired in the puddles of sand that
formed over the ruts; the mules had to strain and pull
the bogged-down coach through drifts a foot or more
high, with the passengers walking—and Magenta grous-
ing—in the sweltering heat behind.

Weary, exhausted, and filthy, they had finally arrived
at the relay station, a good six hours overdue, only to

hear Jim declare the possibility of yet another disaster up ahead.

"Been makin' this y'ere run fivc years now," Jim muttered. "Each time there were trouble, I smelt it right off. There be trouble now, ripe as a whore's arse after a cattle drive."

"What kind of trouble, old man?" Sun Shadow asked softly, knowing the answer already. He had seen the signs all day.

"Injuns." He looked pointedly at the Ute beside him. "Comanche, I reckon. Them devils been all over these y'ere parts lately. Cain't hardly take a piss without one o' them stickin' his head out'n the bush an' takin' a whack at ye. Raided the last train what come through, mostly fer their animules. We don't carry no food, so they ain't touched the coaches . . . so far."

Sun Shadow saw McBride move up beside the driver's box and he vaulted effortlessly out of his seat and landed with a soft thud in the sand. They held a rapid, low-toned conversation in Shoshonean, and when it was over, Jim leaned over from his high perch and spat a stream of tobacco juice between the traces.

"Yus were hired ter ride shot fer me. I ain't holdin' yus to nothin' more. No need to go no farther. I'd as soon have yer company on the way back as lose the pair o' you now."

"You understand my language, old man?" Sun Shadow asked in dialect.

"Near as good as you speak blue-nose English, boy."

Sun Shadow allowed a wry grin while McBride indicated the darkness ahead. "Then you'll agree, if there are still Comanche down there, they will have seen us and heard us by now."

"Agreed."

"And you'll agree that the mules will go no farther. They would never make the trip back to Fort Dodge tonight, and we would have no chance if we had to try to outrun Indian ponies."

Jim sucked air and spat. "Agreed."

"The Comanche," Sun Shadow commented disdainfully, "do not linger after a kill. They run away like frightened children to hide in their mother's skirts."

"I take it he's sayin' we should go for'ard?" Brody mused.

"We're both saying we should at least have a look," McBride replied.

"What is going on out there?" Greaves demanded, showing his face at the window. "If you are making decisions that concern us all, shouldn't we be a part of the discussion?"

Jim Brody snorted. "Might be it concerns yus at that. Might be you have sumpin' *real* important to add to this y'ere discussion. Know much about Injuns, do ye?"

"Indians!" Magenta shrilled from the darkened interior. A moment later, she thrust her head through the window, her blond curls tumbling askew over the wooden ledge. "Did you say Indians?"

"I said what I said, lady. You feel like joinin' us fer a stroll down yonder ter have a closer look-see?"

"You mean they are out there now?" she gasped. "Waiting to attack us?"

"Not if they know'd you was on board," Jim grumbled under his breath. "They'd be harf way through Texas by now."

"Is it true?" Magenta appealed to Christian McBride. "Are we about to be attacked by savages?"

"Like Sun Shadow said," he explained with an amazing show of patience, "the Comanche hit and run. If they had wanted to attack us, they would have done it on the road. On the other hand, it might not be Comanche at all. It might be Kiowa or Apache, and if that's the case . . ." He shrugged and left Magenta to form her own conclusions.

"You seem to know a great deal about the Indians' habits," Greaves said testily. "Maybe too damned much."

It was the first time he had spoken directly to McBride since the incident on the riverbank, and the plainsman had not minded the deliberate snub in the least. Sober, the agent had been content to merely glower threats from his corner in the coach, but since the sandstorm, he had been drinking steadily, and his belligerence grew bolder with every swallow.

"Just what is that remark supposed to mean?" McBride asked quietly.

"Nothing. Just that you and your *brother* here seem a little too eager to leave us and go exploring. Couldn't be you already know what's waiting up ahead, could it? Couldn't be you have more friends waiting down there for us and planned all along to have a share in the spoils?"

McBride stared at Greaves in silence. At length, when he spoke, his words were carefully chosen and delivered in a voice that was as dangerously thin as a rime of early frost.

"I'm going to overlook your stupidity this time, Greaves, but I give you fair warning: if you so much as breathe at me the wrong way again, I'll slit your tongue out of your throat and stake you on the nearest anthill." He turned to Jim and added harshly, "Stay put. Sun Shadow and I will go on ahead and have a look around. If everything is all right, we'll put up some lights. If not, or if you hear any gunfire at all, turn tail and make a run for it."

"But where will we wait for you, Christian?" Magenta asked breathlessly.

McBride glared past Greaves as he adjusted his

Peacemakers and tightened the thongs binding the holsters to his thighs. "A kind thought, ma'am, but if there are Comanche down there, what is left of us wouldn't be worth waiting for."

He broke open the breech of the Winchester and ensured it carried a full load, then, treading so lightly not a dry twig was disturbed in the unearthly silence, the two men melted into the blackness and were gone.

"Asshole!" Magenta hissed, cuffing Greaves on the shoulder with her balled fist. "Will you never learn to keep your big mouth shut?"

"Who's to say I was so far wrong? You have to admit they make a strange twosome. I'm damned if I've ever seen a white man attach himself to a Breed like that."

"I'm damned you can see anything at all from the bottom of a bottle!"

"Well at least I look at more than just the bulge in his crotch," he sneered.

"Excuse me," Aubrey said, making her way past them and out of the coach. Bruster was close on her heels, leaving the songstress and her agent to bicker it out between themselves.

Jim Brody had climbed down from his seat and was standing by the lead team of mules, his gnarled hand stroking one of the bristly snouts.

"Like to take a gun and shoot them two yay-hoos myself," he muttered, sensing Aubrey's presence beside him. "Might do it yet they don't close them windbags they call mouths. Course, I might not have to if the big fella comes back an' shuts them up hisself. Sound carries a fer piece on the desert."

As hot as it had been during the day, the desert had cooled after dusk, and Aubrey, having sweated herself out of the worsted jacket an hour after leaving Fort Dodge, now hugged herself against the inadequate protection of the thin cotton blouse.

"Do you really believe us to be in danger?"

"Dunno, miss. Come across many an old bone y'ere, I have. Yuman an' otherwise. Picked clean too they was, some still with the arrows stickin' straight up out'n where their gizzards ought to be."

Aubrey glanced at the driver. The top of his Hardee hat barely reached the level of her shoulder. The cud in his cheek was fatter than any one area of his wiry frame, and he chewed it with the determination of a housewife working a butter churn.

"It's my guess, Mr. Brody, that if you thought the Comanche were still here, we wouldn't be."

He frowned and met the clear blue gaze directly. She didn't frighten too easily, this one. Didn't whine and caterwaul like the other one, which made her almost tolerable.

"Been a fight, I reckon," he said finally, spitting and wiping his chin. "Smell of a raid stays in the air a spell, so a man cain't rightly tell if'n it were yesterday, or a couple o' days ago. Didn't see no mark, but mebbe the storm blew this way and carried it off."

"A mark?"

"Yep. Comanche always leave a mark behind. Kinda like signin' their names, yer might say, to leave a message fer them what follers. One o' them—a ripe son of a bitch named Quanah Parker, he's been on the rampage the past few months, raidin' all over Texas an' on up the Red River. Ain't heard of him this fer north, but that don't mean he ain't been y'ere. Mind you, ain't a one o' them I'd as like to turn my back on. Parker's jest a notch meaner than the rest, is all."

Aubrey shivered involuntarily and stared off into the darkness.

"Do you think they will be all right?"

"Cain't rightly say. That Injun, he be a smart 'un, though. And the big fella don't 'zactly bring ter mind no tree stump either. Worse comes, I'd stake my life on them."

"I would say we already have, Mr. Brody."

He peered up and screwed his mouth into a grimace. "Ain't never cottoned ter nobody callin' me *mester;* don't 'specially want to start now. Jim'll do jest fine"— he paused and cackled lewdly—"less'n o' course you wanted to use my pro-fessional handle."

Aubrey smiled uncertainly. "Dare I ask how you came to be known as, er . . ."

"Stink Finger Brody?" He cackled again and his beard shifted as he moved his cud from one cheek to the other. "Blastin' rock," he said proudly. "Used to drill a hole yea round, fill 'er with black powder, then tamp 'er down nice an' tight afore feedin' in the fuse. Never did cotton ter the feel o' them proper ramrods, so I used my number-one picker y'ere." He held up a stubby forefinger so she could admire the shortened, blunted tip. "Danged if'n it didn't turn all black on me an' stink to the heavens with blastin' powder."

"And so the name," Aubrey surmised.

"Yep. Jest kinda stuck." He hooked his thumbs into the top of his belt and grinned slyly. "Course, that ain't always the story I tell the fellers, if'n yer git my drift."

Aubrey was saved from answering by the sound of a particularly loud thump and squeal from inside the coach. Jim swore and drew his gun, stalking back to the door of the coach and flinging it wide open. His arrival and the utterance of an especially heinous threat had the desired effect and the two occupants fell silent, albeit not without the additional persuasion of cold gun metal on the back of Darby Greaves's skull.

Aubrey sighed and tried to rub some of the grit and weariness out of her eyes. Bruster was nowhere in sight, so she walked a short way and found a seat alone on a small outcropping of rocks. She sat there for quite some time, marking the slow passing of the minutes by watching the languid path of the rising moon. It was three-quarters full, swollen and glistening with its own importance, and cast a dull white ghost light over the plains and valley. The cratered desert was thrown into relief, etched with dozens of troughs and crests that could have been the relay station, silhouetted with scores of tall cactus that could have been the forms of silently watchful Indians.

McBride and Sun Shadow should have reached the station by now.

What if Jim was wrong?

What if the Comanche were still there? What if they had silenced McBride and Sun Shadow before a warning shot could be fired? What if, even as she sat there pondering the alternatives, the two were enduring some dreadful form of bloodthirsty torment? Stories abounded of the atrocities the Comanche committed on white men. And Sun Shadow? His trial would be even more gruesome.

Aubrey's imagination was promising to unravel in starkly vivid details when she saw a tiny pinpoint of light twinkle to life across the desert. A second light, swinging back and forth in an arc, had her on her feet and running back to the coach. Jim had seen it already and was gathering the reins of the team, preparing to move the coach down on into the valley.

"It's them, isn't it? They're safe?"

"I reckon we'll find out soon enough," Jim said. "All aboard! Don't wake the fancy man; I persuaded him ter rest his brain a spell."

"He struck him!" Magenta hissed as Aubrey and Bruster climbed aboard. "That vile and obnoxious little man actually had the effrontery to strike a paying customer!"

Aubrey took her seat and looked calmly at Greaves's

slumped form. "You're lucky Jim didn't do a lot worse . . . and not just to your Mr. Greaves."

Magenta's mouth dropped open in shock. "Well!"

Minutes later, the Concord rumbled to a halt in front of a mud-brick building that served the stagecoach line as a relay station. The stables and corrals were bigger than the station itself, its main purpose being to supply fresh teams and water for the second half of the desert crossing. There were no special accommodations for overnight guests, since none were expected, and the main bulk of the interior was taken up with the huge water barrels transported by wagon from either the Arkansas or the Cimarron rivers. The roof was mud and prairie grass, with one whole section gaping in a crumbled state of disrepair. There was one narrow door in front and two slit windows that were fixed with heavy shutters inside and out.

"Home away from home," Magenta muttered to no one in particular. "I don't see anyone," she added irritably. "Where do you suppose they are?"

Aubrey glanced out of the coach window and was struck at once by the silence. The stoop was deserted. The door hung crookedly on its hinges and had been left invitingly open, spilling a dull yellow light onto the dust of the yard.

"Oh for heaven's sake, a body could die for want of a few simple courtesies around here," Magenta said, and reached for the handle of the door.

"Clara, wait," Aubrey cautioned, grabbing the other woman's arm.

"I beg your pardon!"

Aubrey was uncertain if Magenta's indignation was due to her touching the brocaded sleeve, or addressing her by her proper name—and she didn't much care.

"Wait. Just wait until we see someone we know—"

"Let go of me this instant. How dare you!"

"It may not be safe," Aubrey argued. "Just wait another minute or two—"

The coach bounced slightly and Aubrey caught a glimpse of Jim Brody's crouched body crabbing cautiously around to the darkness out back of the station.

"Let go of me, you silly little chit!" Magenta cried, and wrenched her arm free. "If you want to sit out here all night, go right ahead. *I'm* going inside."

She disembarked in a swirl of crushed brocade and strode up the path leading to the door of the station. She called out a singsong "Hello?" and when no one answered, she crossed the threshold and disappeared inside.

"What's wrong?" Bruster asked in a whisper. "What's happening?"

"Nothing is happening," Aubrey said grimly, "And that's what's wrong. The light . . . the open door—" She bit down on her lip and frowned. "Jim went around back and Magenta has gone in, but—"

The scream was loud and pure and achingly clear on the chilled night air. Aubrey's skin shrank from the nape of her neck and she swore softly as her hand fell to her pocket and she remembered her gun was not there.

It was Bruster who moved first. He pushed the unconscious Darby Greaves onto his side and helped himself to one of the Smith and Wesson revolvers. After another brief moment of debate, he removed the second gun and handed it to Aubrey before he climbed out of the coach.

"Stay here," he whispered shakily. "I shall endeavor to find Mr. Brody and offer what assistance I may."

"For God's sake—*no*!"

But he was already gone, darting into the shadows with a remarkable agility for a man of his size and disposition.

Aubrey was not about to be left alone in the dark with

an unconscious drunk. She followed Bruster out of the coach, then stood for a moment, her heart pounding in her ears, debating where to go. Jim and Bruster were out back and there were no sounds of a struggle taking place that she could hear. Magenta had gone inside; McBride and the Ute might be anywhere, in any condition.

She blinked, and for a moment, the relay station was transformed into a two-story adobe ranch house. Flames were lapping at the windows and Scud Holwell and his men were inside, pistol-whipping her father, raping her mother.

She blinked again and the coolness of the desert settled over her. She approached the open door with extreme caution, hugging the shadows, keeping well clear of the light streaming out onto the ground. Reaching the outer wall without incident, she risked a glance inside. The room appeared to be empty other than for a mess of overturned chairs, a table on its side, and the smashed remains of an interrupted meal scattered across the floor.

Directly across from the doorway were the splintered remains of a dozen water barrels, some still with a few inches of liquid in their bellies, one of them with the feathered shaft of an arrow jutting out from an oak bracket.

A portion of the room was out of sight, obstructed by the wall of barrels. Aubrey guessed that whatever had happened to Magenta, whatever she had seen to make her scream, had happened there.

Aubrey took a deep breath to steady her nerves and stepped across the threshold. She flattened herself against the wall and stood for several long moments, listening. She took a hesitant step . . . then another . . . sliding herself along the rough surface of the wall until more and more of the rear half of the station came into view. She held the gun straight out, braced by both hands and ready to fire at the slightest need. It followed her eye from the table to the large stone fireplace that edged into sight; from the fireplace to the axe that was embedded in the wall, its handle and blade smeared with dried blood.

At the sight of the blood, her toe missed a delicate placing and crunched solidly on a pile of broken crockery. Aubrey glanced down in horror. A moment later she saw movement from the rear of the station.

Her finger flinched against the trigger even as she brought the gun to bear on the suddenly visible rear door. She recognized McBride at the last possible second and jerked the gun aside, but because of Greaves's experiences as a gambler, he had filed the notch of the hammer so that the trigger would pull at the slightest pressure. Aubrey heard the explosion and felt the kick in her arm as the gun discharged. Her vision was briefly obscured behind an acrid cloud of hot white smoke and when it cleared, she could see McBride gaping at the shot that had thudded into the wall a scant two inches from his temple.

Neither one moved.

Aubrey saw his eyes flick to her hand and realized that her finger was still poised against the trigger. With a gasp she released the breath she had been holding, and lowered the gun, letting it drop from between her fingers to land with a dull *thonk* on the packed earth floor.

"I could have killed you," she whispered.

McBride came across the room toward her. As he walked, he holstered one of the Peacemakers and she was shocked again to realize he had drawn and set himself to return fire in less time than it had taken her to accidentally pull the trigger.

"You could have killed me," she said with greater accuracy.

"Lucky for you I was busy ducking." He bent over and retrieved the Smith and Wesson. "Another one of your natty little accessories?"

"It belongs to Greaves." Her eyes widened and she glanced back at the door. "Dear God, Bruster has the other one. He won't know the trigger has been sweetened!"

"Relax—" McBride caught her gently by the arm. "Bruster's fine. Everyone is fine."

"But Magenta . . . we heard her scream."

"She saw something she wasn't meant to see."

Aubrey looked up and McBride was suddenly quite content to leave his hand where it was on her arm. "The station was attacked two, maybe three days ago. We found the manager out front and the hostler inside. Neither one was a very pretty sight. We lit the lamps and moved the bodies out back thinking we could get them covered before the stage arrived, but we didn't count on the other three bodies we found near the corral. Jim showed up first and saw what we were doing, and pitched in to help. Miss Royale came through next and, well, as I said, the corpses were not a very pretty sight after three days of heat and flies.

"Just when we thought we were in control again, Bruster charged out of the bushes, took one look, and fainted in a heap alongside Magenta. I was coming to head off the rest of you . . . when I very nearly got my ear blown off."

Aubrey was conscious of his hand around her arm. She was also acutely aware of the unexpected tenderness in his fingers as he brushed away a smudge of dirt from her cheek. He was standing close enough to share the heat of his body, close enough she could see the fine rim of white skin along his hairline where the sun never reached.

She parted her lips slightly, although she could not for the life of her think of a thing to say. She could not think of anything other than the overwhelming need she was fighting to simply lean forward and feel his strong arms gather her against his chest.

He laughed softly and tucked his finger under her chin.

"By God, woman, you pick the damnedest time to want a kissing."

Aubrey was startled into taking an abrupt step back, her retreat cut short by the wall. "I want no such thing."

"No? Then it's just as well you told me, because I nearly obliged."

"I'm surprised a simple no would stop you; it didn't before."

"And that disappoints you?"

"Hardly."

His grin broadened. "Well, unfortunately, I don't often come upon a kissing mood in the middle of a burial detail. Next time, however—"

"There will not be a next time, Mr. McBride," she insisted. "Or if there is, I won't trouble myself to correct my aim."

"Correct your aim?" His eyes narrowed and he studied the two clear splashes of vibrant blue that gazed calmly back at him. "A regular Belle Starr, are you? Another Bandit Queen of the Indian Territories?"

"My father thought a woman should know how to protect herself," she said evenly. "He taught me how to shoot when I was a little girl."

"Did he also teach you all about 'sweetening' triggers? And about customized four-barrel .22's? Not exactly a common weapon for a schoolmarm to carry around in her reticule."

"It suits my purpose."

"Which is—?"

She sighed heavily. "Do you plan on giving it back to me?"

"That depends."

"On what?"

"On if you plan on answering any of my questions."

"So far, you haven't asked any that merit an answer."

McBride leaned forward, placing his hands flat on the wall on either side of her head. "Have I told you how much I enjoy unraveling a good mystery? Well . . . I enjoy it as much as"—his eyes wandered to the few jet black wisps of hair that curled against her throat—"as much as I enjoy unraveling a woman's hair and letting it run through my fingers."

Aubrey held his gaze unwaveringly. "In that case, I will be sure to use twice as many hairpins in the future."

"Twice the challenge," he mused. "And twice the pleasure taking them out."

"A handful of steel pins will hardly help you solve any mysteries."

"Ahh, but if it leaves you looking the way you did this morning, I doubt I'd give a damn one way or the other."

"So you're saying . . . if I let my hair down, and I let you kiss me . . . you'll leave me alone?"

"It's an interesting theory. Shall we try it?"

Her focus drifted down to his lips, and the sardonic little smile was there, as she expected it to be. He was like a testy schoolboy, wanting most what he could not have. What would he do if he got it? Take his fill and toss her away with a hearty pat on the rump, no doubt; well, she wasn't interested. Not in him, not in his insincere seductions.

So why was her belly fluttering and her limbs quivering? Why did her mouth feel as tender and swollen as it had this morning after he had kissed her, and why was her body actually *aching* in places she never would have associated with pain? Yet it wasn't painful at all. It was . . . just an ache. A hot, urgent, throbbing ache and she did not want to think of what her body was demanding in order to ease it. She needed a safer subject; something to take the heat out of his eyes.

She cleared her throat and tried to ignore the way his smile followed her train of thought. "Do you think we will be bothered any more by the Indians?"

"My guess would be that they're long gone by now."

"Does that mean we will be continuing on? That we will not be turning back?"

"Are you in so much of a hurry to reach Santa Fe?"

"Naturally, I would like to be there as soon as possible."

"Naturally," he murmured. "You wouldn't want to miss out on any of those eligible, unmarried sodbusters capering around unfettered . . . or was there one in particular you had in mind?"

Aubrey's brow inched upward. "Are you putting yourself forward as a candidate, Mr. McBride?"

"Me?" He looked genuinely startled and flinched back. "Not likely, madam!"

"But you seem to be taking such a perverse interest in my welfare, I only assumed there was a purpose behind it. And then there was the incident this morning by the river—"

"Incident? It wasn't an incident, it was a kiss. It was nothing."

She regarded him coolly. "Where I come from, Mr. McBride, a kiss is indeed *some*thing. As is the suggestion that you might want to repeat it. Now, I realize a man such as yourself fancies he has women falling all over themselves to gain his favor, but I, however, find you a little too much in a hurry, and not at all appealing."

"Not . . . ! Well, I'll be damned," he muttered.

"Be whatever you wish," she added in her most wasp-ish voice. "So long as you take care in the future not to be it around me."

Christian watched openmouthed as she tilted her chin in the air and walked out of the station. He was half of a mind to follow her and throttle the smug expression off her face; he actually strode over to the open door and halted there, staring out over the eerie moonlit landscape. The coach was a dark, silent hulk etched in shadow. The mules stood as still as stones, only their husk-shaped ears twitching this way and that to isolate the various sounds around them.

Aubrey was nowhere in sight, but McBride's eyes scanned the immense, bleak beauty of the desert terrain, his senses straining to hear beneath the low hum of the wind-shifted sand.

One of the mules snorted and lowered his head, reverting his attention to the ball of prairie grass at his feet. McBride relaxed as well, shaking off the tension with an added curse for good measure. He glanced behind him and knew he should return to the business of burying bodies, but he stole an extra few minutes to brace himself with the harsh taste of raw tobacco.

He struck a match on the splintered wood of the doorjamb and touched the flame to the end of a cheroot. He continued to hold the burning match in his cupped hand, staring at the bright, hot center until the sulfur spluttered out.

A rejection he could understand. He had not experienced many in the past, but he could take the logic of one in his stride. Hands off. Do not touch. My chastity or my life. And he certainly had never had to force his attentions on a woman, regardless of his needs or situation. He liked his women warm and willing, eager to please, eager to be pleased. The thought of settling down with one woman—any woman—actually caused a cold shudder to ripple along his spine . . . a shudder that froze his belly to a block of ice as he felt the hard snout of a gun barrel thrust against his neck.

"You should be dead, *yanqui*," Sun Shadow hissed.

The plainsman cursed aloud and waited for his nerves to jangle back into place.

The Ute grinned and lowered his rifle. "Something is troubling you, McBride?"

"Nothing I can't handle."

"You handled her so well, she nearly parted your head from your shoulders."

Christian drew on his cigar and frowned. "She puzzles me," he admitted finally.

"All women puzzle you, my friend."

"She's hiding something; I just want to know what it is."

"Hiding something?" Sun Shadow cocked his head at the howl of a coyote echoing far off across the desert. "Something important enough to make you forget everything you have learned about staying alive? A buffalo could have charged you just then and you would not have known it until his breath was on your face."

"Buffaloes do not walk in the shadows of their feet."

"Nor does a man who wishes to keep his blood in his veins let his whereabouts be known by shooting guns and striking matches."

"The shot was an accident, it couldn't be helped."

"And the way you stand in the doorway now, with the light at your back? Another accident?"

McBride was appalled, and for the first time in more years than he could remember, he felt a flush of stupidity heat his cheeks until they were on fire. He stepped quickly into the shadows outside the door, and for good measure, crushed the partially smoked cheroot under the heel of his boot.

"Damned know-it-all savage," he muttered.

Sun Shadow grinned. "You used to know as much as I did, *yanqui*. The years in prison have made you soft."

"Soft? I'd like to see how soft you would be after five years behind bars."

"It would never happen, *yanqui*," the Ute said with quiet surety. "They would never have taken me alive."

McBride returned the Ute's steady gaze. There was no sign of contempt or sarcasm in Sun Shadow's words, only a plain statement of fact, supported, perhaps, by an underlying disdain for the white man's system of justice. McBride had put his trust in the law and lawyers and had paid dearly for his poor judgment. Sun Shadow had trusted no man, no court of law, no man's justice but his own, and for that, had spent the same five years as free as an eagle in his mountain aerie.

Why he wasn't there still was a subject neither man had broached so far.

"I could have found my way home by myself, you know. You didn't have to risk so much by coming to meet me."

"We are blood, McBride," the Ute said simply. "Your father was my father. I tried to kill you once for the insult, but you were stubborn and would not die, and when the gods smile on a man in such a way, they must have had a good reason. I will keep you in my eyes, *yanqui*, until I learn what that reason is."

"And then?"

"Then—" Sun Shadow stopped and his head turned toward the sound as the cry of the coyote shivered the air again. It was much closer this time, and much too casual for a challenge to the full moon.

The Ute sank onto his haunches, pleased to see that McBride needed no prompting to do likewise.

"Two braves?" Christian asked.

"More."

"How many?"

Sun Shadow shook his head.

"Well now." McBride peered out over the expanse of desert. "What do you suppose they want?"

6

"I vote we go back," Greaves stated flatly. "You say there is still a fair piece of desert to cross before we reach the next station, before the next water and change of horses?"

"That's the truth of it," Jim grunted.

"Then why are we even discussing it? We have to take the way that presents the least amount of danger."

"Egg-zactly! An' that's why we be debatin' it. We be halfway 'tween water, halfway 'tween horses. We be halfway across this blamed hell hole an' whatever way we choose ter go, them blamed Injuns'll be half a step behind us."

Bruster swabbed his brow and sucked furiously on a lemon drop. "Must you shout, Mr. Brody?"

"It's the onliest way he seems to hear me," Jim declared. "Unless o' course, he'd ruther not hear me at all, in which case I kin put him back to sleep in a blink!"

Bruster quickly placed himself between the two men. "Violence amongst ourselves will surely solve nothing, Mr. Brody, Mr. Greaves. We must decide calmly and logically what to do and how best to defend ourselves in the event there are indeed Comanches still out there."

The men were standing by the row of smashed water

barrels; the women sat a little apart, scarcely more than their profiles etched in the weak light of the lantern. McBride had called an abrupt halt to the burial detail and had gathered everyone inside the station, including a surly Darby Greaves, who glowered at Jim Brody and the plainsman with equal loathing. Sun Shadow had slipped off into the darkness for a closer look at the "coyotes" and had recently returned with the estimate of three, perhaps four unwanted visitors out on the desert.

"The next stop is Middle Springs, is it not?" McBride asked, rubbing his thumb thoughtfully along his jaw.

"Thirty miles due south o' here, give 'r take a mule's arse."

"And the Arkansas?"

"Thirty miles north an' east, same mule, same arse."

"But it's land we have been across once, so at least we would know what to expect," Bruster said hopefully.

"Don't know nothin' o' the kind," Jim snorted. "Ten minutes after we passed down the road, it could've all changed. Ye saw for yourself what happened after a little blow."

"But the Indians—"

"Laws o' heaven help me, peddler, if'n yer about to say there was no Injuns behind us. Injuns ride horses, an' horses kin move right damned fast in any direction a Comanch' war hoop sends it."

"What about the soldiers?" Magenta asked through tightly gritted teeth. There were definite signs of wear beginning to show through the tension and fear. The yellow curls were limp, dulled by the dust and heat of the long day; the heavy layer of kohl she applied around her eyes was smudged and resembled dull bruises. "Surely there are regular patrols along the stagecoach routes, especially if they know the Comanche are stirred up. If we are overdue, won't they come looking for us?"

"A patrol of cavalry could be less than a mile away," McBride said matter-of-factly, "and they would still arrive too late to help out if we were under attack."

"Then you're saying we won't make it either way?" she gasped.

"I didn't say that at all. I just said we shouldn't count on anyone but ourselves."

"An' the natural stubbornness of an Injun ter finish what he starts," Jim added dryly.

"But why do we have to go anywhere at all?" Magenta demanded in a shrill voice. "We're perfectly safe right here. If they're going to attack, wouldn't it be better to defend ourselves here rather than out in the open?"

"Five other people thought the same thing," Christian said bluntly. "You saw what happened to them."

"What makes you think they'll just let us drive away?" Aubrey asked quietly.

"I'm not saying they will"—he paused as Greaves cursed and threw up his hands in disgust—"but there's a good chance they might. According to Jim, they haven't actually attacked any coaches lately; we carry nothing they need or want. He also seems to think he recognizes one of the bodies out back, an Indian agent by the name of Hawkins."

"Lyin' thievin' snake if ever there was one," Jim interjected.

"It could be that the Comanche were after him specifically to settle a score, and if that's the case—" He shrugged and for all of ten brief seconds, Aubrey allowed herself to believe it might possibly be true. But the gray eyes were too calm, and too direct, and they were watching her response, comparing it to the blatantly hopeful relief that washed over Magenta's features.

"You mean, if they were just after him, they might leave us alone?"

McBride looked at Magenta. "They might, ma'am. They just might."

"Well then," Bruster said on a gust of expelled air, "perhaps we should depart with all due haste. And since I know absolutely nothing about the Comanche, nor would I feel the slightest bit qualified to render any judgment one way or another as to whether we should proceed or retreat, I gladly defer my vote to you, Mr. McBride."

Christian smiled wanly. "I'm just a passenger like you, Bruster. I can only make suggestions. The final decision is up to Jim."

Brody knocked back his Hardee hat and scratched his scalp. "I'd kinda like ter hear them suggestions, young fella, not that I think I'm gonna much like what I hear."

McBride glanced at Sun Shadow, who was standing by the door, his arms cradling his carbine.

"First of all, if it isn't the whole war party we're dealing with, if it's only a few braves who stayed behind after the raid to see what happened, then it will take time for them to get word back to their main camp, and then more time for them to argue in favor or against another raid. If I was to suggest anything, it would be to take advantage of that time to put as many miles between us and this station as possible. How long does it normally take to reach Middle Springs?"

"Three, mebbe four hours . . . but that's with a fresh, sound team. We'll be pushin' five wore-out mules —the sixth 'un is crippled up too bad to count on pullin' his full load, an' might even slow us down some."

"Then we cut him loose and run with five. We also strip any unnecessary weight from the coach to burden the animals as little as possible. We leave behind everything and anything that isn't an absolute necessity—baggage and gear included."

"All of the baggage?" Magenta exclaimed. "But my clothes, my gowns . . . surely you don't mean *everything?*"

"Yus two are welcome ter stay behind with 'em," Jim declared, hawking savagely and spitting into the dirt at his feet. "Dad-blame cain't expect me ter carry petticoats instead o' water!"

"He's quite right, you know," Bruster said solicitously. "A few frocks are hardly worth your life."

Magenta shot him a withering glance. "When I want your advice, you little prune, I'll ask for it."

Bruster's throat muscles worked rapidly to dislodge the lemon drop he had swallowed, a task accomplished only after he had turned a glorious beet red.

Aubrey glared across the space that separated her from Magenta Royale, and for an instant, would have given anything to be able to scratch the woman's eyes out. Her wish must have been mirrored on her face, for Magenta was quick to raise an eyebrow in mock alarm.

"Save my soul, I do believe the schoolmarm is about to have a fit of pique."

"If I have a fit of anything," Aubrey said ominously, "you'll be the first to know."

"Stop it, the pair of you," McBride commanded. "The last thing we need right now is a cat fight."

Magenta demurred at once to the echo of authority in his voice, leaving Aubrey to bristle under the piercing gray threat of his eyes. She turned deliberately away from him, feeling the heat of his gaze follow her to the far side of the room.

"If'n we be movin' soon, we'd best git to it," Jim announced gruffly. "Them Injuns ain't gonna be takin' their sweet time makin' up their minds. Count on it."

•

The coach was attacked mid-morning. They had not traveled as far as they had hoped, nor as fast. Stink Finger Jim was loathe to push the ragged animals full out; they had suffered through the dry heat and sandstorm of the previous day and were rebelling against each crack of the whip. Traversing the desert at night might have been cooler business, but the going was twice as treacherous, with long stretches of the road disappearing into inky blackness as the shadows thrown by the moon grew longer and wider. For a while it was bright enough to compensate for the lack of lanterns. The dunes and hillocks were glazed as white as china, and the sand glittered like a lake of frozen ice. But as the moon crested and began its rapid slide downward, the light came from behind and the mules began to balk at stepping into their own shadows.

They rested twice, with McBride and Sun Shadow seeking a high point of vantage to determine whether or not they were being followed. A futile exercise in reality, it nonetheless gave the other passengers a few moments of reassurance on their return. That and the first hint of dawn blooming along the horizon nearly overcame the frustration of having another mule come up lame after stumbling over a hidden cavity in the road.

Sun Shadow, riding on the roof of the coach, sensed the approach of the Comanche before he actually caught sight of them, and Jim was not about to question the Ute's instincts. He lashed the whip out over the heads of the four remaining mules, skinning them out of their sullen lethargy with a stream of particularly graphic oaths that had them flattening their ears back and straining for every ounce of speed they could muster. The Concord flew over the rutted earth, jarring the passengers to full alertness and causing several cries of alarm as a body was flung heavily onto the floor.

Christian McBride heard the unmistakable whoops of attack and reached for the Winchester repeating rifle at his feet. He made use of the time before the Indians came into range by rechecking the bolt action of the carbine and ensuring the extra ammunition was within easy reach.

Greaves was dry-lipped and sober for a change. He sat rigid in his seat with his eyes squeezed tightly shut and the oily sheen of sweat popping out across his brow.

Armbruster Shillingsworth was in the painful process of trying to regain his seat, and was assisted perfunctorily with a thrust of McBride's arm.

"You have a gun?"

"I . . . uh . . ."

McBride drew one of his Peacemakers and shoved it into the peddler's chubby hands. "It might not be as 'sweet' as Greaves's, but it gets the job done."

"Oh my. Oh . . . my . . ."

Christian ignored his splutterings and reached across the coach, taking hold of Magenta's arm and urging her forward. "Get on the floor"—he glanced at Aubrey—"both of you. The Comanche are notoriously bad shots but the walls of this coach are so thin they're likely to hit you by accident."

"If you'll give me back my gun—" Aubrey began.

"You want to be useful? Here, take these boxes of ammunition and keep the guns loaded."

"But—" She was about to say she would be of more use at one of the windows, but McBride took it as the beginning of a complaint and dragged her unceremoniously off the seat and pushed her into a heap on the floor.

"Forgive me, I neglected to say please."

Aubrey's retort was drowned by a roar of gunfire. Sun

Shadow, splayed on the coach roof to minimize the target he presented, was firing now at the rapidly closing riders. There were more than a score of them racing into the dust of the coach. Those with rifles or guns fired from a distance, those armed only with bows and arrows hunched low over the backs of their ponies, flailing them to greater speed.

Christian took command of one of the windows and fired carefully, smoothly, needing only a fraction of a second to aim and pull the trigger on the Winchester. Magenta, crouched on the floor, covered her head with her hands and screamed, batting at the spent shell casings as they fell around her. Bruster and Greaves both emptied their guns in a wild barrage that hit nothing but rocks and dirt, and in the time it took them to reload, the howling had drawn up alongside the coach, fanned out on either side of the great cloud of boiling dust raised by the churning wheels.

McBride emptied his carbine and cracked the breech before tossing it down to Aubrey to reload. He changed it for a Peacemaker and returned to the window, flinching back almost immediately as a shot splintered the door and plugged the wood behind his head.

"Son of a bitch!" he muttered, then, "Greaves! They're coming up on your side!"

Aubrey heard the shouted warning and saw a blurred movement as Darby Greaves leaned farther out of his window. He fired off two quick shots and was grinning with satisfaction when he screamed suddenly and jerked himself back inside, clutching a bloodied, damaged hand to his chest. Without thinking, Aubrey caught the gun as it slipped out of his fingers. She scrambled onto her knees, then onto the seat, pushing past the sagging figure to take over his position at the window.

Shock kept her frozen in place for several terrifying moments. The Comanche were whooping and screaming as they thundered along beside the coach. Their faces and upper torsos were painted with red or blue or ocher stripes and lightning bolts; their ponies were painted in a similar fashion, manes and tails tied with strings of red flannel.

Aubrey locked eyes with with one hideously painted warrior whose squat and powerful body was bonded to that of his pony in a way that made their rippling muscles extensions of each other. His thighs governed the pony's movements, leaving his hands free to raise the old army issue carbine and take aim at the pale white face in the coach window. Seeing that the face belonged to a woman, the warrior hesitated long enough to throw his head back and laugh with disdain—a laugh that turned into a choking spray of blood and shattered tissue as Aubrey's first shot tore away half of his throat.

She saw him fall but took only a brief moment to shudder her revulsion before she aimed and fired at another raider. They were close enough to fire bows and arrows now and three wickedly barbed shafts *thunk thunk thunk*-ed into the wood frame of the door, spraying the interior with needlelike slivers. Aubrey felt a warm trickling sensation on her chin and throat, but paid it no heed as she cleared the chambers of the gun and reloaded.

The Comanche veered again, concentrating their efforts on unseating or killing Jim Brody and Sun Shadow. Several of the warriors attempted to close in on the mules, but the Ute read their intentions easily enough and was able to pick off three attackers without suffering more than a minor scratch for his troubles.

As if by prearranged signal, the raiding party sheered away from the stagecoach and pulled to a rearing halt in the midst of the boiling sand and dust. Aubrey watched them grow smaller and smaller in the distance, hardly believing her eyes or her ears as she realized the shooting had stopped.

"We did it!" Bruster cried. "They've stopped, by Jove! We've turned them away!"

"I wouldn't count on it," McBride said grimly. He knocked a fresh handful of shells out of the box and fed them into the warm breech of the Winchester. "You had better all reload. They'll be coming back."

The order had a ring of authority that no one dared challenge. Numbed by the violence and unwilling to acknowledge the reality of what she was doing, Aubrey did as she was told, reloading her gun, then resting the heavy weapon in her lap as she fought to control the pounding in her chest.

". . . outside."

"What?" Aubrey gathered her wits and turned to McBride. What was he doing? Dear God, he had unlatched the bolt on the door and he was—

"No!" She gripped the windowsill as a roll in the trail sent the coach careening drunkenly side to side. "Are you mad? You can't go out there! You'll be killed!"

McBride looked back once before levering his frame out the narrow door. The gray eyes were flashing and his teeth were bared in a wide grin when he saw the concern reflected on Aubrey's face.

"I'll be back," he promised, then swung up and out of sight.

She braced herself against the coach seat, anticipating the scream and fatal thud as he was torn loose from the side of the Concord. When there was no scream and no thud, she allowed her lungs to pump again and risked a hasty glance out of the window.

"My God, is it over yet?"

Magenta Royale. Aubrey had all but forgotten her. She was pressed flat to the floor, her hands shielding her head under the flattened crown of yellow curls. She had

been crying and two black rivers of kohl ran all the way
down to her chin.

"Is it over?"

"McBride doesn't seem to think so," Aubrey said, reverting her attention to the uneven terrain rushing past
the window. There was no sign of pursuit yet, but she
had the uncomfortable feeling that McBride was not
often wrong. Moreover, she had her own frightening
idea as to why the Comanche had pulled back. The
mules had to be all but played out by now; despite the
almost constant cracking of the whip and Brody's best
efforts to drive them on, the beasts were slowing, the
coach was noticeably lagging.

"We've turned off the trail," she said with a frown.

"Oh my God," Magenta groaned. "I never should
have agreed to this madness, Darby. I never should have
agreed to come out to this godforsaken wilderness, and
I never would have if you hadn't *convinced* me it was the
best possible thing I could do. And now look at me.
Look at us both!"

She gasped again as she caught sight of the injured
Darby Greaves crouched down beside her. "Darby!
Darby, you bastard, you're bleeding all over my skirt!"

Greaves grunted as he received a sharp elbow in the
ribs. It was Bruster who came to the agent's rescue,
prying the wounded hand away from his chest to inspect
the damage. Several fingers were bloodied from a gash
that ran from his palm across the back of his wrist.

"Not too bad at all," Bruster said cheerfully. "Be
good as new in no time."

"What do you know about it," Greaves rasped. "Are
you a doctor when you're not selling corsets?"

Bruster, who had taken his big white handkerchief
out of his pocket to offer as a bandage, reconsidered the
gesture and handed it to Aubrey instead. When she
looked back at him, baffled, he leaned forward and

pressed the linen against her cheek, showing her the dark stain of blood that came away.

"Just a scratch," he assured her. "A flying bit of wood, I believe."

Aubrey thanked him with a faint smile. There was a scraping sound on the side of the coach, and moments later, two booted feet swung through the doorway, the rest of McBride's body following, unhampered by the motion of the compartment.

"They're both fine," he said. "How is everyone in here?"

Greaves was in the process of winding his own handkerchief around his hand and wrist, and did not think the question warranted an answer.

"Bruster?"

"Oh fine. Quite fine, really. A few bruises, but otherwise rather invigorated. Miss Blue says we have turned off the road?"

"Jim is heading for a stand of rocks. It isn't much, but it'll give us better protection than . . . you're hurt!"

Aubrey looked up to find the plainsman's eyes on her. "It's . . . nothing," she stammered, shocked by the way her body responded to the concern in his voice—even more shocked by the relief she had felt when she had seen him climbing back through the door. "It's just a scratch."

"Let me see."

"Really, it's just—" She flinched back, but his hand was already there, covering hers, gently angling the handkerchief away from her cheek. It *was* a scratch and had already stopped bleeding, but he took advantage of the opportunity to brush aside the long strands of black hair that had blown free in the wild rush of air. Their eyes met and locked and he was mildly pleased to see the soft tint of self-consciousness return some of the color to her cheeks.

"Then she was right!" Magenta sobbed. "We're going to be attacked again!"

Christian dropped his hand and turned to the others. "If this is the same band that attacked the station—and I see no reason to believe otherwise—then my guess is they're not out here for light entertainment. They're out for blood and they mean to get ours."

Magenta blanched and buried her face in her hands again just as the coach lurched and rumbled to a dusty halt.

"We appear to be here, folks," McBride announced crisply. "Carry as much ammunition as you can."

He was the first out, helping the others and keeping a sharp watch as they ran into the comparative safety of a large formation of boulders and tumbled sandstone pillars. The air was hot and dust-choked, the sun a blinding white disk an hour or so away from being directly overhead. The island of rock spanned several hundred yards in width and rose half that in height, carved with many natural ledges and niches from which to mount a defense.

Sun Shadow vanished into its depths after a hurried consultation with McBride, reappearing a short time later on a ledge high above them. There must have been a breath of dry wind near the summit, for his long black hair shifted forward over his shoulders as he stood motionless, scanning the plains for sight of the Comanche.

"Sun Shadow will give us ample warning," said McBride, "but I'd guess we have about five minutes to set ourselves in place. Bruster—just above you to the left is a ledge that appears to have good cover and a clear view. Get up there and take these two with you—" He indicated Darby and Magenta. "Our ammunition isn't limitless, so make every shot count."

Bruster nodded and for once there was no argument or resistance from the chanteuse and her agent. Greaves was delayed a moment by McBride, who spoke in a voice so low Aubrey might not have heard if fear had not sharpened her senses.

"Whatever happens next, I wouldn't want to see the women taken alive."

It took Greaves an additional few seconds to understand what McBride was saying, and when he did, he glanced at Magenta, then at the Smith and Wesson he carried in his uninjured left hand.

"I couldn't," he whispered.

"Think of it this way, Greaves. She'll die anyway, but it will be a much longer, much more terrible death than a simple bullet in the head. That's Quanah Parker's band of merry men out there. He doesn't take captives; he prefers to see how long and how loud he can make his victims scream."

Darby turned a sickly gray. "Wh . . . what about the rest of us?"

"Don't worry." The sides of McBride's mouth curved in a wry smile. "You, I'll see to personally."

Darby's eyes widened and he wiped the back of his hand across his lips. He backed away a step or two, then turned and hurried up the path after Bruster and Magenta.

"Damned fancy arse," Brody grumbled. "Nuthin' but a passel o' trouble from the day he were hatched, I wager. He'll have 'is britches fouled afore the day is through."

Christian grinned at the wiry driver. "I assume you can pick your own spot?"

"But what if'n them Injuns gits me?" he whined in falsetto.

The grin broadened. "There's not enough hair up top for a decent scalp lock, not enough flesh for a good roasting. My guess is they'll just throw you back."

Jim cackled and ducked into a crevice shadowed by two enormous rocks.

"How can you joke at a time like this?"

Christian glanced back over his shoulder. Aubrey was standing behind him, very tall and very slender, threads of loose black hair curled against her skin by the heat, her eyes very large and very blue in a face dusted pink with fear and anger. He slung a pouch of ammunition over his shoulder and took hold of her hand.

"It isn't a question of joking, Miss Blue. It is a question of survival. If you think you're going to die, chances are you will."

"Considering our circumstances, is there any other way to think?"

"Circumstances can change. Things are never as cut and dried as they look."

He stopped climbing and took a new sighting before he pointed her in the direction of a natural abutment to their right.

"I heard what you said about Quanah Parker."

"Did you now." He was behind her, close on her heels, and she could not stop to look around.

"How do you know it's him? And who is he?"

"He's a renegade half-breed out to prove there's more red blood in him than white. It seems he's sworn to die first and take half of Texas with him before he'll order his people onto a reservation. He's even famous in Leavenworth—that's where the officers who have failed to catch him end up doing duty."

Aubrey reached the abutment and leaned gratefully against the hot stone. McBride took another sighting and grunted in satisfaction, setting down the pouch of ammunition and leaning the Winchester against a narrow shelf of rock. He unslung one of the two canteens he had strapped over his shoulder and took a long, deep swallow before passing it to Aubrey.

The water was tepid and tasted like gravel, but it felt good on her parched lips and throat. She watched McBride make a meticulous check of the rifle and both Peacemakers, perversely fascinated by the almost loving care with which he handled the deadly weapons.

"Do you think Greaves will be able to do it?"

Even though he knew what she meant, he bought a little time by asking, "Do what?"

"Spare Magenta a long and agonizing death."

"You never know what a man is capable of doing until he does it."

"Are you?" she asked softly. "Capable of doing it, I mean."

McBride looked at her. "I won't let anything happen to you, Miss Blue. Not if I can help it, anyway." He paused and reached for her hand again, pressing something cool and metallic into her palm. "But just in case, you might feel more comfortable with this to fall back on."

It was the four-barreled .22 he had taken from her by the river. It looked like a toy compared to his Colts, but the chambers were loaded and the lead just as deadly if fired with any kind of accuracy.

"Furthermore," McBride said, frowning over his own awkwardness, "a lot of what I said was for Greaves's benefit. He strikes me as the kind who fights better when he thinks he's going to die. If he thought we had a good chance to pull this off and walk away, he'd probably crawl into a hole somewhere and look after his own neck."

"Then you think we have a chance?" she asked on a breath.

He debated his answer for a moment, then grinned. "Not a hope in hell. But I intend to give it a good run for my money."

His audacity was getting easier to tolerate and Aubrey

almost found herself smiling. She was still terrified and
her heart still pounded in her breast like a wild thing
she could not contain, yet it was somehow reassuring to
know McBride would look out for her in any eventual-
ity, and that he was not a man who easily accepted
someone else's rules for governing his destiny.

"Are you always so sure of yourself, Mr. McBride?"

He sighed and arched an eyebrow. "Are you always
so stubborn, Miss Blue? Just once, before I die, do you
think you could call me Christian?"

She hesitated, a sudden weakness flooding her limbs.
"I . . . don't think—"

"Exactly," he said. "Don't think."

And before she knew what was happening, she was
gathered into his arms and pulled against his chest. His
mouth claimed hers with a warm, devouring passion, his
lips and tongue quick to smother any attempts at resistance. But there were none. Instead, her lips were as
eager and searching as his, and far from trying to push
him away, she shuddered with the need to burrow herself deeper and deeper into his protective embrace. His
mouth demanded more and she gave it. A mindless
drumming in her blood became a roar as he crushed her
to him, holding her so close she could feel his heart
thudding against hers.

Their mouths came apart, but only for as long as it
took him to sink his fingers in her hair and draw her
back. His lips bruised her with their hunger, then, with
curses as soft as the softest caress, trailed a path of fire
to the curve of her cheek and down along the slender
arch of her throat.

"By God, woman, you pick the *damnedest*
times . . ."

Aubrey gasped and pushed out of his arms. Her skin
flamed everywhere; breasts, belly, and thighs were alive
with sensations she had no means of controlling. He saw

her helplessness and cursed his own even as the heat raged through his veins, confounding him with an equal absence of logic.

Aubrey searched for something—anything to say that might give some plausible reason for her insane behavior, and it was as she tore her gaze away from his terribly compelling hold that she saw the staggered line of Comanche warriors strung out across the plain, sitting just out of rifle range, staring up at the pitifully inadequate bastion of defense.

"Christian . . ." she gasped.

But he was staring in another direction. He was staring at a point somewhere above them, at the coolly disdainful features of Sun Shadow. And when he was sure he had made his opinion of McBride's behavior perfectly clear, he spun on his heel and was gone again, back to his perch near the top of the rocks.

Christian swore and adjusted the brim of his hat, pulling it lower over his face in the hopes of shading the ruddy color he could feel warming his cheeks. He turned all of his attention to the Indians below, squinting into the reflected blaze of sun off the desert sand.

There were twenty-three lined up in the foreground, their ponies still as statues, their riders looking as impressively savage as the bleak beauty of the plains that sprawled out behind them. A smaller group of three stood a dozen yards to the rear, two of them holding tall scalp poles decorated with feathers, braided locks of hair taken from their enemies, and pieces of hide-bound mirror that flashed and winked in the sunlight. The third man was larger and more imposing than the others even at a distance. He had painted his face, arms, and upper torso a gleaming indigo, and rode a pure white stallion.

"You asked me how I knew it was Quanah Parker? That's him; the big bastard in the blue warpaint."

Aubrey found herself edging closer to McBride in spite of their compromising position of only moments before. "Will he order an attack?"

"It isn't up to him. He'll leave the decision to the two medicine men he's with. They will have already consulted the spirits and are probably waiting for some kind of a sign now. He knows he doesn't have to attack. He knows he can just wait us out if he has to. *Shit!*"

As if on cue, four warriors broke from the line and raced forward, not to launch the attack, but to come close enough to where the coach was standing to kill the four remaining mules and ride away again, whooping and screaming their triumph.

McBride heard answering blasts from a ten-gauge and guessed it was Jim Brody expressing his opinion of the underhanded tactics, and, swearing again, the plainsman swung his rifle up and sighted carefully along the barrel, squeezing off two quick shots before the braves were out of range. One of the quartet clutched at his chest and tumbled sideways out of the saddle, his foot catching in the stirrup and dragging him several hundred yards along the coarse ground.

The rest of the line broke and surged forward, their screams echoing off the rocks, clashing with the sound of gunfire and thundering hooves. Christian fired the Winchester until the barrel smoked and his hands blistered from the heat. The Comanche attacked in groups of half a dozen or less, the rest circling and brandishing their weapons, screaming encouragement to the few who rode close enough to taunt their enemies and discharge their carbines. When their guns were empty, they rode back to the circle, passing the freshly reloaded raiders who charged in to take their place.

Dust rose in great white clouds, distorting everything but the sound of men screaming and dying. The stench of sweat and blood and gunpowder hung thickly on the air, not rising, not falling. It choked throats and stung eyes and clung like an opaque veil to the island of rocks. Aubrey fired without thinking, she reloaded without thinking, she watched the frenzy of charging, circling Indians attack again and again without thinking. She could see and hear McBride beside her until he moved farther along the abutment, leaping out of sight as he sought a better position to defend their backs.

The numbers of fallen Comanche grew. Four, five, seven writhing bodies lay in red mud of their own making. Eight, nine . . . someone among the defenders was a remarkable shot, a fact the Comanche could hardly fail to notice as they drew up beyond rifle range and circled among themselves, the two medicine men standing impassive alongside their raging leader.

Aubrey made use of the brief lull, knocking the shell casings out of the Colt and reloading as quickly as her fingers would move. She overturned a box of bullets and hissed at her own clumsiness as she lost most of the skin on her knuckles scrabbling to catch them before they rolled between the crevices in the rocks. She dragged the back of her sleeve across her brow, scarcely noticing the tint of blood that was mixed in with the sweat.

She braced herself as the Comanche came at them again. They seemed to have tempered some of their mindless bloodlust and now hung down by the sides of their ponies, firing their guns from under the protection of their animals' head and neck. Their aim improved as well, the bullets flying closer and truer to their marks. Aubrey felt a lick of hot air brush by her cheek and flinched as the ricochet zinged off the boulder behind her and returned for another near miss.

One of the thick-limbed ponies buckled under the impact of a rifle shot, hurling its rider into the dirt. The Indian came up waving his war club, but he staggered only a pace or two before jerking sideways in a fountain of red spray.

The Comanche reared to a halt again and looked back at the shimmering hillock of sandstone. They raised their weapons in a bone-chilling promise to return, then thundered away on the heels of the two retreating medicine men.

Aubrey collapsed against the hot boulder. She let the heavy gun tilt drunkenly on the rock and leaned her forehead on her crossed arms. She gulped at long, deep breaths, savoring the raw heat that burned along her throat, grateful she still had the wits to feel anything at all.

She lifted her head slowly. The silence was so absolute she could almost hear the faint sifting of the dust as it settled around her. Nothing moved below. Nothing moved out on the plain. There were no cautious heads peeping out of hiding to see if anyone else had survived the horror.

My God, they couldn't all be . . . !

She heard the scrape of a footstep beside her and nearly wept with relief.

"Christian, I—"

She turned and the words froze in her throat. Less than an arm's length away was the blunt and hate-filled visage of a blood-streaked Comanche warrior.

7

Christian McBride ejected the last empty cartridge and lowered the Winchester slowly, watching the cloud of swirling dust that marked the Comanche's triumphant departure—triumphant because no matter how many warriors they had lost in honorable battle against their enemy, the enemy was without the means to pull their coach out of the desert. Without transportation they were doomed, if nothing else, to days of sweltering agony under the cruel sun.

It was not a pleasant prospect.

He sighed and wiped at the sweat on his temples. His hat was lying several feet away, carried there on the wings of a bullet that had nearly succeeded in taking off his head along with it. He dabbed gingerly at the source of a thin trickle of blood and grimaced as he accidentally ground salt and grit into the fresh wound.

Having seen Sun Shadow give the all-clear, the scream caught him completely unaware.

It came from the abutment where he had left Aubrey, and even as he ran along the rocks toward the sound, he could hear the scraping, shuffling noises of a struggle.

The Comanche held Aubrey snug against his chest,

one stocky arm draped tightly around her neck, the other intent upon slicing through the fastenings of her clothes. The buttons on her blouse had already been sprung from their bindings. Her camisole had been torn and there were two vivid red stripes of blood welling on the pale flesh of her naked breast. Her ability to breathe was all but choked off by the force of the Comanche's arm and she could do little more than pluck feebly at the iron-hard band of muscle holding her.

The Comanche saw McBride and the knife was lifted swiftly to the underside of Aubrey's chin. A grin spread across his flat, copper-colored face; anticipation of a kill throbbed in the veins snaking across his brow. His squat upper body was painted with oxblood, his long, dark hair was greased and braided with strips of calico.

McBride felt a cold calm settle over him.

His rifle was empty, but the Indian could hardly know that as he made a pointed show of lowering the weapon onto the ledge of rocks beside him. The bloodshot eyes glowered like two burning brands, watching the minutest curl of a finger as McBride reached for the leather sheath at his waist.

"Just relax," Christian said softly to Aubrey. "He's not going to hurt you when he can have me. When the son of a bitch lets you go, I want you to forget everything you ever learned about being a lady and run like hell."

The Comanche's eyes had narrowed. He saw the knife withdrawn and understood the challenge. His lips curled back over yellowed, overlapping teeth and he snarled a response deep in his throat. Aubrey was flung violently to one side, forgotten in an instant as the Comanche bore down on McBride.

Christian sidestepped the first lunge expertly, but the Indian, who was clearly testing for some such move, quickly reversed and thrust again. It took a costly moment for McBride to adjust to his opponent's superb reflexes, and in that same split second, he came away with the mark of the razor-sharp blade across his ribs.

Aubrey crawled painfully to her knees. Her hair was scattered over her shoulders, torn loose when the Comanche had first grabbed her. Her forehead was scraped and stinging from the heat and fear. Both the Peacemaker and her own small derringer were on the far side of the ledge, as was McBride's rifle, and to get to them she would have to pass by the thrashing pair of men. Fighting waves of dizziness and nausea, she pulled herself upright, clawing at a rock for support, but the moment she tried to put any pressure on her left leg, it buckled under her and she went down again in a jolt of pain.

McBride felt the sickening slither of steel parting his flesh twice more, each the result of a minuscule error on his part. His face and neck streamed with sweat, his shirt clung to his back and chest in darkly soaked patches. His thighs ached from the strain of stalking, circling, lunging, and darting only to recover and stalk again. He knew the game well enough; he and Sun Shadow had played it often as teacher and pupil, and more recently, in Leavenworth, fighting made the difference between eating and starving.

But he could not ignore the fact that he was tiring. Lack of sleep, lack of adjustment to the dry heat of the plains was taking its toll, and he could see the same knowledge reflected in the Comanche's eyes. He had to do something and do it quickly, or the Indian would simply flay at him until enough cuts had been made to bring him helplessly to his knees.

With a swiftness that earned a grudging gasp of respect from the Comanche, he feigned a thrust to the left and spun away at the last moment, managing to slash his knife across the Indian's unprotected belly. The blade came away wet and dripping, and he saw the Indian stagger back in surprise, unable to brace himself for the hard-heeled boot that was driven squarely into the bleeding wound. The Comanche screamed and threw his weight forward, twisting the boot and the foot in it so that Christian found himself sprawled face down on the rock. He saw the silvery blur of steel slashing down toward his face and he rolled awkwardly onto his side, the blade slicing air less than an inch from Christian's throat and skittering on the ground to carve into the pad of muscle on the top of his shoulder.

Snarling with the pain, McBride launched his own knife upward, feeling it punch through flesh and bone. He pushed it deeper, plunging the knife in to the hilt, hearing the bone splinter and crack as the Comanche's weight collapsed over it. He saw the look of utter astonishment on the bronzed face; a cry hissed from between the taut lips, turning to a spatter of blood-flecked foam as he expelled a last breath and lay still.

Christian sucked at a lungful of air and heaved the body off him. There was blood on his hands and blood on his shirt, most of it belonging to the Comanche, and he wiped off what he could in the few minutes it took him to recover his strength and senses. A movement out of the corner of his eye caused him to tilt his head slightly and glare over at where Aubrey sat crumpled against a boulder.

"Why the hell didn't you run when I told you to?" he asked harshly. "Can't you follow a simple order without arguing?"

Aubrey did not answer. Her eyes were wide and round and shimmering with unshed tears. Her blouse and camisole gaped open, the whiteness of the fabric dotted red from the gashes on her breast.

McBride's face softened with self-disgust and he

moved over beside her, wiping his hand again before he reached tentatively for the gaping bodice.

"Are you hurt?"

Aubrey gasped and clutched the edges of her blouse closed, shoving his hand away before he could touch her. "No! I'm not hurt."

His eyes narrowed. "Then why the hell didn't you run?"

"Because I think I wrenched something in my leg when I fell."

He glared at her for another few moments, then glanced down. He lifted the hem of the dour tweed and ran his fingers down one shapely calf.

"Just sit still," he commanded gruffly. "This is no time to plead modesty."

"I wouldn't dream of it," she retorted, "but you are groping the wrong leg."

He shot her a frosty look, then switched his attention to her other knee, calf, and ankle. The black wool stockings and matronly shoes earned another wry scowl, and he removed both without so much as a by your leave.

After a few gentle probes and several involuntary gasps from Aubrey, he sighed and leaned back on his heels.

"Nothing is broken, thank Christ. You may just have bruised the ankle when you hit the rock, or twisted it slightly. Either way, you won't be wearing these for a while." He indicated the shoe and stocking with a frown and added, "Not that I can understand why you would want to in the first place. Couldn't you find anything uglier?"

Aubrey caught her lower lip between her teeth and tried to ignore the icy shivers racing down her spine. Her bare foot was cradled in his lap and his hand was still cupped around her ankle, the long tanned fingers a stark contrast to the pale pink toes and delicate calf. His head was bare and his hair gleamed like tarnished wheat under the sun. There was a dead Comanche six feet away from them and blood drying on his shirt and pants . . . she should have been thinking of any one of a dozen other things at that moment other than the way the heat of his hand was traveling straight up her leg and shooting into her belly.

Their eyes met and held, and she straightened self-consciously.

"Thank you," she murmured. "It feels better already."

"Do you think you can stand?"

"I . . . I think so."

McBride stood first—not an easy task, what with all of his own aches and bruises. He reached down and took Aubrey's hands in his, pulling her up beside him, and yet when she would have thanked him and sought her own means of support, he continued to hold her hands, even tightening his grip so that she was forced to meet his gaze again.

But he wasn't looking at her face. He was looking instead at the torn edges of her blouse. Her breasts were straining the cloth apart and he had a glorious view of the firm, rounded flesh for the two breaths it took before she was startled into tugging her hands free and covering herself.

"You should bathe those cuts right away," he murmured, lifting his smoky gray eyes. "It would be a shame to see something so lovely marked so needlessly."

Aubrey was crimson. "Mr. McBride, you are . . . you are no gentleman."

"Well, that's an improvement over being called a bastard, I suppose." He grinned. "Shall we go and see if we can find the others now? They'll be wondering what has become of us, even though we may not give a damn what's happened to them."

Aubrey's flush deepened, if that was possible, and she shrugged off his outstretched hand, wincing as she hobbled forward on her own strength. McBride watched her for a moment, struggling on the bad ankle and trying to hold her clothing together at the same time, and he laughed.

"You are a confounding woman, Miss Blue."

"Thank you."

"But I really don't have the time to spare on your pride." He scooped her up in his arms and held her securely against his chest. Aubrey looked startled as his hands tightened a little more deliberately than was necessary, and his fingers curved with feigned innocence around the swell of her breast. But her concerns were quickly forgotten as he began to make the descent down through the twisting crevices and sheared creases in the rock. She threw her arms around his neck and clung to him for dear life, her eyes squeezed tightly shut, her face pressed into the comforting shield of buckskin.

8

 The first member of the party they saw was Stink Finger Jim Brody. He was kneeling by the slain mules, one of his gnarled hands stroking a still warm neck. Twin streaks of tears ran from his eyes into the wiry fuzz of his beard and he looked up at McBride as he passed, unashamed at showing he cared more for the faithful, hard-working beasts of the world than he did for most of mankind.

Armbruster Shillingsworth was sitting near the scarred hulk of the stagecoach, his round face bathed in sweat that ran in dirty paths down his neck and stained his collar. His skin was pallid despite the heat, and having lost his derby somewhere along the line, the sun was beaming off the top of his bald head like a beacon. Magenta and Greaves were sitting off to one side, too numb to even bicker. Sun Shadow was walking among the bodies of the dead Comanche, turning them belly up and rifling through the small leather pouches some carried fastened to their belts.

"Is he robbing them?" Aubrey cried, aghast.

"He is looking for anything that might be of some use to us," McBride answered pointedly. "Flints, matches, ammunition—they don't carry too much on them in a raid, but we need just about everything, so . . ." He set her down on a patch of dry scrubgrass and steered her onto a seat on a low rock.

"But robbing the dead—"

"You think they wouldn't do the same to us if the position was reversed? Remember, you're dealing with a whole new set of values out here, Miss Blue. Survival comes first; manners are mighty far down the list."

He left her and walked over to talk to Sun Shadow. Aubrey glanced around at the carnage and shuddered. The bodies were already beginning to take on the waxy cast of death; a few hours in the heat and sun and they would be unbearable. She heard a shriek and jumped, but it was only a big black vulture circling curiously overhead.

"It doesn't take them long to smell tragedy, does it?" Bruster murmured at her side.

Aubrey finished tying her blouse together as decently as she could manage it and only then noticed the odd way Bruster was holding his arm.

"Have you been hit?"

"It's nothing, really. It isn't even bleeding . . . much."

"Take your jacket off and let me see."

"There's no need to fuss, believe me. There appears to be a hole in and a hole out, so I presume it is not as bad as it could be."

Aubrey sighed. "The last thing I need to deal with now is another hero."

"I beg your pardon?"

"You heard me. Your wound may not be bleeding much now, but what if it does later? A few drops an hour is all it takes to leave you as weak as a kitten and then how much good will you be to yourself or anyone?"

"Oh. Oh yes, I . . . I see what you mean. Then . . . then of course, you may do what you think best."

Bruster removing his jacket and Aubrey struggling to her feet took about the same amount of time, and after he rolled up his sleeve, she made him take her seat on the rock. The wound was as clean as she supposed a bullet wound could be, hitting mostly fatty tissue and missing the bone and major arteries. Aubrey looked around for McBride, but he had gone back up the hill to retrieve the guns and ammunition they had left behind.

"I'll see if I can't find something in the coach to clean and bind it."

Bruster nodded, paler now that he had seen, rather than merely felt, the actual damage.

Aubrey hobbled painfully over to the Concord, her misery coming as much from the bruised ankle as from the searing hot sand under her bare foot. Miraculously enough, the huge water barrel strapped to the boot had not been damaged and Aubrey lifted the lid and took a dipperful, drinking some, letting more trickle down the sweltering curve of her throat.

A hand reached out, grasping her wrist, preventing more than a few drops from touching her skin.

"The water you waste now could mean the difference between life and death later."

Aubrey stared up into Sun Shadow's angry brown eyes. They were so much like the eyes that had so recently blazed at her with brutish loathing she needed a moment to remember the Ute was a friend, not an enemy.

"I'm sorry," she gasped. "It was stupid of me. I . . . didn't think."

He saw the red spatters of blood on her shirtfront and frowned. "You were hurt?"

"I . . . no. No, it was just . . ." She looked up and composed herself with an effort. "My ankle is a little sore, that's all. I was looking for something to help Bruster. He's been shot. I thought Mr. Brody might travel with a kit of bandages or some such thing . . . for emergencies."

Sun Shadow released her wrist. "The drummer fought well. His eye is good, his hand steady. He did not always sell women's clothing, I think."

Aubrey held her breath, suffering through the distinctly uncomfortable feeling he was seeing right through her, knew exactly who she was, and why she was out here in the desert.

"McBride tells me you fought well also."

Aubrey attempted a weak smile. "Whatever I did, I did out of fear."

"Only fools have no fear." It was a simple statement, and honest enough to raise a flush of color in her cheeks.

While she stood there feeling foolish, miserable, and hot, Sun Shadow searched the boot of the Concord, but it was emptied of everything save for a few blankets and the express box Jim Brody had adamantly refused to leave behind at the way station. Undaunted, he walked around to the door of the coach, his long hair rippling like a spill of dark silk over his shoulders, and after a moment of searching beneath the seats, emerged with a small carpetbag and a leather satchel that clinked suspiciously with glass.

He offered her the carpetbag, but before Aubrey could look inside, Magenta Royale came hurrying over and snatched it out of her hands.

"What do you think you are doing with this?" she demanded.

"We were going to look inside—"

"I'll just bet you were!" Magenta hugged it possessively to her bosom. "I'm not even dead yet and already you think you can divide the spoils."

Aubrey was dumbfounded. Magenta's face was ribboned with dried tears and grime. She had a sickly odor about her, the source of which was spattered liberally down the front of the emerald silk bodice. Her hair was straggled around her shoulders, and her hands shook visibly as she clutched the prized carpetbag.

"Bruster has been hurt," Aubrey explained with more patience than she was feeling. "I merely thought there might be linens or something I could use for bandages inside."

"Bandages!" Magenta shrieked. "Out of my silk scarves? And I suppose you would want to pin them closed with my pearl cameo? There is nothing you can use in here. *Nothing!* If you are so eager to play nurse, you'll just have to bloody well use your own linens!"

"I haven't any with me," Aubrey said through her teeth. "All of my things were left behind."

Magenta's golden eyes raked over Aubrey's torn blouse, over the makeshift knots in the material that only drew attention to the natural curves beneath. "I see you are managing quite well in spite of the inconvenience . . . or does it give you a thrill to traipse around half-naked in front of *savages*?"

She turned and flounced away, her limp blond curls dull against the emerald silk.

"I will get the case for you," said Sun Shadow, his hand resting lightly on the hilt of his knife.

"No. No, never mind." Aubrey sighed almost regretfully. "I don't imagine silk scarves would be all that appropriate anyway. May I borrow your knife for a moment, though?"

After an uncertain pause, the knife came out of its sheath with a whisper of a sound and settled heavily into the palm of her hand. It was a lethally beautiful weapon, the blade honed so sharp there was no visible breadth to the edge.

Aubrey bent over and luckily did not see the look of

shock on his face as she used his vaunted killing tool to cut away a length of her petticoat.

"Thank you." She returned the knife and glanced hesitantly at the dipperful of water. "Do you think we could spare a small amount to clean Bruster's wound?"

The liquid brown eyes flickered over to where Bruster sat, then to the leather satchel on the step. Opening it, he removed a bottle of Greaves's whiskey and offered it to Aubrey. "Take this as well. The gambler has plenty to spare."

She saw Greaves start to his feet, a protest curling his lips, but a single, warning glance from Sun Shadow was enough to change the agent's mind and Aubrey carried the bottle and the dipper of water back to where Bruster sat burning quietly under the sun.

McBride returned just as she finished washing and dressing Bruster's arm.

"Jim is taking the first watch," he said. "How is the arm, Bruster?"

Bruster smiled wanly. "Apart from these ubiquitous flies who seem determined to pester me to death"—he paused and swatted at a buzzing pair for emphasis—"it feels remarkably well, thank you. Miss Blue has the touch of an angel . . . but . . . my goodness! You should have your own wounds tended to, my good man. I trust not all of that blood is yours?"

McBride followed his gaze to the dark stain on the front of his shirt. When it was dry he would rub it with some of the fine powdered sand, but for the moment he supposed it did look rather gruesome.

"No," he smiled. "It's not all mine."

Aubrey recalled the Comanche's blood-slicked knife. "If you'll take off your shirt, I'll do what I can."

For the first time in their brief but stormy acquaintance, he showed signs of reluctance at the thought of removing his clothes.

"Don't worry about me," he said gruffly. "I've given myself worse cuts shaving."

"Nevertheless, Mr. McBride, it would not hurt to allow Miss Blue to clean your wounds, if for no other reason than to ward off a chance infection." Bruster made the pronouncement as he wiped his brow on the ruffled edge of a piece of torn petticoat. "It wouldn't do at all to have you fall ill. No, not at all."

"Since it doesn't look like I'll have any peace around the two of you until I do," he said irritably, "go ahead, if it will make you happy."

He set the assortment of weapons he carried aside and peeled off the buckskin shirt, baring arms and a muscular torso that appeared to be molded out of solid bronze. The scar Aubrey had noticed earlier under moonlight cut a bold swath from his breast to his belly and made an even more shocking sight under the harsh and unforgiving sunlight. But it was when he turned around and sat down, presenting his back to her with its latticework of crisscrossed weals, that her hand flew to her mouth to stifle the involuntary gasp.

"Not a very pretty sight, is it?" he asked, sensing the reason for her sudden stillness.

"How . . . ? Who did this to you? And why?"

"Let's just say one of the members of the Leavenworth social club wasn't very sociable. Can we get on with this now?"

Aubrey dipped a clean strip of linen in the water and started with the wound on his shoulder. The Comanche's knife had pared away a strip of skin several inches long and it had bled profusely, but it was already beginning to form a scab in the heat and sunlight. A second cut on his ribs was not nearly as bad, but certainly not deserving of the crooked smile that appeared on his face as she leaned over to sponge away the clotted blood and dirt. The graze on his scalp was the last that merited attention, and the one that brought the widest grin to his lips.

"Mr. McBride—?"

He lifted his eyes and she lowered hers, gasping when she saw the reason for his amusement. One of the knots had slipped loose on her bodice, affording him not only an intriguing view each time she leaned over to tend his wounds, but a most disarming view now of the darker peaks of her nipples thrusting against the strained fabric.

Aubrey soaked the square of linen in whiskey and pressed it against his wound.

"Jesus!" He flinched as the burning liquid set fire to his scalp, and grabbed her wrist before she could apply any more. "Thank you, Miss Blue. I think we should call a halt before your halo starts to slip along with your buttons."

She threw the wad of linen at him and whirled around with the intention of storming away, but she was distracted by the sight of Sun Shadow emerging from behind the cover of the rocks, leading one of the dead Comanche's ponies behind him. It was a stout, strong-limbed pinto, with white circles painted around its eyes and jagged stripes of blue dye marking both flanks.

"I'll be damned," McBride muttered. "Where did you find him?"

"Jim Brody saw him from up above. The warrior you fought; it was his."

McBride shrugged into his shirt and walked over to inspect the pony, running an appreciative hand along the muscular chest. "Any chance of catching the others?"

Sun Shadow merely arched a brow.

"Well . . . we'll have to try to hide this one where the Comanche won't be tempted to steal him back."

"Steal him back?" Aubrey asked. "You mean . . . it isn't over yet? They haven't gone away?"

Several possible answers flicked through McBride's mind, and he dismissed each of them under the steady blue intensity of her eyes.

"Parker isn't the type to give up easily. He'll be back. Maybe not today, maybe not even tomorrow, but he will be back."

"Tomorrow?" Magenta stumbled forward, still clutching the carpetbag in her arms. She and Greaves had been lured away from their narrow strip of shade by the sight of the horse, but McBride's words had quickly turned their interest to horror. "What do you mean *tomorrow?* Surely you don't expect us to stay here all night?"

McBride regarded her with genuine curiosity. "Where would you suggest we go? And how would you suggest we get there? The mules are dead, we have no means of pulling the coach."

"We have a horse!" she cried frantically.

"Yes, we do. One horse . . . and seven people—some of them wounded. Even if we were all healthy, and took turns riding, I doubt the Comanche would let us reach the next cover, let alone the ten miles or so to Middle Springs."

"Are you saying we should just stay here and wait for them to attack again?" Greaves asked.

"We've got adequate protection. We've got a couple of days' worth of water in the barrel and canteens, and enough ammunition to mount a pretty good defense if we have to. I'd say staying here gives us the best chance to survive."

"This conversation sounds disgustingly familiar, McBride, only it seems you've changed your tune a little. Seems to me we would have been better off if we'd ignored your advice the last time and stayed put at the way station."

"The choice was yours to make then," Christian said evenly. "And it's yours to make now. The fact that we're still alive means we made the right decision."

"Of course, we don't know that for sure, do we?" Greaves sneered.

"No, we don't."

"And we don't even know if the station at Middle Springs is even there or not. It could have been attacked, just like the last one, in which case we've come all this way for nothing, lost the mules, lost the coach, lost our *lives* more than likely . . . for nothing. But then I'm sure you have another brilliant plan to get us out."

"As a matter of fact, I don't." McBride smiled coldly. "I thought I'd leave it up to you this time."

He turned on his heel and strode away, taking up his Winchester and his Colts, and planting his hat firmly on his head before disappearing into the tumble of rocks again. Sun Shadow glared ominously at Greaves and was a few steps behind McBride, pausing only long enough to hobble the pony securely to a branch of scrub oak.

"Oh dear," Bruster murmured. "Do you suppose they'll come back?"

Greaves snorted. "Where can they go? Furthermore, who put them in charge anyway? We don't need McBride or his damn Breed telling us what to do. And frankly, I don't trust them. Clara is carrying a lot of valuable jewelry with her—worth sending the Comanche to attack us, well worth slitting all our throats now and making it look like it was part of the raid."

Aubrey sighed. "Mr. Greaves, if either one of them had wanted to slit your throat, I doubt they would have waited this long."

"Yeah?" His mouth curled at the corner and he stared insolently at the puckered repairs to her bodice. "Well maybe I'm not surprised either that you'd take their side in this. You and McBride seem awful friendly lately—you're looking less and less like a schoolteacher each day, and he's looking more like the cat licking the cream."

Aubrey's stare was hard and cold, her anger constricting enough to tauten every nerve in her body. She looked from Greaves to Magenta, who seemed to be noticing for the first time the absence of the wire-rimmed spectacles, the soft scatter of black curls over her shoulders, the slender grace of the figure concealed up until then by brown worsted and plain starched blouses.

Even Bruster seemed a little shocked, although he recovered quickly and tried to restore some order to the situation. "Well, I for one freely and openly admit I would have difficulty leading us out of a paper bag, and unless you have some previous experience in fighting Indians, Mr. Greaves, I dare say we must defer to Mr. McBride and his companion. Mr. Brody appears to trust them implicitly, and I rather imagine he has forgotten more about this wretched frontier than all of us combined will ever learn."

"So you trust them too, eh? That and a plugged nickel will get you exactly nowhere."

"No, Mr. Greaves," Bruster said evenly. "It will get *you* exactly nowhere if you persist in using your mouth instead of your brains to think for you."

Greaves spat scornfully into the dirt at his feet. He took Magenta by the arm and started to walk away, halting after only a few steps to return to the coach and pick up his satchel. He tucked it under his uninjured arm and together he and Magenta retreated to their shallow scoop of shade, their heads bowed in an exchange of furious whispers.

Aubrey was too angry to even feel the heat of the sand on her bare foot as she allowed Bruster to help her back to the coach. There, she sat on the lowered step, her face flushed, her hair clinging in damp wisps to her temples and throat.

Bruster glanced around, making very sure they were alone before he lowered his bulk on the step beside her.

A wave of heat rolled past them, bringing the low drone of flies gorging nearby. The sun was a fierce ball of fire overhead and Bruster laid a scrap of linen over his scalp in the hopes of saving it from becoming one enormous blister.

The heat. The stillness. The flies.

He stole a sidelong peek at Aubrey and shifted uncomfortably on the narrow step. His arm was throbbing and his belly was a liquid volcano threatening to erupt.

"Don't say it," she hissed.

"Say what, my dear? I wasn't going to say anything."

"You were thinking it then. You were thinking this was a mistake from the outset and you were thinking I should have listened to you when you tried to talk me out of it."

Lucius Armbruster Beebee chuckled with the wry wisdom of a proven sage and adjusted his arm inside the makeshift sling he had devised from his vest. It was, as his blasted luck would have it, the same shoulder and arm he had dislocated a month ago when he had had a sane and practical reason for abstaining from this ill-fated venture.

"What I said—to be more precise—was that emotion was always an unreliable bedfellow in our line of work, and of all the emotions, revenge is the whore with the hidden disease."

"You didn't want to come. You never wanted to be a part of this."

"I couldn't very well let you make this trek by yourself, could I? What kind of a partner would I be then? What kind of a guardian? I've looked after you for nearly ten years now, taught you everything I knew, coached you, groomed you for greatness . . . how could I simply put you on a stagecoach and let you ride away to battle the mighty dragon by yourself? Hmph! A fine, doddering old fool you must think me."

"Oh, Bruster—" She reached over and slipped her hand into his. "You are neither doddering, nor a fool. And I'm so grateful for everything you have done for me, I hardly know how I can ever begin to pay you back."

"No, no. It was you who breathed new life into me, Aubrey Blue. When I found you out on that desert— God rot that we should find ourselves in similar circumstances again, what?—you were half-starved, half bled to death, and haunted by devils so fearsome a grown man would have faltered under less. But you didn't. You clung to life and showed me what a precious, irreplaceable thing it was, and then later, when you grew stronger, smarter, brighter than the brightest star in the sky, you gave freely of that strength, making an old grifter feel as if he still held the world in the palm of his hand."

"You were the best there ever was, Bruster, and you still are."

"I was good," he conceded modestly "But I was never the talk of five states, not until an urchin with nerves of steel and eyes like liquid purity showed me the meaning of true artistry."

"We won a few card games, sold a few worthless bonds . . ." She smiled wearily and quoted, " 'That and a plugged nickel will get you exactly nowhere.' "

"Ahhh, I wouldn't be too hasty. Your Mr. McBride does not seem to me to be the type to throw in his hand before all the cards are played."

"He isn't *my* Mr. McBride," she said tersely. "And he doesn't miss very much either. His nose was itching an hour out of Great Bend."

"Do you think he suspects a connection between us? I thought we'd been extremely careful."

"We have, and I don't think he does. Mind you . . ."

Bruster arched an eyebrow and waited.

"He . . . seems determined to prove I'm not who I pretend to be. Mysteries intrigue him, or so he says, but so far, every easy solution I've given him, he hasn't believed."

"Could he be a problem?"

"No. Just an annoyance. He has his own secrets to keep, and I doubt he'll even remember my name in a week or so."

Bruster pursed his lips and squinted upward, defying the glare of the sun long enough to isolate and identify the three figures standing in the rocks high above them. All three—McBride, Sun Shadow, and Jim Brody— were easily distinguishable by virtue of their various and varied characteristics, but it was McBride's tall and powerful silhouette that earned the longest consideration.

Aubrey Blue had never let her interest in a man interfere with business before—not that Bruster could immediately bring to mind any man who had earned her interest at all. She was smart and cagey, clever and cool in the meanest situations, and he had no doubts whatsoever that her single-minded determination to seek out Maxwell Fleming and destroy him would tolerate no interference of any kind from any source . . . and yet, the plainsman had made an impression. Despite her brusque dismissal, he might well develop into the wrong kind of problem if she did not acknowledge her attraction and do something about it one way or another.

Bruster sighed and mopped his brow. He had never had any desire to become a father, never planned on forming any permanent attachments or assuming any responsibility for anyone's life other than his own . . . and all for the very reasons that found him out here now, sweating like a crock of pickles, fighting Indians, and worrying about the consequences of a young woman falling in love with a brutishly handsome stranger.

"I should have listened to myself when I said this was a bad idea," he said morosely. "I *should* have left you to your own devices instead of chasing after you like an old fool."

He looked so dejected, Aubrey thought it best to contain her smile. "You certainly did manage to surprise me —shock me, in fact—when you bustled into the stage office in Great Bend. You could have warned me."

"I was testing you, my dear. If you couldn't have kept a straight face under those circumstances, how could you have expected to stand up to Maxwell Fleming? Besides"—he sighed dramatically—"you will need me in this wretched mecca of thin whiskey and Spanish fly —if only to see you properly introduced to Lily Cruise Montana."

"Are you sure she is still in Santa Fe? For that matter, are you sure she will remember you?"

"Remember me?" Bruster's eyebrows arched a little wistfully. "I truly hope she remembers me, for I remember her as clearly as if it was only yesterday that we parted. Sweet Lily. As delicate as a butterfly, with the face of an angel. The only woman I know—present company excepted, of course—who could set my heart racing by the simple act of picking up a deck of cards. A beauty. A rare, ethereal beauty she was, with skin as white as the petals of a gardenia and hands so nimble she could strip a man naked without him feeling a thing. Yes. Yes, my sweet Lily is still in Santa Fe. She has, ah, out of necessity adopted a new name and guise, of course, for there are still some scurrilous sorts who might be vengeful enough to see her dragged before a court of law and made to account for her past deeds, even though, for all intents and purposes, she has retired from the game."

"Then what makes you so sure she will help us?"

Bruster smiled. "One look at you, my dear, and she won't be able to resist. You will remind her of herself twenty years ago—bright and sharp-witted, as sly as a minx with as keen an eye for an easy mark as any I have had the pleasure to work with. True talent, m'dear, always recognizes itself. And in this case, Lily will be looking into a mirror, envying what she sees there. Conversely, you will have a chance to glimpse into your own future, although, God willing, it will come to better purpose than sewing frills and frippery for wealthy, bored ranch wives."

"There is nothing wrong with being a seamstress."

"Did I say there was? I only meant that for Lily Cruise Montana, having known the glitter and celebrity of a much faster paced life . . . hawking needlework must be as dull as watching dust settle."

The name Lily Cruise Montana had not rung any bells for Aubrey when he had first mentioned it, nor did it ring any now. She had supposedly worked the mining towns of Missouri and the Dakotas, and had, according to Bruster's glowing accolades, earned immortal fame in the gaming halls of San Francisco before seeking her so-called life of everlasting boredom and respectability in New Mexico. That Aubrey had never heard of Lily

Montana had not alarmed her overmuch in the beginning; she had not heard of half the names Lucius Armbruster Beebee lauded as pioneers and heroes of their profession.

"Doña Dolores Tules," Bruster said, giving his head a slight shake. "Widow and frockmaker. So must the end come to all of us, I suppose."

Aubrey blotted the back of her hand against the fine beading of moisture that had collected over her upper lip.

"Does this . . . Doña Dolores Tules . . . know we are coming?"

"Well, ah . . ."

Aubrey turned slowly, the look on her face prompting Bruster to wriggle a finger between his collar and throat. It prompted something else—a habit he fell back on every time he needed an extra ration of luck, or prayer. It was a charm, a worthless trinket he had won in a card game years ago. From one end hung a black and white hare's foot; from the other a pair of silver dice studded with tiny bits of colored glass. He was never without it. He would never engage in any game of chance or luck without rubbing the hare's foot first, and he was rarely caught telling the truth if he was feigning intense interest in the dice.

At the moment, he was studying them as if he had never seen them before.

"Bruster . . . she doesn't know we're coming, does she?"

"Well, ahh—" He cleared his throat brusquely. "I could hardly see the purpose in sending a cable after I had made the decision to join you. And it did seem more prudent not to give her too much time to dwell on the less favorable aspects of our venture. But you needn't concern yourself over her loyalty or her willingness to lend an old friend a hand. Lily and I owe certain, er, debts to one another."

"What kind of debts?" Aubrey demanded.

"Of the heart," he assured her, clutching the hare's foot steadfastly. "As always, of the heart."

9

"The idea is for one of us to take the pony and make a run for the station at Middle Springs."

McBride and Jim Brody had come down from their high perch when the sun had lost most of its fury and was beginning to slide toward the horizon. There had been no further sightings of the Comanche, other than the odd flash of a mirror well off in the distance, or a puff of dust from a retreating scout.

Together they had worked for an hour or more moving the dead bodies out of sight, if not out of mind. Jim had turned practical and carved one of the mules hindquarters into steaks, roasting them over a fire while he helped the plainsman with his grisly detail. He presented each of the passengers with a skewer of cooked meat when it was done, telling them they could choke it down for sustenance, or not, live or die; he didn't much give a damn. The water barrel had been moved, taken from the coach and placed in a protected niche where a chance bullet or arrow could not damage it. Jim had salvaged enough canteens and containers from the relay station to issue one to each person, and he told them it would be filled once a day and once only, to be drunk in a sensible manner, or all at once; he didn't much give a damn about that either.

Daylight had kept nerves and tempers on a raw edge, but now that the sun was setting, more than just the threatening chill of the night air began to stir the passengers out of their earlier surliness.

Their sandstone fortress, touched with the last rays of the sun, glowed pink against the massive dark void of the sky. The light was thin, blue, and cool, trapping the vaporous residue of the day's heat in layers that shimmered and rippled like water.

McBride's hair, like the glittering needles of gypsum that caused the sandstone rocks to glow with varying shades of pink and rose and oxblood, burned with threads of gold and yellow and deepest amber as he stood in front of them, his hat in his hand, his one foot raised and propped on a rock.

"It's the best chance we have—for one of us to go on ahead and try to find help. One man on a fast horse can cover the ground in a fraction of the time it would take for all of us to move together."

"But the Comanche," Bruster asked. "Won't they be able to pick off a single man all the more easily as well?"

"It's a risk," McBride agreed. "But the alternative is just to hole up here and wait until they pick us off one at a time anyway. Make no mistake, folks, we were damned lucky this morning. The fact they haven't come back yet only suggests they are giving a good deal of thought as to how they will approach us tomorrow."

"Who do you suggest goes?" Greaves sneered, "As if we didn't know already."

McBride smiled easily. "I actually thought of you first, Greaves, but then I realized that even if your hand was good enough to hold the reins, you probably wouldn't be sober enough to ride in a straight line."

Greaves massaged his bandaged wrist and palm, the rims of his nostrils grew white with loathing. "And if you or the Breed go, who's to say you'll even go out of your way to find help once you're free and clear?"

"Darby, for heaven's sake," Magenta hissed. "Shut up."

"If it was only you, Greaves, I'd be mighty tempted," McBride said, pondering the glowing tip of ash on his cheroot. "But there's only one horse, and, unfortunately I didn't draw the short straw."

"In other words, you've already decided!"

"Since the decision realistically only concerned three of us, we took it on ourselves to save anyone the grief of offering to play hero."

"Is that truly fair to you gentlemen, Mr. McBride?" Bruster protested. "You are, none of you, obliged to carry the burden of risk for the rest of us."

"A generous thought, Bruster, and much appreciated, but you wouldn't be able to tolerate the pain in your arm for more than a few hundred yards, and I can't see any of us standing on the rocks waving so long to one of the women. That leaves only Jim, Sun Shadow, and myself."

"I'm not trusting my life to any bloody redskin!" Greaves declared.

"You won't have to," McBride said through a wide slash of white teeth. "You'll be trusting it to me, right here."

"What about the soldiers?" Magenta wailed. "I still say there *must* be a patrol out looking for us by now. We're two days' overdue at every station between here and Santa Fe. Even if the next one *has* been attacked, the one after that would have been alerted, or the one after that. *Some*one would be concerned about us by now."

"Like I said before, the army could well be out in force right now, but they wouldn't know where to look."

"What do you mean they wouldn't know where to look? We're within sight of the main trail—wouldn't they simply have to follow it until they found us?"

Aubrey saw Stink Finger Jim shift perceptibly behind the shielding bulk of the plainsman and she had a sinking feeling she knew what McBride was going to say before he had found the words to say it.

"The fact is, we're not on the main route, Magenta. Jim took a chance on a shorter cut he sometimes takes across this part of the desert, hoping to shave some miles and time off the trip."

"In other words," Magenta gasped, horrified, "we are lost."

"Ain't lost unless yus don't know where yus are," Jim grumbled. "I know'd where we are, it's jest that no one else does."

"So . . . the army could be looking for us *right now,* searching the road we *should have been on?"*

"Jim will head due west and pick up the main road before he tries for Middle Springs."

"Jim?" Magenta cried. "You're giving that mealy-mouthed, snot-eyed little bastard the only horse we have and you're trusting *him* to lead the army back to us?"

McBride stared into the brittle amber eyes for a long moment before the disgust repelled him. Whatever beauty had turned heads and won her audiences was badly ravaged by the heat and hysteria. Her cheeks were sunken and burned bright red by the sun, her eyes were swollen and puffed from intermittent bouts of weeping and whining. Large, dark semicircles of sweat stained the underarms of her dress and the hem was torn and filthy, shredded by the sand and stones.

By comparison, Aubrey's simple white blouse and practical skirt had held up well despite the Comanche's best efforts and in spite of the hardships of the heat and dust. Her hair had rebelled against any further attempts at entrapment, tumbling in a soft midnight spill around her shoulders, mocking even the constraints of the thin shred of linen she had used earlier to tie it back. The sun had warmed her complexion as well, but not to the painful cherry red suffered by the fairer-skinned Magenta Royale. There was a natural duskiness that hinted at an exotic heritage somewhere in her background— Spanish, perhaps, or . . .

McBride frowned. Spanish?

A drifting pencil line of smoke trailed up from his cheroot, stinging his eyes, causing him to lose his train of thought. He blinked and glared at Magenta.

"Jim is the best man for the job. He knows the territory. He knows the Comanche's habits almost as well as he knows his own. If anyone can get through, he can, and if he does, Miss Royale, he'll deserve not only your thanks, but your absolute respect . . . which I will personally see that he gets."

Magenta sucked in a shocked gasp and clawed her hand into Darby's arm. "Are you just going to stand there and let him talk to me this way?"

The light was almost gone. There was only the burning red of the sandstone, the pale wash of desert sand, and the diamond-bright depths of Greaves's hatred standing out against the encroaching blackness.

"For the time being, Clara love, it seems I have no choice."

"Darby!"

"Come along, my dear. The air is getting a little too full of righteousness for my taste."

Aubrey did not consciously draw another breath until Greaves and Magenta had walked away, and McBride's hand had eased away from the Peacemaker strapped around his waist. The piercing gray eyes continued to

follow the retreating pair, however, and Aubrey had to
reach out and touch his arm before either he or Jim
noticed her still standing beside them in the heavy
gloom.

"When will Jim be leaving?"

"The moon is full, but it's already up and we should
have a fine, dark sky by one or two in the morning. We'll
keep a fire burning up top to let Quanah Parker know
we're still here, and we'll wrap the pony's hooves in
strips of blanket to muffle the sound. With luck he'll get
away all right. If he keeps to the draws and gullies, he
should make it to the Springs long before dawn."

"So close," she whispered.

"Ten miles, or a hundred; it's all the same when you
know there's an empty notch on a scalp pole looking to
be filled."

•

Aubrey stood back from the heat of the fire and
watched the orange and yellow flames leaping skyward,
sending bursts of bright red sparks spiraling higher into
the darkness. The pop and crackle of dry wood seemed
as loud as a hail of gunfire, yet it was nothing compared
to the sound of Jim Brody's snores. He was stretched
out alongside the fire pit, fast asleep, his mouth wide
open, inhaling and exhaling with enough velocity to
draw the rim of his beard in and spray it out again on
each breath. He still had a couple of hours to wait and
had declared the time better spent in sleep than worry.

A fine philosophy if one could forget the war party of
Comanche waiting for him somewhere out on the
plains.

Bruster's arm had started bleeding—a result of his
insistence on helping McBride gather brush and break
up the seats of the coach for firewood. The last time
Aubrey had checked on him, he had fallen into a fitful

sleep, and apart from the raging sunburn on his cheeks and nose, was showing no signs of fever.

Magenta and Greaves had taken their blankets, bottles, and jewels off to a private niche somewhere; the Ute was standing watch, and McBride . . .

Aubrey looked up toward the crown of the rocks, but there was only blackness and stars beyond the glow of the fire, dancing shadows, and ghostly patterns on silent spires and jagged blocks of rock surrounding her.

McBride was somewhere. Like a big, prowling cat, he preferred to go off on his own, and in this company, she could hardly blame him.

Aubrey pulled the edges of the blanket closer around her shoulders. It was cool away from the fire and she turned, on the verge of going back, when she spotted a tiny red pinpoint of light farther along the shoulder of rocks. She waited, watching for it again, finding it difficult to pick out one minute sparkle from the carpet of stars that formed the glittering backdrop. But it came again. A small red blossom of glowing ash. McBride was there, finishing the cigar he had prudently only half-smoked earlier.

He was out there watching.

Waiting?

Aubrey looked up at the stars, then over her shoulder at the golden blaze of the fire. She gazed out at the cool, shifting sand, so white under the moonlight it might have been banks of drifted snow—then back at the distant shoulder of rock, imagining she was staring directly into the steely gray eyes.

The kiss this morning: she had thought about it a good deal. She hadn't demurred, hadn't fought him, hadn't resisted in the least. Moreover, she hadn't wanted it to end, hadn't wanted him to let go of her, and hadn't been able to keep her body from burning with memories every time she saw him walk by. Her reaction could have been chalked up to fear—fear of impending doom would most certainly have contributed to her need to feel the press of warm human flesh. Yes, fear would have made her cling to him, made her respond to his kiss as if her soul was on fire.

She wasn't afraid now, and yet his power and strength and rugged confidence attracted her like a moth to a flame. And despite her earlier opinion of him as a dangerous nuisance and a man too consumed by curiosity for her own good—she could not rid her body of the aching need to be close to him. To not be alone. To know once and for all how much of a threat Christian McBride was to her plans in Santa Fe.

Aubrey moved restlessly into deeper shadows. She walked in stockinged feet, having decided it was much easier than trying to cope with one bare sole and one high-buttoned shoe. Her ankle only ached when she thought about it, and she tried not to think too much about anything as she picked her way carefully around jutting spurs of rock.

After a good deal of effort and several halts to debate her own foolishness, she arrived at the place where she thought she had seen McBride's cigar. Of course he wasn't there. The rocks were cold and barren; she had only the low hum of the dry wind for company. Either he had seen her coming—or heard her, more likely than not—and moved elsewhere, or he had never been there at all.

"I thought I told you to watch the fire."

Aubrey's heart took a sudden leap up into her throat as she spun around. He was standing right behind her, so close her hands brushed against the buckskin fringe of his shirt. She couldn't see much of his face, they were on the wrong side of the rocky island for the moon to have a direct effect, but there were enough stars and cumulative reflections off the stones and sand to give substance to the rugged planes and angles.

"I . . . was watching it," she said, backing away a step, "and decided it wasn't going anywhere."

McBride's hand moved to his waist and she caught a glint of blue light refracted off the metal blade of his knife. "I would have thought you'd have learned from your experience this morning that it isn't the smartest thing to do to go wandering around this place unannounced."

She heard the slick slide of his knife being resheathed and felt her heart take another turn in her chest. "I'm sorry, I didn't think. I just wanted to be by myself for a while. Surely you, of all people, can understand that particular desire."

She sensed, rather than saw, the slow grin relax his features.

"Does this desire for solitude include me? Are you trying to tell me our truce this morning was only temporary?"

"I . . . truce?"

His hand moved again and this time Aubrey felt a whisper of warmth from his fingers as they brushed a stray tendril of hair back from her face.

"I thought we had managed to get past the stage where you wanted to hold a loaded gun to my head."

"Mr. McBride, I—"

He groaned and slumped abruptly back against the rock. "And I *know* I heard you call me Christian this morning, I know I did."

She curled her lip between her teeth and nibbled on the fleshy pad, uncomfortable in the knowledge that far too much had seemed to happen this morning, and she was only compounding her errors now. Of course, he couldn't know she had come this way deliberately, but still . . .

"So, what did you want to see me about?"

"See you?"

He took his hat off and raked his fingers through his hair. "You didn't exactly take the easiest path away from the others, if privacy was all you wanted."

"Mr. McBride, if you are insinuating—"

"Conversation . . . a little human companionship: it isn't a crime, you know. In fact, I was sort of hoping to have a quiet minute alone with you. I'm . . . not much good at apologies, and handing out compliments is right out of my area of expertise entirely, but I wanted to say that I thought you handled yourself well today. You didn't panic. You didn't ask a lot of unnecessary questions. In the coach and later . . . here . . . you did just fine."

Aubrey savaged her lip again, swaying slightly with the unexpected rush of pleasure his words sent spilling down her spine.

"Thank you," she whispered. "But as I told Sun Shadow, whatever I did, I did out of fear."

He seemed mildly taken aback. "You spoke to Sun Shadow?"

"Why, yes. Is that so unusual?"

"It is if he spoke back. He prefers just to glare and look fierce when he's in the presence of most women— all women, for that matter, except for his wife."

"He's married?"

McBride's grin broadened. "Is *that* so unusual a notion?"

"No, of course not," she said, flushing. "It's just . . . I never thought about it, I guess."

"Well, he's very much married, and has four sons to carry on the fierce and glaring tradition. A fifth is on the way, or so he tells me, but I'm hoping it will be a girl, just to keep the smug bastard honest."

"You are very good friends, aren't you?"

He contemplated the rim of his hat for a moment, turning it slowly in his hands. "We were the worst of enemies at one time. I spent half a year tracking him, another half-year dodging his bullets and scalping knife. When we finally came together, he gave me this"—his hand traced lightly down the scar that ravaged his throat and chest—"and a new respect for the meaning of the word survival. I don't know what I gave him, other than a lot of shame and anger and pain."

"I don't understand."

McBride drew a breath and released it on a short gust. "He didn't know, until I found him and told him, that we shared the same father. A grievous insult to any Indian warrior, to be sure; doubly so to a wild and proud chieftain . . . not that I was all that thrilled at the notion myself. Hearing a stranger named in your father's will is enough of a shock without finding out later that he was the leader of the band of renegades that had been raiding our ranch for years. Blood ties tend to weaken under those circumstances."

"You obviously managed to resolve your differences."

McBride looked up and his hands stilled. "We found a third, mutual enemy to hate."

"What about you?" he asked after a moment. "Are there any more like you at home? Any brothers or sisters?"

"Why?" she asked, immediately on her guard.

"No particular reason," he protested innocently. "Just friendly conversation. That's usually how it goes, isn't it? I tell you a little bit about me, you tell me a little bit about you."

"And then you start asking too many questions, and we argue, and one thing leads to another." She stopped and shook her head. "Frankly, I don't trust your idea of a friendly conversation. Maybe I should just go back . . ."

"Aubrey—" His hand reached out, catching her arm as she started to walk past him. "Arguing with you is the last thing I want to do tonight, believe me. I promise, no more questions. We don't even have to talk at all if you don't want to. We can just sit back and watch the show and say nothing."

"Watch the show? What show?"

"The best seats are over here," he said, indicating a sloping shoulder of rock behind her. "If I promise to keep my thoughts pure and my hands in my pockets, will you join me?"

"I still don't know what you're talking about."

"I can't explain it, I have to show you."

He held out his hand and Aubrey stared at it a moment. Touching him voluntarily was the last thing *she* wanted to do and yet she saw the pale, slender thing that was her hand settle shyly into his. When her skin did not instantly erupt in flame or her arm not dissolve in a spray of acid, despite herself, she almost smiled.

McBride, seeing the faint glimmer of the smile, and feeling the cool tremor that traveled up her arm, refrained from making any casual comments about either. She was as skittish as a colt already, and he had no intention of scaring her off just yet. At the same time he had to remind himself that while a little trust was a good thing, too much could be downright dangerous. For both of them.

He held her hand tightly and helped her onto the higher level, cautioning her to watch her step as they climbed toward the rounded dome of the rock. Aubrey saw a break in the smooth symmetry of the stone face, a shallow pocket hollowed out of the sandstone and cushioned with sand carried there by the wind. A darker patch in the center of the shallow scoop proved to be a blanket; beside it lay McBride's rifle and gunbelt.

"Sit down," he invited, doing so himself.

Aubrey glanced around, hugging her own blanket to her shoulders, feeling more than a shade unsteady to be balanced, as it were, on the edge of their little sandstone world. The desert was a hundred feet or more below them, and there was nothing but the starlit vault of the sky above.

"You're blocking my view," Christian said gently.

Aubrey lowered herself gingerly onto the edge of the blanket and tucked her feet up under the hem of her skirt. She could see nothing out on the plains—no lights, no fires . . . no dancing girls or cavorting bears.

"There," he said, pointing straight up.

Aubrey tilted her head back, catching just a glimpse of the fiery tail end of a shooting star.

"I must have counted two dozen so far," he said, then added casually, "It's better if you lie down."

He stretched back and folded his arms under his head, his long legs crossed at the ankles, and Aubrey was terribly, physically conscious of the sleek, powerful lines of his body. His shirt had gaped open to reveal the smooth muscling of his shoulders and chest, and she felt a ridiculous, giddy urge to run her hands beneath the buckskin, to strip it completely aside and bare the hard, gleaming torso to the searching curiosity of her fingertips. She felt a new and different kind of warmth surge into her cheeks and it was disturbingly clear to her that she was no longer the controlled and aloof study of indifference she had supposed herself to be. She could touch and she could be touched with none of the revulsion she experienced in her nightmares. She could look at a man's body and wonder; she could remember the feel of his lips and know desire.

The blush in her cheeks grew hotter. Her heart began to pound with a strange new rhythm and to cover her own ineptness, she sank back down onto the blanket, acutely aware of the way his eyes followed her. The sand was cool and velvety soft beneath her, the little hillocks of fine powder molding to the shape of her body. She looked straight up, her head pillowed on the sand, and it was as if the ground had suddenly fallen away beneath her, as if there were no desert surrounding them, no island of rocks sheltering them. There was only the endless black void all around her, a vast glittering wilderness that beckoned her to leave her body behind and float upward into the stars.

"I think this was what I missed the most, being locked inside," McBride said quietly. "You were right about understanding the need for privacy—there's no such thing in prison. Hell, there were times I didn't think I would ever breathe good clean air again. Times I thought I'd never be free again." He paused and laughed huskily, the sound seeming to come from very far away. "There's a butte in Arizona, must be a mile or more high. I used to lay in the stink and slime of my cell and imagine myself on the top of that butte, with nothing but the wind and the sky and the eagles for company. I think . . . in the end, it was the only thing that kept me sane."

Aubrey drifted to the sound of his voice. She let his words shiver through her, heightening her pleasure and warmth and sensitivity everywhere. As a child she had lain on the sand dunes and imagined she was riding the foaming wake of the clouds but they had seemed close, and there was never any danger of being swept away by one of the ghostly galleons. The stars were so very far away. She raised a hand, her fingers fanned wide, and stretched it upward as if there should have been some substance to the sea of midnight blue, as if there should have been something real and tangible holding her back, preventing her from floating away into space.

She gasped as a bright white slash of light arced across the sky, and she gasped again as it seemed to fly right through her fingers. She felt hot, childlike tears spring into her eyes and she could not have explained them, not to herself, not to the man who reached up and laced his fingers through hers, bringing her back down to earth before she was lost completely.

"You're supposed to make a wish on a falling star," he murmured.

"Did you?"

"I most certainly did. It took two dozen, but you're finally here."

He said it so quietly, she was sure she had heard the words wrong, and far from easing her flush of light-headedness, he only added to it.

She sat up quickly, her heart clamoring in her chest, her breath rushing along a throat that had suddenly gone dry and gritty. She stared at her stockinged feet and ordered them to move, but they would not. She felt the blanket being peeled away from her shoulders and she commanded her hands to snatch it back, but they were too busy clasping each other for courage.

A long, tanned finger collected up the mass of black curls that lay scattered across her shoulder, and dragged them slowly to one side. He pressed his cheek into the silky tangle and bent his lips to the warm satin curve of her throat. His tongue traced a lazy pattern up to the lobe of her ear and Aubrey's eyes shivered shut. The shiver spread heat into her chest and down into her belly, running in a hot, slippery trickle between her thighs.

"Please," she whispered. "Don't do this."

His breath rasped against her ear, the sound lost almost at once as his tongue probed the delicate pink ridges of flesh. Aubrey tried to twist her head away, but his hand was suddenly there, twining itself into the thickness of her hair, forcing her to submit to the unconscionable torment. His other hand cradled her chin for a moment before succumbing to the lure of a greater temptation; its heat and boldness slid slowly downward, riding the gentle slope of her breast, molding around the shape and softness and tracing the wrinkled tautness of her nipple with a broad, calloused thumb.

The strength crumpled out of Aubrey's shoulders and she leaned back against him. He kissed her temple, her cheek, her chin; he nibbled at the corners of her mouth, his assault deft and sure and gauged to the cadence of the ragged cries that escaped her lips.

"You promised . . . to keep your hands . . . in your pockets . . ."

His lips broke away for a moment and he gazed down at her, his eyes, nose, and mouth barely more than dark slashes, cloaked by shadows. Aubrey's face, on the other hand, was dusted in starlight. Her eyes shimmered and her lips were full and inviting. The curve of her throat was pearly white, drawing his gaze down to where his hand was beginning to test the strength of the knots binding her blouse.

"I lied," he said simply. "I don't have any pockets."

He bent his mouth to hers, smothering her gasp with a swift, fierce pressure. Aubrey raised her hands, intending to push him away, but instead of meeting buckskin, they encountered the heat of his smooth, hard flesh.

Her lips parted and his kiss deepened, becoming deliciously wet and suggestive. His tongue darted and caressed and cajoled, sending rivers, *torrents* of sensation flooding downward only to be met and swamped by the richer, lusher waves of pleasure invoked by his questing fingers.

Aubrey drew her legs higher and curled them tighter beneath her, hoping to staunch the flow of heat, but it was no use. His mouth was ravishing her, his hand was peeling away her defenses, and his body . . . his body was radiating heat and strength and passion. She was on fire where he touched her, and where he did not, her flesh seemed to smolder with impatience, waiting for the spark that would burst her into flame.

Christian was surprised by the depth of his own desire. His fingers shook with such eagerness he could barely steady them long enough to free the knots instead of simply tearing the barriers away from her body. The black mist of her hair was in his eyes blinding him, the taste of her was on his lips intoxicating him beyond all sense of reason. It was madness to want what he wanted on a stone bed a million miles from nowhere. She was frightened and vulnerable from the effects of a long, dangerous day and he knew he was taking shameful advantage of her weakness under the moonlight. He *knew* it, damn it, just as he knew she would undoubtedly hate him for it in the morning.

But why should he care? She was nothing to him—a mystery, a challenge, a diversion with flashing blue eyes and a mouth made for kissing. Chances were better than good that none of them would make it off this rockpile alive, so why should he care what she thought or felt about him in the morning? Why, when all he wanted to do was bury himself in her warmth and wetness and send the rest of the world to hell for as long as he could?

He groaned as the last knot sprang free. He thrust aside the crinkled layers of fabric and closed his hand around the soft white mound of her naked breast, holding her close as he felt the shock of unexpected intimacy ripple through her body. Soft. Her skin was so soft. It filled his palm with a cool heaviness, starkly, softly white save for the two thrusting peaks of duskier rose.

His mouth descended again and the fist that was still twined in her hair forced her head back, eased it back until she was no longer cradled against his body but lying down alongside him. His fist tightened further, his eagerness making him rougher than he meant to be as he shifted his weight over her, and for the first time, a twinge of pain intruded on her pleasure.

Aubrey's eyes fought the drugging weight of her lashes and she watched with a kind of stunned fascination as his mouth made a slow, fiery pilgrimage to her breast. The heat surrounded her nipple and drew the engorged flesh inward and upward, his tongue prowling and probing and suckling the raw nerve endings until she was arching unwittingly into the exquisite torment.

Christian smothered another groan as he crushed her to him. She wanted the same thing he did; he could feel the admission in the restless clutching of her hands and the squirming, writhing undulations of her body. His hand skimmed down her thighs, then between them, and he cursed the sturdy brown worsted of her skirt. He cursed the fastening at her waist that he could not find, and cursed the bulkiness of the folds that lay stiff and unyielding between them. Reaching down again, he dragged the hem up over her knees, abandoning it there when he felt the lithe suppleness of a naked thigh. He heard a small gasp and felt her limbs twist away from the intrusion, but he was adamant in his quest, using his knee to trap one slender leg beneath him.

Aubrey twisted again and the heat of his need raged through him. It tainted his impatience with anger and made his fingers resent her efforts to bar his way.

"The game is over, Aubrey," he said hoarsely. "It was fun while it lasted, but I think we both know the game itself is over."

The game is over.

The game is over, sweet thing . . .

Aubrey's eyes opened wide and she stared at the black sky above, hearing the voice from her Dream echoing in her ears. It was Scud Holwell's voice, and

Scud Holwell's rough, prying hands that were ignoring her pleas, ignoring her efforts to avoid the pain and terror.

The game is over, sweet thing . . .

"No," she gasped. "No . . . !"

She jerked her head to one side only to find her hair anchored flat to the ground. In a growing panic, she balled her hands into fists and flailed like a wild thing, her legs thrashing, her body bucking and lurching against the massive weight pinioning her.

Christian caught two sharp blows on the side of his head, but it was the third—a scraping, clawing ambush on the shoulder cut by the Comanche's skinning knife that made him rear back in a sudden flaring of star-studded agony. The shock sent him reeling sideways and in the time it took him to adjust to the fiery transformation from pleasure to pain, Aubrey had scrambled to the far side of the sandy depression. She would have fled farther if her legs had not become briefly tangled in the hem of her skirt, and if the voice behind her had not brought her crashing back to reality.

"Jesus Christ," gasped McBride, doubled over with the burning pain. "Jesus H. *Christ!*"

The tawny hair, the broad sloping shoulders, the long and tanned fingers that clasped his arm in agony did not belong to Scud Holwell. They did not belong to the horror of the Dream and Aubrey pressed chilled fingers over her mouth, waiting for the steely gray eyes to search her out through the gloom.

"I'm sorry," she whispered. "Christian . . . I'm so sorry."

Wordlessly—he was still too close to violence to trust himself to speak—McBride reached under the buckskin and probed gingerly at the wound on his shoulder. His fingers came away slick and wet, the fresh blood gleaming black under the moonlight.

"I'm sorry," she said again, her voice trembling as badly as her hands as she lowered them to clutch the edges of her blouse closed. "I . . . I don't know what came over me."

Christian glared. "Yeah, well, if it comes over you again, you might try a simple *no.*"

Aubrey felt a rush of shame burn into her cheeks. "I said I was sorry. And I did say no, as I recall, but you didn't listen to me. You . . . just kept doing what you were doing. You wouldn't stop."

"I didn't think you followed me out here to discuss the weather," he countered harshly. "And if you did, you should have kept both feet flat on the ground."

She bowed her head, flinching from the anger and sarcasm. She never should have strayed from the fire, never should have sought him out in the darkness, never should have accepted his invitation to lie beside him under the stars. Dear Lord, no wonder he had thought what he had thought; to be any bolder, she would have had to come to him naked.

"It's just that I . . . I don't like being touched."

"You don't like being *touched*?"

He regarded her narrowly for a long moment, then exhaled a muttered oath. "Not good enough, Miss Blue. I can tell when a woman is enjoying what I'm doing to her and, madam—you were enjoying every minute of it."

Aubrey stared at him across the shadowy gap, reading the accusation in his eyes and knowing a denial would be useless—not when her mouth still felt tender and bruised from his kisses, and her breasts still tingled with the memory of his lips and tongue.

No, he was not Scud Holwell, but neither was he the kind of man who was overly generous with either his patience or his compassion. He was blunt, cynical, and self-assured; ex-army, ex-convict, Indian fighter, gunfighter . . . not exactly the type who would understand the nightmares that haunted her, or even comprehend the horror and revulsion those nightmares instilled. A man without weaknesses of his own could hardly be expected to tolerate them in others.

Aubrey tasted blood from her lip and looked down at her hands. They were still clutched around the folds of her blouse, and with a small, weary sigh, she forced them to move, retying each of the knots with painstaking care.

"Would you like me to look at your shoulder?" she asked quietly.

"No, Miss Blue, I would not. I would not recommend you touch me, or even come near me again tonight—not unless you want to find yourself flat on your back with my hand over your mouth and your skirt up around your waist. In fact, I'd say you have about ten seconds to get out of my sight completely, or I'll start thinking this was all just another part of the performance; that you didn't really want me to stop, you just didn't want it to look like you were so eager to rut with the likes of a vulgar lowlife like me."

Aubrey looked over, stunned. "That wasn't why—"

"Nine seconds, Miss Blue."

"You don't understand—"

"Eight."

Aubrey scrambled to her knees. Her hair spilled in a tumbled black mass over her shoulders, concealing most of her features, and while it could have been the waning light playing tricks on him, Christian thought he saw the bright sparkle of a tear trapped in the sooty thickness of her lashes.

"Seven," he said slowly.

Aubrey turned and fled. He could hear her stockinged feet snagging on the rough surface of the stone, and the worsted wool of her skirt tearing at the few tufts of mesquite and bunchgrass that managed to survive in the fissures of rock. The wound in his shoulder was throbbing furiously and the ache in his groin made him angry —too damned angry to do more than watch her disappear over the crest and stumble out of sight.

It was just as well. Another hour or so and the moon would be gone, it would be dark enough for Jim Brody to make his break for Middle Springs. As it was, the shadows thrown by the cactus, rocks, and tiny hillocks of sand were stretched out in eerie distortions of their original shapes, blending into and joining other encroaching shadows until it was almost impossible to find a clear patch of pale sand. And in Christian's anger and frustration, he almost missed the one shadow that moved independent of the moon's influence—a shadow that took the shape of the Indian paint, its hooves wrapped in strips of blanketing, its reins held in the hands of Darby Greaves.

10

 "Give me one good reason why I shouldn't kill you here and now," McBride demanded, his gun cocked and aimed dead center of Darby Greaves's forehead.

He had followed Greaves out onto the desert, ironically applauding the agent for having had the sense not to try to run the horse at a gallop until he was well away from their defenses. McBride caught up to him a mile out on the plain, and less than a minute after Sun Shadow had leaped out from behind the cover of some rocks and brought the agent careening out of the saddle.

Greaves had landed hard, the wind knocked out of him, and Sun Shadow had been on him between one heartbeat and the next, his knife unsheathed and gleaming purposefully at the agent's bare throat. McBride loped up behind them, his urgent hiss the only thing that stopped the Ute's blade from slicing through cartilage and stretched sinew.

"The horse, dammit. Forget this bastard for a minute and go after the horse."

Sun Shadow glared down at Greaves and exerted just enough pressure to leave a glistening wet promise over the agent's windpipe. Greaves wailed at the feel of the cold steel slithering over his skin, but that was quickly forgotten as the Ute sprang away and the greater threat of McBride's gunbarrel filled his vision.

"One good reason, you stupid bastard," Christian snarled.

"I w-was going for help, I swear it. I was tired of waiting around and I knew I could ride well enough to be of more use here than back at the coach. You would have needed Brody's gun if the Comanche had attacked again."

McBride grinned. "You expect me to believe that, you piece of crap?"

"It's the truth, I swear it. I was riding for help. I would have made it too if you and that bloody savage hadn't stopped me. Or was that the problem—you didn't want anyone else playing hero!"

McBride cursed and hauled Greaves to his feet. "You want to play hero? Be my guest. You start running now, they might give you a hero's welcome at Middle Springs by noon tomorrow."

"Running? On foot?"

"On your feet, or on your ass, I don't much care, Greaves, but you're on your own from here on out."

"You can't do that! You can't just leave me here! What about the Comanche?"

"What about them? If you could dodge them on horseback, you can dodge them on foot. And besides, a smooth-talking fellow like yourself should be able to win them over easily enough. Be real nice to them and they'll only make you scream a day or two before they kill you."

Greaves blanched. He seemed to sag against the support of McBride's fist, but in the next instant, his uninjured left hand was reaching beneath his jacket to make a desperate play for his gun. McBride was almost disappointed. With ridiculous ease, and no small amount of personal pleasure, he grasped the agent's shattered right hand and squeezed, the welter of sheer agony causing Darby to scream with such bloodcurdling excruciation, the two shadowy figures emerging from the rocks behind them cringed back and dove for cover.

Christian heard the shuffle of feet on sand and dropped into a crouch, abandoning Greaves to the pain as he spun around and took aim on the rocks. Both Colts blasted simultaneously, the noise and blue-white flashes of powder followed a split second later by the sound of bullets zinging off stone.

"Hold up there! Hold up, dammit! We're soldiers! Soldiers in the United States Cavalry, J Troop, Lieutenant Faraday DesLaurier commanding! Hold up, I say!"

Christian, belly out on the sand, had his fingers on the triggers ready to fire again. "Show yourselves, boys . . . *real* slow."

The tops of two heads edged cautiously over the rim of rock. Arms and hands raised, the two soldiers showed enough of themselves to earn a guttural curse from McBride's throat.

"Soldiers," Greaves gasped. He was on his knees, cradling his injured hand, but at the sight of the two blue-coated troopers, he staggered to his feet and ran forward, as much to greet the newcomers as to distance himself from Christian McBride. "Soldiers, thank God. Thank God, you've found us."

"Found you? We damn near took a bead on you ourselves till we heard yous arguing in good old Texas English. Might be you want to identify yourselves before we go any further?"

"We're passengers on the Kansas Stage Line," Greaves said eagerly. "We were ambushed yesterday by Comanche. I was riding to get help when . . . when . . . Good God, but there can't be just the pair of you out here on the desert. Where is your camp? Where is the rest of your troop?"

"Yonder," one of the soldiers replied succinctly, his suspicions returning now that there was no longer any apparent need to fear having their heads blown off. "This here's the outer picket line you crossed. We thought we saw an Injun."

"You probably did," Christian said, rising slowly and brushing the sand off his pants. "He's one of us. A Ute. He's gone after our horse, so I'd be much obliged if you didn't shoot him when he comes back."

Sun Shadow reappeared as if on cue, the paint walking docilely by his side. Moments later, the thunder of more horses' hooves brought a dozen soldiers riding out from the camp to investigate the source of the gunshots. Greaves, McBride, and Sun Shadow were escorted back to the camp and introduced to a sleepy-eyed Lieutenant DesLaurier, who, upon learning there were defenseless women and a wounded man stranded back at the redoubt, gave orders for the company to break camp right away. Within the hour, as the first streaks of dawn were beginning to light the sky, the entire troop of one hundred and twenty men was riding double time across the arid plain.

•

The men of J Troop were not the only ones to have heard the gunshots. The echo of the distant pops had reverberated across the utter stillness of the plains, startling Aubrey and causing Stink Finger Jim to spit, miss, and hit his own sleeve with a splatter of tobacco juice. Having been woken earlier by McBride's hasty dash past, Jim could only hope and speculate that it was the plainsman's guns meting out prairie justice to the yellow-livered fancy man, and not the guns of Quanah Parker claiming a victim.

He, Aubrey, and Bruster—the latter feverish but alert
—took up their positions in the rocks, but it was Magenta Royale, searching frantically for the missing
Darby Greaves who saw the galloping line of blue-
coated soldiers first and ran joyously out onto the trail
to meet them.

Jim gave a resounding whoop and fired both barrels
of his shotgun in greeting. Bruster's grin stretched ear to
ear and he sent a hearty wink in Aubrey's direction before he followed Jim down onto the flats. Aubrey was
the last to make the descent, happy enough to smile at
McBride with genuine relief and pleasure—a smile that
faltered badly as the plainsman acknowledged her with
a single, perfunctory nod before turning his attention
elsewhere. He dazzled Magenta Royale with his best,
most charmingly handsome smile and presented her
with a canvas pouch containing biscuits and chunks of
thick yellow cheese.

None of them had eaten anything for two days aside
from the nearly unpalatable mule steaks, and it was with
true theatrical melodrama that Magenta Royale wept
over the first mouthful of soft white biscuit. Fully a score
of awestruck soldiers flocked around her like big blue
birds, some offering water, some offering other sweet
tidbits. A few noticed Aubrey and hastened over to accord her the same aid and succor, but her silent nods of
thanks and strained smiles were no match for Magenta's
effusive praise and gratitude. The soldiers, most of
whom had been on patrol for a month or more, fell
easily, painlessly under Magenta's spell, even the most
hardened veterans wiping at the corners of their eyes
after hearing of her selfless bravery in the face of the
attacking hordes of bloodthirsty renegades.

The appearance of men, so many men, worked an
amazing change on the blond songstress. She fussed
apologetically with her hair, wept dramatically over the

two cuts and a bruise she was able to find, and generally used all of her plentiful stores of feminine wiles to ensure her captive audience remained captivated. She needed only to accidentally brush up against a muscular arm or thigh and she could have asked for the world and gotten it. The wordless promise was there for every man to see in the sultry amber eyes, and every man who saw it could have sworn it was meant only for him.

Much to Magenta's surprise, Christian McBride seemed to have lost his air of detachment and was pleasantly attentive. Magenta's renewed energy brought with it a flush of generosity and she was more than willing to overlook his former hostility. She was, after all, the Jewel of New Orleans, and it must have placed an inordinate amount of strain on his sense of chivalry to know he had been, in part, responsible for her safety. She forgave him instantly his surly tempers and sarcastic remarks. She even forgave his brief and inexplicable attraction to the schoolmarm. Women who acted and fought like men were understandably fascinating for a short while, but the fascination usually ended the moment the woman appeared more interested in wearing the breeches, not just seeing what was inside.

To that end, Magenta made certain that McBride knew how truly grateful she was, how helpless and foolishly female she had admittedly been throughout the two-day ordeal. She even went so far as to make the supreme gesture, one she felt sure to earn his admiration. She stood solemnly by the tall and stoic Ute and laid a delicate hand on the bronzed arm.

"Thank you, Sun Shadow. We owe you a great deal as well and I hope you can find it in your heart to forgive our little peccadilloes. You risked your life so many times for us, and took so many heart-stopping chances: you are a true credit to your race and your people."

Sun Shadow glanced at McBride and took a deep

breath as he read the unmistakable mirth in the gray eyes. He was not about to acknowledge the foolish *yanqui* woman's condescension, yet with so many soldiers hanging on her every word—including the fawn-eyed Lieutenant DesLaurier—it would not have been wise to rebuff her either. He settled for a curt nod and folded his arms across his chest, subtly breaking contact with the soft white hand.

Magenta was nonplussed. She merely switched her favors to McBride and slipped her hand through the crook of his arm, smiling vindictively in the direction of a shocked and glaring Darby Greaves. The agent had been leery of finding himself alone with her since his return with the soldiers, and for a damned good reason too. He hadn't troubled himself to mention he was taking the horse and leaving. Nor had he troubled to mention he was taking along her satchel of jewels for safekeeping.

Part of his shock, she felt confident, was also due to the discovery of his precious cache of whiskey bottles smashed to smithereens. It was a petty act of retribution, hardly worthy of her true capabilities, but equally as effective as her open flirtations with McBride and the young army lieutenant in command of J Troop.

"I suppose I must take some of the blame for having put you at such risk," DesLaurier was saying now, blushing furiously as Magenta's eyes lavished him with attentiveness. "My men and I have been shadowing Quanah Parker for several weeks now, always a few steps behind, a few days late in preventing a tragedy. I'm afraid we've driven him well north of his own territory, and out of spite, he's leaving us a bloody trail to follow."

"Knowing you were so close behind explains why he didn't come back for the kill," McBride said, lighting a cheroot. Magenta's hand was like a clamp on his arm, and he would have liked to shrug her off, but he was aware of another pair of watchful eyes observing their small group.

Conversely, DesLaurier stared at the slender white fingers with envy and sighed. "I swear he sniffs his information off the wind. We have three of the best trackers in the army working with us to find Parker, and we've never come close enough to find soft droppings—er, begging your pardon, ma'am. I'm worried that if we don't catch up to him soon, he'll start to swing south again, and if he makes it back into the Oklahoma Territories, we'll be looking at a long winter campaign to try to run him to ground."

"Then we shouldn't delay you any longer than necessary. If you can spare us enough horses to pull the coach, we'll be on our way and out of yours in no time."

"Leave us alone again?" Magenta gasped, forgetting her benevolence for the moment and digging her nails into McBride's flesh. "Surely you can't be suggesting the lieutenant abandon us to our fate again? I couldn't bear it! I couldn't bear to be so frightened again!"

"I would never dream of abandoning you again, Miss Royale," DesLaurier assured her hurriedly. "Why, I would sooner cut my own hands off as do any such thing. It was my intention to provide you with an escort as far as Middle Springs. Farther, in fact," he added hastily, seeing the tears spring into Magenta's eyes. "All the way to Taylor Springs, in New Mexico, if necessary, or until you can meet up with another patrol out of Fort Union. Believe me, Miss Royale, you are perfectly safe now. Quanah Parker is our concern from here on out, not yours. The rest of the stage route is clear all the way into Santa Fe."

"Of course I believe you," Magenta said, blinking the wetness from her lashes and smiling tremulously. She caused another million or so blood vessels in the young lieutenant's body to dilate with ecstasy as she drifted from McBride's side to his and melted herself around his arm. "How could I not trust myself implicitly in your care?"

"You say Parker passed by Middle Springs but didn't attack?" McBride asked dryly.

"Yessir. The stationmaster keeps on friendly terms with the local Kiowa and Comanche. He had plenty of warning that Parker was in the vicinity and managed to button himself up tighter than a drum. He had some livestock run off and a few shots fired into his stockade, but it would have taken Parker a week or more to do any lasting damage. At any rate, Sir Percival was the one who alerted us to the fact that your stage was overdue, and suggested we search along this route instead of the main trail. It seems he harbors a certain admiration for Mr. Brody's ingenuity and spunk."

"Sir Percival?"

"Yessir." Faraday grinned. "A real live baron or duke or count, or something. He took over the station a couple of years back, and damme if he doesn't have the locals singing 'God Save the Queen' every morning. He has his own private cannon—one of the main reasons I'll wager why Parker didn't get too close—and serves high tea precisely at four o'clock every afternoon. He'll be thrilled, ma'am," he said, turning to address Magenta, "to know he has a genuine celebrity as a guest."

Christian exchanged a glance with Sun Shadow and clamped his teeth down savagely over the butt of his cigar.

High tea and cannons; boys who hadn't yet seen the sharp side of a razor in charge of army troops; two women as exasperating as any he'd met, a drunk, a corset salesman, and a stage driver who wept each time he passed the corpses of the dead mules . . . was it just him, or had the whole world gone mad?

•

The madness took on an even more eerie aura of unreality as the Concord rumbled through the stockade gates at Middle Springs. The original way station, built on the site of an old trading post, had been refurbished, rebuilt, and reinforced, expanded into a comparatively large and sprawling compound situated at an elbow of the Cimarron River.

Dry, arid plains had gradually given way to the greening influence of the river. Instead of the browns and grays and dusty flatness of the past sixty miles, there were ragged draws and low, sharp-crested hills marking the landscape on either side of the Cimarron. Luxuriant stands of cottonwood, willow, and wild balsam trees stood regally along the banks of the river; blooming wild currant and morning glory, larkspur, and wildflowers in bright pockets of yellow, red, and blue atoned for the bland vale of the desert crossing.

The Cimarron itself raged swift and deep and blue, as welcoming a sight to the hot and dusty travelers as the solid defenses surrounding the compound. Inside the tall, spiked walls there was a new, well-stocked trading post and smithy, stables large enough to house a small herd of horses and mules, the way station itself with sufficient rooms to accommodate a dozen guests, and, most incongruous of all, a tiny but neatly maintained two-story house complete with wrought-iron fencing and a flowering rose garden.

Sir Percival Fortesque, a duke as it turned out, had emigrated from England with not much more than his title and a bristling sense of adventure. Booked on the Kansas Stage Company as a passenger, he had disembarked at Middle Springs four and a half years ago, and had been there ever since. What little money he'd had had gone into "civilizing" the outpost; the enormous profits he'd made since in trading with the Indians he'd poured back into transforming a mere way station into a tiny monarchy.

He was a tall, ramrod-stiff man with a waxed handlebar moustache and a pencil-thin nose that was perpetually strained and white-rimmed from being held so high in the air. He affected the use of a monocle and carried an ebony walking stick under his arm, not the least hesitant to apply it to the rump of a recalcitrant mule or the ear of a dozing hostler. His wife, Lady Prudence, was as diminutive as her husband was brusque, prone to talking a great deal but saying very little that was audible above a breathless rush of nervous excitement. There were eight little replicas of Lord Percival and Lady Prudence, each with pinched nostrils and heads trained to be held at slightly elevated angles.

True to Faraday DesLaurier's prediction, the host and hostess were both overcome with awe upon learning the identity of Magenta Royale, Jewel of New Orleans. Lady Prudence was all aflutter as she danced nervously back and forth across the narrow path that led into the way station, and after a hand-wringing consultation with her husband, insisted the celebrated chanteuse would be much more comfortable as a guest in their house rather than in the spartan accommodations of the station. Magenta was swept away like royalty, leaving Aubrey to follow the shy smiles and hand signals of an Indian girl who led her to her room in the common building.

She was not offended. If anything, she was relieved to finally have some privacy, for like everything else that was strictly regulated at Middle Springs, there were separate women's quarters inside the station, and Aubrey had her choice of the biggest, coolest of the rooms. There was also the luxury of a private tub and all the steaming hot water and soap she could endure. Unfortunately, she barely had the energy to enjoy it. She managed to scrub away the accumulated layers of grime and sweat and slip into the clean chemise the Indian girl brought her, but before she could finish dressing or enjoy more than half a cup of the sweet, hot chocolate she was given, she sank wearily onto her cot and drifted off to sleep.

Stink Finger Jim had made good time crossing the last ten miles of desert, and so it was only a little past nine o'clock in the morning when Aubrey closed her eyes. The clanging of a loud brass bell some seven hours later brought them popping open again, but not even the lure of hot tea and cucumber sandwiches could convince her to relinquish her cozy nest of blankets and toweling.

She was vaguely aware of Magenta's tinkling laughter somewhere in the distance, and once she thought she detected a whiff of aromatic tobacco smoke wafting through her room on a slight draft. But if someone had come to check on her, or if a hand had gently tucked aside the mist of black hair that had tumbled over her cheek, she could not have said for certain if it was real or just part of another dream.

11

"Don't let her get away!"

Aubrey ducked low and crawled toward the deeper thickets, ignoring the sharp thorns and stiff scrub brush that tore into the flesh of her arms and legs. She could only pray that the shadows were dark enough to hide her. Her heart was pounding in her ears, her legs so weak she feared they would not hold her even if she saw her chance to break free and run. The voices were all around her: front, rear, right, left . . . She was trapped!

She sobbed again as her nightdress snagged on a thornbush. She remained crouched on the ground, inching forward on hands and knees over the rough terrain, feeling the sting of pebbles and jagged earth beneath her.

"Over there!" someone yelled.

The voices were moving in the opposite direction. Aubrey swallowed at the lump of terror in her throat and leaned against the cool bark of a tree to catch her breath. The bark moved. The tree shifted, and, as she looked up, it took on the grotesque features and bulbous face of Scud Holwell.

"The game is over, sweet thing. Thought you could

get away, but you couldn't. The game is over. The game is over."

Aubrey opened her mouth to scream, but no sound came out. She turned and ran again, but the ground had suddenly become a quagmire of mud, slimy and sucking, and she could not lift her feet. She fell in an agony of desperation and her hands sank to the wrists in the ooze. She could hear Holwell laughing behind her. She could feel his heat bending over her, smell his putrid breath on the back of her neck as he grasped a fistful of her hair and dragged her beneath him.

"The game is over, sweet thing," he hissed. There was more—more words and more pain, and the choking sensation of his tongue ramming down her throat.

"No," she gasped, twisting frantically, struggling mightily against the pressure holding her arms trapped by her sides. "No!"

"Aubrey?"

No, no! It was a trick. He didn't know her name, had never used it before!

"Aubrey, wake up. You're having a nightmare."

She twisted again and flailed out wildly with her hands, striking something solid, striking something that flinched back and swore with more vehemence than a mere specter could be accorded. The pressure on her shoulders eased and Aubrey was able to scramble blindly back into the darkness. Scud Holwell's ugly face loomed before her a moment longer before a brilliant flaring of orange and yellow light caused it to swell and expand and burst into a million scattered fragments.

Christian McBride held the match aloft and let it blaze long enough for the dilated centers of Aubrey's eyes to narrow against the effects of whatever it was that had started her clawing and fighting like a wildcat. Even so, even with his features illuminated against the shadows and the tranquil beauty of the moon-washed Cimarron behind them, it took half an eternity for Aubrey to release the breath she had been holding and half as long again for her hands to relax from the frozen claws they had formed.

She remembered. She remembered.

Sometime after dusk she had finally wakened, hot and smothered by the airlessness of her tiny room. She had heard voices and laughter and someone singing to the accompaniment of a badly strummed banjo, and she had quietly dressed and slipped unnoticed out the rear door of the way station. With the threat of an Indian attack past, the huge stockade gates had been left open and she had wandered down to the riverbank, lured by the rushing sounds of the Cimarron. There, she had walked in knee-deep salt grasses and cattails, weaving in and around the stooped grace of tall willows. Finding a particularly secluded patch of grass and shadow, she had kicked off the moccasins she had been loaned and, with the heat and grime of the desert still imprinted on her mind, if not her body, she had shucked the gingham dress supplied by Lady Prudence, and had waded into the inky, cold water.

On the riverbank again, she had stretched out on the grasses, letting the desert moon dry her skin just as she had done so many times as a child. Thinking as a child, behaving as a child, she had closed her eyes and the nightmare of the half-child, half-woman had returned once again to torment her.

That was how McBride had found her, roused out of his own brooding solitude by cries of terror so convincing he had approached at a dead run, guns in hand. Now, he knelt by her side, a second match sizzling to charred ash as he saw her eyes fill with tears and her hands lift to cover her face.

McBride released his own bated breath and responded instinctively to the sob that shook her slender shoulders. He drew her forward and took her into his arms, and when he met with no outward resistance, he gathered her closer, held her tighter, burying his lips in the cloud of midnight curls. He kept holding her, kept rocking her gently, kept kissing her and whispering endearments in barely audible Shoshonean, knowing she would respond more to the reassuring sound of his voice than to anything he said.

When her tears stopped and her trembling gave way to quavering sighs, he eased his grip slightly, but kept stroking one hand through the shiny thickness of her hair.

"That must have been quite the nightmare," he murmured.

"It always is," she admitted, her voice muffled against the crook of his neck.

"Always? You've had it before?"

She was still for a long moment, then nodded. "My parents were murdered when I was thirteen years old. I saw the whole thing. It . . . comes back to me every now and then if I've been frightened or . . . or if I'm worried about something."

Christian's hand slowed. This was not only the first glimpse of her past she was sharing, but also the first time she had risked exposing a vulnerable underside to her emotions.

"Well, you're perfectly safe now; you have nothing to be frightened or worried about. Not when you're with me."

Aubrey sighed again and nestled her cheek deeper into his shoulder, making him alarmingly aware of the fact that she was almost naked. The linen chemise she wore was ill-fitting and left nothing at all to the imagination, being too short to do more than cover the rounded curves of her bottom, and cut too low in front to conceal the view of her breasts plumped warm and soft and alluringly against his chest. The image of her caught in the glow of the sulfur stick was burned on his mind, making him wonder how he had ever thought her to be plain and homely. Sloping white shoulders, a narrow waist a man could span with two hands, legs that were long and smooth and seemed to go on forever. They were curled beneath her now, outlined starkly against the darker grass, tempting him to reach out and run his hand from hip to ankle, from ankle to calf to knee to thigh . . .

A sniffle and a shuddered sigh dragged his thoughts onto safer territory and he tried to sound fatherly, or brotherly, even as the softness shifted in his arms and burrowed unashamedly deeper into his warmth.

"We missed you at teatime. Bruster expressed his concerns over a mouthful of scones and clotted cream—whatever the devil that is. I went to check on you, but you hadn't moved an inch since noon, so I didn't have the heart to disturb you."

Christian McBride with a heart? Of course he had one—couldn't she hear it beating solidly within the chamber of his chest?

"You came and checked on me?" she asked through a hiccup.

"Several times," he admitted.

"You didn't sleep?"

He lifted his lips from the crown of her head and smiled wryly. "I never sleep, remember?"

"Oh. Yes. Only one eye at a time—" She paused through another soft sniffle. "I r-remember."

He buried his smile in her hair again and let the clean, sweet fragrance tantalize his senses. His hands ached to gather up fistfuls of the wild black stuff and rub it over his naked skin. He wondered how it would feel spilling over his chest and belly; he wondered how it would look fanned out beneath them, the curls catching the moonlight as their bodies moved together, locked in passion.

"Damnation," he muttered, aware of his blood beginning to quicken with images that were neither fatherly nor brotherly. What the hell was wrong with him? What the hell was there about this woman that made him behave like a green and ungainly schoolboy who was just discovering the tightness in his pants for the first time? He wasn't even sure what had drawn him to her in the first place, what had made him crush her spectacles or tear the steel pins out of her hair. Magenta Royale was more his kind of woman—fast, loose, and brassy, with a tongue like a snake and a body that would siphon a man dry and not take shame in the pleasure of doing so. With a woman like that he could be as rough and vulgar as he pleased, take what he wanted with a smile and a nod of thanks. He neither wanted nor needed the responsibility or the distraction of a conscience interfering with his pleasure. He did not want the memory of an Aubrey Blue clouding his judgment, haunting him with the violet blue of her eyes, the sulky softness of her mouth, the incredible seductiveness of her body pressed close to his. A woman like Aubrey Blue would expect declarations of love and undying affection, not to mention a commitment to the other kind of prison he was determined to avoid at all costs: marriage.

He had no qualms about saying the words, if that was what a woman wanted to hear through a long dark night. But that was all it was to him, just words. And the last time he had said them to a woman with his clothes on, her brothers had stalked him halfway across New Mexico with a ten-gauge shotgun. That had been a long *long* time ago and he still carried a few pellets of birdshot in his ass to remind him of the fine line between wanting a woman badly and needing one.

So far, he hadn't needed one. He wanted Aubrey

Blue, but on his terms, not hers, and surely not if it meant giving away any more of himself than he could afford to lose.

The hand stroking her hair stopped at the nape of her neck, the long fingers stilled with the realization that she had tilted her face up and was looking at him, the frown on her brow intimating that she too was becoming aware of her state of undress.

"Well, Miss Blue," he murmured. "I wonder what I should do with you now."

"Do with me?" she asked on a breath.

"Mmmm. Knowing you don't like being touched, I find myself wanting very much to touch you. Knowing you don't like being kissed, I want very much to kiss you . . . kiss you and touch you until you forget how much you don't like being kissed or touched."

His eyes glowed with a strange, silvery fire that had nothing to do with the moon's luminescence and she felt the promise in their depths melting down her spine and pooling hotly in her belly. She noticed also that one of her hands was curled around his neck, the fingers twined in the careless waves of tawny hair. He had changed his buckskins for a pale-colored cotton shirt and cord pants, both indecently tight-fitting, the former so much so that most of the buttons had been left undone and a great deal of solid muscle lay bare before her eyes. It should have frightened her. So much man, so much obvious virility, so many fresh and disturbing memories of his hands, his body, his mouth . . .

Aubrey looked at his mouth and felt the heat in her loins ripple upward, ripple downward, ripple outward until it seemed her whole body was in subtle motion, aching everywhere, throbbing everywhere, tingling everywhere, hot and cold at the same time.

"Why do you keep doing this to me, McBride?" she asked softly. "What is it you want from me?"

"I already told you," he answered, his thumb brushing lightly over the whispered question. "A kiss."

"A kiss?" She said the word as if she had never heard it before, knowing she was in the arms of a man who had already proven he could not be trusted with any manner of compromises. "You've already kissed me. More times than you should have."

He shook his head slowly, the moonlight tarnishing the thick waves of his hair. "Not nearly enough, by my reckoning."

His lips were too close. They were too warm and too smooth, too firmly shaped and far too knowledgeable in the ways and means of undermining a woman's concentration. Aubrey tried not to look at them, but that was impossible. She tried not to recall how they had felt roving hungrily over her flesh, but that only sent a hotter flood of confused desires through her body. Was it only last night she had pushed him away? Only last night she had lashed out at him, punishing him, punishing them both for something that had happened a long time ago? She had feared the pain and brutality of the act that was to follow, but in truth, his touch had neither frightened her nor been brutish. If anything, she had been lost to the sensation of being in his arms before she had even thought to be frightened of being there.

Just as now.

Dear God, she was so tired of being alone, so tired of holding it all inside—the pain, the hurt, the humiliation, the anger. She was tired of never feeling safe, never trusting anyone with her true emotions, or *any* emotions at all, for that matter. Not even Bruster. Dear, sweet Bruster; he had tried to convince her she was not crippled forever by Scud Holwell's actions, but she hadn't really believed him. Not until Christian McBride had taken her into his arms and forced her to realize she

deserved something more than anger in her life . . .
maybe even *wanted* something more.

"A kiss," she murmured. "I think I would like that
very much."

Christian smiled and gallantly obliged. His lips moved
over hers without urgency, without demands, content in
the beginning just to feel her body lose its incredible
tension and melt slowly into his embrace. He nipped at
the corners of her mouth and let his tongue leisurely
explore the soft contours, not even certain himself of
exactly when the casual act became anything but. The
blood began to flow in a fiery river through his veins. He
became acutely aware of her breasts crushing up to his
and of her hand tightening around his neck, imploring
him to hold her closer, and closer still.

Aubrey's lips parted willingly beneath his and she
could taste the salty residue of her tears moistening the
sliding thrust of his tongue. Spiraling showers of sharp,
bright sensations whirled through her body and she
shuddered with the joy of it. There were tremors in his
hand as he moved it from her nape to her shoulder, and
she felt the tightness gathering in her chest, the chill of
erotic pleasure anticipating the path his fingers would
take . . . if she allowed it.

"Aubrey—" His voice was a low throb against her
lips, half threat, wholly a warning. "I won't be able to
stop this time. If you're going to run, you had better do
it now."

A staggering flood of heat poured downward into her
limbs and she opened her mouth to speak. She opened
it, but the words refused to come and he took shameless
advantage, kissing her as she had never been kissed before, kissing her until both her breath and her senses
had deserted her.

A wisp of hair fluttered across her cheek, stirred by
the motion of his hand as it rode her shoulder down to

her elbow, then crossed the heated space to where her breast pillowed against his chest. Her eyes shivered closed as he insinuated his broad, calloused palm between her breasts, her lips slackened around a moan as his thumb circled the proud rise of her nipple. She tilted her head back, arching her throat in a helpless surrender to his lips, and she did push him away, but only far enough to give his hand the freedom and access to chase down the row of pearly white buttons that fastened the front of her linen chemise.

Aubrey looked up, looked into the gray gleaming eyes and part of her tried not to see the hunger smoldering there. Another part of her drew a deep breath, swelling her chest so that when the parted halves of the chemise were pushed aside, her breasts rose proud and free into the ravishing heat of his gaze.

Christian caught his breath and held it. He could feel his resolves slipping, could feel himself forgetting all about not saying the words, any words that would make her his. His darker hand hovered a moment over the silky whiteness of her flesh and when he touched her, the shock raced up his arm with nearly the same force as the gasp that was expelled from her lips. He bowed his head and captured the soft sound of a plea. His hand stroked her breast and his tongue foraged a damp and devastating path to the delicate pink curl of her ear.

Aubrey was aware of his voice, of the muted, shapeless words traveling from her ear, along her throat, and lower onto the smooth plane of her chest. The wet heat closed around her nipple as he molded and shaped her flesh for his pleasure, and she was certain he could feel her heart clamoring with each rolling thrust of his tongue. Every breath was like swallowing flame, every suckling swirl of his lips and tongue made the flames grow hotter, brighter, made her limbs quake and writhe and curl against the corresponding heat of his body. She arched against him, alternately holding her breath, then releasing it in a series of dry, shallow whimpers. And, when the tension became almost unbearable, when she felt his hand skim down from her breast to her thigh, she had no thought to resist him, only to urge him to bring relief to the restless ache within her.

Even so, when his fingers stroked lightly into the downy triangle of dark curls, the contact jolted her. Her groan was harsh and guttural, her body a mass of hot, steamy sensations that grew impossibly hotter with her determination not to falter.

Christian steeled himself as the shivering, liquefying heat of her flesh closed around his fingers. He slid them slowly into the soft, moist recess, dragging them back and forth over the tiny nub of live nerve endings, knowing by her broken cries when to press deeper and harder, and when to hold back, feathering her with the lightest touch he could manage. It was cruel work, bringing her to the brink of ecstasy with his mouth and hands when it was his body crying out for the privilege. Crueler still when her hips began to move unself-consciously with the rhythm of his fingers, tentatively at first, then faster and bolder, thrusting into them, clenching around them, using them to heighten her sensitivity to explosive proportions. He groaned as she groaned. He shuddered as she shuddered and, hissing a mixture of Spanish and Shoshonean, he lifted himself away and tore at the buttons on his shirt, sending most of them skipping off into the darkness in his haste to rid himself of the barriers that kept their bodies apart.

Aubrey's hands clutched at the tufts of long grass as she watched him peel back the cotton shirt, baring skin that gleamed like bronze under the moonlight. Her lips parted on a choked breath and she wondered where the shadows had gone. She wondered at the hard bunches of muscle that swelled and rippled with the movements of his hands as he swore over the strained buttons on the cord pants. She wondered at the powerful musculature of his chest, the lean hardness of his belly and hips. His legs were thewed with muscle and sinew, even his calves had the threat of power in them—all of it tanned and weathered, toughened by years of sun and sweat, all except the formidable stretch of pale flesh that began below his waist and ended just above his thighs.

Now, she thought. *Now the fear will come again and this time I will not be able to stop it or push it aside. The moment he touches me the nightmare will become real again, the fear will wipe away all of the pleasure that has gone before, and I will be lost. I will be lost!*

Christian reached out a hand and touched a blunted fingertip to the tear that slipped from the corner of her eye. He brushed it to the side, carrying it into the disheveled glory of her hair as he cupped his hands around her face and drew her lips slowly up to his.

Now, she thought wildly. *Now . . . !*

His kiss was deep and bold and evocative, his tongue filling her mouth then retreating, filling it and retreating, entreating hers to follow, inviting her to do the same. He drew her against him, his arm circling her waist and bringing her closer than she thought it possible to be held in someone's arms. Close enough to feel the tautness in his body and to know the rearing impatience of his flesh. The enormity of his arousal pressed into the cleft between her thighs and should indeed have frightened her, but the gasp that pulled her mouth away from his and caused her to look deep into the scorching heat of his eyes was a gasp of pleasure—pleasure so pure and sharp and uncompromised, she could feel her body opening wider for him, spreading and blossoming like the dewy petals of a flower.

It was the heat that astounded her the most, though. The heat of his body easing down over hers, the heat of

his male pride so thick and insistent it should have
scalded her, destroyed her. Yet it only seemed to ease
the way. The more heat, the sleeker the friction, the
swifter and deeper the penetration of flesh into flesh.
He seemed to hesitate a moment, as if expecting to find
something that was not there, but the moment passed,
taking all vestiges of hesitation with it, and he stretched
within her, plunged within her, filling her so completely
she had to tear at her lip to keep from screaming out
her pleasure. The harsh rasp of his breath was against
her neck and the tension that kept his arms and chest
rigid above her made her brace herself instinctively,
made her arch and twist slightly to prepare herself for
what was to come. But it was hopeless, of course, and
she acknowledged her folly with a shivered groan. Nothing could have prepared her. Nothing.

He started to move and she was pulled, sucked forward and back with the slow, deliberate motions of his
body. Her fists brought clumps of torn grass with them
as she propped them against the bulging muscles of his
chest. Her fingers splayed wide, luxuriating in the
smooth texture of his skin, marveling at the power and
prowess she could feel gathering and trembling tighter
and tighter on each delicious stroke. Of their own voli-
tion, her knees edged higher and higher and began to
clutch at his thrusting flanks. Her heels gouged into the
soft earth and she discovered how to bring him even
deeper into the well of her body—a discovery that
nearly brought him shivering out of his skin.

Christian swore again—it was either that or sob like a
madman. She was moist and tight, an agony of squeezing, grasping little muscles that adjusted to his shape
and dimensions, sheathing him in a raw caress of silky
heat. The blood pounded in his temples, blinding him.
His body shook with the force of his own potency—a
force unlike anything he had felt before. The pleasure

caromed through him in volleys and he reached down to
hook his hands around her knees, urging them higher,
doubling them almost to her waist and holding them
there until he felt his very soul beginning to spurt into
her, hot and thick and rich with his life's essence.

Aubrey tried to tear herself away, to detach her mind
if not her body from the moving, thrusting pressure
within her, but it was no use. The heat was too strong,
too overpowering and she cried out in her helplessness
and her awe. Christian sank his fingers into her hair,
forcing her to cry his name against his lips and to taste
the echo of her own. She gave a last sob of stunned
disbelief as the ribbons of fiery ecstasy lashed through
her, spinning one into the other, hurling her toward
some unseen, unknown peak. She could no longer
breathe through the spiraling flames, she could no
longer think through the rushing intimacy of their two
bodies fusing together as one. She could only obey the
commands of his hands and body as he coaxed her,
urged her, soared with her into an erupting maelstrom
of pure sensation.

From somewhere, Christian found the strength to
open his eyes and and look down into Aubrey's face. In
the luminous glow of the stars and the moon, he could
still see her lips shuddering around the shape of his
name, saying it over and over, without sound or substance, and he continued to hold her, continued to move
within her until her soft groans were not caused by the
heat and flame, but by the warm, slippery wonder of
shared passion.

•

Aubrey lay perfectly still, her breathing finally
calmed, her heartbeat almost back to normal. She was
cradled against the warm crook of Christian's body, her
head resting on his shoulder, her hand draped limply

across his chest. She wasn't exactly sure how she felt—
numb, exhilarated, shameful, shameless. She was even
less sure how she was supposed to feel. The tension was
gone, certainly. The fear was vastly diminished, if not
gone entirely. There was, perhaps, still a degree of ap-
prehension remaining, but more over what to say and
do next rather than what had already been said and
done.

Christian was silent. Thoughtful. She imagined she
could hear his thick lashes blinking now and then as if
he was staring up at the sky and sharing her consterna-
tion. *Most* of the tension had left his body. Occasionally
his hand would stroke absently through her hair, but on
the whole, he appeared to be quite content just to lie
there on the grass with the moonlight dappling their
bodies and the cicadas scolding them from the bull-
rushes.

She thought she slept for a time. The moon was well
down toward the horizon, visible through the lower
branches of the willows. It hung there, swollen and glistening, ruing its departure, blurred around the outer rim
by the vapors rising off the earth.

Christian drew a deep breath and carefully, carefully
began to slip his shoulder free. Aubrey was not yet certain she was ready to confront him, and so she kept her
eyes closed, hoping she gave a good imitation of a person still lingering on the edge of sleep. He folded his
pants into a pillow to replace the comfort of his shoulder and he draped his shirt over her body to compensate for some of the lost heat before he walked down to
the river and waded into the roiling waters.

Aubrey listened to his movements for a few minutes,
but they were too difficult to distinguish from the rush
and burble of the water itself. Curiosity won out over
her reservations and with a sigh, she pushed herself upright, lifting the weight of her hair off her face as she

turned and scanned the river. He was there, midstream, his head and shoulders shedding sheets of crystalline water as he dove beneath the surface and rose again several yards farther on.

And that was that, she thought. She did not know whether to frown or smile as she watched him. He had made a mockery of her fear. He had laid to waste a decade of nightmares and dread with a few strokes of his hands, and now he frolicked in the swift-moving currents like a boy, blithely unaware of the tremendous upheaval he had wrought.

Aubrey smiled.

She cast a halfhearted glance around the shadows but could not immediately locate the gingham dress Lady Prudence had provided. She slipped her arms into the sleeves of McBride's shirt, her smile turning wry as she held up her hands and saw that the cuffs drooped several inches over the tips of her fingers. She rolled them as best she could and closed a button for modesty's sake, then cautiously tried standing, not entirely trusting the strength remaining in her legs.

A breeze had sprung up over the past few hours, dry and cool, smelling faintly of the desert sands it had crossed. The grass beneath her feet felt like long satin ribbons that caught between her toes and slithered along her ankles, tickling her calves and knees where it grew taller nearer the water.

With one eye on the naked plainsman floating well out in the river, Aubrey waded in as deep as her knees, wary of the slippery-smooth rocks underfoot. She crouched down and chased aside a floating weed, then raised a cupped handful of water to her mouth. It was cold and sweet, tasting of distant mountains and green forests, of melted snow and hot sunlight, and miles of unspoiled wilderness. She splashed some on her face and throat, then carried another hesitant cupful to the tops of her thighs, almost reluctant to rinse away the evidence of their expended passions. She would have worn it like a badge if she could, a placard announcing that she was whole again.

Other splashing sounds drew her gaze to the middle of the river. McBride had seen her and was swimming back to the shallower water, his arms stroking cleanly, effortlessly against the strong currents. He jackknifed and swam underwater the last few strokes, surfacing again when his feet touched bottom and he could walk the rest of the way to shore.

"Feeling cold, clean water on my skin is something else I missed for the past five years and can't seem to get enough of," he said, standing unabashedly in front of her, his muscles gilded in silver, his hair clinging to his face and throat in slick, dark streaks. He laughed at her bemused expression and shook his head like a frisky terrier, sending a spray of diamondlike droplets in a wide circle, some of them spattering the front of Aubrey's shirt. "Come on. A little deeper and we can scrub each other's backs."

Aubrey took a hesitant step back. "No . . . thank you. I'd rather not get wet again tonight. The air is a little chilly, and—"

"I don't mind warming you when we're finished, if that's all that's stopping you."

He grinned with all the charm of a vagabond prince and Aubrey took another step back. "No. Really, I just don't want to get wet."

His eyes narrowed and the white slash of his smile widened. "A stubborn slip of a thing, aren't you."

Aubrey's eyes popped and she scrambled back as she saw him take two stalking steps toward her. She managed to splash her way almost to the riverbank before he caught her; a shriek of alarm greeted the arm that snaked around her waist, but it turned quickly to a peal of laughter as he swung her around and scooped her up against his very wet body.

"Put me down," she gasped. She wriggled a moment or two, but in the end, acquiesced with another small laugh, this one causing a noticeable stillness in the tall, broad body. It was the first time he had heard her laugh, and he liked the sound. It was also the first time Aubrey could remember laughing in a long while. His stare unsettled her and her smile faded. The awkward silence stretched for another full minute before Christian's mouth bent to hers, displaying proper appreciation for her lapse. Rendered breathless and more than slightly light-headed, Aubrey squirmed against the pressure of his arms and haltingly laughed again.

"Please put me down. I really *don't* want to get wet again."

"You don't, eh?" His eyes glowed with a queer mix of humor and deadly earnest. "Then you had better put your legs around my waist."

"What?"

He shifted her weight in his arms, lifting her higher so that her eyes were level with his. "You heard me: put your legs around my waist. If you truly don't want to get wet, you'd better wrap them tight and hold on."

"McBride! McBride, for God's sake, what are you doing? *Where are you going?*"

He was walking back into the river, heading it seemed, straight for the deepest, blackest part of the water. Aubrey wrapped her long legs around his waist, dismayed to see his smile and to feel his hands obligingly cradle the softness of her rump. He was knee-deep, thigh-deep, almost waist-deep before he took an abrupt turn and waded right into the heart of a tall and swaying forest of cattails. At its center was a flat oasis of grass and moss, an island of smooth green surrounded by a curtain of gently rippling rushes. The sounds of the swirling river were all around them, the light from the moon-drenched shadows was blue, cool, and liquid, making it seem as if they were standing underwater.

McBride knelt on the moss, lowering Aubrey with him, but instead of relinquishing his hold on her body, he simply shifted it, scoffing aside the single button binding the front of the shirt and skimming his hands upward, engulfing the full shape of her breasts.

"McBride—" she began weakly.

His mouth replaced his hand and Aubrey pressed her head back into the soft cushion of moss. She stared straight up into a sky painted with stars, the canvas framed by the tall rushes. She gasped and twisted to one side, not daring to look down, not daring to challenge the hot path his tongue and lips were forging downward, down to where the wedge of his body ensured she could not have denied him his pleasure had she the strength or wit to do so. The heat of his breath was on her thighs, then between them, and she gave a violent start at the first flicker of his tongue. Her knees parted limply, then spasmed tight to his shoulders again as he took the most precise care in ravishing every soft fold of flesh, in chasing after every moist shiver that shuddered through her. He brought her to the very brink of rapture and retreated again, over and over until she was trembling with a sweet, senseless surrender.

Only then did he rise bold and brazen above her. With the starlight and passion glowing in his eyes, he levered her purposefully into his arms. Gentling her, reassuring her in a deep, throaty murmur, he began lowering her over the rampant spear of his flesh, his hands guiding her knees to either side of his hips, her arms around the solid rack of his ribs.

"Hold on to me, *querida*," Christian murmured. "Don't be afraid to take what you want."

"I . . . can't," she gasped. "I don't . . . know what to do."

He gave a soft chuckle and gripped her firmly around the waist. He showed her exactly what to do, drawing her hips forward, pushing them back, pulling and pushing in a slow, rolling motion that made him thank every star above that he had slaked his most urgent needs on the riverbank. Not that he was laying any claims to sainthood now, for she was hot enough, sleek enough, wet enough to destroy the best of his intentions. And, after it became more than evident that she was an adept pupil, he abandoned her hips to their own recourse and collected twin fistfuls of her hair, forcing her head to tilt back, baring the swanlike arch of her throat.

Aubrey rocked against the combined assault of his lips and body. She reeled with the first wave of white-hot pleasure, the heat and ecstasy so intense she felt the threat of a faint clouding her senses.

"Open your eyes," he commanded. "Look at me."

Aubrey shook her head drunkenly, her body a mass of raw, quivering nerves and sensations.

"Open your eyes, *querida*. They'll tell me what you want, even if you can't."

Aubrey's thick lashes opened slowly. He was waiting, all muscle and hard, bronzed flesh. His arms were like bands of steel around her, his thighs rocklike and bulging beneath her. She looked down, looked at where the whiteness of her flesh stroked and undulated against the tautness of his belly . . . at where the dark explosion of hair at his groin meshed damply with her own thrusting, silky black curls.

Drenched, drowning in her own heat, she looked up again, bereft of words, helpless in her ecstasy, floundering hopelessly in the knowing depths of his eyes.

"Ahh, *mi querida, mi querida*," he rasped. "I did give you the chance to run, did I not?"

He lowered her quaking body onto the moss and smothered her ragged cries beneath his lips. In the final, brief moment of sanity, it came to him in a wry burst of irony that he should have taken his own warning to heart. He should have been the one to run—as far and as fast as he could.

12

 "Sir Percival has managed to pursuade Jim Brody to lay over here an extra day," Christian said as he stamped a foot into his boot. "I'm not saying Magenta had anything to do with it, but Lady Prudence was winging around like a headless chicken, insisting that both Bruster and Greaves needed the additional time to recover from their wounds, and that both you ladies would benefit from ah, more civilized company. His timetable is shot to hell anyway, so is the front axle on the coach; both of which probably carried more weight in his decision than any wailings or weepings Lady Prudence might have bombarded him with."

Aubrey smiled faintly and returned to the infinitely difficult task of buttoning the bodice of the gingham dress. Her fingers were somehow too thick and too clumsy, and each tiny button seemed to take an eternity to capture, straighten, and feed through the corresponding loop.

Christian watched for a moment then gently brushed her fingers aside. "Let me do that. I've always wondered how it felt to button a woman *into* her clothes."

Aubrey took care to avoid his gaze, although she

knew her cheeks were maintaining the warm flush they'd glowed with since dawn had roused the naked lovers out of their secluded blind. They had bathed together in the swirling water, the sky as red as flame behind them, the distant rim of mountains burning gold against a tumble of low-lying cloud. They had reluctantly waded ashore to restore some sort of order to their appearance, and while they dressed, McBride had brought her up to date on what she had slept through the previous day, talking, she supposed, to try to smooth over the frequent, uncomfortable lapses into silence.

Now he even gave up the pretense of conversation as he lifted his hands away from her bodice and threaded his fingers into the shiny black tangle of her hair.

"You look like a temperance advocate struggling with a hangover," he said with a sigh. "Was it so terrible to show a little human weakness?"

Solemn blue eyes met his and sparkled a moment over a fierce "Yes," then softened reluctantly with a barely audible, "No."

"I see. Yes and no; that averages out to a maybe."

"Maybe I just don't want to talk about it."

She started to pull away, but he would not let her. "And maybe I think it's high time we did talk. It occurs to me we've come this far on the merits of a handful of arguments and a hell of a lot of moonlight. A little conversation might be in order, wouldn't you say?"

"I've never been against having conversations with you, McBride, but you never seem to want to talk, you only want to ask questions."

"Maybe that's because I want to know a little more about you."

"It works two ways. For all the questions you ask and expect—no, *demand* to have answered, you haven't told me much about yourself."

"I told you I was in prison—not exactly the kind of admission one makes on a casual acquaintance."

"There was nothing casual about the way you admitted it. It was more of a challenge. You wanted to shock me."

"Did I succeed?" he asked mildly.

"It isn't the kind of admission one accepts blithely, like a comment on the weather, or a compliment about one's appearance."

"Your appearance didn't deserve a compliment. Not then," he added, fondling a curl that had become twined around his fingers. "And I'm still damned curious to know why you went to the trouble of presenting yourself like the Wrath of All Spinsterhood. You wouldn't care to enlighten me now, would you?"

Aubrey sighed expressively. "There, you see what I mean? You've done it again. You've steered the conversation away from yourself and turned it onto me. And no, I don't feel like enlightening you. You've become quite enlightened enough about me over the past several hours."

McBride stared at the sullen determination in the set of her mouth and wanted to kiss it into compliance again, but he shrugged instead and took a deliberate step back, removing any other temptations or distractions from within his grasp.

"Okay. What do you want to know?"

Aubrey regarded him suspiciously. "Just like that?"

"Just like that."

She turned her head a bit and looked out over the river. The red blush was fading from the sky, replaced by the pale, clear blue that foretold another day of blazing sun and heat. The color of the Cimarron had changed as well, losing its inky blackness to the greens and blues and aquas of filtered daylight.

"Who are you?" she asked, turning back. "Where are

you from? What did you do to earn five years of hard labor in Leavenworth? I mean, I know you said you killed a man, but why? Why did you kill him and what did you mean when you said you killed the wrong man?"

Christian gave a low whistle of appreciation. "You must have been saving those up for a long time."

She did not comment, nor did her gaze waver or back down in the least, and in the end, McBride indicated a seat on an uprooted tree trunk. He began with his full name, Christian Stanfield McBride, delivered with the cynical twist that had become so familiar. Seeing it, Aubrey fully expected a tale fabricated with the same verve and authenticity as a penny dreadful, but he lost the smile after a few minutes. He lost the air of easy arrogance as well and drew Aubrey into the telling of his story, so much so that neither of them noticed a silent observer standing in the shadows of the trees.

With the exception of a few modest reservations, McBride recounted a youth that seemed as normal as could be expected growing up on the wild frontier of New Mexico. His father had been a rancher, one of the tens of thousands who had emigrated west during the frenzy of the gold rush in '52, but had never made it farther than the lush foothills west of Fort Union. He and his wife had raised five sons and two daughters, the latter both happily married and living in California. The eldest son, James, had died at Shiloh, the youngest of yellow fever when he was only two years old. Of Christian's two remaining brothers, the younger one was, the last he had heard, raising hell somewhere in Montana. Jefferson had never shown any affinity or affection for the hot, arid plains of New Mexico and he had lit out for the fur and timberlines of the cold north some eight or ten years back. Ethan McBride was older than Christian by nine months to the day, and while it was said they were as close in appearance as two peas in the proverbial pod, their characters had developed as differently as day and night.

Where Ethan was quiet and serious, accepting without reservation the responsibility of being the successor to the McBride name and nominal fortune, Christian had been wild and irrepressible, wanting to know as much about stocking a herd and running a ranch as he did about flying to the moon. Where Ethan's nose was always in the books, Christian's was sniffing after trouble, from dipping girls' pigtails into inkwells, to toppling outhouses with the occupants still inside. Ethan, up until the age of twenty-two, had still been a virgin, whereas Christian—said with the modest humility of a man who took such things for granted—had found himself in bed with his schoolteacher at the tender age of fourteen.

"Possibly why I feel an instant attraction to all schoolmarms," he added in a wry aside. "At any rate . . ."

By the time he was eighteen, he was almost out of control. He had acquired a certain amount of skill with a gun and used it to finance his other bad habits: gambling, women, and fine whiskey. He might have ended up sprawled face down in a puddle of his own blood, dead in a showdown over a barroom whore, if the war in the East had not lured all the young hotheads into enlisting.

His first hard lesson in life came while he was riding by his brother's side. Both of them had joined the cavalry, both of them had thought themselves immortal and indestructible. James had died in his arms at Shiloh, and there were still some nights he could feel the sticky heat of blood on his hands and smell the strong cordite stench of exploding cannon shells. Anger had made him even more reckless—the army reports called it being courageous under fire—but by the end of the conflict, he found himself longing for the solitude of the New

Mexico plains, the terrible beauty of the malpais—lava
fields—and the omnipresent savagery of the Sangre de
Cristo Mountains. He was homesick and couldn't wait
to muster out of the cavalry, yet after he had ridden
halfway across the country, it was only to discover that
the greedy warmongers and profiteers had already entrenched themselves in the best grasslands, eager to
capitalize on the preoccupation of the army.

He also found his father ill and his mother's grave
freshly turned. Ethan was a man of peace, and had his
hands full just coping with the rustling and the blood-
shed. Wells on the Double M were being poisoned and
the rivers dammed; cattle were being slaughtered or
driven off by Indians—impartial thieves, so the law
claimed, who struck indiscriminately by night and vanished into their hideouts in the mountains by day.

It took Christian almost a year to hunt and track
down the raiders responsible. By then, his father had
seen the hand of God reaching out for him and, in a fit
of conscience-cleansing, had admitted to a dalliance
years earlier with a beautiful Ute woman. A son had
come from that union. A son who now rode at the head
of the raiding renegades.

Finding Sun Shadow, and coming damned close to
killing him as well as being killed himself, cost McBride
another six months. During that time, his father had
died and his brother Ethan had taken over the running
of the Double M. Christian returned to the ranch with
Sun Shadow, partly to make peace, mostly to have the
other ranchers in the valley listen to what the Ute had
to say, namely, that he and his band were being well
paid by one of their group to harass and pressure the
others into selling off their lands and rights. Since the
testimony of an Indian was not admissible in any court
of law, the only justice to be gained was through confrontation.

"The rancher in question was not the kind of man to stand up and confess outright that he had been guilty of any wrongdoing. In fact, he laughed outright at Sun Shadow's allegations and accused my brother and me of making the whole thing up to cloud the truth about our father's philandering with 'a dirty Indian whore.' Guns were drawn, shots were fired, and when the dust settled, a man was dead and the law was pointing the finger at me."

Christian fell silent a moment, frowning over the stalk of saltgrass he was shredding in his fingers.

"You said before that you . . . shot the wrong man?"

He looked up and nodded grimly. "I don't miss what I'm aiming for very often, but that night there was a lot of shouting, a lot of confusion. Someone else fired first and took out the lights before he turned his guns on me and Ethan. I just aimed at the spot where I last saw Maxwell Fleming standing, and by chance missed him and hit one of his hired guns by mistake. An ugly son of a bitch albino by the name of Whitey Martin."

Aubrey sat very still. Just as in the pages of a penny dreadful, she had been anticipating the climactic ending of the tale—part of her had even anticipated the revelation of the villain's name: Maxwell Fleming. How she had known, she could not have said then or later, but it was just as well she *had* known, or at least prepared herself for the possibility, otherwise she might have screamed, or fainted, or done something worse to make a complete fool of herself.

As it was, the shock of hearing names so familiar spread through her like a cold, sluggish slick of oil. She could not move her arms or legs for the sudden weight of them, nor could she move her lips or find the right command to make her tongue come unglued from the roof of her mouth. She wanted to ask him if he was sure of the name, Whitey Martin, and if he was positive the man was dead . . . but she couldn't. She couldn't.

Someone observant might have noticed an added tautness around her mouth, or a brittle quality to the intensity of her stare, but McBride was engrossed in twisting and untwisting the morsel of saltgrass and probably would not have noticed a stick of lit dynamite smoldering nearby.

"Fleming screamed murder, naturally, and with a body bleeding all over the floor, and a few more of Fleming's guns ready to challenge any discrepancies, there weren't too many witnesses who would swear to just who fired first. Ethan hired the best lawyer he could find—or maybe I should say, the best one he could find who was not scared shitless of walking down a dark alley at night. Unfortunately for me, both the prosecutor and the circuit judge *were* terrified of alleyways, and, as a result, I spent the next five years vacationing in Leavenworth. I probably would have been hung outright except that the McBride name still carried some weight with the army and Fleming wasn't stupid enough to risk drawing too much attention to his little ring of thieves. Now, of course, he wouldn't suffer from any such qualms. If what I've heard is true, he not only owns most of the Pecos Valley, but half of Santa Fe as well."

After another lengthy pause, he threw away the tatters of grass and squared his shoulders.

"And that's about it, Miss Blue: the sum total of who and what I am. Not very pretty, not very genteel. Probably not even very civilized by Eastern standards—and I haven't even gone into the vacation years at Leavenworth."

Aubrey met the silent challenge of his pride as he stared at her and waited for her reaction. It was odd, but she wanted to go to him and put her arms around him. She wanted it more than anything else on earth, but she didn't dare. Not now. Not after he'd stripped away the arrogance and bravado and let her see a glimpse of the real man underneath.

If she went to him, if she touched him and felt the warmth of his arms offering their protection, she would be tempted, damned tempted to blurt out her own story of Maxwell Fleming's involvement in her life. If she did —and Lord knows, she wanted to—she had the distinct feeling that her hurts would somehow become his hurts and he would want to take a hand in solving them without any participation on her part.

Furthermore, if she told him why she was going to Santa Fe and what she planned to do when she got there, she would also have to explain what she had been doing before she boarded the coach in Great Bend. He would want to know about the murder of her parents, her flight across the desert, her rescue by Lucius Beebee and her subsequent education under his selective tutelage.

How did one go about confessing to a war hero and a noble victim of circumstance that she was a thief, a cardsharp, and confidence artist? How did one confess to years spent in smoky saloons watching and learning a thousand ways to cheat a fool out of his money? Or about graduating from organizing penny-ante shell games to participating in million-dollar lotteries for phony railroad stock?

Back at the stage office in Great Bend, it had amused her to see the wanted posters hanging on the bulletin board. An alert for two con artists last seen in Louisiana had been prominently displayed—as well it should have been. She and Bruster had left there with over twenty-five thousand dollars' worth of the governor's property.

In truth, she had never thought her way of wreaking revenge on the world was wrong until now. She had been so full of anger, so full of bitterness toward all mankind, she had never once thought it wrong to steal or cheat or connive against any of them. The fact that she excelled at it with her quick hands and quicker wit had made it seem even more ludicrous that they should consider themselves the superior sex. And if a man was that stupid and that blind, he deserved to be made a fool of, deserved to be humiliated and chastened and sent slinking away with his tail between his legs where his manhood had once been.

McBride was neither stupid nor blind. He had seen through her almost from the outset, scoffing at the notion of her being a schoolmarm, equally belligerent about her hiding behind spectacles and tweed. What would he think of her if he knew the truth? He had spent five long, lash-ridden years in prison for killing a man in self-defense; what would he think of someone who had committed real crimes nearly every single day of his forced confinement, yet had never spent so much as an hour recanting behind bars? Would he see it as an irony, or would he see it as a deeper offense to his pride?

The answer drained whatever color there was remaining in her face and she clasped her hands tightly together in her lap, wishing with all her might that she could be the one to just slink away now without ever having to confront those noble gray eyes again.

"You wanted the truth," Christian said quietly, perplexed by her silence. He was also troubled to see a complete absence of the compassion and understanding —even the relief he had hoped to see. Instead, it was as if stronger, thicker shutters had been drawn closed over her emotions, guarding them against any manner of intrusion whatsoever.

Why?

She'd certainly had no such reservations during the night. Her softness and vulnerability had been as open and honest as the raw beauty of her passion. She had certainly seemed to give herself completely to him, not once asking for any promises or expecting any declarations in return.

Again: *why?*

He had to think it was because she might have heard them all before. Discovering she had not been the dry, spinsterish virgin she had given all good impressions of being had surprised him somewhat last night, but now, in hindsight, it went a long way toward explaining her cool disdain for men. Had someone made her promises before, only to break them once the heat of passion had waned? Had some bastard taken the gift of her virginity and innocence, then laughed it aside afterward, hardening her against ever letting her guard down again? It would explain why she tried to deliberately downplay her own beauty. It would also explain her aversion to being touched and caressed and being treated like a warm convenience on a cold desert night. And he, bastard that he was, had not yet given her any real reason to believe she was anything else to him.

"Aubrey—" He moved forward and crouched down before her on one bent knee. "I'm not going to abandon you if that's what you're worried about."

There. He'd said the words while they were both fully clothed and the sunlight was breaking over the plains. He was acknowledging his responsibility and admitting to a conscience—both heady new sensations for a man determined to avoid either. It probably wasn't *exactly* what she wanted to hear, but it was the best he could do, what with the iron vise clamping around his chest and the chivalric tremors rattling his hands.

Aubrey could see the panic gripping him, and in a strange sort of way, it helped restore a measure of control to the situation. Establishing what was distinctly and irrevocably out of the realm of possibility, made it that much easier to accept what was. It was possible to thank him for what he had done in releasing her from a nightmare of horror and aversion—and she did, by laying a hand tenderly on his cheek and kissing him with her heart and soul pressed to his lips. It was possible to acknowledge her response as a woman who had discovered within herself the capability of expressing passion and desire, and she did this too by smiling at the instant rush of pleasure that tingled into her breasts and thighs. And it was possible to hold that smile, to fix it firmly in place even though her heart was splitting in two and she was certain it would never be entirely whole again . . . only because she knew what she had to do, and she knew how she had to do it.

"You dear, sweet thing," she said, giving what she hoped was an excellent imitation of Magenta Royale's seductive purr. "Is that a proposal of marriage?"

McBride clenched his jaws so tightly together, she could feel his teeth grinding beneath her hand. "I hadn't planned on it being one, but I suppose—"

Quicker than a dying heartbeat, Aubrey covered his mouth with two fingers and cut him off short.

"I suppose you think you owe me some sort of . . . compensation for what happened here tonight? I confess, you surprise me. I didn't think you were the kind of man who would be contemplating a hearth and home, church meetings, children—"

"Children!"

"They usually do appear some time after a marriage," she pointed out.

"Children," he repeated, his voice softened by shock. "I hadn't really thought that far ahead."

"Nor do you have to, Mr. McBride," she assured him gently. "What happened tonight was as much my fault as yours. My eyes were wide open, so to speak, so you needn't feel you have to oblige me with any offers of marital salvation. And anyway, I would not be free to accept."

McBride frowned. He curled his long fingers around her wrist and slowly pulled her hand away from his cheek. "What do you mean . . . not free to accept?"

Aubrey moistened her lips. "I appreciate your offer, McBride, truly I do . . . I just can't accept it."

"May I ask why not?" he grated.

"No. I mean . . . would it really make you feel any better to know?"

"I'll let you know after I hear it. And you can drop the simpering Southern belle routine; it doesn't suit you in the least."

Aubrey blinked. He wasn't going to make this any easier.

"Very well, if you insist. But I believe I already told you why I was going out west."

McBride frowned, his mind searching back over the numerous verbal jousting matches they'd had, wondering which one had borne a shred of truth.

"The land of golden opportunities," she prompted softly. "You said it yourself: rich cattlemen, streets paved in gold dust. A girl could do worse—your very words, McBride."

"My words, yes, but I didn't think . . . I mean, I thought you were just playing along with me."

"Flirting?" she suggested sarcastically.

No, McBride thought. No, she had done everything but kick dirt in his face in order to throw him off the scent. Aubrey looked away and Christian felt a cold surge of disgust grip him.

"By God, that really is it, isn't it? You've come west in the hopes of landing yourself a rich cattle baron for a husband."

"I have come west in search of a better life than the one I left behind me," she said succinctly. "And since the best you could appear to offer is, no doubt, a back room in a dusty little cantina somewhere . . . well, I'm afraid this"—she dismissed the sunrise and the river and the night of spent passions with an impatient flick of her wrist—"simply isn't enough. I'm sorry. Truly I am. But I never deliberately sought your attentions or encouraged them in any way."

Christian let every word soak into his brain. He was dumbfounded. He was more than that—he was furious. Outraged! Damned near homicidal! Not enough? He had spilled his guts, opened himself to her pity and ridicule and . . . *it wasn't enough?*

"I never wanted it to go this far," she said, softening her voice, twisting the knife deeper by letting her sympathy chafe salt into his already wounded pride. "I honestly don't know what came over me last night. Perhaps it was all the danger and the fear that had come before . . . I suppose I was just too exhausted to fight you anymore."

"No," he mused, "you certainly didn't fight me, but don't worry—the added wear doesn't show. If anything, it probably helped. Whoever told you that Western men like their women plain and decent was obviously not talking from experience. Where you're headed, the more you flaunt your talents and the better you display the goods, the better your chances of snagging the top prize. And from what I've seen"—his eyes fell with deliberate scorn to rest on the swell of her breasts—"you should have no trouble competing for the brass ring."

Aubrey bit her lip to keep the flush from rising in her cheeks. "Why thank you for the advice, McBride, although . . . considering the extent of your own experiences over the past five years, I'm not sure your expertise is without flaws of its own."

McBride pushed to his feet. He had heard enough— more than enough. Any more and he might be tempted to give in to the urge to squeeze her throat until her eyes bulged and the forks in her tongue turned as black as her heart—or should he say as green? As green as the money she so obviously valued above all else.

He was angry. Quite possibly angrier than he had ever been in his life and he did not trust himself to speak or to remain too near her. With a controlled calmness he was far from feeling, he started to search for his hat in the long grass, and that was when he caught a movement out of the corner of his eye and saw Sun Shadow standing under the awning of a willow.

It was not possible for the Ute to have missed a single word of their exchange, not with the keenness of his ears, and McBride flushed through yet another towering surge of rage. He glanced down at Aubrey and the loathing in his eyes was more brutal a blow than anything his fists could have dealt.

"I hope you find what you're looking for, Miss Blue," he hissed savagely. "I hope you find it and I hope it makes you as happy as seeing the last of you will make me."

He turned and strode away, his boots cutting the grass like scythes. As he passed by the Ute, his gaze warned against any attempt at conversation, whether humorous, consoling, or otherwise. Sun Shadow's expression did not change. He merely waited until McBride's fury had put a few healthy steps' distance between them, then fell in behind him, his long black hair rippling in the growing sunlight.

Aubrey's lips slackened. She released the breath she had been hoarding and let the pain wash through her in a bright-hot wave. She had hurt him badly. She had taken his pride and trampled it underfoot, grinding it so far into the dust, there would be no retrieving it. Not for her, anyway.

She stood, but her legs would not support her and she

slumped back down again. She would have cried, but there was nothing to cry about: she couldn't lose something she had never had, and she had never really had Christian McBride. She had had his body for a while—a long, bittersweet while under the desert moon.

But the moon was gone, and so was McBride.

When she finally worked up the courage to return to the way station, she was told that the plainsman and the Ute had purchased saddlehorses from Sir Percival and had left without so much as a glance back over their shoulders.

Part Two

Each man for himself.
—Geoffrey Chaucer

13

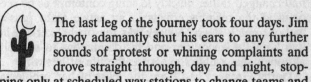The last leg of the journey took four days. Jim Brody adamantly shut his ears to any further sounds of protest or whining complaints and drove straight through, day and night, stopping only at scheduled way stations to change teams and wolf down a plate of hell-fire hot beans and fried fatback. They had acquired a relief driver at Middle Springs, compliments of Lord Fortesque, as well as three additional passengers, missionaries who had been set upon by thieves and left stranded on the banks of the Cimarron.

They followed the river south and west for eighty-five miles, then began a two-hundred-mile climb through rocky foothills gored by mesas, canyons, and cliffs. At the small and dusty town of Las Vegas, they lost both the shotgun driver and the missionaries, the one refusing to even consider navigating the treacherous Apache Canyon by night, the latter three deciding the perils of thin air and hostile Indians were preferable to the risk of hurling headlong down a sheer drop to the accompanying whoops of a tobacco-chewing madman who farted like thunder and cursed like the devil.

While Aubrey would never say she had become accustomed to Stink Finger Jim Brody, or even comfortable with his knowledge of the Trail, she and the others were at least partially numbed by virtue of their shared experiences together. Even Greaves, emboldened by the absence of McBride and the Ute, drank less and leered more, winking now and then when he caught Aubrey's eye and knew that Magenta's head was turned. Back at Middle Springs, Greaves had, as luck would have it, been emerging from the room occupied by the Indian servant just as Aubrey had been attempting to return to her own room unnoticed. His start of embarrassment had changed rather quickly to smug contempt as he recognized the obvious effects of an active night passed without much sleep. Aubrey was reasonably certain he had kept the encounter and his deductions to himself, although she couldn't guess for the life of her why.

Darby Greaves had been the least of her problems, however, as the Concord rumbled through the wooden stockades of Fort Union. The stop was as brief and perfunctory as the others, with Brody changing the mule team and shoveling food into his cheeks between bellows for the passengers to void their bladders and board up or be left behind.

On horseback, McBride and the Ute would have reached the fort a full day or two ahead of the coach. He had claimed to have had business there, or at least, had only booked passage this far, but if he was, indeed, within the staked timber walls, Aubrey saw no sign of him. And once they left the fort behind them, fading into a cloud of dust, she refused to think about him.

If Bruster suspected anything, he wisely kept it to himself, and Magenta was too busy bemoaning the loss of all of her beautiful clothing. Her luggage, as reported dutifully by Lieutenant Faraday, had been stolen or destroyed by the Comanche. She had managed, by sheer strength of will, to squeeze herself into an altered gown

belonging to Lady Prudence—a gown that was styled
suspiciously without shape, as if meant to conceal a
woman's figure in the final months of pregnancy. The
only other option was to wear the calico or homespun
frocks stocked by the trading posts along the Trail (there
was not much call for silks or satins among the home-
steading women) neither of which had touched Magenta's skin, she shriekingly declared, since she had
become the Jewel of New Orleans. The skirt was notica-
bly too short and the bodice dangerously tight, but Magenta had cinched the waist to savagely trim proportions, determined to arrive in Santa Fe in a froth of silk
tulle and yellow curls, as gaudy a resemblance to her
normal self as was possible.

Stiff and cramped, weary from the effects of fighting
the heat and motion sickness, none of the passengers
seemed able to rouse themselves to any great level of
enthusiasm when Jim Brody announced they would be
in Santa Fe before noon. The announcement was made
mid-morning, accompanied by a gnarled finger pointing
to a jumble of tiny, pale white buildings clustered well
down in the valley below them. With the advantage of
their height in the mountains, they could also see across
the blue void of the plateau to where the silver ribbon of
the Rio Grande snaked along a canyon. West of that,
the red and purple land slanted off into infinity, with
only an occasional mesa or butte standing solitary guard
over the vast plains.

Half a day's travel downward seemed to bring them
no closer to their destination. Only a marked absence of
tall piñon trees and a return to sparse grasses and stands
of forked chaparral suggested their torment was indeed
drawing near an end. Aubrey peered, like the others,
out the coach windows, but aside from a few scattered
adobe huts, the view was mainly obscured by clouds of
dust—fine white alkali dust that sifted through the tight-

est weaves of cloth and chafed the skin like a coarse abrasive.

And then, with a jubilant blast from Jim Brody's trumpet, they were there. The scattered adobe homes became rows and clusters, which started to take the shape of streets. The streets followed the course of three deep arroyos—dry riverbeds gouged out of the earth centuries before by the snow melting out of the mountains.

Nearing the center of town, the more ancient and graceful homes were half hidden behind concealing adobe walls, each private dwelling separated by narrow *calles* that bisected the streets like picket fences. There was very little green to break the monotony of white caliche dust on the roads and walls. What few trees and plants survived the heavy-wheeled and pedestrian traffic were deliberately cultivated and archly defended by rings of stone bleached as white as skulls.

The business and social heart of Santa Fe was the main plaza, a large area of some three or four acres in size, dominated at one end by the arched gates fronting the mission of San Miguel, and at the other, the Palacio de los Gobernadores—both adobe structures more than two hundred years old. The remaining two sides of the square were lined with businesses and storefronts, and, tucked into a far corner, La Fonda: inn, trading post, cantina, and, by virtue of its being one of the oldest established businesses in Santa Fe, the official terminus of both the Santa Fe Trail and the Kansas Stage Line.

Aubrey remained in her seat long after the Concord drew to a halt. She watched the swirls of dust settle, the finest particles hanging suspended in the air like a mist. She had not been altogether certain what her reaction would be to the once familiar sights and sounds of Santa Fe, and as it turned out, she was too exhausted to feel more than simple relief.

The plaza was crowded with shoppers and merchants. The stone fountain in front of the *palacio,* boasting the only two trees and therefore the only source of shade, was obviously a favorite place to gather and rest and exchange gossip. Soft Spanish music filtered through the air. Farmers in flowing white shirts and baggy trousers hawked their produce from huge straw baskets slung over the backs of weary-looking mules. Their women wore flaring, brightly colored skirts topped by loose, low-cut blouses that scorned the very idea of whalebone corsets and layers of stifling wool and linen. Some were barefoot but most wore sandals of wood and braided leather thongs.

Contrasting the poorer citizenry there were merchants and ranchers going about their daily affairs, dressed in neatly tailored gabardine and sturdy corduroy. Cowboys in from the Goodnight-Loving Trail lounged against the hitchrails, winking and flirting with the well-dressed young ladies who strolled past under the watchful gazes of their mantilla-draped *dueñas.* These rowdy young men, eager for ways to release a head of steam, were in turn watched by elaborately garbed *caballeros,* the sons of rich Spanish families who had little better to do than strut and boast and issue silent challenges to the indolent gringos.

And everywhere, children. Grub-faced urchins in hand-me-down pants and shirts too flared to fit their thin frames. They trailed pedestrians in packs of three and four, constantly haranguing for the privilege of earning a few pennies carrying packages and parcels. They begged theatrically from the strolling *Americanos* and suffered the insults and cuffs from locals if they tried to pinch an apple or an orange from an overflowing basket.

The children had swarmed the coach as soon as the huge wheels had rumbled to a stop. They converged in a babbling, chattering mass around each passenger as he or she descended, briefly discouraged but not deterred in the least by Jim Brody's cracking whip and voracious oaths.

Aubrey smiled as they scattered and regrouped, recalling a time when she used to run barefoot and grimy alongside the black-haired, brown-eyed children who belonged to her father's *vaqueros*. She had often been mistaken for a Mexican child herself, with her dark hair and suntanned complexion, and for all that her blood was half Castilian, she had felt like one of them, born and bred for generations on the arid New Mexico plains.

Sighing, she prepared to disembark. She stepped down onto the talcumlike dust of the street and turned a purely professional eye toward the Alameda, the adjoining artery that ran into the main plaza alongside La Fonda and housed the rows of saloons and gaming establishments that had sprung up in the wake of encroaching civilization. She felt her first thrill of anticipation, for she was no stranger to streets like the Alameda. Saloons were the same everywhere; noisy, smelly, and crowded, their customers as greedy for the big win as they were susceptible to the big loss.

Somewhere in that hub of activity was Maxwell Fleming's newest pride and joy, the Golden Eagle. Built to meet the needs of ranchers, cowboys, miners, gamblers, and merchants alike, the casino would be Fleming's greatest source of ready cash. It would also be his soft underbelly, the place where he was most vulnerable to influences beyond his control. No doubt the tables were rigged and there were "sharps" hired to control the so-called games of chance like poker and monte, but for someone with a quick eye and a quicker hand, these were trifling obstacles. And Aubrey had both—quick eyes and quick hands. Coupled with Maxwell Fleming's greed and his arrogant belief in his own infallibility, she had known exactly what form her revenge would take.

Now, she felt a warm, heady rush of eagerness. Now, she needed a moment to catch her breath and bring her racing pulse under control.

"Well!" Magenta stood on the boardwalk just ahead of Aubrey, and brushed irritably at the dust streaking her skirt. "Doesn't this just make you want to leap up and down for joy!"

"I find it all rather rustic, in a charming sort of way," Bruster chimed in. All but fully recovered from his encounter with the Comanche, the only sign of his travail was the neat white sling cradling his wounded arm. Among his purchases at Middle Springs had been a bowler hat to replace the one he'd lost out in the desert, but it was too small for the roundness of his head and sat perched on his balding dome like an overturned teacup.

"I find it appalling and filthy," Magenta declared. "And one can only hope there is more to Santa Fe than . . . than *this*."

She waved a hand in exasperation, condemning the plaza and everyone in it, then, without missing a beat or breaking the momentum of her hand, altered its direction and boxed the ear of a particularly grimy urchin who had sidled close enough to paw at her skirt.

"Look at this! Barefoot and begging in the middle of the street! Get away, you filthy little creature. Darby? *Darby!* Where in God's name *is* that fool?"

"Perhaps I can be of service?"

Aubrey, still facing out over the plaza, felt something akin to a filament of a spider's web dragging across the nape of her neck. She had never seen Maxwell Fleming before, never heard his voice, and yet she knew, without needing the confirmation of the sudden, complete silence around them, that the softly modulated voice

coming from the shaded doorway of La Fonda belonged
to no other.

The urchins froze where they stood. Heads turned
and stared from across the plaza and, as if by some
unspoken command, the pedestrian traffic steered a
wider berth around the immediate area in front of the
depot. Men quickened their step, tugging at the brims of
their hats to show respect. *Dueñas* scooted their charges
along the boardwalk, hissing at them in muted Spanish
to keep their heads averted and their eyes lowered.

Magenta's hostile expression lingered, but only for as
long as it took the well-dressed gentleman who owned
the voice to stroll out of the musty shadows and join her
in the sunlight. He was a tall, leanly built man in his
early forties. Black hair curled out from under the rim
of his hat, framing a face more accustomed to lamplight
than sunlight. The mouth was a straight, hard slash under a nose that was thin enough and sharp enough to
cut the face cleanly in half—not a handsome face by any
measure, but mature, and sensual in a cruel, predatory
fashion. And although subdued by the shade cast by his
hat, she could see the powerful gleam of his eyes—eyes
that were a blend of golds and greens, and penetrating
enough to make her feel as if her clothes could be
stripped away at a glance.

"Miss Royale, I presume?" he murmured, removing
his hat and bowing formally. "We were informed of the
troubles you encountered on your journey. I trust you
yourself were not injured in any way?"

"Miraculously, no," Magenta said, her gaze drawn to
the enormous diamond stud that glittered from the lobe
of his ear. His fingers, as long and elegantly lean as the
rest of him, were not lacking in rings, and the horse-
head clip that held the knot of his string tie neatly beneath his collar was carved from a single large nugget of
gold.

"But I am forgetting my manners. Allow me to introduce myself . . . Maxwell Fleming, at your service."

His hand was warm and dry, his lips very deliberate as they brushed the back of her fingers.

"I'm . . . so very pleased to meet you, Mr. Fleming. And embarrassed. I . . . did not expect you to meet me in person. I . . . I . . ." She lowered her lashes with a helpless flutter. "What a perfectly dreadful sight I must be. All of my things—my lovely, beautiful things were stolen by those . . . those *savages* who attacked us. I was forced to borrow this *rag* from an innkeeper along the way. In truth, I don't even know how I've managed to keep my bodice decently closed."

Fleming's smile and obligatory glance downward assured her that she had not.

"Replacing a lost wardrobe is a small matter and one for which I have already made provisions. I have taken the liberty of arranging to have one of Santa Fe's finest dressmakers placed at your immediate disposal, and have had my own private stores of silks and satins made available for your selections."

"Well . . . I . . . hardly know what to say. Naturally, I will be only too happy to reimburse you for any expense incurred—"

"The expense, madam, could have been far more devastating had anything happened to you or your companions. The gift of a new wardrobe is the least I can do to apologize for the brutish conditions you have had to endure. I have also taken the additional liberty of arranging for a suite of rooms for you in my hotel, and a maid to tend to any personal needs you may have."

"Making arrangements for Miss Royale's accommodations and personal staff has always been my responsibility," said Darby Greaves, stepping up beside them. "I'm sure you can appreciate the need for caution and discretion when one has the fame and reputation of an *artiste* like Miss Royale to consider."

Fleming's expression did not alter noticeably in any way, yet there was an instant and ominous gleam of dislike in the depths of the molten eyes. He took in Greaves's appearance from the bandaged hand to the frayed cuffs of his jacket and the soiled collar of his shirt, and it was apparent, from the way the slender nostrils flared around the rims, that he was repelled by more than just the smell of stale whiskey and sweat.

"And you are . . . ?"

"Greaves. Darby Greaves. Miss Royale's agent and close *personal* friend."

Fleming's lips flattened into a suggestion of a smile. "Of course. Mr. Greaves. Naturally, I did not intend any offense; I merely sought to make Miss Royale as comfortable as possible as soon as possible. The maid is from a very respectable family, and the dressmaker . . . well . . . you can judge her workmanship for yourself. It is beyond reproach, as you can see."

Both Magenta and Greaves turned at the sound of a soft rustle of silk. A figure neither of them had noticed until now emerged from the gloomy doorway of La Fonda and stopped beside the much taller, broader frame of Maxwell Fleming.

The woman was an exquisite beauty, almost childlike in her delicacy of face and form. Alabaster white skin contrasted sharply with the abundance of blue-black hair that hung in a straight, sleek curtain almost to her knees. Eyes as dark as her hair, thickly lashed and accented with kohl, emphasized her Oriental heritage; the gown of dragon green silk she wore accented her other attributes, and with such startling indifference to the accepted modesty of the current fashion she might have been standing there naked, shielded only by a spill of shimmering green water.

"This is Anna Lee," Fleming said by way of an introduction. "Unfortunately she neither speaks nor understands any English aside from a few basic phrases, so you will have to forgive her silence; it does not come from rudeness, I assure you. Mr. Greaves . . . perhaps you would do me the favor of escorting Anna Lee while I further my attempts to convince Miss Royale that we are not all savages and barbarians."

Greaves, caught off guard, was torn for a moment between his need to establish his authority as Magenta's agent, and his ill-disguised fascination with Anna Lee. He missed, where Magenta did not, the subtle nod from Fleming that sent the dainty white hand sliding around the agent's arm. And Magenta, unsure herself over how she should react to the exotic beauty, found her own hand grasped firmly and tucked into the crook of Fleming's elbow.

"My carriage is this way," he said, indicating a gleaming black surrey pulled by a pair of matched grays. The driver, a tall thin Negro, was rigged out in a suit of livery that would have rivaled that of an English lord. Other carriages driven by other servants clipped along the bustling streets, but none were so clearly stamped with the owner's wealth and position in the community.

"Now then, where were we? Ah yes, I was about to ask how soon you might be up to announcing the date for your opening performance. I certainly wouldn't want to rush you in any way, but your arrival has been anticipated with nothing short of a general frenzy. I was hoping for something along the lines of a week or so; that would give you time to settle in and—"

The two couples moved toward the carriage, Fleming's voice blending into the sound of the traffic moving by in the crowded plaza. Two burly figures stepped into line behind them; men with faces like quarried rock and

eyes that warned all but those with a premature death
wish to keep a respectful distance.

Aubrey watched the carriage with its escort of
mounted gunfighters roll away from the boardwalk. Her
stomach was churning, her muscles and nerves taut
from the strain of standing frozen for so long. She
breathed slowly and painfully, forcing the air in and out
of her lungs, tasting as she did, the bitter, coppery tang
of the blood that flowed from the shredded pad of her
lower lip.

"So that was him," Bruster murmured. "He seems
rather taken with himself, wouldn't you say?"

"I suppose he has good reason," she said quietly.

"Mmmm, yes, well . . ." He looked up, his eyes twin-
kling from beneath the beetling brows. "Care to speculate on how much that little bauble in his ear is worth?"

"Enough to change your mind about the merit of
making this trip?"

"Mmmm. I will admit, it is beginning to make a certain macabre sense. Why don't you find yourself a bit of
shade, my dear, while I make a few discreet inquiries.
Time squandered is time lost forever, you know."

Aubrey knew, all too well.

She took Bruster's advice and sipped a lukewarm
glass of lemonade inside the cantina while she waited
for him to find out if there was a Doña Dolores Tules
living in Santa Fe. One after another, three hot and
obviously irate customers approached the wire-fronted
desk that served as the ticket office for the Kansas Stage
Company and demanded to know when the stage would
be ready to begin its return run back east.

Stink Finger Jim Brody, his voice echoing off the
walls of La Fonda before his body came stumping
through the rear doors, came into view with a half-eaten
loaf of bread in one hand and a heaped plate of frijoles
in the other.

"Well, Rodriguez? You find me a gun yet? I ain't a goin' nowheres without a gun. Man cain't be expected ter ride six hunnerd miles with no gun an' no relief. That blamed coach'll jest set there where she be till I gits me one, takes a week o' Sundays to do it!"

He glared around, relishing the shock he saw on the passengers' faces as he asserted his absolute authority from the outset. He caught sight of Aubrey Blue seated against the window and, after a moment of contemplation, winked.

Aubrey was tempted to wink back, and minutes later, in the shuffle of passengers boarding and luggage being strapped to the boot of the shiny new Concord coach, she even admitted to a little sadness. Jim Brody was her last link with the east. When he rumbled away, she knew there would be no turning back.

14

The neatly carved sign tacked to the adobe had obviously been rewarded with a recent coat of fresh paint. The sign was one of the few things that distinguished this one squared, flat-roofed dwelling from the scores of others just like it that lined the narrow street. The other incongruity was that the sign itself was painted a bright marigold yellow, a splash of color where there were only drab grays and whites.

There was no name etched into the wooden plaque, only the symbols of a needle and spool of thread. The windows, like all the others on the street, were closed and shuttered against the sweltering afternoon heat, but a closer inspection through the angled wood slats revealed more colors on the other side of the glass—samples of fabrics, perhaps, or garments already made and displayed for sale.

The street was deserted, quiet but for the buzz of flies and the whine of an addled honeybee searching for nectar in the creases of the yellow wood. Aubrey glanced down both sides of the street, catching Bruster's nod from a doorway several houses down. She gave her head

a resigned shake and knocked quietly on the heavily
paneled door.

Nothing.

She waited, wary of the bee's growing frustration, and
of the dampness growing between her shoulder blades
as she stood in the uncompromising heat.

She knocked again, louder this time and flinched out
of the way as the honeybee took offense and whizzed by
her nose. The door jerked open at the same time and a
bright green eye appeared in the gap.

"What the devil do you want, banging on my door this
time of the day? Land sakes, gal, ain't you ever heard of
siesta?"

"I . . . I'm sorry if I have disturbed you," Aubrey
began.

"That you have, gal, in spades." The green eye narrowed and seemed to shoot a small barrage of sparks
out into the street. "You one of Rosita's new gals? If'n
you are, you can damn well march right back where you
come from and tell her, from me, that I ain't so hard up
for business I'll start taking on her second-string *putas*.
Christ in green boots, where did she find you anyway?
No, don't even answer, cuz I ain't interested in knowing.
You just get on back and tell her what I told you to tell
her and add, for a bit of flavor, that if she tries a trick
like this again, I'll spit right in her eye. *Adiós, putata.
Hasta la vista* and all that crap."

The door slammed shut, leaving Aubrey staring at the
peeling flakes of whitewash on the door.

"I'm . . . looking for Doña Dolores Tules," she said
haltingly.

"She died last week," came the muffled retort. "Go
away."

"But I've just got off the stage. I've just arrived in
town."

"My condolences, dearie. There'll be another stage out again in a day or two."

It was furnace-hot standing in the glare of the sun and Aubrey could feel the sweat beginning to slide down her back and soak into the waistband of her skirt. Her face felt slick with oil and heat, and the top of her head was frying. Her hair had been scraped back into a dusty, tangled knot at the nape of her neck and the frazzled wisps that had escaped were glued to her skin in tight curls.

Bruster, too far away to have heard the initial exchange, was fluttering his hands at her, frowning at her apparent lack of perseverance.

Aubrey glared at the door. "If, as you say, Doña Dolores died last week, perhaps you would know where I could find Miss Lily Cruise Montana instead? And if *she* isn't here"—Aubrey raised her voice—"perhaps I should make my inquiries at the local *alcalde*'s office."

The door opened. A large, remarkably strong hand shot out and grabbed Aubrey by the arm, hauling her inside before the gasp of surprise had left her lips.

"All right, missy. Who the hell are you? Who sent you? And who sent you here banging on my door?"

Aubrey blinked at the lingering blobs of sun floating before her eyes and tried to stall her answer long enough to make the adjustment to the gloomy, half-lit interior. Her initial supposition about the scraps of fabric on display in the front window was justified. Moreover, there were shelves lining all four walls, crammed full to overflowing with bolts of material in every color and fabric imaginable. Paper patterns, yellowed with age, and sketches of fashions a decade out of style were nailed to any spare wall space, while tables placed in the middle of the floor were heaped high with a selection of lace and ribbons and beaded trimmings that glittered like fallen stardust.

Aubrey absorbed most of this in the first few seconds of clarity. It took considerably more time to acknowledge the enormous bulk of the woman who stood in front of her like a galleon in full sail. At least as wide as the door she was blocking, and equally as round in the girth, the only faint resemblance she bore to Bruster's enthusiastic description was the mass of curly red hair piled on the top of her head.

"Are you . . . Lily Cruise Montana?"

The green eyes narrowed—a remarkable feat in itself, considering the roundness of the face and the plump folds of flesh already puffing the lids close together.

"Where did you hear that name, missy, and who told you to come banging on my door using it?"

Aubrey swallowed. Her lips were dry and her skin was wet. The air in the shop was markedly cooler than in the street, but she couldn't seem to catch a deep enough breath to take advantage.

"Beebee," she whispered. "Lucius Beebee. He told me . . . he said I would find you here. He said . . . I could trust you. He—" She stopped and pressed her fingers to her temple. She squeezed her eyes tightly shut for a moment, but when she opened them again, the green sparks were still flying at her without a trace of sympathy. "Don't you . . . know Lucius?"

"I know him. Lucius Beebee is a no-good, low-down cow-bellied snake of a coward, bastard-born to a mother who liked to fornicate with coyotes. What is he to you?"

"Just . . . a friend."

"Hah! That skunk doesn't have any friends, none that walk on two legs, at any rate."

Aubrey swayed slightly at the derision in the woman's voice. "Could I possibly trouble you for a drink of water?"

"You ain't going to faint on me, are you?"

"I . . . sincerely hope not. If I could just have that drink . . . ?"

The woman set her round face in a scowl and thundered past Aubrey, her anger setting her feet to the floor like truncheons. She disappeared behind a curtained doorway and came back a moment later clutching a tumbler of water in her fist.

She watched in silence as Aubrey drained the contents, then snatched back the empty glass as if she suspected it would vanish into the folds of Aubrey's sleeves.

"You got a name, gal?"

"Blue. Aubrey Blue."

"You got a *real* name?"

"I have the one I was born with," she said quietly, "but I prefer to use the one I gave you."

"But you come here bandying other folks names around as if you had a right to it. No, never mind. I don't want to know it anyway. In fact, I don't want to know *nothing* about you, missy, and goddamn that Lucius for thinking I might. I ain't in that line of business anymore. I don't have and don't want anything more to do with the likes of him—*or you, if you're in cahoots with him*—and if you know what's healthy for you, you'll leave before I start to take a *real* dislike to having my siesta disturbed."

"Bruster thought . . . I mean, he didn't intend to get you involved in any way; he just thought you might be able to give me some information."

"Well he thought wrong. I don't know nothing about nothing and that's the way I like to keep it. And the day Lucius comes to me saying he *only* wants this or he *only* wants that will be the same day the cows sprout wings and *fly* up the Goodnight-Loving Trail. He was wrong to send you here, wrong to think I owed him so much as a snap of fly dung for all the pain and heartbreak he caused me. Near broke my heart, he did, up and leaving without so much as a peck on the cheek good-bye. And not a letter or word in the ten long years since! I counted him dead long ago and vowed if he ever did work up the sweat to show his skinny arse to me again, I'd kick it so hard he'd be wearing his balls for earbobs. Kick it all the way back to San Francisco for him too."

"San Francisco?"

"That's where he went, wasn't it? Lily-livered, horse-nosed swine. Up and leaves me without a thought to what I'd do or what would become of me, and all so he could chase after some dream about making the big score. How many times"—she raised her pendulous arms to the ceiling in a gesture of supreme exasperation —"did I hear that one? 'I can feel it, Lily. I can taste it, Lily.' Paugh! Selfish swill-boweled mule of a day-dreamer, that's what he was. I could have chosen a better husband out of a barnyard, not to mention a better partner."

Lily paused to thrust back a curl that had flopped over her eye and Aubrey stared, starting to feel the room spin like a top around her.

"Husband?" she asked in a whisper. "Did you say . . . husband?"

"I did. We were married right here, in the mission of San Miguel, June 19, in the year of our Lord Jesus Joseph Christ, 1864. He left me three years later and, until now, has shown some of the God-given sense he *wasn't* born with to keep his face and his name out of sight and mind. But does he show the sense to keep it that way? Hell no. He up and sends you along, hollering a name I ain't heard in a dozen years, and hollering it loud enough for the governor hisself to choke over his enchiladas. Damned nerve of him! And I tell you again, you made a mistake in coming here. He was dead wrong to send you and you'll get nothing out of me. Not help, not information, not even another glass of water. Now, out you get. Out! Go back to wherever you came from and take this"—she leaned over and spat voraciously onto the plank flooring—"to him from me."

Lily Montana opened the door and started to make a sweeping gesture with her arm to herd Aubrey out into the sweltering sunlight again. Her arm stopped mid-sweep, however, when she saw the hapless figure standing alone in the middle of the street, his tea-cup bowler held in his good hand in front of him, his face glowing red over and around the drooping ends of his moustache.

Lily closed the door with a bang and stood for a long moment staring at the wood panels in much the same way Aubrey had a short while ago.

The tousled frizz of red curls turned slightly as she glanced back over her shoulder.

"Tell me that ain't him."

"I'm afraid it is."

Two measured breaths later the rounded face was as dark as a thundercloud.

"Did he send you on ahead to soften me up?"

"No! I mean, yes, he sent me on ahead, but no, he neglected to mention you would need 'softening up.' He neglected to mention quite a few things, in fact—like the part about his being your husband."

More thunder rumbled in Lily's throat. "And why should that surprise you? You sweet on him or something?"

The room took another sudden lurch and Aubrey had to reach for the edge of the table to help smother a giddy surge of laughter. "Me? And Bruster? Heavens—" She swallowed hard and averted her eyes "—no."

"You said you were friends, honey. That usually means something more than just *friends.*"

"In this case, that's all it means. He . . . he saved my

life, and if anything, he's been sort of like a father to me ever since."

"A father?" Lily snorted and showed the first trace of genuine humor. "Tarnation and damn, I would have liked to have seen that, gal."

She turned away and stepped a little to the side so that she could peer through the slats in the shutter.

"He's porked on a little weight, I see. And he's still wearing that confounded hairy handlebar over his lip."

In the scant light shed from the window, Aubrey could see that Lily sported a good size moustache herself, the fine red fuzz glinting with the same gold and russet threads as her eyebrows and eyelashes.

"What did he do to his arm?" she asked softly.

"He didn't *do* anything. He was shot. The Comanche attacked our coach and Bruster—"

"Shot! By Comanche! That was you? The two of you were on that stage? But I thought I heard it was the Kansas line got ambushed."

"It was. We left Great Bend seven . . . no, eight days ago. Or maybe it was nine," Aubrey mumbled, rubbing her temple again. "I'm honestly not sure anymore, and too tired and too confused to figure it out. But yes, we were on the coach and we were ambushed by the Comanche, and Bruster was shot in the arm while he was helping to defend us. He didn't panic, he didn't act like a coward—in fact, he . . . he even offered to try to cross the desert alone to go for help, wounded arm and all, but we wouldn't let him and . . . and in the end, he stayed behind and, with hardly any help from the others, he held off a second attack and stood firm against the Indians until the cavalry arrived."

There were bits of truth in what she said, enough to keep the fatigue from twisting her tongue into too many knots, and, while Lily might not have believed her absolutely, she believed enough for the hard lines around her mouth to soften into a scowl of concern.

"You look about ready to fall in on yourself, child. Come on along into the kitchen and set yourself down where it's cooler."

"No. Thank you, but I can't leave Bruster standing out there all on his own. He's just as tired and just as hot . . . and probably twice as scared as he ever was out on the trail."

Lily's mouth stayed firm a moment longer, then twitched slightly at the corner. "Don't you think he deserves to be?"

"Truthfully . . . yes. But in another minute or two, he'll be reduced to jelly."

"Good. I'm partial to jelly. Make my own out of mint and a kind of gooseberry that grows down here."

Aubrey managed a weak smile. The entire conversation had had an unreal quality about it all along—why should she not be standing here listening to a casual description of how Lily Cruise Montana went about making her gooseberry jelly? And just because the room began to tilt on an awkward angle, it was no reason for her to stop and wonder what she was doing here, or why she suddenly found herself in a small heap on the floor.

She was dimly aware of Lily yanking the door open and shouting to Bruster to come give a hand. The harsh light hurt her eyes, though, and she closed them, just for a few blissful seconds of quiet darkness. When she opened them again, she was lying on a bed and there was a wonderfully cold, wet towel draped over her forehead, and someone sitting beside her dabbing another wet towel on her wrists and arms.

"There she comes. She's coming back to us. Poor thing—when was the last time she had a decent meal? She's nothing but skin and bone and so tired she about fell asleep on her feet. Get away!" There was the sound of a slap and Aubrey pried her eyes open long enough to see a chastened Bruster Beebee jerk his good hand away from the bed.

"Are you certain she doesn't require the services of a doctor?"

"She needs peace and quiet and a deal of sleep," Lily declared. "And she doesn't need the two of us hovering over her like buzzards. You can just flap your wings on out of here right now and wait for me in the kitchen. I'll strip her down—God in heaven, where did she ever come by this tweed?—and tuck her in, and by then you'd better have some damned good explanations ready, Lucius Beebee. Good enough to keep me from carving off the parts of your body you won't be using anymore. Not that you ever did use them to any good effect," she added under her breath.

"Lily?" Bruster had paused in the doorway and his voice was softer, gentler than Aubrey could remember ever hearing it.

"Lily . . . you haven't changed a bit, my dove. You are still as beautiful as you were the day I lost my heart to you."

Lily's jaw worked fiercely a moment. "And you're just as bad a liar as you ever were. Now get on out of here before I start breaking things."

•

Aubrey wasn't sure how long she slept, she only knew she opened her eyes once and there was daylight showing through the window; again and there was darkness. A third time there was a rim of crimson framing the deeply carved sill and she managed to swing her feet over the side of the bed and make use of the enamel chamber pot tucked beneath the nightstand. She stood at the open window for a time, remembering other mornings so long ago, when she had watched the sunrise breaking over the crest of the Sangre de Cristo mountains, when the tops of the ridges had burned red, as if a line of glowing coals had been strung along them; when the mountains themselves were blue and misty with shadow, and here and there, a higher peak jutted forward, the tips catching the stronger light and glowing with the yellow and gold of the aspen forests that crowned them.

There was no sight quite like it back east, and no way to describe it to someone whose idea of raw wilderness had been the sparsely populated stretches of road between one crowded city and the next.

Aubrey curled back into the warm nest of blankets and closed her eyes with a sigh. She half-expected the Dream to stalk her again, but it didn't. The only images that came to her were of a desert moon, swollen and glistening in a midnight sky; a bank of lush green moss by the edge of a river; and two naked bodies twined together in a passion as deep and raging as the river that flowed beside them.

And once, for a fleeting moment, she thought she wakened to the faint scent of tobacco drifting through the open window. It wasn't real, of course, and there had been no one standing there smoking a thin black cheroot, but the image lingered, and so did the taste of his name on her lips.

15

"You're mad. You're stark raving insane and I hold you personally to blame for the whole idea, Lucius Beebee," Lily said, thrusting a fat finger under his nose. "It sounds just like something you'd dream up. Run a scam on Maxwell Fleming? Why you wouldn't even get close enough to smell his boots never mind try to take the shine off them. As for that little slip of a girl in there, she wouldn't last ten minutes face to face with Fleming. Hell, she barely lasted five with me, and I don't particularly like chewing on raw liver for breakfast."

"Lily, I swear, you have me all wrong," Bruster protested. "It wasn't my idea to come here. Er, certainly not for the sole purpose of skinning Maxwell Fleming, at any rate. I had never even heard of the chap until a month or so ago."

"You ever seen a cow with wings?" Lily demanded.

"What? I . . . er, ah . . . no. No, I can't say as I have."

"Neither have I. And like I told that gal in there, until I do, I ain't about to believe a word you say to me."

"Oh come now, Lily, my sweet. My little dove . . ."

"Don't you sweet dove me nothing, Lucius," she

warned, the finger bunching into an ominous knot alongside three others and a thumb. "You find me a cow that flies and I'll believe that child in there dreamed up this whole crazy scheme."

Bruster looked as if he might attempt a rejoinder, but a movement in the doorway caught his eye and he glanced over with no small show of relief as Aubrey came into the room.

"Well, good morning, sleepy-head—or should I say good afternoon. We were wondering if you were ever going to leave your bed."

Bruster beamed and Lily frowned as Aubrey tried unsuccessfully to stifle a yawn.

"How long have I been out?" she asked.

"Well, you introduced yourself to my floor the day before yesterday around threeish, and here it is . . . near seven in the evening."

Aubrey glared at Bruster. "You let me sleep that long?"

"Lucius had a notion once or twice to go in and wake you, but I convinced him to let you be. I told him your own body would tell you when you'd had enough. And it's not as if you had anything better to do with your time!" This last sentence was said with enough vehemence to start Bruster squirming in his chair.

He had, Aubrey noted, done away with the sling on his arm.

"How is your hand?" she asked.

"It is recovering its strength. About ninety percent, I should think, and fully a hundred by the end of the week."

Aubrey nodded and glanced balefully at the empty plates that sat before Lily and Bruster. The sight of crumbs and blobs of dried egg yolk started her stomach rumbling loud enough to win a knowing snort of satisfaction from their hostess.

"That's the next thing your body tells you it needs: fuel. Set yourself down, gal, and I'll see if I can't scrape up a bit of food for you. Lucius *might* have left something in the pantry. Then again, his jaw hasn't stopped chawing since sunup, so I can't promise more than a few biscuits and gravy."

"Just a plain biscuit would be fine," Aubrey said wistfully. "With a little of your gooseberry jelly, if you have it?"

It was Lily's turn to beam as she disappeared into the pantry, and Bruster's to frown as he cast a blatantly curious eye in Aubrey's direction.

She merely shrugged. "What is it they say about catching more flies with honey than vinegar?"

"My dear girl, I have been smearing my every word with syrup and lying prostrate at that woman's feet since noon yesterday—the first time she would allow me back through her hallowed doorway—to no avail. She is a bulwark. Unassailable."

"She's also your wife," Aubrey said evenly.

"And a holy shrew she was when I married her. Odd, how the mind only remembers what it wants to remember, like the sweetness and the beauty . . ."

"The delicate body of a butterfly and the face of an angel?" Aubrey finished wryly.

"Just so," Bruster sighed, obviously missing the sarcasm as well as the glaring deficiencies in his previous description of Lily Montana.

Lily returned at that point, bustling through the room like a rampant tumbleweed in gingham. Pots banged and pans clattered, and in no time at all, the small kitchen was filled with the aroma of sizzling bacon and fried beans. A platter mounded high with wedges of cheese, hot peppers, and flat tortilla cakes was placed in the center of the table along with enough sliced mutton to satisfy a family of ten.

"Dig in, child; help yourself. Don't waste any time on manners or you're liable to go hungry."

Aubrey doubted that. Not with the amount of food that kept being piled on the table. She filled her plate, and filled it again, and somehow, between eating and listening and talking and eating some more, the mountain of food dwindled and the plates were swabbed clean of every last morsel.

Bruster groaned and massaged his belly at the end of the meal, declaring he could eat nothing more for fear of bursting. Lily promptly produced a cherry pie and Bruster's napkin was thrust back into his collar, his fork licked clean of residual gravy and his plate presented for the first slice.

Lily ignored it and turned to Aubrey. "Miss *Blue*?"

"I couldn't possibly eat another thing. And please, call me Aubrey."

She hadn't missed the sarcasm dripping off the use of her name, and felt suddenly extremely self-conscious—a feeling that had nothing to do with the fact that she was wearing nothing but one of Lily's tentlike nightdresses. Still, to cover the awkwardness of the situation, she plucked at the loose cotton of a sleeve and arched a brow.

"I couldn't seem to find my clothes."

"The shirt was filthy and I gave the skirt away to the old *mamasita* down the street—she needed a new blanket for her mule."

"You gave my skirt away?"

"A godawful thing it was, too. Poor mule probably won't even thank me."

"I'm not sure I will either."

"Don't go getting your ears all in a flap. Bruster is going to treat you to a fine new set of duds, so he tells me."

Bruster choked delicately on a crumb of pastry and

wiped the dribble of cherry juice off his chin. "Actually, what I believe I said was that Aubrey would be requiring a few new outfits of suitable clothes." He caught the fomenting look of battle in Lily's eye and added a hasty amendment. "Which of course, I will most happily finance."

"In gold. In advance." Lily said flatly.

"Does this mean . . . you will help us, my dove?"

"It means that business is a little slow and I'd be a damned fool to send her to someone else, now wouldn't I. It also means I'll have time, between the cutting and the fitting and the sewing to try to talk her out of whatever hare-brained scheme you've concocted."

Aubrey took a sip of the strong wine cordial Lily had set on the table, and acknowledged its potency with a small gust of approval. "But you don't understand; the hare-brained scheme was mine. I was the one who talked Bruster into coming to Santa Fe."

"You sat in a hotel room in Kansas City and decided to come west to run a game on Maxwell Fleming?"

"Actually, it was Wichita. And I don't play games, Miss Montana. I mean to ruin Maxwell Fleming. I mean to take him for every penny he has and to watch his little empire come tumbling down."

Lily smiled at the casual audacity of the statement and Bruster held his breath, catching a glimpse of something more than mirth behind the green eyes.

"My word, Lucius, this is a treat. Where did you say you found her?"

"I didn't, my dove, but if you truly want to know"—he glanced askance at Aubrey and waited for her permission before continuing—"I found her about twenty miles from here."

Lily's smile faded. "Twenty miles?"

She looked sharply at the mane of jet black hair, at the faintly olive-hued complexion that sheer exhaustion had previously bleached white. The blue eyes were a bit of an oddity, but not all that rare in families whose bloodlines went back to the days of the old Spanish grandees.

"Maybe you'd better start at the beginning," Lily said slowly. "And mind you don't leave a damned thing out, or you'll both find yourselves on the street with a potload of piss up your ass for the insult."

•

An hour later, Lily knew everything . . . including some things she didn't want to know. The bottle of cordial was empty and she walked into the pantry to fetch another, but instead of opening it right away, she sat with the bottle clutched in her hands, her forehead pleated in a frown, her mouth pressed into a thin line. She found herself wondering exactly what a cow with wings would look like, but pushed the image aside in favor of staring at Aubrey with a cautious new respect. And, truth be known, a shiver of the old excitement.

She shot a glance at Bruster. "You should be hung by your toenails, you old fart, for not handing her over to an orphanage where she could have got a proper education, and maybe made something of herself."

"She has made something of herself, my dove. To you, she may just look like a fragile slip of a thing, but to me she is the best—*the very best* I have seen in the business, now or ever. Present company *not* excepted."

Aubrey sighed. "Bruster tends to exaggerate a little."

He leaned forward. "On the other hand, she *is* wanted in three states. Quite possibly four by now, if the governor of Louisiana was planning to present the family diamonds to his new bride as a wedding gift. She won them in a poker game, but no doubt the scallywag will have claimed theft."

Lily continued to stare, continued to deliberate while

she strummed her fingers lightly on the side of the bottle. Having reached some sudden decision, she abruptly stood and slid open a drawer in the sideboard. A moment later, a deck of cards lay face down on the table in front of Aubrey.

"If Bruster says you're good, you probably are, but if you have some notion of going up against Maxwell Fleming, you gotta be more than just good. Now then" —she tapped the deck with a crooked finger—"shuffle them once and deal out three hands. Keep in mind, I like to win."

Aubrey took a deep breath and flexed her fingers. She caught Bruster's eye as she reached for the deck, and he gave her a broad, smug wink that made her want to fan the cards in his face. She fanned them on the table instead, laying them out in a long, uniform line. Lifting the last card, she used it to upend the others and guide them in a controlled ripple to the opposite end. With the cards face up now, she reversed the process, drawing the ripple back down the line and leaving only the diamond-patterned backs showing. It was a cheap huckster's trick, but one that allowed her a quick glimpse of the positioning of the cards.

She collected them into a neat pile again and squared the edges. She shuffled them and dealt fifteen cards, placing five face down in front of each of them.

Bruster, eager to show his protégée's prowess, turned his five cards face-up, overturning three aces in a bold row across the table, and chuckling in anticipation when he turned the fourth and fifth and saw the pair of jacks.

"The very hand she dealt me in Boston and earned us both a very sweet pot of . . . how much, my dear?"

"Twenty-two thousand . . . which you turned around and lost again the very next night."

"A touch of the rheumatism," Bruster said with an apologetic shrug. "It slows me down sometimes."

Aubrey's hand was nothing special (she was better with her rings on, she interjected dryly). Lily, who had not taken her hawk's eyes off Aubrey's hands during the shuffle or the deal, showed a genuine flicker of surprise as she turned her own cards over. The missing ace of spades, the ten of spades, the five of spades, the jack of spades, and the two of spades. A flush. Not particularly royal, but good enough to have won the hand.

"I saw you marking the aces," Lily muttered, "but I honestly didn't see the flush."

Aubrey was impressed—and annoyed—that Lily had even noted the gentle pressure she had exerted on the edge of each ace to mark it while she had been rimpling the cards back and forth.

"Like I said, I'm better with my rings on. Did you really give my skirt away? They were stitched into a pocket in the hem."

The dumpling face flushed unexpectedly, then Lily pushed herself to her feet and waddled over to a cupboard beneath the wash trough. She drew out the folded bundle of tweed and scowled to cover her embarrassment.

"Real English tweed is hard to come by in these parts. Be damned if I'd give it away for some jackass to wear."

Aubrey felt along the padded thickness of the hem until she found the three little humps; a snip with a paring knife freed them into her palm. Each circlet of gold was small and dainty, the mounted stones neither gaudy nor particularly valuable. Each had a special abrasion on the back of the band—a tiny point or a niche in the gold by which a card could be secretly punctured, scratched, or roughened to distinguish it in some way from the rest of the deck.

"It's still only card tricks, honey, and Fleming knows them all. Besides, he never plays the tables himself. Never gambles, not so much as a hand of poker. If you were aiming to take him that way, you're plumb out of luck already."

"It takes away some of the personal pleasure, to be sure," Aubrey admitted with a faint smile. "But it isn't enough to stop me. I assume he does allow outside gamblers to run some of the games?"

Lily nodded. "He'd have to, or he wouldn't stay in business very long. But whatever they win, they turn most of it back in to the house and keep only a small percentage as their cut."

"No doubt he also hires gamblers to front games and make it look as if anyone with a few coins in their pocket could walk in off the street and break the bank."

Lily's eyes screwed down to slits. She looked from Aubrey to Bruster, back to Aubrey again. "You ain't thinking what I think you're thinking . . . are you?"

"Can you think of another way to get inside the Golden Eagle?"

Lily thrust out her jaw. "No, but I can sure think of better ways of getting out than inside a five-foot pine box! Just cuz you're a woman, don't go thinking he won't have one of his hired apes plug you right between the eyes if he even *starts* to suspect you ain't on the up and up."

"I don't intend to do the slightest thing to make him suspicious."

"He hires gunfighters and keeps 'em armed to the teeth while they watch everyone who comes and goes. They watch the players *and* the dealers, and, honey, some of them boys were playing with six-shooters before they learned to play with themselves. Fleming has the meanest, ugliest, worst lot of scum working for him that the good Lord ain't got around to sweeping out in the garbage yet. Cock-a-roaches who'll be trying to get up your skirts and down your bodice the first time you bend over. What's more, you ain't asked yet, but he's still there. Scud Holwell. The meanest, lowest son of a bitch of them all. What's going to happen to all your fine plans the first time you lay an eye on him?"

Aubrey blanched. She knew Lily was hoping to shock her, and she also knew she didn't have an answer to the question.

"I don't know what will happen," she said honestly. "I only know what will happen to me if I come this far and just run away without trying. I saw Fleming and I didn't fall apart, so maybe—"

"You saw Fleming? Where? When?"

"At the stage depot when we arrived. He was there to meet Magenta Royale."

"The so-called opry star he's been making such a big to-do about?"

"I don't know how much of a star she is, and I've never heard her sing, but yes, that's the one."

"Hmmm. She dark like you?"

"I beg your pardon?"

"Her hair: what color is it?"

"Blond. Very pale blond . . . why?"

But another cryptic "Hmmm," was the only response forthcoming.

Aubrey began to suspect that at least part of what Bruster had told her about Lily Cruise Montana was true. The fine edge of larceny was not entirely out of her blood yet, despite the years of padding and respectability. As if on cue, Lily scooped up the deck and began riffling it in her pudgy hands. The fingers, swollen to the size of sausages, worked quickly and deftly, cutting the cards and shuffling with the ease of familiarity.

Bruster leaned forward, his moustache twitching with eagerness. "Lily . . . my luscious little dove . . . my lovely, soft, dumpling dove . . . does this mean you might be willing to help us in our endeavor?"

Lily glanced up from beneath her auburn brows. "You

want to feel my fist rammed up the inside of your nose,
Lucius Beebee, you just keep calling me your little anything."

"But . . . ah, my precious, my heart . . ."

"Dolores. Both of you can call me Dolores. Ain't nobody around hereabouts ever heard me called anything
but. As for helping you—I still say you got your nerve
showing your ugly nose here after ten years, sashaying
through my door like you never gave a second thought
to how it might end up flattened against your face. Now
you want my help? Ten years I've been living here,
quiet, respectable, and alone. I don't go looking for ag-
gravations, and they got no call to come looking for me.
I ain't exactly rolling in gold or greenbacks, but I ain't
starving either and I ain't jumpin' out of my skin every
time a splat of bird crap hits a tin can.

"On the other hand"—she heaved her bosom forward
on a voluminous sigh—"I sell maybe one, two pretties a
week. I made a mistake once—that's all it takes with
hombres the ilk of your Mr. Fleming running things—
and customers who used to come see me regular for
their frocks and gewgaws are too scairt to even nod at
me from across the street. Oh, there's one or two sneak
over at night from the whorehouses, cuz they know they
can talk me out of a bolt of fine silk for the price of
twopenny cotton, but I'm getting damned tired of seeing
my life savings squandered on filthy drifters and lecher-
ous cowboys."

"Then you *will* help us?" Bruster cried triumphantly.

"No," she said bluntly. "I won't lift a finger to help
you, you short-assed bag of hot wind. I'll help the girl,
here, but only for as long as it takes to get her headed in
the right direction. Once she's on her way, I'll want ten
thousand dollars in cash—a thousand for every year I
slept alone in my bed—and then I'm gone. I'm out of
here. *Adiós* and *hasta la vista.*"

"Ten thousand dollars?" Bruster gasped weakly.

"And that ain't including what it's going to cost to put this gal in clothes decent enough to get her through the front doors of the Golden Eagle."

"Ten thousand," Bruster spluttered. "Why that's . . . that's . . ."

"More than fair," Aubrey interjected calmly. "And if you tell me where you're headed when you leave here, I'll arrange to have ten thousand more wired to any bank you choose."

Lily drew herself upright, smiling at Aubrey. "*Now,* you remind me of myself twenty years ago. *You* never did have style, Lucius. Talent, yes, and a fair eye for spotting an easy mark, but you were always too busy counting pennies to remember how to spend a dollar. Stand up, child. Can't tell too much about a body's shape and size when she's out cold and limp as a fish. Lucius, you get the hell on out of here and don't come back until you're sent for."

"But, Lily, my love—"

Quicker than her bulk would have suggested, Lily reached over and grabbed hold of one of Bruster's ears. She used it to haul him upright, the pain forcing him up onto his toes.

"I told you, the name is Dolores," she hissed. "And if I have to tell you again, you'll be doing all of your whining out the other end."

Doña Dolores Tules led the tippy-toeing Bruster out of the kitchen and through the darkened shop, oblivious to his arms flailing and his mouth squeaking against the indignity. At the outer door, she paused and swung around to glance at Aubrey.

"Anything else you want to say to him before he says good night?"

Aubrey was biting her lip, trying hard to keep from

laughing. "No. No, I'm sure he knows how to put his time to good use over the next few days."

"Um-humph." Grasping Bruster's other ear in her fist, Dolores dragged her huffing, red-faced husband forward and planted a large, wet kiss smack over his lips. She released him, ears and all, and sent him reeling out the door without a further comment or consideration.

"Now then," she said, dusting her hands together for a job well done, "where were we, gal? Shuck that nightdress and let's have us a look-see at what we've got to work with."

16

Maxwell Fleming lounged back in his chair and absently flipped open the gold facing on his pocket watch. It was a little after ten in the morning, one of his favorite times of the day, when the doors to the Golden Eagle were still closed to customers and he could enjoy the rich opulence of his newest pride and joy without the annoying distraction of noise and milling crowds. The crimson velvet curtains were drawn across the multipaned windows, the enormous mahogany tables stood quiet and clean, the roulette wheels gleaming from a fresh coat of oil. The bar that ran the length of one wall was backed in mirrors, the shelves lined with full bottles and stacks of clean glasses. Overhead, imported crystal chandeliers hung on long chains from the domed, gilded ceiling two stories up. The balcony that circled the entire second floor, also draped and carpeted in red and gold, could be seen and appreciated without the usual thick haze of smoke. The wall opposite the bar was a solid sheet of crimson velvet framed by an arch of shorter lengths fringed in heavy gold tassels. Behind these layered curtains was the stage, its wooden floors polished and buffed to a high gloss in anticipation of the much-heralded debut of Magenta Royale.

Around the circumference of the main salon and the balcony were private alcoves, some slated for high-stakes games of poker and monte, others closer to the stage to be reserved for special guests more interested in the performances going on than in the gaming tables. Fleming sat in one of those alcoves now, his private booth, and, when he had managed to bring his surprisingly strong surge of excitement under control again, he closed the lid of his watch and met the stunningly blue eyes of the young woman who sat across from him.

His initial surge of interest—purely physical and therefore easy to master—had started when he had first seen the woman standing in the door and demanding an audience with the owner. Towering a full head and shoulders above her, the bartender had explained, in terms guttural enough to have sent the strongest heart quailing back into its mouse hole, that his boss, Mr. Fleming, did not like being disturbed this early in the day, but if she was looking for a job in the back rooms, *he* would be more than happy to audition her. She hadn't quailed. She hadn't even blushed at the insult. She had looked straight over to the booth where Fleming sat and arched a brow in an age-old manner that more or less challenged him to look her over and see for himself if she was worth having his solitude disturbed.

Fleming had accepted the mute challenge. He had even been mildly amused by her boldness in coming to Santa Fe's biggest and brashest saloon dressed as if she had just stepped off the pages of *Godey's Lady's Book.* Her lavender day dress was made with a tight basque, scalloped to a deep vee almost to her waist. The vee was in turn filled with lace, a soft waterfall of pale gray, the combination and effect duplicated in the gently belled cuffs of her sleeves. The skirt could have no more than one or two petticoats beneath so that it drew attention to the incredible slimness of her waist and delicate curve of her hips. Gray kid gloves matched the dainty felt hat that nestled in a gleaming mass of ebony curls; bands of lilac ribbon fluttered from the back rim of her hat, made of such fine silk they seemed to move without benefit of breeze or motion.

How could he have done less than beckon George to let her pass? His curiosity had been roused, and, in savagely short order as she came closer and the lights from the overhead chandeliers revealed the breathtaking beauty of her face, the rest of his body along with it.

It was not as if he had not seen a beautiful woman before. Another well-deserved boast of the Golden Eagle was that he employed only the most exquisite and talented beauties east or west of the Rio Grande. Jet black hair and cornflower blue eyes were a rare sensual treat, to be sure, but it was the shocking resemblance to another hauntingly ethereal face out of his past that had caused a marked lapse in his concentration. He had seen those eyes, the sweep of those thick lashes, and the bow-shaped lushness of that mouth before. He had seen it, he had had it, and he had lost it before he'd even realized what he had cast away.

Aubrey Blue. The name meant nothing to him, and after the initial pounding of blood through his veins had subsided, he could see that, although her features were similar in many ways, there were also differences— enough that he could listen rationally to the business proposition she was calmly laying out for his consideration.

"Miss Blue, are you suggesting my tables are rigged in some way? That I do not run honest games?"

"I'm certain you do, for the most part, or you would not be in business very long. I'm only suggesting you

must have certain . . . stoppers . . . in place to ensure against too long, too lucky a winning streak."

"And you think you could be one of those stoppers?"

Aubrey nodded and Fleming gave in to a small laugh.
"Miss Blue . . . forgive me if I seem a little dubious,
but . . . are you telling me you have done this sort of
thing before?"

"I can give you references, if you like. Names of the
places I have worked."

Fleming's grin broadened. "I'm not looking to employ
a nanny."

"Nor am I looking to hire on as one," she said coldly.
"I abhor children as well as childish word games which
serve no purpose but to waste my valuable time." She
stood up and adjusted the folds of her skirt. "I shan't
waste any more of yours, either. Good day to you, sir."

"Wait a minute. I haven't said no, have I?"

"You haven't shown the interest in the proposition
that I expected. I was told you were an enterprising
businessman with a keen eye for profit. I was also told
you were a fair man to work for, and better for . . .
than against."

"Against?" He said the word softly, almost as if he
wasn't quite sure he had heard it correctly.

"The Golden Eagle is not the only establishment of
its kind in Santa Fe. I imagine there would be others at
least willing to see what I could do for them before they
showed me the door."

Fleming's gaze moved lower, settling openly and
speculatively over the swell of her breasts. "What exactly can you do for me, Miss Blue?"

"I can bring a lot of business into the Golden Eagle,
Mr. Fleming. Or I can draw a lot of business away. I'm
offering you first choice."

"Rather bold words for a . . . schoolteacher, wasn't
it?"

So he did remember seeing her at the stage depot; Aubrey hadn't been sure. He had either asked Magenta Royale about the other passengers, or else he made it his business to know everything that went on in his town.

"Miss Royale was the one who made the assumption that I was a schoolteacher. A rather . . . hasty departure from Kansas necessitated the use of some . . . adjustments . . . to my appearance, and, well, frankly I didn't see any harm in letting her believe what she wanted to believe."

That won another grudging smile, as well as a glimmer of conjecture in the hazel eyes. "You are not welcome in Kansas anymore?"

The best lie was the one that stayed closest to the truth: Bruster's words.

"Let's just say a certain gentleman of some importance did not take too kindly to the way I relieved him of the burdens of his financial responsibilities."

Fleming laughed outright and signaled the bartender to bring over a deck of playing cards. "All right, Miss Blue, I'll give you a chance to show me what you can do. Do it well enough, and you can start Saturday. Do it poorly and you can still start Saturday, but you'll be working for George."

Aubrey looked at the bartender, who winked and rubbed a hamlike hand over the bulge at his crotch. She sat back down and slowly, daintily peeled the kid gloves off her fingers.

•

An hour later, Fleming was seated alone at the booth, deep in thought. His long fingers thumbed through the three decks of cards in front of him, but he was damned if he could account for all of the subtle markings that had allowed Aubrey Blue to deal hand after hand of winning combinations. He hadn't seen her mark them. He hadn't found more than half of the infinitesimal scratches and nicks she claimed were there for a blind man to feel. Not even when the decks were stacked side by side and the edges compared, were there any noticeable discrepancies. Certainly none that would cause even a trigger-happy cowpoke to draw his gun and cry cheat.

She was cool, she was clever, and she was beautiful. She was also starting to work Saturday night, right here in his own private booth, the price he had paid to call her bluff on a hand *he* had dealt.

Fleming downed his drink and pushed away from the table. An hour exchanging silent, sensual challenges with those clear blue eyes had made him restless and he wondered where Anna Lee was. Probably with Greaves again, keeping him distracted and out of everyone's way, which was just as well. Five minutes in the company of that pompous fool was enough to make his hands itch to draw a gun.

Fleming smiled again. When he had questioned Aubrey Blue as to her ability to handle trouble if it arose, she had quite calmly produced a small derringer from her reticule and laid it on the table in front of her. So much for trouble.

Fleming nodded to the bartender and climbed the carpeted steps to the upper landing. To his right, through wide double doors, was a long corridor with private rooms furnished in the same taste and opulence of the casino. The girls who worked for him were not only the best in the city, but they charged the most for their services—a fee more readily parted with from the tumbled bedsheets of a feather mattress than from a squeaking iron cot.

To the left was another set of doors, these leading to his own private rooms and his office. Standing guard was a big brute of a man whose features had been put together like a patchwork quilt. One eye was blue, one eye brown. A full, thick beard grew on his chin, but not over a cleft upper lip that gave him a perpetual scowl. The shaggy, unbroken line of his eyebrow stretched the width of his Neanderthal forehead, with an arrow-shaped scar on his temple pointing irreverently to the stub of a severed ear.

Fleming chose his brutish-looking gunmen with the same care as he chose his women, only using ugliness and a capacity for viciousness as a guide rather than beauty and sexual prowess.

"Mr. Fleming." The guard nodded his head respectfully as his boss approached.

"Clay. I heard you had a little trouble last night."

Clay Wilson shook his head. "No trouble, boss. Just a bit of a misunderstanding. The Kid handled it okay."

Fleming followed Wilson's glance over the railing to where a gangly youth was just swaggering up to the bar. His spurs jangled as he propped a foot up on the boot rail, and as he shoved his hat to the back of his head, he released an unruly tangle of reddish-blond hair that stuck out at various odd angles around the boyish face. He winked a pale blue eye at one of the girls sashaying by and earned a squeak of annoyance as he pinched her through the layers of her skirt.

"He seems to be fitting in easily enough."

"He'll do. Still kicking the saddle dust out of his pants, and he don't have too much to do with the other boys yet, but he'll come around."

The hired gun under discussion sensed their scrutiny and responded by raising a shot glass full of whiskey in their direction, toasting them over his shoulder without troubling to turn around.

"Cocky little bastard too," Wilson muttered. "Makes

me want to scratch all over when I can't see where he is."

Fleming smiled. William Bonney had come to him highly recommended, displaying an exceptional skill with a handgun that set him apart from the usual wild guns who roamed the Territories. As fast as most of Fleming's boys were, Bonney was faster, drawing and firing in a single fluid motion that left his opponents gaping in shock—or horror. At least two of the Eagle's former patrons who had had the misguided notion to challenge Bonney's speed now had shattered hands to show for their lapse in judgment—a fate much worse than death for a professional gambler. Word of Bonney's prickly temper and queer sense of humor had spread quickly upon his arrival, with most men giving him a wide berth, or, like Clay Wilson, taking care not to criticize him in too loud a voice.

"I like him," Fleming declared. "And he's of much more use to me here than out on the Pecos counting cattle. What about Holwell?"

"I told him what you said; that he'd best cool his heels and stay low for another week or so, until the fuss with the girl and the priest blows over. He's up in a cabin in the hills, gettin' meaner every day, shootin' holes in trees and chewin' on anything on two or four legs that comes near."

"Witnesses?"

"None stupid enough to testify to anything they seen."

Fleming drew a slim black cigarillo out of a silver case, but held it unlit in his hand. An unfortunate piece of business, that, and poorly timed. Holwell had let his perversions get out of hand—not for the first time—and the girl had nearly died. During her recovery, she had "found God" and when she was well enough to walk again, she had walked right into Fleming's office when no one was watching, and had stolen an accounting ledger from his desk, to use as insurance, no doubt. Inside the ledger were lists of names—lawyers, judges, assay clerks, even politicians who were not averse to accepting bribes in exchange for turning a blind eye to certain land transactions and political maneuverings. Men like himself who had seen the wisdom of acquiring land and water rights in the fertile Pecos Valley. Men who turned unprofitable farmland and fouled sheep pastures into vast ranges for grazing cattle. Men who would sooner shoot a homesteader than tolerate so much as a mile of barbed wire fencing.

Governor Axtell's name was in the ledger. So were the names of most of the prominent citizens in the county. Fleming's own tracks were covered well enough, but there were some entries his "partners" might not understand. Or appreciate. Even a rumor of the ledger's existence could have far-reaching repercussions. There were already reports that the army was starting to poke its nose where it wasn't wanted. Ex-soldiers driven off the plots of land promised them at the end of the war were screaming foul. Envoys from Washington were beginning to question court verdicts, to investigate the shootings and lynchings that were the mainstay of keeping the sodbusters under control.

Holwell had tracked the girl to a nearby mission where she had taken refuge with Fray Rodriguez, a self-righteous, self-appointed savior of the poor and down-trodden. Scud had retrieved the ledger and silenced the girl, but had been uncharacteristically sloppy in trusting the fire to finish off the priest. Only one charred corpse had been found in the wreckage; the priest had taken a week to track down and silence permanently. For his sloppiness, Fleming had ordered Holwell to stay away from Santa Fe until he was sent for; a dressing-down he would not take in the best of spirits.

"Was there something else, boss?"

Fleming had been unaware of letting his mind drift. "As a matter of fact, there is. Tell Billy I have a job for him. There's a woman I want him to check out for me. She calls herself Aubrey Blue and she came in a week ago on the Kansas line, same coach as Miss Royale. I want to know where she's staying, who she sees, where she eats, *what* she eats . . . in other words, everything about her. I want to know everything about Miss Aubrey Blue, and I want to know it by Saturday night."

17

"Think this might be of any use to you, honey?"

Aubrey turned from the window, her face softly illuminated by the glow of lantern light outside. That same glow sparked along the thin steel blade of the knife Dolores was holding out to her.

"Them damn Mex's sure know how to enjoy themselves, don't they?" she asked, peering over Aubrey's shoulder. The street outside the shop was ablaze with lights and music. There had been a wedding that afternoon and most of Old Santa Fe was helping the happy couple celebrate. The *caballeros* were decked head to toe in their finery; embroidered jackets stiff with fancy braid and barrel buttons, tight-fitting *calzones* flared from knee to ankle glittered at the seams with tinsel lace and filigree beads. The women, not to be outdone, wore wide, multilayered skirts frothed by crinolines of lace and taffeta. Bodices were cut daringly low, hair piled impossibly high and held in place by sparkling tiaras and fountaining *mantillas*.

Aubrey dropped the curtain back in place and took the dirk from Dolores's hand. It was sharp and deadly, with an abalone-shell handle that reflected all the colors of the rainbow.

"I'm not very good with knives," she confessed, turning the blade over in her palm.

"What's to be good or bad about? Stick a knife 'tween a man's legs and they tend to think good and hard about saying or doing anything that don't set right with you. And you can always cut 'em a little, by accident, to show you mean business. It won't hurt none to take it along, whether you need it or not . . . and besides, it's more a lady's weapon than that there squint-sized pepper box you carry around with you."

"All right." Aubrey smiled. "Thank you."

Dolores planted her hands on her hips. "I reckon this means you're bound and determined to go through with this? I haven't managed to talk you out of it?"

"You gave it a good try, but no. I'm bound and determined."

"Hmphf." Dolores thrust out her jaw in a fairly good imitation of Stink Finger Jim confronting one of his recalcitrant mules. "Well, I guess if you have to do it, you have to do it and nothing shy of hitting you over the head with a cast-iron fry pan is gonna have any effect. You all ready underneath?"

Aubrey shed the wrapper she was wearing. The pantalets and chemise Dolores had provided were pale blue silk, so sheer and cool against Aubrey's skin they made her shiver. Her stockings were black, held up above the knees by blue velvet garters. Dolores had fussed an hour over Aubrey's hair, using tongs and hot crimping irons to arrange a spill of glossy curls that fell from crown to nape, leaving a few blue-black ringlets draped seductively over her shoulder.

"Grab hold of the doorjamb, then, and hang on tight."

Aubrey did as she was told, bracing herself as Dolores

settled a whalebone corset around her waist and started pulling the laces tight.

"Never thought I'd see the day a gal would come along skinny as Marita Gonzales. Guess it's a good thing for you she up and died before she could collect all the frocks and things she ordered. Suck it in, gal, suck it in."

"I'm sucking," Aubrey said through her teeth. "Any more, and I'll have no ribs left."

Dolores chuckled. "Under twenty inches she was, and ate like a pig. You ain't done so bad in that department either, come to think of it. That's probably why you're havin' so much trouble now."

The trouble, Aubrey thought, was that Dolores had thought to save some time, effort, and materials—while charging Bruster for all three—by squeezing Aubrey into a trunkload of dresses she'd had stored for six months. The gowns were beautiful, no denying, but Aubrey hadn't had a twenty-inch waist since her early years.

"Up," she ordered, nudging Aubrey's arms.

Aubrey inhaled slowly and tried to stabilize the fog of stars swimming in front of her eyes. She raised her arms dutifully, however, and the room disappeared briefly under a billow of linen petticoats. They were tied by ribbons to the corset cover, then gathered flat across the stomach and pinned at the rear to add even more volume over the wire bustle.

"Not bad," Dolores declared, standing back to admire her work. The corset had effectively reduced Aubrey's waist to nothing while pushing her breasts so high they looked about ready to pop out of the chemise. "Up again."

Aubrey raised her arms a second time and felt the slippery satin of the gown float over her shoulders and settle around her waist. It was dark sapphire blue in color, with sprigs of sequined flowers following the alarming décolleté of the bodice and edging the sleeves, which were short and fit like caps over her shoulders. The satin hugged her waist and lay in draped folds over her stomach and hips, the fullness gathered over the bustle and accented by more clusters of glittering flowers.

From Aubrey's viewpoint, all she could see was the aggrandized plumpness of her breasts.

"Marita had a snap less fullness there than you do," Dolores agreed dryly, "but you'll be fine so long as you don't plan on bending over and touching your toes."

The image was so incongruous, Aubrey laughed. The excitement sparkled in her eyes and, for a moment, Lily Cruise Montana felt a rush of pure envy.

"Damn, I wish I was going in there with you. I wish . . . well, never mind what I wish, I just wish it, is all. You got your rings?"

Aubrey wiggled her fingers so that the gold and semi-precious stones winked in the lamplight.

"And everything else you might need?"

Aubrey bent over—carefully—and picked the .22 derringer off the table. She slid back the barrel and double-checked that it carried loads in all four chambers, then slipped it into the special pocket Dolores had sewn near the hem of the skirt. There were also two decks of cards on the table. After seeing the brand Fleming used at the Golden Eagle, Bruster had purchased a couple of "cold decks," which Aubrey had painstakingly marked in some small way so that, even under Dolores's penetrating stare, she could pick every card in the pack and call it without missing a one.

"You maybe shouldn't take them with you tonight," Dolores advised. "You'll have to run as square a table as you can the first few nights. Some of them hot-ass sharps might take offense to a pretty thing like you horning in on their territory. They might even take it to mind to turn you end over end and see what falls out alongside your family jewels."

"If anyone tries to turn me end over end, they'll earn all four barrels for their trouble."

Dolores cackled and nodded, her stiff red curls bouncing like wood shavings. "Still and all, the more honest you look and play, the bigger the suckers you hook. Hook 'em good the first few nights, and you'll be reeling 'em in regular after that. *Not* that anyone will be looking any higher than your neck the blessed night long anyway. Maybe we should tuck a bit of lace down front so you don't catch your death of a cold from all that heavy breathing."

Aubrey went to stand in front of the cheval mirror. Having worn only modest cotton blouses and dull colors over the past few weeks, seeing bare flesh and a voluptuously molded figure was a shock. She reached up and ran her fingers lightly across the ruffle of sequined flowers and, for one wild moment, wondered what Christian McBride would think if he saw her dressed like this.

She was still staring when Dolores pinched her on the arm.

"What is it, gal? You look like you just swallowed a mouthful of ripe jalapeños."

"I . . . I think you're right. Perhaps it needs something."

"Mmmm." Dolores studied the flush crawling up Aubrey's throat and frowned. "I might have just the thing. Don't move; I'll be back in a spit."

Aubrey turned slowly back to face her reflection. McBride's face was still there, the cynical half-smile curling his lips, the light in his eyes harsh and critical. The heat was still there as well, deepening the flush in her cheeks, causing a shortness of breath that had nothing to do with the lacings of her corset.

"Here! Land sakes, child, you're as jumpy as a cat.

Now isn't this just the prettiest thing you ever saw? It's one of the few things Lucius never got his fat hands on and was never able to toss into a pot or gamble away on a bad throw of dice."

Dolores tied a cameo broach, pinned on a deep blue velvet ribbon, around Aubrey's neck and stood back to admire the effect.

"Perfect," she pronounced. "And you've got your gold piece tucked in your shoe for luck? All you need, then, is a quick toast and a *hasta la vista, vaya con Dios,* and all that crap. Don't take no plugged nickels, don't take your eyes off the table, and never, ever, play against a hand holding a one-eyed jack."

Aubrey accepted the glass of cordial and smiled over the rim, her gaze straying back to the mirror. Hers was the only face she saw, and she looked exactly the way she felt—strong and confident and comfortable in the knowledge that success was finally within her grasp.

•

Aubrey stood in the entrance of the Golden Eagle, every nerve in her body tingling, every drop of blood in her veins singing with excitement. The saloon, sumptuous to excess when she had seen it nearly empty, was teeming now with men from every walk of life. Well-heeled, respectable-looking ranchers stood beside rough miners in dirty old flannel shirts, and Mexicans wrapped in their blankets smoking cigaritas stood next to cowboys spitting and chewing and gambling away their wages. The curtains on the stage were open and held aside by thick gold cords. A raucous group of six musicians in striped shirts and red pants were banging out an energetic version of "Goldpan Annie."

All of the tables were occupied, with men elbowing their way this way and that trying to find a likely place to gamble some of the silver dollars they shuffled restlessly from hand to hand. There were tables of roulette, black-jack, faro, and vingt-et-un. And special booths where men could change the bulk of coins or gold dust they carried into red and white playing chips. The bar was just as cramped with the greedy and unwashed. Cowboys lolled over their whiskeys and tried to haggle the working girls down from their quoted rates. Gamblers took a breather from their games to partake of the platters of free food set out on long wooden tables.

The air was hazy from the quantity of tobacco smoked and strongly impregnated with the fumes of whiskey. The chandeliers glittered. Shaded lamps in the alcoves pulsated a muted red. The mirrors behind the bar seemed to double the length and breadth of the already cavernous interior, while at the far end of the room, a half-circle of ornate brass footlamps cast giant shadows of the musicians against the garishly painted background scenery.

"Miss Blue?"

Aubrey gave a small start and turned to find a young, towheaded gunslinger standing beside her. His hair had been neatly and precisely parted down the middle and slicked flat with neat's foot oil, but there were one or two stubborn licks that stood straight up at the crown, like quills on a porcupine. He appeared to be noticeably uncomfortable in a starched white shirt and gold braid jacket.

"William Bonney, ma'am. Mr. Fleming asked me to keep an eye out for you and to show you into his private salon when you got here."

"His private salon?"

"Yes, ma'am. Near everyone else is there already . . . if you'd like to foller me . . . ?"

Aubrey did not move. "Who is . . . everyone else?"

"Why, Mr. Fleming's invited a passel of real important folks tonight on account of it's Miz Royale's opening night. The guv'nor's here, the mayor, the sheriff . . ."

Aubrey had almost forgotten about Magenta Royale's much heralded debut, and William Bonney was looking at her as if she had just emerged from a winter's hibernation.

"I, er, didn't expect to be included among his . . . real important folks."

Bonney grinned, shaving another five years off his face. "Well, hell, I reckon he just thought, since you and Miz Royale traveled here on the same stage and all, that you'd be a friendly face in the crowd. Kind of to relax her, you know?"

Aubrey refrained from smiling. Hers would be a familiar face in the crowd, all right, but whether or not Magenta would regard it as being friendly, or comforting, was another matter altogether.

Mention of friendly faces in the crowd prompted Aubrey to steal a moment to glance past Bonney's shoulder and scan the sea of Stetsons and derbys. Bruster was nowhere in sight.

"Ma'am?"

"Lead the way, Mr. Bonney; I'm right behind you."

Billy started toward the stairs. Where others had difficulty passing through the heavy congestion of gamblers, Aubrey noted that neither she nor Billy Bonney had any trouble at all. Granted, a few of the men gave way out of respect for the amount of cleavage passing by, but most saw only Billy and stepped quickly aside to avoid catching the lanky youth's eye.

As they climbed the stairs to the second floor, Aubrey noted the four additional gunmen posted around the upper balcony. They wore sidearms and carried rifles slung in the crooks of their arms. None of them looked as if they had cracked a smile since infancy; all of them noticed her progress up the stairs with open curiosity.

At the carved double doors, Billy turned and tugged on a forelock.

"I'll leave you here, ma'am, if you don't mind. I don't cotton much to strangers, and for some reason"—he grinned and winked broadly—"they don't cotton much to me."

"So you're deserting me, are you, Mr. Bonney?"

"Oh no, ma'am. Mr. Fleming said I was to watch out for you the whole night long. I'll be right downstairs when you need me." His pale eyes slid into the soft, deep vee of her bodice and he blushed a painful red. "And I'd be real obliged, Miss Blue, if you'd just call me Billy. Hell, I won't even punch you out none if you call me Kid."

"I'm relieved to hear it," she said, disarmed again by his smile. "But I think I can manage to remember 'Billy.' "

He raised his eyes with an effort and gave a wistful nod to the guard at the door. Aubrey walked through and started down the hall, following the sound of voices and laughter. On her way, she passed the closed door on her left marked OFFICE and noted, farther along, a second door with no markings at all. But on her right, wide doors were opened to a large, elegantly decorated drawing room, complete with fireplace and chandeliers, a half-dozen settles and chairs placed in cozy groupings. Aubrey paused at the entrance, struck by the fact that there was no other apparent exit from the hallway or the room; no way in or out without passing the guard at the outer doors.

"Ahh, Miss Blue." Fleming strolled away from the group of men he had been talking to and greeted Aubrey at the door. "I was beginning to wonder if you'd changed your mind, but if you come into my casino looking as lovely as this every evening, you may be as tardy as you please."

Aubrey allowed him to take her hand and press it to his lips. He was impressively dressed in dark blue trousers and jacket, his lean form flattered by the addition of a silver brocade vest embroidered with tiny green vines. The diamond stud glittered in his earlobe, competing with the oily sparkle of his small white teeth.

"Do come in and join us," he invited. "I'm afraid Magenta has not yet deigned to grace us with her presence but, hopefully, some time before midnight, she will."

His guests offered hearty laughs, as they were expected to do. There were a score of men and five or six women, the latter gowned and bejeweled for an audience with royalty.

"Miss Blue," Fleming explained to those closest, "is a personal friend of Miss Royale's. They traveled west on the same coach and had the good fortune to survive the associated perils together. Miss Blue will also be working for me, although not on stage, and not"—he crooked an eyebrow in response to the immediate surge of interest in several of the men's eyes—"at the bar."

"Ee-gods, man, what's left then? Surely not the kitchens!"

Fleming turned to the speaker, one of the gentlemen he had been talking to when Aubrey had arrived. "Surely not, Samuel. It might interest you to know she has the coolest poker face I have seen since"—He looked speculatively at Aubrey—"since Lily Cruise Montana worked the coast back in '64."

Aubrey met his gaze and saw the subtle arch to his brow, and she knew he had not simply mentioned the name by coincidence. That and the fact that Billy Bonney had known her on sight suggested Fleming was a very thorough man indeed. It would be interesting to know if he had wired Kansas City to verify her story about having to depart in somewhat of a hurry.

"A lady gambler?" The gentleman's snow-white moustache bristled over a smile. "How sporting of you, Maxwell. A diversion to take the sting away while one is being divested of one's hard-earned cash."

Fleming laughed. "And she is going to be under my express orders to divest you of every penny you possess, Samuel, and to show no mercy for your age or your position. Miss Aubrey Blue, may I present our governor —and my personal friend—Mr. Samuel Axtell. Samuel . . . Miss Blue."

"Delighted." The governor took Aubrey's hand in his and stroked a thumb over her slender fingers. He was sallow-skinned where once he must have been robust, with a blustery frame turned to soft fat by the excesses of an easy life. "You will of course permit me to be the first to be fleeced by so pretty a pair of hands?"

"It would be my pleasure," she said, dimpling her cheeks.

Fleming, observing, felt another jolt—swifter and fiercer than the one he had experienced the first time he had seen Aubrey Blue. On that occasion she had been modestly elegant, unsettling him by appearing to be so obviously at odds with her surroundings and her purported profession. Lavender velvet and delicate gray kid gloves had left an impression, but one that was savagely erased by the shimmering, low-cut sapphire satin. The color of the gown brought out the hue and sparkle of her eyes; the sensual expanse of creamy white flesh across her shoulders and breasts made the breath scorch along his throat and burn into his lungs.

Only once before had he seen such exquisite perfection. Only once. A woman who was as beautiful dressed in rags as she was in silks and fur. Fleming had come as close to loving her as he could have loved any woman, but his lust for her had been preempted by his lust for land and wealth and power. She hadn't understood his needs, nor supported his efforts; her fire and spirit had waned and proved too weak a match for his own.

There was fire in Aubrey Blue. And spirit. Enough to make his hand tremble slightly as he indicated a table nearby stocked with bottles of wine and brandy.

"May I offer you some refreshments? Something light, perhaps? Champagne?"

"Just some lemonade, if you have it. I prefer not to drink when I'm working."

"Lemonade it is."

A dark-haired man standing close by had turned at the sound of Fleming's voice. He glanced casually at Aubrey, then looked again, long and hard, his eyes raking her from top to bottom, then climbing slowly and deliberately to the top again.

"Well I'll be my great-granddaddy's uncle," he grinned. "It's the schoolteacher!"

18

"Mr. Greaves," Aubrey said tautly. "What a surprise."

The ebony eyes moved insolently across her bared shoulders and paused over the half-moons of her breasts. "Miss Blue. I hardly recognized you. May I assume you have recovered from our little travail out on the desert?"

"I am adapting."

Greaves himself was resplendent in a suit of dark gray broadcloth. He looked tanned and healthy and remarkably sober for nine-thirty in the evening. Fastened to his arm like an ornament was the same Oriental beauty Aubrey had seen with Fleming at the stage depot, and she could only surmise that he had been given a new toy with which to amuse himself and thus keep out of Fleming's way.

"Have you seen Magenta yet?" Greaves asked, not bothering to reintroduce Anna Lee.

"No," Aubrey said. "I have not yet had the pleasure."

"Pleasure?" His smirk broadened. "The pleasure is going to be all mine, believe me. I, uh, suppose it's a little late to be asking this now, but . . . just what the hell do you teach, Miss Blue?"

"Greaves," Fleming said quietly. "Why don't you go and see what is taking Magenta so long? She has been keeping my guests waiting for almost two hours already."

Greaves laughed and shook his head. "I make it a firm rule never to go near sweet Clara when she's preparing for a performance. *Especially* an opening night performance. She has been known to scream the curls out of a pickaninny's hair for preparing her bathwater too hot, and the devil take pity on the man who squeezes too much lemon in her throat wash."

The chiseled jaw tensed and Aubrey had the feeling this was not the first time "sweet Clara's" foibles had grated on Fleming's nerves.

"Nevertheless, I suggest you—"

Whatever he had been about to say was lost under a sudden and thunderous ovation. All eyes in the room were directed at the doorway, where a golden-haired vision in bright crimson silk was standing . . . or posing, as it would appear. Every inch of the watered silk gown dripped beads and sequins. The bodice plunged in a deeply curved slash almost to her waist, making it impossible to conceive of there being any garments concealed beneath. The glittering sheath of beaded fabric molded to her hips and thighs, and was cut in an equally revealing swath from hem to knee—a necessary device to enable her to walk. The blond curls were piled high on her head, surmounted by ostrich plumes dyed the same shocking red as her gown.

Magenta Royale, Jewel of New Orleans, held out an imperious hand and waited for Fleming to cross the room to greet her. The guests were still applauding and Magenta accepted their accolades with a regal bowing of her head. She rested the merest tips of her fingers on Fleming's arm and undulated into the center of the room, sequins flashing with every step, her eyes roving the rapt faces with a haughty benevolence that implied she could have been anywhere else in the world, but instead, had chosen these few lucky mortals to grace with her presence.

As Greaves had done, Magenta skipped past Aubrey, dismissing her in favor of playing to the ogling eyes of the men. She was, in fact, midway through her introduction to the governor when Aubrey saw the amber eyes widen and move slowly back to where she stood in the corner.

Disbelief. Shock. Curiosity. And finally, rage. Each reaction was imprinted on Magenta's features, the last one lingering the longest and bringing the slow heat of color into her cheeks. To her credit, however, she carried on through the introductions, smiling and greeting each guest in turn; laughing at their stammered flattery, forgetting names and positions as soon as she moved to the next in line. By the time she had made a circuit of the room, the heat of her anger had turned frosty cold, and she was able to address Aubrey with a measure of control.

"Of course, you already know Miss Blue," Fleming said, bringing the two women together.

"Of course. The schoolteacher."

Aubrey smiled. "I'm afraid—as I was telling Mr. Fleming—I have been guilty of a small deception. I was rather pressed for time when I left Kansas and thought it best not to draw too much attention to myself. Posing as a schoolteacher seemed harmless enough, although, since I knew you had seen through my disguise from the outset, I must thank you for keeping my sorry secret."

Magenta's venom was effectively staunched with the flattery over her perception. However, it was well worth the cut Aubrey gave to the inside of her lip to see the expression on the songstress's face as she added, "And now that we'll be working together, I just know we can become even better friends than we were on the Trail."

"Working together? Maxwell . . . what does she mean: *working together?*"

"She means I have given her a job here in the casino, as a dealer at one of the tables. She has promised"—he looked at Aubrey and a strange softness came into his voice—"to make herself indispensable to me."

If it was possible for Magenta to become even more incensed, she did. Tiny flecks of hatred came to life in the depths of her eyes and her skin turned as white as chalk beneath the heavy layering of stage makeup. Fleming's eyes came alive as well—with surprise and alarm. He hadn't anticipated a cat fight, and was not about to jeopardize his star's opening night performance with a temperamental fit of jealousy.

"Ladies and gentlemen—if I might have your attention for one more moment before we adjourn downstairs? As you know—" He took Magenta by the arm and gently steered her toward the middle of the room. "I have been awaiting the arrival of Miss Magenta Royale with no small measure of pride and excitement. Luring such an exquisite talent this far west was no small feat either, I might add, and, what with the calamity of an Indian attack on top of the usual perils one encounters on the trail west, we are indeed honored and awed by Miss Royale's commitment and dedication to her profession.

"I realized at once that Miss Royale would unquestionably become the crowning jewel on the stage of the Golden Eagle, dazzling in her own right, to be sure, and yet"—he reached to an inside pocket of his jacket and withdrew a slim leather case—"in need of a crowning jewel of her own."

He opened the slim box and Magenta's gasp was not entirely theatrical. Nestled on a cushion of pure white velvet was a broach, the center stone a square-cut emerald as large as a hen's egg, framed in a halo of diamonds, each better than a carat in size. It had been threaded onto a black velvet ribbon, which Fleming lifted out of the box and proceeded to drape around Magenta's throat.

It was one of the most difficult challenges in Magenta's acting career to refrain from clapping her hands and squealing in glee, but she managed it, her cheeks flushed and her breasts laboring under the strain. Aubrey's cheeks reddened as well, then drained just as quickly to a bloodless, waxen cast as she stared at the emerald broach. It was the same broach—*there could be no mistaking it*—her mother had taken out of its delicate filigreed box on special occasions and allowed her to hold it up to the sunlight to see the sparks of green fire burning in its depths. It was the same broach Luisa Granger had died trying to preserve for her daughter. The same broach Aubrey had last seen being slipped into the filthy pants pocket of Scud Holwell.

Aubrey shivered. The sweet lemonade she had sipped turned bitterly sour in her stomach and came halfway up her throat in rebellion. She set her glass down in haste and, while the others were flocking closer to Magenta to inspect the beautiful broach, Aubrey hastened toward the door.

"Miss Blue?"

Fleming's voice.

She stopped and closed her eyes briefly, willing her expression blank.

"A true gambler's spirit, I see," he murmured. "Anxious to buck the tiger, are you?"

"I'm . . . anxious to make up for lost time, Mr. Fleming. Gambling is my livelihood after all, and I do have rent to pay at the end of the week."

"Ah yes, Lily Montana. Or should I call her Doña

Dolores? An odd choice of rooming houses, I must say."

Aubrey offered what she hoped was a casual shrug. "A mutual friend from back east gave me her name and suggested I look her up when I got here. It isn't the most ideal arrangement, I agree, but it's quiet and the rent is fair."

"Why don't you take a room in my hotel?" he suggested. "I can promise you the rent will be more than fair, and you won't have to walk through half of Old Santa Fe to get here."

"Why don't we see how things work out first? Who knows, you may fire me after a few nights. You may fire me after tonight if I don't get downstairs and start to earn my wages."

Fleming reached out as she turned to leave. His grip on her arm was firmer than necessary, but it eased after only a moment and changed into something more like a caress.

"I doubt very much if I'll fire you, Miss Blue. Not until I know a good deal more about you, at any rate."

Aubrey risked a glance up into the strangely mesmerizing eyes. She hoped he did not feel her shudder of revulsion as his fingers stroked her arm, or, if he did, that he interpreted her reaction as something other than the deep and utter loathing it was.

•

Fleming had wanted her to start with three-card monte, not so much because he did not believe she was capable of drawing poker players or running a large table of faro, but because he did not want to upset the balance of power with his other dealers. Newcomers usually began with a monte table and if they lasted a full week without being shot or tarred and feathered as a sharp, they were accepted by the others with good humor and hearty wishes for good luck in the future. There were occasional personality clashes between gamblers, each insisting he was the best at his game. These disputes were settled in marathon games that lasted four and five days, or, more simply still, with a bullet.

Aubrey's practiced eye could spot the professionals at each table and a few moments' study revealed their peculiar methods. The man who stared intently at the back of his opponent's hands had probably added secret marks to the design of the cards that would identify each number and suit. Other sharps imperceptibly felt the edge of each card as it was dealt, looking for the subtle scratches or watermarks they had used to distinguish the high-value cards. Their fingers would be sandpapered to the point of drawing blood, so that they would not miss a scrape or puncture. Still others used holdouts, devices that secreted extra aces up the sleeve of a jacket, or held them tucked under the lip of the table.

Aubrey could see the mechanics so plainly it was always a wonder to her that the other ninety-nine percent of a gaming hall's clientele could not. Even Bruster, who was intimately familiar with most methods known for cheating at cards, was a blind sucker when it came to faro. With his pockets bulging with winnings from monte, poker, and vingt-et-un, he would be fleeced as neatly as any tinhorn yokel as soon as he sidled up to a faro table. Gambling was in his blood and he could no more have lived without it than he could live without air, whereas Aubrey never gambled without a purpose, and she would be quite blissfully happy if she never had to pick up a deck of cards again.

She half-expected to see Bruster firmly entrenched at a faro table now, but she was wrong. He was standing at the bar sampling the various tidbits of food he had loaded onto his plate. He had seen her descending the stairs and had acknowledged her faint nod by adjusting the broad triangle of the napkin he had tucked into his collar.

Aubrey twisted her hands together as she made her way toward her booth. The encounter with Greaves and Magenta, not to mention seeing her mother's emerald broach sparkling around another woman's throat, had turned the contents of her belly liquid. Her hands felt cold and clammy, her mouth was dry with an unaccustomed nervousness. George, the bartender, handed her an unopened deck of cards and stared hard down the front of her dress. The booth was empty, but the soft sheen of sapphire satin soon drew curious eyes and strolling players to her table.

She started out slowly, knowing the men were more attracted to the oddity of a woman dealer than they were to the prospect of laying any serious bets. They laughed good-humoredly when she shuffled the cards and her anxiety caused them to scatter across the table-top. They laughed again when she executed a poorly turned sleight of hand and lost twenty dollars to her own clumsiness.

The ancestor of three-card monte was the shell game, played with three walnut shells and a pea. The operator put the pea on the table and covered it with one of the half shells then placed the two extras on either side. He then moved the shells back and forth, over and around, shuffling their positions as quickly as his hands could manipulate the shells. When he stopped, he invited the onlookers to bet on the shell most likely to be concealing the pea.

Three-card monte worked on the same principle, only using two low cards and a "winner" for placing bets.

"You will have to forgive me, gentlemen, if I am a little nervous tonight. It is my first night working here and I've been told I have to make a good impression."

"You've already made a fine impression with me, little lady," one of the onlookers chuckled, his eyes fixed firmly to her bodice. "But that don't mean I won't take your money all the same."

Aubrey sighed, tried to ignore her churning stomach, and started into her patter. "Very well, gentlemen, here you have the queen of hearts; the winning card. Watch it closely, follow it with your eyes as I move it around the table. Here it is"—she stopped shifting the cards and flipped the one on the left—"and now here"—she turned it up again on the right—"and now . . . oh." She turned up the card on the left again, plainly expecting to see the queen, and flushed when a round of guffaws greeted the lowly two of spades.

Her next shuffle was better, quicker, but she still lost track of the queen, and her carelessness cost her another ten dollars. The callous laughter that greeted her ineptness began to grate on her nerves. It also began to draw the unwanted attention of the bartender, and a few of Fleming's men who were watching the proceedings with a critical eye. Laughter and ten-dollar bets were not going to win her any accolades over the course of an evening.

"Fine," she said, moistening her lips. "Who will bet me twenty this time?"

"Twenty? Darlin', you can earn yourself an easier twenty by leading the way to the back rooms."

Aubrey glared at the outspoken player and smiled tightly. "I have to play for twenty dollars. If you lay your bet and pick the right card, you beat me. If not, I beat you and take your money. Twenty dollars, sir. Twenty to take the chance."

Bruster's short, stout, moustachioed figure pushed forward, wiping his chin with the large white napkin. "I'll take that bet, my dear. I've no qualms about making easy money tonight. Twenty it is. Let the lovely lady of hearts dance."

Aubrey maneuvered the cards and lost again. Bruster waved aside the twenty-dollar gold piece she produced from her cache and let it ride with the one he had played previously. Aubrey slid the cards back and forth and let Bruster choose where he supposed the queen of hearts to be, but before letting him turn the card, she clapped a hand over his wrist and smiled defiantly. "I'm obliged for your participation, *sir,* but you wouldn't care to double your bet again, sight unseen, would you?"

The men exchanged looks and smirks and for the first time, began to pay more attention to the money being wagered—and won—than to the velvety soft cleft between her breasts.

"Done," Bruster said and flipped the card. He crowed delightedly at the sight of the queen of hearts and started fishing in his pockets for more money.

Aubrey scowled and glared at the cards. "I don't understand," she muttered. "I've heard of bad luck before, but this is ridiculous."

"Well, before it changes," Bruster chuckled, "I should like to double the stakes again . . . er, if you are willing, that is."

Aubrey looked up sharply. She also glanced sidelong at the bartender, her expression clearly torn between cutting her losses and calling it an early evening, or remaining and having to explain her ineptness to the humorless George.

Bruster, meanwhile, took advantage of her distraction and, moving his hands almost too quickly to see, flicked a thumbnail over the edge of the queen, marking it plainly for everyone around the table to see. With a broad wink to his fellow conspirators, he cleared his throat and drew Aubrey's attention back to the three cards.

"Well, my dear? Play up or . . . as this gentleman previously suggested . . . find yourself an easier way of earning a living and leave the big games to the big boys."

Aubrey's lips set into a grim line. "I'll cover your bet, sir. Keep your eyes on the cards—*if you can.*"

This time, with the queen of hearts plainly marked, Aubrey's loss drew more silence than mockery. Avarice and greed began to erase any traces of sympathy the men might have been feeling for the beautiful lady gambler. She was obviously an amateur and there was a killing to be made before the bartender signaled someone to have her removed or replaced.

"How much you got left in that there pretty purse of yours, little lady?" a gruff individual asked.

Aubrey had to tear her eyes away from the sizable column of gold coins vanishing into Bruster's pockets.

"Excuse me?"

"I said . . . how much you got left to wager?"

"I . . . I don't know exactly," she whispered.

The man grinned and reached into his pocket. "Well, I got me sixteen hundred in cold cash here—" He slapped a sheaf of bills on the table. "Fifteen to cover a bet, and an extra hundred to cover *you* for the rest of the night."

Aubrey's hand trembled visibly as she pressed it over the cameo at her throat.

"Well?" He arched a brow. "Like you said before, I pick the wrong card, you win. I pick the right card, I win the money, and you . . . win a damn fine recommendation to your boss from me."

The other gamblers laughed enviously along with the speaker. Aubrey took a firm grip on herself and reached down to start shifting the cards. Her hand movements were sharper, angrier, but it made no difference to the gambler who followed the faintly notched card to the center, to the left, to the right . . .

When she stopped, he drew a deep breath and stabbed a triumphant finger at the marked card. Aubrey turned it, her eyes closed over a murmur of words that were half prayer, half curse, and when she opened them again, she could not stifle the cry of relief when the upturned card proved to be the four of clubs.

The gambler snatched the card out of her hand. "Wait a minute! This is the wrong card! This isn't the same one he—" He caught himself a breath away from admitting he had seen Bruster mark the card and had been trying to take advantage. Moreover, when he looked down at the other two cards, he could see that they both now bore the same faint notch in the corner.

"The wrong card?" Aubrey blinked her eyes, all innocence and confusion. "But you picked it out yourself, sir. You set the terms of the wager and you chose the card yourself."

The gambler looked at the card in his hand, then at the faces of the dozen or so men around him. The short, fat peddler was nowhere in sight, nor was there any sympathy or support on the expressions of the others. The laughter was turned on him this time, and since he could not very well accuse Aubrey of cheating when he had been attempting to cheat her himself, he had no recourse but to quietly pay up the sixteen hundred dollars.

Aubrey acknowledged the man's angry stare with a faint tilt of her eyebrow. She tucked the money into her purse and discarded the three marked cards with a small smirk of disdain. She shuffled the remaining cards in the deck with an expertise that left the gamblers smiling, then fanned three new cards onto the table: a ten, a three, and the one-eyed jack.

"For certain, an unlucky card," she laughed. "Shall we try again?"

She was about to drop the three cards in the discard bin when a large, tanned hand reached out and caught her wrist.

"I happen to find jacks extremely lucky, ma'am. Maybe you'd make an exception for me?"

Aubrey froze at the sound of the all-too-familiar baritone. Her gaze was equally reluctant to make the long journey from his hand to his elbow to his shoulder to his face; noting at each stage the absence of soft leather buckskins, the lack of gleaming twin Peacemakers, the missing wide-brimmed hat with its sweat-stained band of braided thongs.

The Christian McBride who returned her stare was tailored and refined, handsome enough in his dark brown broadcoat and fawn trousers to draw the openly interested smiles of several of the painted beauties working in the saloon.

19

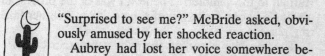

"Surprised to see me?" McBride asked, obviously amused by her shocked reaction.

Aubrey had lost her voice somewhere between recognition and recollection of their last meeting. Waves of heat and cold washed through her. She felt dizzy, unsettled, sick. She fought hard to bring a deep lungful of air to her rescue, but the whalebone stays prevented her from taking more than rapidly shallow gasps. His hand was warm and firm around her wrist, causing a multitude of conflicting responses to shiver up her arm: fear, panic, suspicion, uncertainty, and, most unnerving of all, excitement.

She could feel the blush holding fast in her cheeks as they continued to stare across the silence. His tawny hair had been tamed by scissors and curled softly along the curve of his throat. His eyes were clear and bright, his smile never more charming or seductive. His clothing accented the breadth of his shoulders and the leanness of his waist; his shirt was as white as the slash of his teeth, the cuffs and front placket an elegant, ruffled contrast to his dark skin.

Aubrey's lips parted on yet another helpless gasp and she saw him, not as he stood before her now, but as he had stood before her on the moonlit banks of the Cimarron, naked and virile, a threat beyond all conceivable proportions.

"I should have known you would not have the good grace to stay away from me, McBride," she said, finding her tongue at last.

"How, in all conscience, Miss Blue, could I have done that?"

"Hey." A couple of the gamblers were becoming restless. "Are we going to play cards or hold a reunion?"

Christian's grin remained relaxed and easy as he turned to the gambler. "I believe I was in the process of calling a bet on jacks, but of course, if you'd rather take my place . . . ?"

The gambler absorbed the subtle undercurrent of a threat in McBride's smile and wisely backed off. "Can we get on with it then and stop jawing?"

McBride turned back to Aubrey. "Miss Blue? I said I preferred to chase the jack, if you didn't mind."

Aubrey gently twisted her wrist out of his grip. "I don't mind how you lose your money, *sir.* Place your bet."

McBride set a fifty-dollar gold piece on the table. Aubrey centered the jack between the ten of diamonds and the three of hearts. She turned them facedown and began shifting them back and forth, positioning and repositioning the three cards until she was satisfied they were confusingly misplaced. McBride, still smiling, reached forward and pointed at the card on the left, shrugging good-naturedly when Aubrey triumphantly upturned the three of hearts.

Another gold piece glittered on the table and Aubrey shifted the cards again, vindictively taking McBride's money as he picked wrong a second time. His third and fourth attempts were no more successful, and by the fifth, Aubrey's sense of victory was giving way to anger as it became obvious that he was miscalling on purpose. A sixth and seventh gold coin was added to her cache before her patience expired on a sigh. "Isn't there some other game you would prefer to play, *sir*?"

"My money isn't good at this table?"

Aubrey looked around in exasperation. The group of men had thinned considerably, the serious gamblers moving on to tables not monopolized by one player.

"McBride—"

"Yes, Miss Blue?"

He looked at her in a way that made her limbs go molten, his eyes holding hers, questioning, accusing, and finally freeing her with a blink of the dark lashes.

"Fifty dollars is the bet," he said quietly.

"No."

"Excuse me?"

She snatched up the three cards and threw them in the discard bin along with the rest of the deck. "I'm taking a short break now. You'll have to find some other way to amuse yourself."

She moved away from the table and pushed through the crowds of gamblers until she had gained the bar. Her heart was pounding in her chest and her ribs felt like they were being crushed inward. If she didn't get a deep breath of fresh air soon, she genuinely feared she might drop into a dead faint.

George, acting out of habit, set a shotglass of brandy on the bar in front of her. Aubrey stared at it for a moment, then picked it up and swallowed the contents in a single gulp, welcoming the rush of sweet fire into her belly. She signaled for a refill and downed it just as easily, aware of the looming presence of McBride behind her, his reflection mirrored in the gilded glass behind the bar.

"Why are you doing this?" she hissed. "Why can't you just go away and leave me alone?"

"I told you: I'm a curious man. You were so eager to reach Santa Fe, so adamant about wanting to better your position in life—" McBride's eyes met hers in the mirror. "Yet here you are, in a most *un*refined establishment, dressed—and I use the term loosely—for anything but improving your situation."

"What I do, or don't do, and where I do it or don't do it, is none of your business."

"Two weeks ago," he agreed blithely, "it might not have been. But now . . . considering you might be carrying my child—"

Aubrey spluttered the contents of the second refill halfway across the waxed surface of the bar. Choking and coughing, she heard McBride's low laughter as he pounded her gently on the back and called for a glass of water. Most of that was dribbled down her chin and streaked wetly into the cleft between her breasts, but when McBride attempted to blot the spillage with a cloth napkin, she batted his hands out of the way and glared up at him.

"What? What did you just say?"

"You want me to repeat it louder?"

"No! No, I do not want you to repeat *anything.* I would just like to know why you think . . . how you would dare to think . . ."

"You were the one who mentioned it first, if you'll recall, along with church meetings, hearth, and home . . ."

His smile was infuriating and Aubrey's anger threatened to choke her again.

"I wasn't *serious.* And neither were you, as I *do* recall. You turned as pale as a sheet and broke out into a cold sweat at the very notion of fatherhood and marital responsibilities."

"I've had a chance to think about it since then. I think I could accept it a lot more readily than I could accept"

—the humor vanished from his eyes as he glanced coldly around the saloon—"this."

"Well, you can rest assured, Mr. McBride, that you don't have to think about *this* or anything else. I told you then, and I'm telling you now, as outlandish as it may seem to your male pride, I want nothing more to do with you! We're both adults, we had a pleasant evening together . . . can't you just leave it at that?"

This time, she made it as far as the main doors before a fresh surge of customers came into the casino, pushing her back, forcing her to seek refuge near one of the private booths. She gasped as a hand, very hard and very determined, curled around her upper arm with enough pressure to bruise the tender flesh. McBride dragged her into the closest velvet-draped niche, then spun her around, holding her with her back against the crushed curtains, unmindful of the laughing crowds passing by.

"How dare you!" she cried. "Let me go at once!"

"Not on your life, lady. Not until I get a few answers."

"I don't have to answer to you or to anyone else!" She tried to shove past him, but he had grasped her by both shoulders and was pinning her to the wall with enough force to negate what little breath and composure she was managing to hoard.

"When I said, back at the Cimarron, that you should break out of your tweeds and matronly scowls, I had no idea you would take my advice so literally."

"You were hardly in a position to advise me about anything."

Christian laughed. "So I see. You seem to have been able to adapt quite nicely all on your own."

Aubrey flushed hotly as his gaze lingered long and hard on the wide expanse of bare flesh across her bosom.

"I needed a job," she spat.

His eyebrows shot upward. "And this was your first choice?"

Aubrey pushed forward and was slammed back again, and when she looked up, her eyes were sparkling with outrage.

"Let . . . me . . . go!"

"The little game you were running back there: it didn't look to me as if you just picked up the knack this past week."

"McBride—" Where was Billy? One word to him and the plainsman would be removed, with or without force.

"I just want to know if there are any more surprises tucked up those lovely sleeves of yours."

"If there are," she answered venomously, "you will be the last to know."

"That's what I'm afraid of."

"You hardly have anything to fear from me, Mc-Bride."

"Unlike you?"

Aubrey's mouth opened, then snapped shut again. He was too damned close, too damned tall, and the brandy she had consumed, she had consumed too damn quickly to even let her think clearly, let alone keep pace with him in an exchange of wits or insults. Moreover, although his voice was as calm as water on a windless day, she could detect the treacherous undertow beneath the surface. He was, she suspected, a hair's breadth away from exploding; anger smoldered in his eyes and kept the smoothly sheathed muscles in his jaw as tight as leather. The pressure in his hands had not decreased noticeably and her arms had very little feeling left in them from the elbows down.

"I lost my fear of you some time ago," she insisted evenly. "Now, if you don't mind—"

She started to twist free again, but a loud hail of applause from the saloon startled them both into turning around. Maxwell Fleming was striding out onto the lamplit stage, holding his arms high to encourage the cheering and raise the already taut level of anticipation.

"Ladies, gentlemen, as you know, we have a special treat for you this evening." He smiled slickly through a resounding wave of applause and used his hands to temper it. "Without further ado, the Golden Eagle is proud to bring you, straight from the finest opera houses in New York, Boston, Savannah, and New Orleans, the brightest jewel of the entertainment world . . . *Miss Magenta Royale!*"

The cheering and howling rose to a crescendo as Fleming turned and extended his arm toward the right of the stage. From behind the folds of the crimson draperies came the even brighter, more breathtaking flush of bright scarlet as Magenta walked slowly onstage, bowing and smiling her acceptance of the crowd's adoration. Even the hardened gamblers who rarely lifted their eyes from the green baize tops of the tables paused and watched Magenta's undulating progress. Hearts pounded and eyes bulged throughout the cavernous saloon as the blond chanteuse took a deep bow, her yellow curls glinting, her feathers dancing, her voluptuous curves catching the full glow of the brass foot lamps.

"If you had to interfere with someone's life, McBride," Aubrey asked over the swell of noise, "why couldn't it have been Magenta's? I'm sure she would have been whatever you wanted her to be, for however long you wanted her."

"But I didn't want Magenta," he replied quietly. "I wanted you. And God only knows why, but it seems I still do."

Aubrey stared up at him with eyes that had not given him a moment's worth of peace. His hands slid up and sandwiched her face between them, holding her while he brought his mouth down over hers, kissing her with all of the pent-up anger and frustration he had no other means of venting. She stiffened slightly in resistance to the spreading pleasure that moved over her, but his tongue had already forced her lips apart, reminding her with deep, deliberate thrusts, that the shivers she felt now were nothing . . . nothing compared to the rapturous ecstasy their bodies could unleash.

She moaned helplessly as her fingers curled into the narrow lapels of his jacket. His body crowded closer and she could feel the strength and power, the heat and the intensity of his hunger.

"Leave here," he murmured. "Leave with me now."

Her soft, despairing cry was lost under the firm possessiveness of his lips and she could feel herself slipping, sagging weakly under the onslaught of his mouth and body.

"I swear to Christ I won't ask any more questions, and you don't have to tell me anything you don't want to tell me . . . only . . . just get the hell out of here with me now."

Aubrey opened her eyes slowly. They were burning with unshed tears and her lips tingled and throbbed from his caresses. But she uncurled her fingers from the front of his jacket and splayed them flat on his chest, pushing him firmly and irrevocably away.

"It's a tempting offer, McBride," she admitted softly. "But a wasted one, I'm afraid. I don't *want* to leave here. Not with you, not with anyone else. You can take this as truth, or not, however you please, but *this* is why I came to Santa Fe. *This* is what I do. *This* is who I am. You deserve a lot better, McBride, and I mean that sincerely."

Christian stared at her long and hard for another few moments, but in the end, let his hands fall slowly away. He continued to stand and stare and Aubrey continued to remain pressed against the crush of velvet curtains, her heart aching within her breast, her senses reeling under the growing chill in the silvery-gray eyes.

"I see. You enjoy this kind of life, do you? You enjoy these *people;* you enjoy their company? Tell me . . . do you enjoy them all equally, or do you get more enjoyment from the ones who pay more?"

Aubrey shook her head, her eyes so wide and bright and blue that he could have drowned in them.

"Your *friend* back there offered you a hundred dollars for a trip upstairs. Is that part of your job as well?"

Aubrey should have slapped him for the insult. Indeed, she could see that he was half-expecting—hoping? —she would try, and when she didn't, she could not tell if it was a resurgence of his anger, or a bristling new wave of self-disgust that caused him to draw even farther away.

"By God," he said hoarsely, "when I called you a chameleon, I didn't know how truly good you were!"

"Why don't you just go away, McBride. Go away and leave me alone!"

He started to comply, but on an afterthought, stopped and fished a hundred-dollar greenback out of his pocket. "Here. I don't particularily like owing anybody anything. Especially favors."

Aubrey averted her eyes. She saw the strong fingers crumple the money, then move forward and tuck it into the ruffle of silk flowers that edged her bodice.

"Don't be so modest, Miss Blue. You earned every penny."

She turned back, dug the bill out of her bodice, and lifted her fist to throw it back into his face. Christian saw her eyes flick over his shoulder, saw her expression change from total fury to dispassionate blandness in less time than it took to blink, and, surprised, he wheeled around to search out the cause.

Standing behind them, his own face a mask of shocked hatred, was Maxwell Fleming.

•

Fleming had left Magenta in the capable hands of the crowd and the musicians and, pleased with the response, had made his way onto the floor of the casino to see how his other newest attraction was doing. With Magenta's astonishingly sweet voice holding the audience rapt with a stirring rendition of "Annie Laurie" he had noted the glaring absence of a crowd around Aubrey Blue's table, but could see no trace of the slender, dark-haired lady gambler.

He looked up at one of the guards stationed on the second-story balcony and, as if sensing his boss's query, a casually returned glance indicated the niche by the main doors. Fleming saw a splash of rich sapphire silk set against the crimson draperies and tried to catch her eye, but she was engrossed in a conversation with a tall, fair-haired man whose broad shoulders blocked most of Aubrey's view of the room.

Blocked it with somewhat more deliberation than Fleming thought necessary. His possessive instincts roused, he cut through the clapping audience and headed for the niche, arriving just in time to see the hundred-dollar bill being tucked into Aubrey's bodice. Fleming had also caught a glimpse of the man's profile —a glimpse that made his footsteps slow and his fists clench so tightly the white bones of his knuckles glowed through the skin.

He had heard that Christian McBride had been let out of Leavenworth; he just hadn't expected the bastard to have had the guts to show his face in Santa Fe so soon.

•

The air crackled instantly with tension as the two men came eye to eye for the first time in five years. They were of an equal height, so their gazes were level. McBride had an advantage in sheer volume of muscle, but Fleming compensated with the weight of implied power and lethal authority. Neither man was visibly armed. Both glowered with the quiet threat of explosive violence.

Christian forced a lazy smile. "Hello, Max. Nice place you have here."

"McBride. I suppose I should be flattered. All those years at Leavenworth . . . they must have left you with a taste for luxury."

"Five years and ten days, to be exact. A lot of luxury to be catching up on. I was trying to get a head start with Miss Blue here, but she seems to have become a mite less friendly since we left the Trail."

Fleming's glance slid from McBride to Aubrey, back to McBride. "It must have been a crowded stagecoach."

"It was anything but dull," McBride agreed, extracting a cheroot from his pocket. "Smoke?"

"Not if they're the same penny weeds you burned hunting buffalo."

"The same," Christian grinned. "They seemed to work keeping the varmints away back then; I kind of hoped they would work the same now."

Fleming's eyes glittered savagely. "Am I interrupting something?"

"No," Aubrey said quickly. "No, Mr. McBride was just leaving."

Fleming looked at the hundred-dollar bill clutched in her hand. "Alone?"

Her flush darkened and McBride laughed. "Unfortunately, yes. It appears Miss Blue appreciates my company as much as you do, Max."

"Then she exhibits extreme good taste."

"Still and all, she's going to have to get used to unsavory types like me if she plans to work for you much longer. And passing up a hundred dollars . . . tsk tsk. Just plain bad business all around."

"Mr. McBride, you are becoming tiresome," Aubrey said with a sigh. She stuck the hundred-dollar bill in his coat pocket and, as deliberately as he had done a few minutes earlier, found a two-bit piece in her reticule and pressed it into the palm of his hand. "Here. I'm sure this can help you find someone more suited to your tastes out in the alleyways. My treat."

Fleming laughed and slid his arm around Aubrey's waist. "You'll never learn, will you, McBride? You just keep poking your nose where it isn't wanted."

McBride stared at Fleming's hand, settled snugly around Aubrey's middle, and his voice came out like a sheet of ice. "Maybe I should try to be more like you . . . just take what I want and damn the consequences. Ethan tells me you've run out of ranches to burn and you've started on missions. I wouldn't have thought there was much profit to be made in roasting padres."

Aubrey felt the tremor shiver through Fleming's arm, even though outwardly, he remained calm enough to give the appearance of engaging in a conversation with an old friend.

Fleming's eyes narrowed. "You should have stayed in Kansas. Or gone east to see the sights. I have the feeling you are going to get in my way again."

"Well, if I do . . . you can always try to stop me . . . again."

"McBride . . . if you get in my way, I *will* stop you. Only it won't be for a measly five years this time. It will be for good."

"Any time, any place, Max—assuming you haven't forgotten how to use a gun."

"I haven't forgotten. And I haven't forgotten that you like to shoot your enemies in the dark, in the back."

Christian regarded Fleming over the flare of the match he held to his cigar. His teeth gleamed whitely through the cloud of smoke, his grin as sardonic as the arched tilt of his brow. "When I come for you, Max, it will be a face to face meeting; that much I promise you."

"Is that a threat? In front of witnesses?"

"It's a promise." Christian turned to Aubrey, his eyes distant and unforgiving. "Good night, Miss Blue. And good luck; working here, you'll need it."

He bit down on the end of his cigar and strode away. Fleming watched him move through the crowd and exit without a care for his unprotected back.

"I must apologize." Fleming dragged his eyes back to Aubrey. "Ours is a private quarrel and we had no right to air our dirty laundry in front of you."

"That's quite all right. From my own personal experience, I must say Mr. McBride can be rather bothersome when he wants to be."

"Nor is he the type of man you should be affiliated with, for whatever the reasons. He was in prison for the past five years. For murder."

"Yes," Aubrey said carefully, "I know. He seemed quite boastful of the fact. As if it was some kind of an accomplishment. If you ask me, however, the greater accomplishment is for one to stay *out* of prison while still getting what one wants."

Fleming looked at her and smiled, obviously approving of the sentiment.

"Just now," she continued with a wry chuckle, "he offered me a hundred dollars so that I would not have to 'degrade' myself at the gaming tables. I suppose, in hindsight, it was foolish of me not to accept it—you would have been that much more impressed with my first night's work. My first *hour* for that matter."

She opened her reticule and lifted out the wad of money she had won at the monte table. Fleming *was* impressed, and told her so.

"Unfortunately"—she glanced at the stage, where Magenta was warbling a bawdy ballad to rousing cheers of enthusiasm—"there seem to be just too many distractions tonight."

Fleming took the wad of money and peeled off two hundred dollars' worth of bills.

"For the annoyance," he murmured. "And for handling yourself so well under the circumstances. You will, of course, let me know at once if he bothers you again?"

"McBride?" She glanced at the door and exhaled a shallow breath. "Somehow, I don't think he will." And, sensing Fleming's eyes on her, she laughed suddenly and slipped her hand through the crook of his arm. "Not as long as he can feel that two bits chafing up against his pride, at any rate."

Fleming's expression relaxed. She was clever, beautiful, and independent. A woman confident enough in her own abilities to extend his interest beyond the initial challenge of merely getting her into his bed. The notion that had been taking shape in the back of his mind since he had first seen her standing in the entrance of the casino, grew by leaps and bounds, and he knew, beyond any shadow of a doubt, that it was unthinkable for anyone other than himself to own such perfection. The radiant, graceful wife he had often envisioned sharing his empire had a face now; an uncommonly beautiful, regal face surrounded by a spill of midnight black hair.

20

"I want her out of here," Magenta declared, pacing an angry length of Fleming's office. "She's a nuisance and a distraction and I cannot concentrate with either a nuisance or a distraction around me."

Fleming was sitting at his desk. He hadn't said much since Magenta had flounced into his office a quarter hour ago; he hadn't had the chance. She had come through the door complaining about the rowdy customers, too much smoke in the air, the poor lighting, the *dreadfully* inadequate musical accompaniment, the lack of appreciation for her singing talents as opposed to the continuous requests for the bawdy, lewd songs that inspired nothing but a steady stream of traffic to the upper rooms. It was unsettling and disconcerting to someone of her refined skills. She was accustomed to singing in theaters where the audience was respectfully silent and behaved with the dignity and decorum she deserved. She was *not* accustomed to drunks yelling for more titties, or with trying to outshout dealers calling for fresh bets.

"I'm paying you twice what you earned in your last theater booking."

"Money isn't everything," she pronounced imperiously. "I have standards to maintain, a reputation to uphold."

Fleming's gaze raked her slowly from the angry, tapping toe of her shoe to the top of her head. She had changed out of the crimson dress and had come to him wearing a frilly, feathered tulle wrapper and—he suspected—not much else. Her hair was still piled impossibly high and stiff on the crown of her head and her face was still garishly powdered and painted. The emerald broach glittered at her throat, a splash of cold green fire amid the profusion of purple ruffles and feathers.

"And just what is your complaint against Miss Blue again? I'm not quite sure I understood it."

Magenta paced to a halt in front of Fleming's desk. "I don't like her; is that plain enough? She's sneaky and underhanded. Why, if you could have seen the Miss Priss act she put on during that deplorable stage journey out here! She insulted me day and night with her high-handed airs of propriety. She even had the gall to call me a cheap saloon hustler."

"Well—" Fleming spread his hands in a placating gesture. "You may be justified there. I'd hardly call the Golden Eagle a cheap saloon."

Magenta huffed and straightened. "I want her out of here. The mere sight of her nauseates me and . . . and I doubt very much if I could bring myself to perform every night if I have to stare out over the audience and see *her* standing there laughing at me out of the side of her mouth."

Fleming pursed his lips and toyed with a paperweight on the desk. "I'll move her to the rear of the casino, far enough away that you won't even see her."

"I'll *know* she's there," Magenta said icily. "I'll know it by the number of backs I see facing the stage."

Fleming smiled inwardly. Aubrey Blue's table had attracted the largest crowds of gamblers all night long. Men had been climbing over one another to throw their bets on the table, shouting and jostling for position in the hopes of winning a smile from her. The last time he had checked, she had taken in over eight thousand dollars, clear. By far the most profitable monte table in the casino. If she maintained that rate six nights a week, his debts—which had accumulated to a staggeringly huge amount with each gilded chandelier added to the Golden Eagle—could be cleared within the year, and without his having to resort to any more drastic measures.

"Well?" Magenta demanded.

"Well?"

"Are you going to get rid of her?"

"No," he said evenly. "I'm not."

Magenta stiffened. "I see. Then you'll be wanting me to go?"

"No. I most definitely will not be wanting you to go anywhere . . . except, perhaps, into the next room."

"The next room?" She glanced at the adjoining door that led to his private suite of rooms. "What on earth would I do in there?"

"Probably what you do best."

"I *beg* your pardon?"

Fleming stood and walked slowly around to the front of the desk. The lamplight caught the diamond stud in his ear, refracting a glint as cold and hard as the glint in his eyes.

"Your hearing is excellent. As excellent, no doubt, as the rest of your body functions, so shall we cut through the penny-ante seductions and get right to the point? You've been parading yourself in front of me since you got here, in various stages of dress and undress, expecting me to what? Fawn all over you like a three-legged schoolboy? You're a beautiful woman, Clara, but I've got beautiful women hanging from the rafters. Beautiful, willing, eager women who come through that door with their mouths shut and their legs open whenever I want them. That's how I like my women, and that's how I'll expect you to behave from here on out."

Magenta swung sharply, intending to slap the smirk off his face, but he was anticipating the move and caught her wrist with a gruff chuckle. "I don't really think you want to do that, do you?"

Magenta opened her mouth to spit a response, but a sudden, violent tightening of his fingers around her wrist had her gasping in pain instead. She tried to wrench out of his grasp, but he only squeezed his fingers tighter, increasing the pressure and the pain to the point where her skin burned and the nerves, veins, and tissue were mashed flat to the bone.

With his free hand he loosened the belt that held her wrapper snug around her body. He had guessed correctly in thinking she was next to naked beneath. A skimpy lace chemise did little to contain or conceal her breasts, as ripe and full as two half-melons. The hem of the garment barely reached the top of her thighs.

"I see you came prepared to negotiate."

Magenta swore and managed to rake her nails down the side of his throat. She failed to break the skin, but she did shatter his cold calm and in the next instant found herself shoved brutally back over the desk.

Fleming swept the papers to one side. He ignored her cries and frantic writhings and pushed her flat on the hard wooden surface. Without troubling to do more than loosen his trousers and push the broadcloth aside, he wedged himself between her thighs and pulled her forward, shoving himself so deep inside her that her other pains became incidental.

"Get off me! You bastard! You have no right—!"

Fleming laughed and slapped her fists aside. He

clamped his hands around her waist and jerked her against him, again and again, grunting his full length into her. He caught her arms when she continued to flail at him, shoving them down on the desk, pinning her hands above her head and using them as leverage to thrust himself even deeper. Magenta arched and squirmed. She tried to gouge her heels into his flanks, to kick him or unseat him, but it was a futile effort and one that only helped to augment his gratification, not hinder it. Worse, it augmented hers as well, and somewhere between a curse and a cry, her legs stopped thrashing and twined greedily around him, and she began to work with each thrust instead of against it. Her eyes closed and her breath came on gusts of unbelievable pleasure. He plunged repeatedly, explosively into the hot, pliant flesh, and their bodies bucked and lurched in tandem, scattering papers, startling splashes of dark ink out of the crystal well.

Magenta screamed hoarsely as the first throes of rapture began to streak through her. She sank her nails into the thickness of his coat sleeves, unaware of when he had released her wrists, unaware of anything much aside from the feel of his body pounding her to a feverish frenzy. She screamed and screamed again, half-laughing, half-sobbing her way through an orgasm so intense it was a breath away from agony.

As abruptly as he had taken her, Fleming released her and jerked his weight away, leaving her panting and quivering on the shambled chaos of his desk. He stared down at her for several moments, a faint flush in his cheeks the only sign that he had enjoyed the sensual violence.

Calmly, he refastened his trousers and straightened the front of his shirt and waistcoat.

"Not bad," he said matter-of-factly. "For a whore."

"You have . . . no right to speak to me like this,"

she gasped, her mouth dry, her body drenched and shivering.

"Read your contract, Miss Royale. I have all the rights I need. I can do or say whatever I damn well please to you for the *next two years*. I own you, body and soul. And if you don't believe me, ask your Mr. Greaves what attributes he sold along with your singing abilities."

"No. No, Darby would never—"

"Your Darby is a greedy man. I believe he would sell his own mother into a brothel for a nickel and a good bottle of whiskey. Tell me if I'm wrong, though, by all means, do."

Magenta couldn't tell him any such thing. "I'll leave. I'll get on the next stage out and—"

"How far do you think you would get? Where do you think you would end up when my men brought you back?" He reached forward and smoothed his hands over her big breasts, his thumbs rubbing the velvety soft aureoles until they strained hard and wrinkled through the lace. "You've seen my back rooms. I'm sure a lot of my customers would pay handsomely for the chance to climb on top of the Jewel of New Orleans. Ten, twenty, even thirty men a night; easily. Hell, I could probably earn more off you that way than I can keeping you strictly on stage."

Magenta's mouth sagged open. "You wouldn't dare."

He laughed and pinched her nipples, twisting them until she whimpered involuntarily from the pain.

"I do pretty much what I like to do in this town," he said. "And frankly, I'm surprised you still doubt that."

"I don't doubt that you're a bastard. A cold, unfeeling, heartless bastard," she agreed, a sound very much like a sob choking in her throat. This was not going the way it was supposed to have gone. *She* was not the one who was supposed to be sprawled in an ignoble position awaiting the pleasure—or pain—of his next whim.

Fleming must have known exactly what she was thinking, for he sighed and straightened again, but not until he had removed the emerald broach from around her neck.

"I'm sorry you feel that way, Clara. Here I thought we were on the verge of forming a beneficial working relationship."

He left her lying flat on the desk, her legs dangling limply over the side, her hand clutching at the bare arch of her throat. She lay there quite still, quite uncertain of what to expect next, and when, after several long moments of silence, he did not reappear in her line of vision, she pushed herself awkwardly upright and looked around the room.

He was standing over by the opposite wall, and as she watched, a part of the decorative paneling that formed the wall opened and swung away from the others. Behind it, gleaming dully in the low lamplight, was the metallic faceplate of a wall safe. She heard the sound of tumblers clicking through a preset combination, then a solid, heavy *thunk* as the locking mechanism released and the door of the safe was opened.

Magenta climbed gingerly down off the desk, wincing and cursing under her breath as she rubbed the bruised flesh at the backs of her thighs. She would have black and blue marks by morning. Her skin was chafed red from the abrasive fabric of his trousers; her belly and breasts had been scratched by the metal edges of his waistcoat buttons.

Fleming had removed a large laquered chest from the safe and seemed not to notice or care when Magenta sidled up quietly behind him. A second lock was released with a slim gold key, and when the lid of the chest was raised, she could see it was divided into compartments, each designed to hold leather cases similar to the one that had held the emerald broach.

"Would you like to see true beauty?" Fleming asked, startling Magenta into flinching half a step back.

Without waiting for her answer, he placed the chest closer to the light and removed one of the cases. He opened it, along with another, and set them side by side under the full glow of the lamp.

Magenta's eyes bulged and her jaw sagged.

Nestled on beds of plush velvet were two necklaces, each comprised of a score of large stones—rubies in the one, sapphires in the other—set into intricate patterns and accented by delicate webbings of filigreed gold. A third case—presented as reverently as the first two and larger than both—contained a complete set: necklace, bracelet, earrings, and ring, all of glittering, dazzling white diamonds, their sparkle and brilliance almost painful to behold.

"This is beauty, Clara. This is what is rare and exquisite and worth moving mountains to obtain . . . and to keep."

Magenta stretched out a hand, at his invitation, and ran her fingertips over the faceted surfaces of the gems. A *fortune* in gems, she estimated, and there were at least a dozen more unopened cases inside the black laquered chest.

"What did you mean when you said . . . a beneficial working relationship?" she asked, her throat so dry she could barely work it.

Fleming smiled and started to close the three cases. He held back his answer until the lid of the chest was closed and locked and the box itself returned to the safe. He gave the metal dial a swift twist to scramble the tumblers, then closed the outer panel and turned to face Magenta.

"I meant exactly what I said. I am not an ungenerous

or an unfair man, Clara, but I do demand absolute obedience, absolute loyalty in return. For those who want to be more . . . exclusively employed, shall we say . . . they would naturally have to prove to me that they want and deserve special treatment. Not by flaunting themselves in front of me or my men. Not by issuing demands and threats and throwing fits of temper. Certainly not by coming in here half-naked and expecting me to drool over something I have seen and used a thousand times before. You are, undeniably, the most voluptuous beauty I have encountered in some time—that was why I brought you out here in the first place. Moreover, I had every intention of enhancing that beauty by lavishing you in furs and jewels and the most devastatingly gorgeous gowns money could buy. But, I'm sorry to say, you haven't exactly impressed me with your enthusiasm so far."

"And if I do?" Magenta moistened her lips. "Impress you, I mean?"

Fleming smiled. "Why, you would no longer be known merely as the Jewel of New Orleans, my dear. You would be the Queen of Santa Fe, the Empress of the West. Moreover, if you continued to please me"—he reached out and touched a silver-blond curl with the backs of his fingers, tracing its shiny length down to where it rested on the ample swell of her breast—"you would indeed become the crowning jewel of my collection, complete with all the wealth and fame you deserved."

His hand continued moving lower and paused at a torn bit of lace on the hem of her camisole. "I apologize for my methods of explaining myself, but you do understand, there can be no middle ground. I either have you fully and completely, or I do not have you at all, in which case, you can make your own arrangements with George."

"No!" Magenta said quickly, her eyes still dazzled by the brilliance of the jewels. "No, I . . . I don't want to deal with George."

"You would rather deal with me?"

"Yes," she whispered. "Oh yes."

"And you think you can please me?"

Magenta could tell, by the flood of sticky fluid on her thighs and by the flush of color still high in his cheeks, that she had already pleased him more than he was prepared to admit. This knowledge, coupled with the fact that he had no real inkling of the enthusiasm she was • capable of displaying when jewels, furs, and silk gowns were at stake, brought a genuine smile of eagerness to her lips. She moved closer, shrugging the sleek purple folds of her wrapper off her shoulders. Her hands, pressed flat on his chest, slid slowly down his body, undoing buttons and buckles until he was naked from his belly to his thighs. With her eyes locked firmly on his, she sank onto her knees, and, after a few minutes of concentrated effort, the soft tinkle of her laughter welcomed his grunting, sweating form on the floor beside her.

"Can I please you?" she murmured, her mouth hovering over him again. "Until you scream for mercy, lover. Until you scream for mercy."

21

Aubrey gathered the folds of her shawl closer around her shoulders and moved swiftly along the shadowy street. She had decided she had had enough—enough of the stale, smoky air, enough of the grasping, ogling gamblers who mentally stripped and ravished her at every glance. She hadn't told anyone she was leaving, she had just left. The casino was still full of customers and would be until the bartender swept them out with the morning refuse.

She had done surprisingly well for her first night, considering all of the interruptions and distractions. Discounting the two-hundred-dollar bonus Fleming had given her, she had made close to four hundred from her percentage of the takings. A tidy night's earnings. Not as tidy as keeping the whole amount, but an earned percentage was a sure thing, whereas, on her own, she could have worked the casino once, maybe twice, before Fleming's dealers had branded her a sharp and delivered her to the stage depot with his compliments.

Being caught in the middle of a confrontation between McBride and Fleming had been a surprise she had not anticipated. Both men had tempers that were unpredictable, and while she was thankful McBride had

not elaborated on their "friendship," she knew she had
not escaped his wrath by much. Handing him an insult
along with the two-bit piece had been like waving a red
flag in front of a bull and she could only blame her
extreme foolhardiness on the two quick shots of brandy
she had downed on an empty stomach.

But she had survived and Fleming's suspicions had
been averted—she hoped. She had to tread carefully for
a while, and treading carefully did not include rousing
the jealousies of two powerful antagonists. She honestly
had not expected to see McBride in Santa Fe so soon;
certainly not walking as brazen as brass into Fleming's
casino. It would be just like the arrogant, prideful fool
to shoot Maxwell Fleming out of hand and ruin everything—not to mention getting himself thrown into jail
again—or worse.

Aubrey welcomed the cool, brisk night air. She would
have welcomed it more if she could have inhaled it
deeply enough. The thought of finally unclamping the
iron vise around her ribs infused her tired feet with new
purpose and she was well away from the Alameda and
starting to cut through the deserted streets of the private sector before she became aware of the second figure keeping apace with her, some twenty yards or so
behind in the shadows.

When she stopped to adjust her shawl, she noted that
he stopped too. She turned and tried to stare him out of
the shadows, but whoever it was kept well back in the
darkness of a doorway.

Aubrey patted the reassuring bulk of the .22 derringer. It was barely past midnight; surely if she screamed
or fired the gun, someone would hear her and come to
her rescue. She started walking again, so intent on listening to the spurless crunch of boot steps behind her,
that she rounded a corner and ran headlong into a man
leaning against the side of a hacienda wall.

"Oh! Excuse me! I'm sorry, I didn't see you standing there, and I . . . I . . ."

Muted light from the main street glazed his tawny hair with the same unearthly glow that set his teeth gleaming white against the bronzed darkness of his face.

"McBride? Is that you?"

"You were rushing to meet someone else, perhaps?"

"I wasn't rushing to meet anyone, I was—" She turned, a flash of alarm crossing her face as she heard the sound of boots approaching the lane at a run. McBride frowned and followed her gaze, and without waiting for consent or direction slung an arm around her waist and pulled her into the shadows of the recessed gate. The gate was partly open and he pushed her further out of sight behind the adobe wall, then swung the wrought iron closed behind him and flattened himself into the shadows beside her.

Whoever had been following her ran past and stopped at the far end of the short laneway. They could hear him curse and take several steps in one direction before backtracking and trying the other. Something was flung onto the ground in great disgust—his hat, probably—and another curse brought him back toward the main street again.

McBride kept Aubrey pinned against the wall until the angry steps had faded well away, then cautioned her to remain in place while he made sure the man was gone.

He was back in a few moments—hardly long enough for Aubrey to bring the pounding in her temples under control.

"Another one of your admirers?" he asked in a harsh whisper.

She ignored the question and the sarcasm. "What are *you* doing here, McBride? Why are you following me?"

"In case it skipped your notice, Miss Blue, it was you

who ran full speed into me. I should be asking you that question, not the other way around."

"Me? Following you? Are you out of your mind? What possible reason would I have for following you?"

He folded his arms across his broad chest. "Well, since I don't imagine it is because you've had a change of heart, I might guess it had something to do with unfinished business."

"Unfinished . . . ? We have no unfinished business, McBride. We have no unfinished anything between us, not now, not ever, and if you don't leave me alone *this instant,* I'll . . . I'll—"

"You'll do what?" he asked, lowering his arms and crowding her against the wall. "You'll scream? Go ahead; try it. People scream on the streets of Santa Fe every night, the local residents are used to it."

"I'm warning you, McBride, I'll—"

"Shoot me?" He laughed and caught her wrist, twisting the derringer out of her fingers with mocking ease. "You tried that once already, remember. And if you try it again, I may not find it so amusing. I might just find it downright aggravating and stick all four barrels somewhere *real* unpleasant."

"Crude," she spat. "Vulgar. Nothing you would do would surprise me."

"It might pain you a little, though." He pocketed the gun and leaned forward, his hands braced on the wall on either side of her head. "And you would for sure end up telling me what I want to know."

"I have no intentions of telling you anything, McBride, now or ever. In fact, I have no intentions of ever *speaking* to you again if I can help it. Now, if you don't mind—"

His arm dropped to her waist, effectively cutting off her first route of escape. She twisted and attempted to dart the other way, but his left hand was just as swift, just as effective in keeping her trapped against the adobe.

"I want to know," he said evenly, "exactly how friendly you are with Maxwell Fleming."

"Exactly? You want to know *exactly*?" It was tempting, and it was there, on the tip of her tongue, to blurt out that they were lovers, but something stopped her. Something that recognized and respected the depth of McBride's anger. And something within herself that could never have said such a thing, not even out of spite. "I work for him. He gave me a job."

"As a whore?"

Aubrey's fury strained the tightness of her corset. "What possible business is that of yours?"

Christian's hands rose from her waist to her neck, cradling her chin roughly, squeezing so tightly she gasped from the pain.

"You made it my business, lady. When you said I wasn't good enough for you, you made it my business."

"McBride—"

He squeezed his hands tighter and forced her head back against the wall. "Christian, damn you! The name is Christian. You said it often enough and loud enough when I was between your thighs. Say it now. Say it with that sweet little tongue of yours and keep saying it, or by God—"

"Christian . . . please . . . you're hurting me . . ."

"Again," he snarled.

"Christian."

"Again."

"C-Christian," she gasped.

His lips covered hers, muffling her cry, smothering her efforts to resist or fight him. He kissed her deeply, savagely, using his mouth like a weapon to destroy her senses.

"Again," he insisted.

"Christian," she whispered.

He angled her head higher and buried his lips in the curve of her throat. "Again."

Aubrey's head was swimming. Her body was on fire and her ability to think and counter the powerfully erotic workings of his mouth and body was drifting away on a wave of heat. His hands held her fast and his mouth . . . dear God, his mouth was burning her flesh, scorching it, scalding it wherever he touched.

"Christian," she sobbed. "Christian . . ."

His mouth plunged down over her lips again and Aubrey's knees buckled beneath her.

"Tell me you're not a whore. Tell me you're not *his* whore!"

"I'm not," she sobbed weakly. "I'm not his whore. Dear God, I'm not anyone's whore, I swear it."

He only kissed her harder, deeper, bruising her lips with a terrible intensity that should have frightened her, would have frightened her if not for a more nightmarish blackness that was threatening to swamp her completely.

"Christian! Christian . . . please! I can't breathe! I can't . . ."

The weakness in her knees turned into a swoon and her body started to go limp in his arms.

"What the hell—?"

"I . . . can't . . . breathe . . ."

The words were pressed against his lips as he found himself holding an armful of wilting female. He cursed and spun her around, using his one arm to support her while he tugged at the fastenings down the back of her dress.

"No," she managed to gasp.

"Shut up. I've never understood why women strap themselves into these things anyway."

The bindings on the dress gave way under his impatient fingers, as did the taut lacings of her corset. Aubrey gasped, then gasped again with near-ecstasy as she was able to expand her lungs and gulp mouthful after mouthful of clean, cold air. She leaned forward, her hands braced on the wall, her cheek pressed against the cool adobe, and all she could think about was the ludicrous picture they made should the owner of the hacienda step out onto his terrace for a breath of night air.

"Better?" Christian asked from behind her.

Aubrey opened her eyes slowly. The world was still spinning, but at least it was upright, and so was she.

"Dolores was . . . a little over enthusiastic when she was helping me dress tonight. I haven't been able to breathe properly all evening."

Christian could feel the tortured ridges of flesh through the silk of her chemise and he used his thumbs to gently massage the creases the corset had left down her back.

"As I said, I never could understand why a woman would want to bind herself up in an iron vise. Especially a woman who hasn't got a reason to bind anything or alter anything in the first place."

"Good God; was that a compliment?" she muttered wryly.

His thumbs worked into the small of her back and he grimaced. "I guess it was, wasn't it?"

"You'll spoil your image, McBride"—she gasped as his thumbs gouged an amendment from between her lips—*"Christian."*

His thumbs and fingers resumed a gentle stroking, kneading motion and Aubrey let her eyes drift closed again, savoring the sensation. She began to savor it a little too much, and so did he, and after a few moments, she straightened from the wall and held the crush of sapphire satin modestly against her bosom. The movement brought her back against the heat of his chest, while at the same time, tempting his hands forward beneath the loosened edges of the corset. Startled, she felt his fingers, then his palms circle and engulf the silk-clad fullness of her breasts. He began stroking and kneading with the same tenderness he had used on her back, caressing her flesh through the sheer layer of her chemise.

"Christian . . . I don't think . . ."

His hands tugged at the neckline of her chemise, finding the three tiny ribbons and slipping them with an authority she could not deny. Aubrey pressed her head back against the curve of his shoulder, knowing it was wrong to let him do this; knowing she should stop him before it went any further. Nothing good would come of it. Nothing at all.

"Christian . . ." The soft plea turned into a softer moan as she felt the roughness of his calloused hands chafe the far-too-sensitive flesh of her breasts.

"Someone could come along—"

"Someone could," he agreed, his mouth pressed into the nape of her neck. "But the lights are all out inside, and I think if we're *real* quiet . . ."

"You can't be serious!" she gasped.

She tried to turn around, tried to dislodge his hands, but he only pressed hotter kisses into her nape, seducing her ruthlessly with a flood of memories from their other night together.

"Lower your arms," he commanded huskily.

She fought the sensual manipulations of his hands and lips a few brief moments longer, then slid her hands downward, obeying the throaty timbre of his voice. Her breasts were abandoned for as long as it took him to peel her sleeves and bodice down to her waist, and to unfasten her skirt and petticoats, and push the entire tumble of linen, lace, and gleaming sapphire satin into a pool around her knees.

"Turn around," he murmured against her throat.

Aubrey swallowed hard and shook her head, clinging steadfastly to the finger-holds she had found in the adobe. She heard him sigh and felt his hands launch a fresh assault on her flesh, this time skimming beneath the trembling silk of her pantalets.

She tried in vain again to deter him, but even she could not decipher the meaningless scramble of sounds and whispers that broke through her lips. His hand curved into the soft vee of her thighs, his fingers teasing and tormenting her, wickedly proficient in bringing the first flush of ecstasy coursing through her body.

She looked down, shamed by the motion of his hands, mortified by the corresponding undulations of her hips as she pressed against him.

"Very stubborn, and very selfish of you not to share," he mused, holding her when the spasms became too intense for her to support on her own. He laughed suddenly, the tremors in his arms belying any humor in the situation, and Aubrey felt herself lifted slightly, and the tangled profusion of her clothing swept aside so that he could guide her down and back over the hard bulge of his thighs. She flailed out wildly with her hands, but there was nothing but the adobe to grasp hold of, and nothing, it seemed, to deter him from taking what he wanted one way or another. He brought her down, brought her back over his bent knees, and it was no longer his fingers probing her moist softness, but something far more determined to win her complete surrender.

Aubrey felt the slide of his flesh within her and she gasped with surprise. He was thick and impatient, solid and slick, and he surged up within her, leaving her no room to move or maneuver, no choice but to take him as deep as he cared to go.

She bowed her head and moaned softly, the pleasure

defying her, defeating her. "Christian . . . please . . ."

He surged again and she arched her head back. She pushed her palms against the adobe and she used what leverage she could to take him even deeper; trembling, shuddering, melting inside on a series of hot, thrusting stabs that filled her, stretched her, impaled her to the very limits of belief.

"Why . . . are you doing this to me?" she gasped.

Christian pressed his forehead into the slender valley between her shoulder blades and wrapped his arms more tightly around her, wishing he could answer, wishing he knew what the answer was. But he could only hold her and pray to keep his sanity even as her drenching wetness hurled them both into a mindless, reeling void of ecstasy.

•

The tension in Christian's arms ebbed slowly. He still held her, but without the rocklike urgency that had caused him to climax with the speed and eagerness of a fumbling adolescent. Aubrey panted lightly, cradled in the circle of his arms, her back cushioned against his chest, her knees and thighs folded alongside his. She still wore her stockings and garters, she noted with wry alacrity. Her camisole gaped open over her breasts, her pantalets lay in a sad, torn heap on the ground beside them. Loosened spirals of her hair trailed over her shoulders like spills of black ink, clinging to her damp skin as well as to the sleeve of his broadcloth jacket.

He hadn't even undressed.

She hadn't even noticed . . . or cared . . . until just this minute. And she only cared now because she could feel his heat throbbing and pulsating within her and she wished she could feel the heat of his skin elsewhere. She wanted to feel his flesh and the rippling power of his muscles bared beneath her fingertips.

"I'm sorry," he whispered. "I hadn't planned that. It just . . . happened."

"You had to spend your two bits," she said haltingly.

His arms slackened and he lifted his head out of the crook of her shoulder, but only for a moment, and only for as long as it took to press a soft oath into her throat.

"I guess I deserved that."

"Yes. You did."

"It just made me so damned mad seeing you there. Seeing Fleming. Seeing the two of you together." He groaned and bent his forehead to the mass of black ringlets at the back of her head. "Please . . . don't tell me he was the one. Don't tell me he was the one you came west in the hopes of luring into a wedding chapel."

Aubrey almost smiled. "No. No, he isn't the one."

"Thank God," he said, releasing the breath he had been holding. "That was the only other explanation I could think of, and kept thinking of for the past few hours while I was waiting for you to leave that hellhole."

"So! You *were* following me."

He had the sense to keep quiet and not try to worm his way around a lie.

Aubrey closed her eyes and savored a delicious flush of warmth inside.

"Fleming might have shot you."

"He might have."

"He had guns all around. Any one of them would have picked you off had he given the signal."

"Probably."

"Then why did you go? What did you hope to gain by antagonizing him?"

"Why, Miss Blue." He tilted his head to one side to catch a glimpse of her face. "Is this a note of concern I detect? Here, I could have sworn I heard you say you didn't care what happened to me, didn't give a hang where I went or what I did . . . or who I did it with."

Aubrey detected his smile and his sarcasm and pushed brusquely out of his embrace. "I *don't* care. I was just . . . curious, that's all."

Standing was a wobbly affair at best and she had to reach for the low-slung branches of a nearby cottonwood to accomplish it on her own. Her legs were shaky and her thighs quivered from the recent outpouring of heat and energy; she had lost a dainty satin slipper somewhere in the volcanic debris of her clothes and for some illogical reason, it became the crucial thing to search for first.

"You know—" His voice came out of the shadows, startling her, and she straightened too quickly, sending a tumble of hair over her eyes. "I don't believe you're anywhere near as tough as you pretend to be."

"Oh?"

"Granted, you're a good actress. Damned good, in fact—but I think I've already told you that before. I imagine you're used to fooling a lot of people a lot of the time."

"But not you."

"Not me. Not entirely, anyway. Oh, I'll admit you had me going in the beginning—mostly in circles."

"But now you have me all figured out?"

Christian grinned and shrugged his big shoulders out of his jacket. "Not by a long shot, lady. Not all of you, at any rate. Parts of you, yes. The parts that count . . . I hope. You see"—he craned his neck forward to unfasten the top button of his collar—"I figure it's all in the eyes. You can say all the right words and make all the right moves and gestures, but if it isn't in the eyes . . . well . . . you just have to say the words with your eyes to make me believe you."

"What words?" she asked suspiciously.

"Oh . . . that you want me out of your life. That you want me to leave you alone and that you never want to see me again . . . or touch me . . . or have me touch you."

McBride's shirt joined his jacket where it was draped over the branch of the cottonwood and he started pulling at one of his tall leather boots.

"What are you doing?"

He looked down. "I thought that was rather obvious. I'm undressing."

Her eyes widened in alarm. "Why?"

"I thought that was rather obvious too," he said quietly.

Aubrey's hands fell limply by her sides and she felt a curl of heat slide down from her belly, puddling where she was already hot and damp and slippery with the proof of his recklessness.

"I know," he murmured. "You probably think I should be happy with what you've just done for me, and I suppose, under other circumstances, with other women, I might be. Tension's gone. Pressure's eased. I don't feel like killing the first ten men I see. Hell, I can almost hold my hands steady"—he held them out, palms up, fingers spread wide—"until I look at you, that is, and then—" He paused again and their eyes met, and she could see his fingers fold tightly inward. "Well, it just won't do, Miss Blue. It won't do at all."

Aubrey shook her head, but denying the weakness she could see in him was like denying the weakness she could feel flooding through every vein in her body.

"I . . . didn't want anything like this to happen," she insisted softly.

"You think I did? You think I didn't leave prison determined to remain a free man the rest of my life? But I'm not free, and I don't think I will be free again until I either find out what put you in my blood or find a way to get you the hell out."

Aubrey backed up a step. He just stood there, his trousers slack and gaping, the starlight dusting the incredible breadth of his shoulders, taunting her into admitting how beautiful he was, how ruggedly breathtaking each hard, sculpted muscle was and how much she longed to run her hands over every bold inch of him.

They made a fine pair, standing in some stranger's walled garden, McBride threateningly half-naked and challenging, Aubrey clad in stockings and garters, and a shivering wisp of silk that was her only defense against the heat of his eyes. Overhead, a million stars twinkled like bits of gemstones, and between the two still bodies swirled a breeze laden with the heavy scents of oleander and honeysuckle. Aubrey swore she could hear the desert air mocking her, and she could feel the fine sifting of caliche dust caressing her ankles.

"It won't change anything," she whispered.

"Ahh, there's where you're wrong." He moved dangerously closer, narrowing the gap between them. "It will change the way you feel when you go to sleep tonight, and it will change the way you feel when you wake up in the morning. That's about all I can offer you for now, Aubrey Blue. Question is: is it enough?"

He wasn't touching her, not quite. But he might as well have been for the way her body undulated and rippled with sensation. It was enough, she thought, and closed her eyes as she moved forward. It was enough to breathe the words against his fingertips and then to feel those same fingertips trace a slow, deliberate path from her chin to her throat, to the quivering plane of her belly.

There was fire in his flesh, and where he touched her, she flared with the brilliant heat of wanting and of being wanted. She had never even realized a sensation like this existed, where desire became everything and the world around them exploded into stardust. She should have known. On their island fortress in the desert, she had almost become part of that stardust, and later, on the mossy banks of the Cimarron, there had been very little keeping her earthbound.

The fire slid lushly into the soft cleft of her thighs and Aubrey reached for him. She smoothed her hands over the satiny hardness of his flesh, stroking over the muscles that tensed and trembled with the same fierce heat she could feel consuming her. She leaned forward, pressing her lips against his skin, smothering the words she wanted to say, but dared not even acknowledge.

He cradled her chin and angled her mouth up to his for a kiss that was raw with emotion, intoxicating in its tenderness. She tasted his husky groan as she pushed the waist of his trousers down and freed the bold thrust of his flesh; she let herself be drawn down onto the bed of crushed skirts and petticoats, and then he was beside her, he was between her thighs, he was moving into her, joining them together under a deluge of swift, liquid pulsations. His powerful muscles corded, his breath came ragged and hot against her throat as he thrust himself to her again and again, deep and hard, consuming her, ravishing her, stretching her beyond the limits of caution. Her flesh clutched at him in spasms and her head arched back into the softness of their makeshift bed, the ecstasy crashing through her, inundating her with one molten wave of white-hot delirium after another. She did not think she could bear it. She *knew* she could not bear it in silence, and her cries came in thin slivers of sound that vibrated through the darkness. Her entire body convulsed, sweet and long, her legs rising to clasp around him, her hands clawing his shoulders, her nails scoring the already scarred slabs of muscle. There was no beginning and no end to the tumult; the waves of

pleasure simply crashed one into the other, the last into
the first, over and over, peaking and cresting with each
savage thrust.

Christian rolled without uncoupling and the thickness
of her hair twined around him, binding them together.
His hands remained taut around her waist, guiding her,
holding her, fighting to control something that had already gone far beyond his ability to comprehend.

He cursed with the helplessness of it all and rolled
again, his mouth covering her keening soft cries, their
bodies eager and hungry for the shivering rapture that
was only a breath away. Aubrey felt her body open in a
melting rush. She *was* melting—dissolving, drowning,
liquefying in the flood of his passion and she wondered
if someone could die of such pleasure. She could have
sworn she did die, gloriously and blissfully, and when
she had taken all there was to take and given all there
was to give, she felt the swimming blackness engulf her.
She succumbed with a soft, mewling sigh, her contentment so rich and deep, it continued to ripple gently
from her body to his long after they had collapsed together under the glittering awning of starlight.

22

The row of adobe dwellings was blurred by the predawn gloom and only the distant baying of a roving coyote broke the heavy silence. Aubrey remained standing under the archway of the shop door and watched Christian McBride melting away into the shadows. Her mouth was still warm from his parting kiss. Her body felt pleasantly loose-jointed and she was moderately surprised that she had been able to walk back to Old Santa Fe under her own strength. Christian had, naturally, insisted on accompanying her all the way to the shop door, scoffing openly at the very notion of their parting outside the terraced garden.

"If someone saw you looking the way you do, it would be like waving an open invitation to every *caballero* out looking for trouble."

Aubrey had looked down at her disheveled state—her skirt and petticoats wrinkled beyond casual salvation, her hair tumbled around her shoulders and her bodice only partially fastened due to the fact that he had been unable—or unwilling—to properly lace her corset back in place.

"How either of us looked didn't seem to concern you

a few hours ago," she reminded him, glancing pointedly up at the darkened windows that overlooked the garden.

Christian had only smiled and handed her the slipper she had searched for earlier. "A few hours ago, I wasn't thinking too clearly."

"And now you are?"

"Let's just say I have other things to think about."

"Such as?"

"Such as . . ." He watched her balance herself unsteadily while she put on her slipper. "What happens now?"

"Now?"

"Yes, now. Today. Tomorrow. What happens tomorrow? Do we go back to playing games, or have we finally managed to get past that point?"

Aubrey stalled her answer, buying time by combing her fingers through her hair, but he had recognized the tactic and had shaken his head in a way that suggested he would have preferred to take her by the shoulders and shake *her*.

"Tell me," he asked quietly. "Is there anyone you *do* trust?"

Aubrey looked up and the pain in her eyes startled him. "No. No one has ever given me any reason to trust them. Not completely, anyway," she amended, for even Bruster, as much as he had done for her when she was younger, had always considered his profits before committing his loyalties.

That was why, despite how warm and safe she felt in Christian's arms, a part of her had remained wary enough to lead him to the wrong doorway on the wrong street, and had waited until he was well out of sight before hurrying along a connecting laneway and finding her way to Dolores's shop.

Aware of the lights blooming to life in nearby windows, Aubrey sighed wearily and entered the shop as quietly as she could. She tiptoed around the cluttered display tables and paused a moment at the curtained doorway to the back rooms. Dolores was asleep in a chair, her head lolled forward, her lips spluttering around snores that were gusty enough to ruffle the collar of her dressing gown.

Aubrey gathered her skirts and edged past her sleeping hostess, knowing she was in no condition, mentally or physically, to withstand the full-scale inquisition that was sure to come. Happily, she made it into her room and managed to close the door without so much as a rustle of linen or silk, and was offering a small prayer of thanks when a scraping sound came out of the shadows behind her.

"Aubrey?"

It was barely a whisper and she was instantly alert, her fatigue vanishing on a rush of alarm.

"Bruster? Is that you?"

"In the flesh . . . or what there is remaining of it."

The shutters on the window had been drawn closed and the room was pitch black, the air thick with the smell of sweat and fear. Aubrey groped along the wall until she located the nightstand and was able to find and strike a match. Holding it high above her head, she directed the bright yellow glow into the corner where the whisper had originated.

Bruster was slumped on the floor, his back pressed against the wall, his legs stuck straight out in front of him. He looked deathly pale, even in the flickering light, and Aubrey raised the match higher, her eyes going to the narrow, streaky smear of blood on the wall that had followed his shoulder down.

The match spluttered and singed her fingertips before she waved it out and struck another. The tang of the sulfur jolted her senses enough to find the oil lamp and touch the flame to the wick.

"Bruster . . . dear God . . . what happened?"

"A slight miscalculation, I'm afraid. And a gunman with a mean disposition."

"Oh, Bruster." Aubrey sank down beside him and reached gingerly for the blood-drenched lapel of his jacket. "What have you gone and done?"

"I was progressing quite nicely, I thought," he said, his eyes brightening for a moment. "What with your success at the monte table and mine with a rather scurrulous faro dealer."

"Faro!" Aubrey dropped the lapel back into place and simply stared, too furious to trust herself to speak. First McBride had shown up unexpectedly, nearly ruining the setup at the casino, and now this, with Bruster . . . !

"I can see you are jumping to all the wrong conclusions," he said, his lower lip a little unsteady, "because I won, you see. I won. Look . . . look there, on the bed . . ."

"Bruster . . . what . . . happened?"

He swallowed with difficulty, and moistened his lips. "Well. As I said, I won. With considerable success too, I must say, for even though the dealer was as crafty and cunning as they come, I was like a veritable panther, stalking in for the kill and leaping at just the right moment! He was setting me up for a fall as surely as we had set up our own sucker so brilliantly, and so, you see, I knew what was coming." He could also see the coming storm in Aubrey's eyes and hurried on without further embellishments. "To celebrate my triumph, I, er, decided to treat myself. There was this most dazzling beauty by my side for most of the evening. Lush and soft and sweetly dispositioned. She was my lucky charm, I warrant, and so delectably attentive . . ."

Like most whores, Aubrey thought, especially when a customer is winning big.

". . . how could I not have succumbed to her tender charms?"

Aubrey would have told him how, in no uncertain terms, but he was looking up at her like a child caught with his hand in the pudding pot, his chins quivering his moustache drooping, and she knew she was the last one who should be lecturing anyone on restraint.

"And so we, ah, retired up the stairs," he continued warily. "A journey well worth the extravagant stipend, I assure you. Sweet Florinda. She made me feel . . . well . . . *manly* again. I am only human, after all, and what with all the danger and excitement of the past few weeks, and seeing Lily again . . . well . . . Can you understand what drove me to such recklessness? I mean"—he paused and dragged the back of his hand across his damp brow—"I know I am not an Adonis descended from Mount Olympus, but neither am I the complete churl Lily has taken great delight in painting me. I am not inept, nor am I past my prime or usefulness."

"I never thought you were," Aubrey said gently.

"Perhaps not. Perhaps not. But it was such a simple task you set me to tonight and, well, I must admit, I have been feeling sorely put out by the way Lily has been monopolizing all of your time."

"Bruster—"

"Let me finish. I know it was foolish to feel this way, but I did, and after I won so grandly both in and out of Florinda's arms, I thought . . . well . . . I thought I should take it upon myself to prove I was as vital and useful as I felt."

Aubrey raised a trembling hand to her temple. "But you *are* useful, Bruster, and you *were* a vital part of my plans. I just wish . . ."

"I found out that Fleming has an inherent distrust of banks—even his own. It seems it was robbed once in the past, and . . . well . . . he prefers to safeguard his money and valuables where no one would dare touch them."

Aubrey lowered her hand slowly and looked over at him.

"He has a safe in his office. He keeps all of his ready cash there, as well as—according to Florinda—a rather impressive collection of pretties—jewels and such that he has used as collateral against the equally impressive and staggering loans outstanding against his gilded casino. Moreover, most of his personal holdings have either been sold or mortgaged to the maximum in order to pay for the building and furbishing of the Golden Eagle. His own bank has approved the loans—a practice which I suspect is somewhat illegal. Also, he has made liberal use of other accounts entrusted to him, fully intending to repay the amounts before anyone becomes the wiser. The governor, for one, might be excessively interested to know his bank balance only balances on paper, as do the accounts of several important businessmen who are already leery of our greedy saloon-keeper.

"There is more," he continued. "A small matter of a girl and a priest, and a ledger of some kind that contains a full record of all of Fleming's debts, bribes, and transactions, legal or otherwise. Attempting to steal it cost the poor girl her life; attempting to pass the ledger on to the proper authorities, cost the priest his. An ugly affair on all counts, and the only reason I mention it at all is because Florinda identified Scud Holwell as the man who beat and mutilated the girl, then burned the mission to the ground. Fleming ordered him into the hills until the furor died down, but just tonight, Florinda heard the order rescinded. Fleming has dispatched some of his men to fetch Holwell back to Santa Fe . . .

to see to some unfinished business. My first thought, naturally, was that *you* were that unfinished business. That through some means or another he has recognized you. Is it possible, do you think?"

Aubrey shook her head, albeit not as confidently as she would have liked. "No. No, I don't think he would make a connection now, not after all these years. He would have taken it for granted that a wounded child out on the desert would never have survived the heat, the coyotes, or the vultures. No," she said with more conviction. "He has no reason to suspect me of anything."

"Nevertheless . . . I thought . . . if I could just get into his office and gain entry to his safe, I could abscond with everything he had of value, and thus there would be no further need for you to place yourself in such an untenable position."

"You tried to break into Fleming's office?" she asked incredulously.

"Indeed—" His expression turned dour. *"Tried* was the pivotal word. Florinda hinted at a secret stairwell leading from the stage to Fleming's suite of rooms, but when I attempted to gain entry, a seething hulk of a giant with one ear and no personality to speak of did not believe my claim of being lost. What's more, the faro dealer had been waiting for me to emerge from Florinda's room, and, well, I was left with few options but to bolt for a nearby window. I jumped and they shot, and here I am, alive only by the lucky happenstance of a hay-filled ice wagon standing in the alleyway below. By the time the giant came down by more conventional means, I was three blocks away and moving as if the hounds of hell were snapping at my heels—a not unworthy comparison if I do say so myself."

Aubrey stared, reduced to speechlessness for the second time in as many minutes.

"I knew I dared not return to my hotel room, so I came here, arriving an hour or so ago. You, of course, were not here, but since I could not conceivably bring myself to face Lily, I thought it best just to wait here until you returned."

He closed his eyes and leaned his head back against the wall, drained by lengthy explanations, relieved to have passed the burden of knowledge into Aubrey's capable hands. She would think of a way out of this mess, just as she always did.

Aubrey was staring at those very capable hands, noting the slippery smears of blood on her fingers. Things were getting out of control; she felt as if she was losing her center of focus. Nothing was going the way it was supposed to have gone. In the past, she'd had her rage and anger to fall back on, her pain and humiliation to keep her softer emotions well repressed. Now, everything seemed to hurt, everything seemed to make her want to cry. Every single emotion that had been thawed after so many years clad in ice made her want to run. And they made her want to run straight back into the strong arms of Christian McBride.

But of course she couldn't. She had to think of a way out of this mess—for both their sakes; hers and Bruster's.

"I should not only make you face Lily," she said slowly. "I should tell her where you've been and what you've been doing to make yourself smell of cheap perfume. I suspect she might be a little harder to elude than a one-eared giant with a poor personality."

"Aubrey . . . my dear child . . . you wouldn't."

Under his baleful gaze, she stood and rinsed her hands in the porcelain washbowl, then carefully removed the satin gown and set it out of the way over the far corner of the bed. In doing so, she caught sight of the folded sheaf of money Bruster had tossed on the coverlet.

"Eighteen thousand, five hundred and twenty-two dollars," he said proudly, following her glance.

"Eighteen thousand! No wonder the faro dealer was waiting for you!"

"A sore loser," Bruster agreed, "as well as a poor cheat."

Aubrey chewed on her lip. "You'll have to leave Santa Fe; you know that don't you?"

"And leave you to face the blackguard alone? Never!"

Aubrey ignored the feeble protest and carried the washbowl over to where he sat. "As far as anyone knows, our only connection is that we rode into town on the same coach. I don't *think* anyone will put us together tonight, although even if they do, you'll be long gone and out of reach of anyone wanting to ask too many questions."

Bruster looked offended. "Hot coals placed under my tongue could not bring forth any incriminating information!"

"I'd feel better not taking any chances," she said dryly.

"You're coming with me, of course."

Aubrey bent over him and started to ease the bloodied sleeve of his coat off his arm. "No, I'm not. I'm staying right here and seeing this damned thing through. I'm *not* going to run away again, not when I'm this close."

Bruster, distracted from his own miseries for a moment, seemed to notice her dishevelment for the first time—the disarray of her hair and the slightly puffy, chafed redness around her mouth. "Close? Close to what . . . or should I say *who?* Good God, you haven't

. . . you haven't been ingratiating yourself *that* way; not with—"

"Not with Fleming, no!" Aubrey said quickly. "I haven't sunk quite that low, for heaven's sake."

"Then who—?"

"Bruster . . . !" Her gusted breath of exasperation was met with steely-eyed determination and she knew there was nothing to be gained by lying or avoiding Bruster's query. "McBride is back. He was at the casino tonight . . . you didn't see him?"

"To my utter dismay, no I did not. Had I seen our inimitable hero of the desert, I might not have acted so hastily, no indeed. But what—?"

"If you ask any more questions," she warned through her teeth, "I may just be tempted to shoot you in the other arm."

He weighed the consequences against his curiosity, and after a moment, clamped his lips firmly shut. He remained wisely silent while Aubrey swabbed the blood away from his shoulder and inspected the extent of the damage. It was clean, as far as she could see: a neat hole in and a neat hole out, the bullet having hit mostly flesh and muscle, missing any major bones or arteries. He had lost a lot of blood, however, and was undoubtedly too weak to get very far on his own.

"Unfortunately, we're going to have to tell Lily anyway. She'll know the safest way to get you out of town."

Bruster sighed expansively. His face and throat streamed sweat from the effort it had taken to help Aubrey ease his coat off his shoulders, and he knew she was right. He dreaded the thought of it, but he knew she was right.

"She won't have to know *all* the details, will she?"

"I'm sure we could spare her one or two."

"God love me, to be at that woman's mercy after all this time—" He shuddered and felt his toes curl up inside his shoes. "A wretched thought. Simply wretched. She'll find some way to shackle me hand and foot, you mark my words she will. The Lord may have said 'vengeance is mine' but he hadn't yet unleashed Lily Cruise Montana on the world."

Aubrey tried unsuccessfully not to smile. "Would it really be so terrible? You have eighteen thousand dollars now, which about matches the twenty Lily will be leaving here with—enough, I would say, to give the both of you a chance to start over. To forgive and forget?"

"Lily? Bah! She'll never forget. And as for forgiving . . . ouch!"

"Sorry."

"As for forgiving," he continued, "she's as mule-headed as someone else I know."

Aubrey switched a bloodied cloth for a clean one. "Maxwell Fleming was responsible for the deaths of my mother, my father, and two brothers. He wanted our land and because my father wouldn't sell, he had them murdered and our home burned to the ground. He destroyed everything I held dear. He almost destroyed me as well. Are you suggesting I should forgive him for what he has done, or merely forget about seeking any kind of revenge?"

"I'm suggesting . . . that I don't want to see you get hurt," Bruster said sincerely. "And I'm simply afraid that if you go any further with this scheme of yours, you will be. You say McBride is back in town—*use* him! A word from you and he would be only too happy to assist you in ridding the world of this vermin once and for all."

"I don't want to *use* him. If anything, I have to think of a way to delay him."

"Delay him?"

"He's made no secret of the fact that he'd like nothing better than to kill Fleming, for reasons of his own."

"Well then goodness gracious, my girl, just stand out

of the way and let him have a clear shot. You're not exactly destitute yourself. You've more than enough squirreled away to give the two of you a fresh start somewhere where the law won't go looking."

"He isn't the kind of man to run away and hide," she said softly. "He's come back for justice, not revenge."

"It would be a justice to kill Maxwell Fleming," he said seriously. "And it would have been a greater justice had I indeed given you over to an orphanage. Neither one of us would have been in the pickle in which we find ourselves now had you learned to tat lace instead of how to deal into a straight flush."

Aubrey reached out and touched his cheek. "No, but it wouldn't have been half so exciting either, would it? Come on now, help me get you into bed before we both turn sentimental and start blubbering in each other's arms."

Bruster strained and grunted with the pain, but he managed, with his good arm slung around Aubrey's shoulders, to haul himself to his feet and stagger to the bed. Aubrey drew back the covers, pulled off his boots, and set his precious derby on the nightstand alongside the fat sheaf of money.

Bruster's head collapsed gratefully against the support of the soft pillows and, before she could rearrange the covers, his eyes had drifted shut and he had slipped into an exhausted sleep. Aubrey sagged onto the nearby chair and propped her arm on the dresser. She knew she had to go and wake Lily, she knew there would be a chaotic storm of questions and accusations she wasn't sure she had the strength to answer. Bruster needed a doctor—one who could be trusted to keep the location and identity of a wounded man to himself. He also needed a fast and safe way out of Santa Fe, preferably under cover of darkness, which meant he would have to remain hidden here throughout the day.

Aubrey lowered her head and rested it on her arm. The first streamers of early morning sunlight were slicing through the slats of the window shutters, catching a spider hard at work repairing the filaments of the web Bruster had torn apart during his unorthodox entrance. It was the same spider, the same web Aubrey had torn and brushed away every morning, and if she thought about it, she supposed she would find a lesson there somewhere about perseverence, or stubbornness . . . or just plain stupidity.

But she couldn't think; she was too tired. Earlier today, tonight, she had been so confident, so cocky she could pull this thing off, but now she was not so sure. Losing Bruster was a blow she might not be able to overcome. Despite his feelings of inadequacy, his role in the days to come would have been extremely crucial. She needed him inside the casino. She needed *someone* inside the casino who knew the setup and knew he would be playing for the win of his life the night she decided to break the house. That had been the plan all along; to play along with Fleming's rules until he let his guard down, then give Bruster the go-ahead to win and win and win until Fleming's golden house of cards came tumbling down.

But now Bruster was out of it, and she was on her own. Alone. Too tired to admit she was frightened—that would come later. Bruster had said Scud Holwell was due back in town any day now; the nightmare, living and breathing and close enough to touch.

Aubrey buried her face in the crook of her elbow. Had it only been an hour ago she'd felt so safe and warm and protected in McBride's arms? Where was he now? Where had he gone after he'd left her? Why *hadn't* she told him what he wanted to know—told him everything? He would feel only contempt for her, contempt for what she was, but Bruster was probably right:

he would kill Maxwell Fleming without a second thought and she would be free.

Free.

She was too tired to even appreciate the taste of the word. Too tired to bother contemplating what else could possibly go wrong.

•

Less than a mile away, something was very wrong indeed. Christian McBride sensed, rather than saw, the movement behind him but as superbly honed as his instincts were, his reflexes had been dulled by the hours of lovemaking. The cold barrel of the gun was pressed against the back of his neck before he could make any counter moves to avoid it. The click of the hammer sounded as loud as a cannon and he braced himself for the explosion to come. Fleming had obviously not taken his promise too lightly and had dispatched one of his thugs to remove the threat before it became a reality.

The expected blast at the base of his skull did not come, however, nor did the last glimpse of his blood and brains spattering on the wall. Instead, the nose of the gun dug deep into his flesh, accompanied by a hissed command to move into the shadowy gap between two buildings. McBride flexed his hands as he obeyed. His Peacemakers were back in the hotel room, and he had returned Aubrey's derringer to her when he had left her at the shop. He had a knife sheathed at the small of his back—too far to reach with a gun cocked and ready to answer any sudden move. He'd been caught out in the open like a novice, still smugly nursing a warm feeling in his groin. He'd been thinking about breasts and soft white thighs, and the palpable little flutters that race through a woman's belly a few moments before she reaches orgasm.

Aubrey. At least she was safe.

The gun moved away from his head. "You can turn around now, sucker," the voice hissed, "but keep those hands reaching for the sky. I see them drop a hair and you'll be face down in the dirt with a hole between your eyes."

Christian turned slowly, his anger visibly heightening the color of his complexion when he saw the tow-headed youth who leaned insolently against the side of the building. He had been stalked and cornered by a mere boy, for God's sake, one whose grin was nearly as big as the fully cocked Colt .45 he held lazily in his left hand.

"Hello, McBride. I heard they let you out of Leavenworth a few months early." William Bonney's pale blue eyes raked indolently up and down Christian's form. "You're looking pretty fit for a walking dead man."

"I feel pretty fit, thanks. Breaking rocks twenty hours a day tends to keep the muscles toned."

"All them friendly boys sweatin' and strainin' alongside you—they keep all the other parts toned as well?"

McBride grinned coldly. "Nah. I thought I'd wait and see if you'd grown up enough to handle me."

Billy waved his Colt airily. "Seems like I done it."

"Seems so. But then, you're working for Fleming now, so I guess you're getting good at back-shooting."

Billy's boyish expression did not change; it was the sudden hard gleam in his eyes that aged him far beyond his years.

"You got no call to go insulting me, now. I ain't never shot no one in the back—ain't never shot no one unless they deserved it."

"We'll put that on your tombstone, shall we? Here lies Billy: The kid who never shot anyone who didn't deserve it."

Billy sighed and shoved his hat off the back of his head so that it dangled by a thong around his neck.

"Aww, shit. You and Ethan both get me right up the ass sometimes. A man can't hardly have any fun anymore."

Christian lowered his hands—cautiously—and laughed. "A man isn't a man until he shaves more than once a month."

"I shave every damned week, you bastard." The twinkle returned to Billy's eyes and he uncocked his gun and holstered it, then clapped his arms around Christian in a bear hug. "How the hell are you, anyway? Damned if you don't look like you put on twenty years whackin' them rocks."

"Sometimes it *feels* like I've put on twenty years. You're even wearing spurs, for Christ's sake, and I still didn't hear you."

"Had you cold and six feet under, if that's where I wanted you," Billy agreed jovially.

"Weren't those Fleming's orders?"

Billy shrugged. "Might be, I dunno. I ain't spoken to him since early last night."

"So why were you following me?"

Billy screwed up his face and scratched through a thatch of sandy-blond hair. "Well, I wasn't. Not in the beginning, anyway. I was . . . ah . . . supposed to be keeping an eye on someone else, but I . . . ah . . . kind of lost her in the dark last night. Figured out later she must have ducked into one of them haciendas along the way. Figured too, that she met someone, maybe. Met someone she knew too, judging by the kinds of noises they were makin' when I went back to have a second look."

Christian's face clouded ominously. "You enjoyed yourself, did you?"

"Hell, I ain't no preevert; I didn't stick around. Besides"—his grin returned in full force—"I knew where she was staying, so I just kind of hung around and waited to see who brung her back. Imagine my surprise when I saw it was you swappin' spit with her in the doorway. And while we're on the subject, do you always kiss a woman that long? I mean, don't it get kinda hard to breathe after a spell?"

"Only if they insist on saying good night at the end."

"Yeah, well, she couldn't exactly invite you in, could she? 'Specially not when she didn't live there."

Christian's jaw tensed. "What do you mean?"

"Just what I said: she don't live there. She don't even live on that street."

Christian took a deep breath and released it before playing into Billy's obvious amusement. "Mind if I ask where she *is* staying?"

"Next street over, halfway down. A dressmaker's shop. Belongs to a woman who calls herself Dolores Tules, but her real handle is Montana. Lily Cruise Montana, to be exact, and she didn't always make dresses. Her and her husband—he's dead now, I hear—used to work the saloons around Taos until Fleming shut 'em down. No love lost between them, far as I can tell."

"In that case, I like her already."

"Yeah, well, seems she's gettin' real popular all of a sudden. I also seen the peddler climbing in one of her back windows."

"The peddler?"

"The short, fat guy who worked the monte game with Miss Blue last night. He crawled through a back window 'bout an hour or so before Miss Blue got there. Ask me, he didn't look none too healthy either. He was limping and favoring his right shoulder, and when I kind of moseyed on over to have a closer look, I saw blood on the ground and the ledge."

Christian digested this news without any humor whatsoever. He had seen Bruster Shillingsworth in the casino, but hadn't really attached any importance to his presence. Anyone could be taught to front for a game of monte, and she and Bruster had been getting friendly out on the Trail. But getting shot . . . and seeking out Aubrey's help afterward . . . ?

What the *hell* was going on here?

"So—" Billy asked mildly, "how come you came back here? Didn't you think Fleming might get kinda nervous having you around?"

"I was hoping he would. He and I have some unfinished business between us—five years' worth of unfinished business, if you know what I mean. What about you?"

"Me? Hell, I just needed a job for a while; it don't mean nothing. I bang a few heads over to the Eagle once in a while, fuss with a few señoritas—" He shrugged. "Easy work. Easy pay."

"Easy way to make a reputation for yourself too."

"Yeah, well, you shouldn't complain. You should be thankful it was me following your lady friend last night and not someone else who wouldn't have stopped to fart before hightailing it back to Fleming with the news."

Christian acknowledged the truth in Billy's words with a wry smile.

"Besides," the Kid added. "I owed you. You done me a favor once, and now was as good a time as any to repay it."

"I would hardly call my giving you a few meals and a dry bedroll a lifetime debt."

"You would if you were twelve years old, livin' off roots and berries, and soaked clear through to the bones for nigh on two weeks running."

"In that case, remind me to share another campfire with you some time."

"It was more than just a campfire. You let me ride with you for over a month."

"Yes, and as I recall"—Christian's eyes narrowed—

"you repaid my generosity by lighting out in the middle of the night with my best horse."

"I sent him back soon as I found my way clear!"

"I still could have had you hung for a horse thief."

"Yeah, well . . ." Billy screwed up his face and scuffed up a clod of dirt. "So I owe you twice. Shit . . . and it was an easy job too." He sighed profusely and spread his hands wide. "I guess I just changed me sides, though."

"Or maybe not," Christian said thoughtfully.

"You sayin' you don't want my help?"

"I'm saying . . . that maybe I want you to go back to the casino and act as if nothing unusual has happened."

"You want me to spy on Fleming?"

"I want you to keep an eye on him for me. Let me know if he makes any plans that might interest me."

"Watch out for your back, you mean."

"Something like that. Unless you have something better to do . . . ?"

Billy grinned. "Hell no. I was beginning to think things were getting a little dull around here."

"I'll see if I can't liven things up then. Just for you."

"You done that already," Billy assured him. "And with Scud Holwell due back in town any day now—" He arched his eyebrows and gave a low whistle.

"I was getting around to asking you about that—I haven't seen his ugly face anywhere yet."

"You will. Fleming won't have to give him any orders to go and hunt you down. He and that albino were like this"—he crossed his fingers—"and he's one *hombre* who holds a grudge a long, long time. A right mean bastard with women too. Can't get it off unless he breaks a bit of skin first. Fleming uses him sometimes to keep his girls in line—another thought you might want to take to heart . . . or even pass on, if you know what I mean."

Christian thought of Aubrey and Holwell together and his gut tightened. "There are quite a few things I want to discuss with Miss Blue; you can be sure I'll add that to the list."

Billy glanced around as a sliver of sunlight broke over the gate at the end of the alley. "You won't be discussing nothing with nobody if we stand around jawing much longer. I'll give you a count of fifteen for a head start." He held out his hand and chuckled. "And don't worry none about your back; I'll take good care of it."

"Thanks, Billy." Christian returned the firm handshake. "Oh, and next time you sneak up on a man—" He pulled Billy forward and brought his other hand up to press the point of his knife into the soft depression above the slimmer man's belly. "Make sure you disarm him *before* you uncock your gun."

Billy cursed good-naturedly and watched McBride move out into the bright morning light. A fat, iridescent fly buzzed by looking for something rotten to gorge on and, without looking away from the street, Billy's hand shot out and scooped the insect out of the air. He held it in his fist, letting it tickle the palm of his hand for a moment, then squeezed his fingers closed until he felt the sticky *pop* of the exploding body.

He muttered, "Fifteen," aloud and sauntered out onto the boardwalk, wiping his hand down his pants as he carefully scanned both ends of the street. This time of the morning the only signs of life on the Alameda were the drunks sleeping it off in a friendly doorway, and the odd horse whose owner had abandoned it for the gaming tables or the bars.

It was hot and getting hotter with every dry gust of dust-laden wind. Billy settled his hat over his head and rooted in his pocket for a plug of tobacco, then casually strolled away in the direction opposite the one McBride had taken. He, like McBride, did not notice the face in the hotel window across the street. Nor did he notice the curtain dropping back in place, released by the same, slightly unsteady hand that lifted a full glass of whiskey to his lips.

"Well, well, well," said Darby Greaves. "Now what do you make of that? The Kid and the plainsman together this time of the morning, laughing and chatting like old friends."

He turned from the window and his naked body glistened with a faint sheen of sweat in the heat. He looked at the bed and tossed back the contents of his glass, then set the empty tumbler aside and walked across the room.

Anna Lee watched his approach without pleasure or disdain—without any emotion whatsoever. The effects of the opium she had smoked earlier were still making her feel weighted and sluggish, as if her body were suspended in a clear, heavy liquid. She did not mind being given to Greaves. He was more handsome than most of Fleming's soft and paunchy business associates, and not too demanding in bed, especially when he had been drinking a lot. When he drank, he talked. He talked and he talked and he talked . . .

Anna Lee stretched and yawned. The bedsprings sagged beside her, but he didn't touch her, not right away, and she knew she'd have to endure more talk before he'd take an interest in her.

"Thinks he's smarter than me, does he?" Greaves mused. "Thinks he's rich and smart and powerful enough to know *everything*. Well he doesn't know everything, does he? There's things he don't know about Clara and me, and there's things he don't know about the schoolteacher that would cause him to take a hard crap if he knew."

Greaves turned his head to look at Anna Lee, not really expecting any response. Her face was blank, inscrutable as always, her eyes empty of any comprehension.

"What do you think he'd do if he knew his good friend McBride had already been to the well a few times? Filled her up pretty good too, damn near every night between Kansas and here." He grinned slyly and pinched Anna Lee's chin between his fingers, forcing her to face him. "What do you think, sweetheart? Think he'd be interested in knowing he's got McBride's woman working for him?"

He searched the glazed brown eyes for any sign of shared humor, then released her chin with a good-natured curse. He grabbed a fistful of the gleaming black hair instead and steered her head down and over his groin.

"Sweetheart . . . talking to you is like talking to a warm wall. Only one other thing you do well besides listen, honey, only one language we both understand. That's right, baby, start talkin'. You talk and I'll think and maybe we'll come up with the best way to make use of what we know."

23

 Aubrey woke with a start. Someone nearby was banging pots and pans, and humming a tune that combined three or four songs into one. She blinked when she saw Bruster stretched out on the bed and it took several moments of hard thought before she remembered how they came to be in their respective positions.

After standing and slowly straightening an arm that had gone numb from the elbow down, Aubrey reached forward and checked the makeshift dressing she had placed over his wound. The bleeding seemed to have stopped, but the edges of torn flesh were red-raw and looked sickeningly like uncooked meat.

She gathered up the dirty cloths and the basin of water, rinsing the former and emptying the contents of the washbowl out the window before she worked up the nerve to go and fetch Dolores. Judging by the height of the sun, it was between ten and eleven o'clock, and she quickly closed the shutters again, blocking out as much of the stifling heat and dusty sunlight as she could.

Aubrey had her hand on the latch of the door when she heard the sound of a bell tinkling on the outer door of the shop. Dolores's humming left the kitchen and faded through the shop, breaking off completely for a shout of greeting to whoever had come through the door. Aubrey glanced back at Bruster, asleep and unmoving, then at the wavering reflection of herself in the fly-spotted mirror. She was still dressed in the loosely laced corset and petticoats. Her hair was a wild black mass of tangles around her shoulders and her eyes were puffy and red from lack of sleep.

She dropped her hand away from the latch. It wouldn't help matters any if she burst out into the shop looking as if she had spent the night in a brothel. Dolores would have enough questions about Bruster without setting her fomenting curiosity loose on Aubrey's appearance.

With one eye on Bruster and one ear on the sounds coming from outside the door, Aubrey stripped off the corset and the fancy underpinnings and donned a single plain cotton shift before pulling a gingham dress over her head. Her hair required a savage volley of brush strokes and a hastily skewered pair of combs to tame the curls back from her temples, but when she was finished, she looked decent enough, if still a little too flushed for comfort.

She ventured out into the kitchen the same instant Dolores came sweeping through the curtained doorway.

"There you are! Land sakes, gal, it's almost noon and I've about chewed through every fingernail and toenail waiting for you to come on out and tell me all the gossip. Lordy, don't you look like the wrath of God!"

"Dolores—"

"_Not that I've_ had a chance to sleep the morning away. My shop's been buzzing like a hive since the crack of dawn, with everyone either wanting to know what I knew about the fancy new singing star over to the Golden Eagle, or all about the bee-you-tee-ful young dealer who almost stole the stage out from beneath her!

I've had three ladies and two whores—not that you can put too much store in *their* opinions—coming in here with orders for me to make copies of that there dress you wore. I tell you, my door ain't swung for so much traffic since the old governor's wife found out his mistress bought all her gewgaws off me."

"Dolores, I have something to tell you—"

"I should hope to Hades you have something to tell me, gal, and—damnation! There goes that blamed bell again!"

Beaming ear to ear, Dolores disappeared behind the curtain again. Aubrey rubbed her throbbing temples and poured a cool glass of fresh milk out of the pitcher. She had only half finished it when Dolores came back, the huge smile still in place, her red curls bobbing this way and that as she shook her head.

"Here now, that's no kind of a breakfast to speak of," she scolded. "Set yourself down and I'll fry us up a mess of cheese tortillas—"

"Dolores . . . Bruster is in my room. He was shot last night and didn't know where else to go, so he came here. He's lost a lot of blood, and—"

Dolores dropped the fry pan she was holding. The *clang-g-g* reverberated in the silence for several seconds, almost drowning out the tinkle of the shop bell.

"Lucius was shot?"

Aubrey glanced at the curtain. "In the shoulder. I managed to clean it and get him into the bed, but I don't know . . . he might need a doctor, and I . . ."

Heavy, even footsteps were pacing the wooden floor out in the shop and Dolores joined Aubrey in staring at the curtain divider.

"You see who it is," she hissed, already on her way to the bedroom. "Give 'em the old heave-ho quick as you can and bolt the door behind them; I'll tend to Lucius. And for God's sake, pinch some color into your cheeks.

If it's the law, it won't do for you to greet them looking guilty as a ghost."

Aubrey was startled. She hadn't even considered the possibility of the law searching after Bruster, but if, as Dolores had taken great pains in explaining previously, Fleming and his associates *were* the law in Santa Fe, then it could make a bad situation even worse.

"But shouldn't you be the one—?"

"Nope." Dolores reached over, without warning, and unfastened the top few buttons on Aubrey's bodice. "They'll want to believe anything you go and tell them far quicker than they'd swallow anything I had to say. Now go on. And smile. This ain't the time for either one of us to fall apart."

Aubrey waited until Dolores was behind the closed bedroom door before she braced herself with a deep breath and walked out into the shop. Her sense of panic wilted like a collapsing balloon when she saw two women bent over a bolt of cloth and exchanging furious whispers. It returned with the heated rush of a brushfire when she saw whom they were whispering furiously about.

Christian McBride stood just inside the door, his broad, buckskin-clad shoulders framed against the brilliant flare of light from the street.

"Buenos dias, señorita," he murmured, then removed his wide-brimmed hat as he turned to acknowledge the other two customers. "Señoras. A lovely morning for shopping, is it not?"

Aubrey released her breath on a gust. "What on earth are you doing here?"

McBride smiled innocently and looked around. "Well now, I surely hope I've come to the right place. I was told that Doña Dolores Tules had one of the finest selections of fancy wear in all of New Mexico. Might you be . . . ah, Doña Dolores?"

Aubrey was conscious of the blush creeping into her cheeks and of the dead silence on the far side of the room.

"Doña Dolores is busy at the moment. Is there something *I* could help you with?"

"Why, I'd be much obliged, ma'am. You see, it's my little sister's birthday—she's turning fifteen and thinks she's all grown up, so I thought I could find her something . . . you know . . . all grown up. I confess, I'm a mite shy when it comes to buying gifts for a young lady. I can tell you a general size and shape—why, it's very much like your own, in fact—but when it comes down to choosing what's right and proper, I tend to get my feathers and my ribbons mixed."

The women tittered and were quick to agree that men were hopeless when it came to shopping for a lady. Reasonably assured he had not come into the shop to wreak havoc or shoot holes in their bonnets with the enormous guns he wore strapped to his waist, they bent their heads over the bolts of cloth again, urging Aubrey to serve the gentleman ahead of them.

Her face hot and her blue eyes threatening physical harm, Aubrey was forced to play along and steered him toward a table displaying several finely worked lace mantillas.

McBride barely gave them a glance.

"At least look as if you really came to buy something," she hissed under her breath.

"Oh, but I did," he said, pausing here and there to admire a swatch of silk or satin. He came, as Aubrey should have known he would, to the special shelves of dainty undergarments, and managed to pick out the skimpiest, sheerest article on display.

"What is this?" he asked as the slippery red silk unfurled between his hands.

Aubrey snatched it away. "A nightgown. And not at all what you're looking for, I'm sure."

"You're absolutely right," he agreed. "The color is all wrong. Now this—" He held up an almost transparent version of the same gown in blue. "This would match her eyes, right down to the sparkle they get when she's angry. They're about the same color as yours too, ma'am, do you mind?"

Before she could answer, he was holding the gown up in front of her. It was sheer enough, even with a double thickness, to reveal every wrinkle and crease in Aubrey's gingham dress, and she could tell by the look in his eyes, that he was having no difficulty imagining the effect against bare flesh.

"I'll take it. How much?"

She swiped it out of his hand. "For you, *sir?* Twenty dollars."

"Twenty dollars?" He whistled softly. "For that much, I could buy a good buffalo robe."

"In that case, I suggest you look elsewhere. You won't find anything here priced much cheaper."

She refolded the gown and started to return it to the shelf, but stopped when he held out a shiny gold double eagle.

"For that much, I presume it comes wrapped?"

Aubrey glanced over at the two women, then back at McBride.

"Fine. I'll wrap it for you." She lowered her voice to a fierce whisper and added, "Then will you leave?"

She fetched a square of brown paper, folded, wrapped, and tied the parcel with twine, conscious all the while of Christian's eyes boring into her. When she finished, she pushed the package across the top of the counter, careful not to brush hands with him.

"I have to talk to you," he said quietly.

"You are talking to me."

"Privately."

"I don't think that would be such a good idea."

"You'd rather talk here, then? In the back room, perhaps? I would have thought it was getting a little too crowded for comfort."

Aubrey met the steely gray eyes. There was no mistaking what he was saying. He knew Bruster was back there—how, she had no idea, but he knew.

"When can we meet?" he asked evenly.

"I'm . . . busy all day."

"Tonight, then."

"I have to work."

"Before you go to work."

"Really, I don't see what this will accomplish—"

"There is a smithy at the edge of town—Ortegas. Do you know it?"

"No."

"I'm sure you are resourceful enough to find it. Be there at seven o'clock sharp."

Aubrey bristled at the order. "And if I'm not?"

He leaned over the counter and smiled. "I'll just have to come and get you."

He touched the brim of his hat and started to back away. Dolores chose that particular moment to come sweeping through the curtain. She saw the two women and drew up short. She saw the tall plainsman and her eyes flew so wide open, they nearly popped from her head.

"Well, if this ain't the damnedest morning for surprises," she murmured. "Christian McBride. I thought the buzzards would have got you long ago."

Christian's smile was politely puzzled. "Beg pardon, ma'am? Do we know each other?"

"Hell no, you'd have no call to know me unless you was in for a dress fittin', but I sure as shootin' know you. Ain't a warm-blooded soul in all of Santa Fe don't know the damned fool who up and shot Maxwell Fleming's pet albino. Not that a single one of us grudged him that bullet, mind, him being one of the meanest orneriest varmints ever took to walking upright on two legs. No one thought it none too fair, either, that the judge sentenced you to five years for doing all of us a favor, but there you go. Grease a palm sweet enough and I warrant the pope himself could be found guilty of fornication, and Fleming never did have no shortage of sweet grease. What the devil are you doing walking around in broad daylight? And why"—she looked around as if recognizing her surroundings for the first time—"are you walking around in my shop?"

Christian held up the wrapped parcel. "Miss Blue was kind enough to advise me on the purchase of a gift."

Dolores glanced at Aubrey and saw the double eagle lying on the counter. "Must have been a hell of a gift."

"Worth every penny, I expect," he grinned. After a long, last look at the flush blooming in Aubrey's cheeks, he tipped his hat again and strode out the door. Dolores followed as far as the window to peer out after him, craning her neck out of its creases to see through the slats in the shutters.

"Well, Lord and Christ, if that don't just beat all. Between him and his damn fool of a brother—" She turned and came eyeball to eyeball with the two female customers who had remained quietly intrigued through the entire exchange. "Well? You two planning on buying something, or just standing there and taking up floor space?"

The women gasped and hurried to the door. Dolores closed it behind them with a loud enough bang to ensure their indignant choler for the rest of the day, then slipped the bolt to guard against any further interruptions. She did not look happy at all and Aubrey decided the best tact would be avoidance.

"How is Lucius?"

"He'll live, more's the pity. I was just coming out to fetch a needle and some stout thread to stitch up the holes in his hide. I didn't know we were holding a convention out here. And *you* never mentioned you knew Christian McBride."

"He was on the same stage from Kansas," Aubrey confessed. "But he only went as far as the Cimarron, then left us. I was as surprised as anyone to see him at the Golden Eagle last night."

"He was at the Eagle? He and Fleming were under the same roof together?" Dolores's bright green eyes narrowed, noting that Aubrey's face and throat were still stained a soft, uncomfortable pink. "What else is choking on you, gal? Spit it out."

Aubrey shook her head. "There is nothing else. I'm just tired, is all."

"Hmph! And I'll bet every last wrinkle and grass stain in that fine satin frock, I know why. Fair is fair, though," she said, holding up a pudgy hand. "You don't have to tell me anything more if you don't want to, and I'd be the last one to poke my nose where it wasn't wanted, but if you'd care to remember, I already know a pile more than I care to know, so it won't change the shape of the world for me to know it all. Besides, child—" Her voice softened and her brows lifted a little bemusedly. "You look about fit to bust needing *someone* to talk to, and whether you like it or not, I'm about all you got next to Lucius, and *he's* about as useless as tits on a bull right now. Even if he comes around in the next hour or so, I'll be knocking him silly again just to save myself the aggravation of listening to him whine."

"Are you certain he doesn't need a doctor?"

"Bah! Old Doc Langtry wouldn't do anything I can't do with a threaded needle and a healthy dollop of whiskey. Come along now, honey; you can talk while I stitch, and when we're done we can both sit and think of a way to get that old bag of wind out of town. I reckon he's pretty safe where he is until nightfall, but after that . . . well, that's when Fleming's hounds start to get a real keen scent for blood. What's more, I just heard, not an hour ago, that Fleming's prize bloodhound was seen not ten miles from town!"

•

Even as she spoke, three riders were trotting down the outlying streets of Santa Fe. They rode abreast, straight down the middle of the road, the hooves of their horses churning up clouds of fine white dust in their wakes.

The rider in the middle was a thick-set, coarsely dressed man, ugly beyond redemption, and familiar enough to the local residents to send them scurrying behind walls and out of his sight. His face was a mass of mottled pockmarks, his nose a swollen, grotesque bulb of deformity, broken so many times there was no longer any bridge or slope dividing the wide-set eyes. His jaw was square and stubbled, his shoulders bowed like an ape's. He wore a tall, black beaver hat, the rim crushed and torn on one side, the crown wrinkled and canted like a tired old stovepipe. One of his eyes suffered from heavy scarring, the lid welded half-shut, the ball of the eye coated in a leaky white film that had, in recent years, begun to limit his vision on that side to blurred shapes and colors.

The thickening cataract did not impede either his effectiveness as a gunslinger, or his general viciousness to all of mankind. He asked for neither sympathy nor pity, and usually killed anyone foolish enough to offer it. Quick to respond to any insult, real or imagined, he wore a shotgun slung across his back bandolero-style, the barrel sawed six inches shorter than the maker's design. He wore Colts strapped to his thighs and carried a Sharps carbine in a saddle sling. There were other weapons tucked and sheathed beneath the folds of his clothing—a pair of knives, a set of brass knuckles, a length of knotted wire handy for garroting throats—but he preferred to use his fists in a close fight. He liked the sound and feel of flesh crushing, tearing apart between his fingers. It gave him pleasure to hear a man or woman scream, and it gave him a sense of power to see his victim's eyes fill with pure terror.

Scud Holwell turned his horse onto the Alameda and fixed his one good eye on the gilded arch of the Golden Eagle saloon. It had been ten days since the episode with the whore and the priest, and Holwell felt a chilling shudder of anticipation slither into his loins. As much as he fought to deny it, as cruelly and brutally as he strove to disprove it with every whore and harlot in Santa Fe, he could not completely repress the heat and sickness of the hunger he felt each time he looked upon the elegantly handsome features of Maxwell Fleming.

Fleming had no idea, of course. No one had any idea that Scud Holwell's obsessive loyalty was based on anything other than just that: the allegiance of a dumb beast to its master. But ten days away from Fleming had been a worse torment than anyone would have imagined. And his need to redeem himself in his master's eyes was so overwhelmingly potent, he had ridden the last few miles into town with a bulge the size of his own two fists straining the front of his pants.

He was glad Fleming had called him back for a specific reason, and he was almost maniacally pleased the reason was Christian McBride. Only once before had he given way to his perverse desire to sheath himself in another man's flesh, and that had been because the other man had harbored an equally aberrant lust for Scud Holwell's brutal ugliness. Whitey Martin had bided his time until Scud had been drunk enough, weak enough with hunger for Fleming, and had slavishly played the whore, offering his pale body in groveling supplication that had made Scud ill each time the glazed pink eyes dared him to deny the memories . . . or the pleasure.

Holwell had taken advantage of a crowded room and a lot of confusion to close those telltale eyes permanently. And, since the murder had conveniently put McBride behind bars, Fleming hadn't even questioned the necessity of killing a good man.

Hunting down McBride now would put the memories to rest once and for all. Hearing him scream, feeling his blood pour hot and steaming over his hands would make up for the clean, fast shot that had ended the albino's miserable life.

Holwell reined his horse to a halt in front of the Golden Eagle. The two men who had accompanied him into town noted his discomfort as he dismounted, but ribaldly credited it to the lack of female company in the foothills. Holwell grunted his agreement and wondered, absently, if the new monte dealer they had been telling him about was half the looker they claimed her to be.

24

Aubrey arrived at the smithy a few minutes before seven o'clock. She was determined to make the meeting as brief as possible and to keep it as unemotional as possible. Unfortunately, she was not at her best, having spent a restless afternoon contending with every calamity a vivid imagination could project. Between Dolores's unsympathetic I-told-you-so's to her own growing sense of impending failure, she was on a decidedly short fuse and not altogether confident about the wisdom of seeing McBride.

The doors to the smithy were open, the interior dark and empty aside from the bellows, fire pit, and clutter of tools associated with the blacksmith's trade. There was a small lean-to stable out back of the smithy, and behind it, separated by a dozen long paces, a compact adobe dwelling with a low-hung door and a chimney trailing an opaque finger of smoke up into the purpling twilight.

The door was ajar and she saw Christian right away, standing in front of the cooking fire, one foot braced on a low bench as he prodded the coals with an iron poker. Talking to him was an older Mexican she did not recognize; small of build, his face a mass of weatherworn creases and crags, all but camouflaged behind an enormously bushy moustache. Neither man saw her and she was content to stand for a moment and observe.

She could no longer deny the instant flush of warmth that spread through her at the sight of McBride. Dressed as he was now in the familiar buckskins, or as he had been last night in the refinements of broadcloth and linen, there was power, pride, and sensuality, bold and unyielding, in every hard line of his body. He was handsome almost beyond decency, noble beyond endurance, as well as arrogant, cynical, courageous, tender . . . more vulnerable and less indifferent than he probably cared to admit to the feelings she had no idea how or why she had roused in him.

". . . *I'm not free and I don't think I will be free until I either find out what put you in my blood, or find a way to get you the hell out . . .*"

His words, but she might well have said them. She did not know if this tightness in her chest and this helpless numbness that coursed through her body was love, but it was the closest she had ever come to it. She wished, standing there in the dusk and shifting desert breeze, that the admission and the acceptance had come to her a week and a half sooner. A week and a half ago, on the banks of the Cimarron River, revenge had been the single most important thing governing her choices and her life. It still mattered, here in the chilling shadows of the Sangre de Cristo mountains, but not nearly as much as hearing him repeat his pledge not to abandon her.

Love, she thought, was too much to hope for, but if he asked her just to ride away with him now, or if he promised only the warmth and comfort of his arms and his body, she would accept them gladly and not even take the time to turn and look back.

Aubrey was startled out of her musings by a movement beside her. She looked up to see Sun Shadow's stark features bathed in the errant beams of lamplight that strayed out the open door. His expression was as implacable as the planes of his face; there was neither surprise nor anger nor pleasure mirrored in the dark brown eyes. She could have been a complete stranger to him for all the reaction he showed.

"Christian told me you were anxious to see your wife again," she said. "I hope both she and the baby are well."

The slightest frown creased the regal brow as he debated whether or not to be offended by the extent of her knowledge of his personal life. It changed into wide-eyed shock when he realized she addressed him in his own language.

"Some women," he remarked dryly, "are far too clever for their own good. And they keep far too many secrets from the wrong people."

Aubrey smiled. "I have a feeling that's about to change."

Christian came to the door when he heard their voices.

"I'm glad you decided to meet me," he said to Aubrey.

"Did I have a choice?"

The gray eyes lingered on her face a moment then he sent Sun Shadow back into the thickening twilight with a slight nod. He invited Aubrey inside the tiny, one-room dwelling and indicated a seat by the fire. The Mexican was introduced simply as "Manuelo"; he bowed with a polite "señorita" and discreetly left them to talk alone.

Aubrey declined the offered chair and waited for the door to close behind Manuelo before she took a more detailed inventory of the room. Aside from the chair, there was a handmade bench and table, and a narrow rope-slung cot in a far corner. A large black kettle hung steaming over the fire, and beside the mantel, a single

shelf held the spartan extent of a bachelor's dreary existence—a bowl, plate, cup, and a scattering of cooking
utensils. A spare change of clothes similar to the shapeless white cotton shirt and trousers Manuelo had been
wearing hung on pegs beside the bed. It was neat and
utilitarian, and had probably looked much the same
through several generations of Ortegas, married or not.

"Well?" She turned to McBride. "Now that you have
me here, what was so important that you wanted to discuss?"

"I was hoping you would tell me."

"Me? What would I possibly have to tell you?"

"Oh . . . who you are, for a start. *What* you are
might also rate a more detailed explanation, along with
your precise relationship to Armbruster Shillingsworth.
But if nothing else, I am most intrigued to find out what
the hell you are doing in Santa Fe, and why, every time I
think I have you figured out, you go and pull another
quick change so that I'm left feeling like I'm standing
there with my jaw—and my pants—wide open."

He was angry. Angrier than she had ever seen him,
and instinctively, she took a step back toward the door.

"It won't do you any good," he said bluntly. "The
door is locked and both Manuelo and Sun Shadow have
orders to keep it that way until they hear otherwise from
me."

Aubrey retreated another step, whirled in disbelief,
and ran to the door. The wooden latch gave freely
enough to her outraged tugs, but the door itself did not
budge. Something or someone was locking it in place
from the outside.

"How dare you!" she cried, whirling again to confront
him. "You can't keep me here against my will! It's . . .
it's *kidnapping!*"

Christian crossed his arms belligerently over his chest
and leaned one shoulder on the adobe wall. "It's a

warning, madam. A warning that I am about at the end of my tether . . . and good humor."

Aubrey stared at him and whatever warm, sentimental feelings she'd experienced a few minutes ago went up in the smoke of her erupting temper. *"You* are at the end of *your* tether? Excuse me, but I seem to be the one who cannot turn around without bumping squarely into *you!* You don't own me, McBride. I don't owe you *any* explanations, and I demand that you open this door at once, or I'll . . . I'll—"

"You'll what—scream? Go ahead. No one will hear you. Draw on me again? Try it, and you'll be flat on your back with two blackened eyes . . . for a start."

"It wouldn't surprise me one bit to know you'd raise your fists to a woman," she said coldly. "After five years in prison, I imagine brutality is your first response to just about anything."

"Or we can just stand here trading insults," he continued blithely. "I can't say for certain where *you've* been for the past five years, but judging by your performances both in and out of your clothes, I can make a pretty good guess."

Aubrey spun away and rattled the door latch again, more out of frustration than out of any hope it might magically have come unbarred. *She* was angrier than *she* could recall being in a long time, and she bowed her head forward, banging it lightly on the wood in a gesture of utter disgust.

"Knocking yourself out won't win any sympathy or open any doors either," he remarked casually.

Aubrey's shoulders sagged slightly and she shook her head in weary resignation. "All right, McBride: you win. What exactly is it that you want from me?"

"A little truth. A little honesty. Maybe even a little trust." He saw her hands clench into fists where they pressed against the door, and he added in a softer tone,

"I know you told me no one has ever given you any reason to trust them . . . but have I ever given you any reason *not* to trust me?"

In the taut, lengthy silence that followed the question, Christian saw her fists unclench and the fingers spread flat on the wood, then curl and draw up tight again as if the answer might cause physical pain.

"You're giving me one now," she whispered.

"Chalk this up to the act of a desperate man," he countered. "Have I ever given you any *other* reason to treat me like something you just scraped off your shoe?"

Aubrey turned around, but kept her back pressed up against the door. "You wouldn't understand."

His anger surfaced with a brief flush of red and it took a massive effort to control it as he walked slowly toward her. "I can't understand what I don't know, and I don't know what you won't tell me."

Aubrey faltered under his approach and slid sideways along the wall, the cloth of her bolero jacket snagging on the rough patches of adobe. He cut her off in a blur of fringed buckskin, his arms shooting past her shoulder to block any further retreat.

"I'm in no mood for games, Aubrey," he warned. "Verbal or otherwise."

Aubrey met the steely gray eyes and felt her heart slide into the pit of her belly. "You won't like the answers."

"Let me be the judge of that."

She lowered her lashes, took a deep breath, and raised them again. "What do you want to know?"

"Bruster Shillingsworth. What is he to you?"

"A friend."

"What do you mean by . . . *friend?*"

"Well, he isn't a relative. He isn't an uncle or a

brother or a nephew or a cousin. He isn't my father or my lover. That leaves . . . a friend."

Christian grit his teeth. "All right, so he's a friend. But you didn't just meet him in Great Bend, did you?"

"I really don't see where this is leading."

"This"—he placed more of his weight on his hands, bringing his face and torso closer to Aubrey—"is leading to the fact that if I could figure out that you and Bruster were more than casual traveling companions, then others can figure it out too—specifically Maxwell Fleming."

"Why should he care if I knew Bruster before Great Bend or not?"

"So you're admitting you did know him?"

"No. I'm merely wondering why it would interest Fleming if I did."

Her gaze was steady on his, her eyes so cool and deep and blue he could feel himself wanting to glance down at her mouth, and he had to catch himself, stop himself from thinking about the taste and feel of her.

"It would interest Fleming, my little chameleon, for the simple reason that he would be interested in anyone who conspires to cheat him out of eighteen thousand dollars."

"I had nothing to do with the eighteen thousand," she insisted, saying it with enough genuine bitterness to win a faint smile from McBride.

"Went against orders, did he?"

"I don't give Bruster orders," she said evenly.

"Since you don't take them very well, either, the 'friendship' must be a damned interesting one at times. Which brings us back around to my original question: How long have you known Armbruster Shillingsworth?"

"Since we boarded the coach at Great Bend," she replied truthfully. A heartbeat later, when she saw the thin white line tauten around his lips, she added calmly,

"However, I've known Lucius Beebee for ten years, give or take a few months."

"Lucius Beebee?"

"Lucius Armbruster Beebee, to be *precise*. He changes the first and last names around, depending on where we are and what we are doing, but he likes to keep a common nickname so that neither of us stumbles accidentally."

Christian's frown deepened. He wore the look of a man who had just taken a shot in the dark and scored a direct hit.

But what had he hit?

And why, suddenly, did it feel as if a blindfold had just been whipped away from his eyes?

"Son of a bitch," he muttered, straightening slowly. "Son of a goddamn bitch!"

"If all you are going to do is swear—"

"Don't!" He held up a hand, the forefinger pointing threateningly. "Don't say another word. You just stand there real quiet and maybe—*maybe* you'll get through this with your neck in one piece."

He stood back and raked his hands through his hair. He paced to the hearth, stopped, opened his mouth to speak, then shut it again as if the words were simply too implausible to say.

"What is it you are struggling to comprehend, McBride?" she asked dryly. "The fact that Bruster and I work together, or the fact that we work very well together?"

"Obviously not well enough," he snapped. "Bruster caught a bullet last night, didn't he?"

"How did you know that?"

"The same way I knew you were staying at the dressmaker's shop and the same way I knew he snuck through a back window last night and got there about an hour before you. Is he still there now?"

"It's kind of you to ask about his wound," she said archly. "Unfortunately, it was bad enough we didn't think he should be moved until tonight, when it would be darker and safer."

"We?"

Aubrey smiled tightly. "His wife and I."

Another small piece of the puzzle slipped into place as Christian remembered something else Billy had told him that morning, although God only knew what the whole picture would look like when it was finished.

"Lily Cruise Montana . . . is Bruster's wife? And you still don't think Fleming will make a connection?"

It was on the tip of her tongue to ask how he knew about Lily, but she refused to take the bait. "Why should he? *I* didn't even know they were man and wife until we got here."

"Ahh, and so we arrive at the next pair of question marks. Why the two of you came here in the first place, and why the need to pretend you were traveling separately as a *schoolteacher* and a *corset salesman?* It seems odd you would have gone to so much trouble to establish separate identities on board a stagecoach full of strangers."

Aubrey bit her lip and averted her eyes—gestures that were becoming familiar enough to McBride to tell him to back up a step and look at the question from another angle.

"You weren't trying to avoid a connection on the coach," he speculated slowly. "You were more concerned that no one should recognize you leaving Great Bend together."

She glared up at him with a sullen frown. "You're obnoxious when you gloat, you know."

"And you look like a ten-year-old when you sulk. Just answer the question."

"I didn't think you were asking one. I thought you had it all figured out."

"Humor me. *Were* you trying to avoid someone back in Great Bend?"

Aubrey took refuge behind the thick shield of her lashes. "It wasn't anyone important."

"Aubrey," he said warningly.

"Well he wasn't. He isn't. Not here in New Mexico, anyway. At least I don't think he has jurisdiction . . ."

"Jurisdiction?"

Her lashes lifted a fraction. "He is an associate of Alan Pinkerton."

"The detective?"

"And close friend of the governor of Louisiana, we learned belatedly."

Christian shook his head. For every inch of progress he was gaining, he seemed to be losing a foot.

"Why," he asked with supreme patience, "is a Pinkerton detective after you?"

The cool, dark blue of her eyes met his boldly. "Because he disapproves of our line of work."

"Which is?"

She sighed in exasperation. "Really, McBride . . . do you need it spelled out? If so, let me explain it as plainly as possible. Bruster is a hustler and a cheat. *I* am a hustler and a cheat. We work at hustling and cheating together, in gambling houses, riverboats, hotels, and two-bit saloons; wherever there is a deck of cards or a ripe mark waiting to be fleeced. We have run lottery games and swindled phony railroad stock. We can deal, play, and cheat at more games of chance than you probably know, and in dry times, can pick any lock on any safe and be in and out of a room without disturbing so much as a speck of dust."

Christian stared at her without blinking. The color

ebbed from Aubrey's cheeks, then flowed into them again, darker and hotter than before.

"I told you you wouldn't like the answers," she said tersely. "Are you happy now, or is there anything else you're having trouble understanding?"

"Only one thing," he said quietly. "Why?"

"Because we're good at it," she snapped. "Because it was what Bruster did when I met him and . . . and at the time, there didn't seem to be anything wrong with taking advantage of someone else's greed and stupidity."

Christian seemed to need another long moment to absorb the full impact of what she was saying. He hadn't moved a muscle throughout her declaration, and he was still as a statue now, his hair lighted in a nimbus of bright gold by the fire, blazing like the fiery halo of a righteous archangel.

"You said you've been with Bruster for ten years," he murmured. "How old are you now?"

"Hardly a polite question to ask a lady."

He smiled the same smile he wore when he faced down the Comanche warrior. "I'm not feeling very polite, and right now, I'd say you were stretching the definition of a lady."

"Twenty-three," she said narrowly.

"So that son of a bitch has had you working in saloons . . . since you were thirteen?"

"No. He didn't have me *working* at all, not in the beginning. I was an orphan and he took care of me the best way he knew how."

"Please." Christian drew a deep breath. "Spare me the hard luck story; the one about the poor little orphan girl saved from the gutter by a sweet, generous old fool who tried—and failed miserably, to his everlasting regret—to turn her into a proper young lady of genteel breeding."

A dull red heat crept up Aubrey's throat and into her cheeks. "Go to hell, McBride."

"I'm undoubtedly bound there already on an express train. It's *your* soul we're trying to salvage here."

"What makes you think I want salvaging?"

"Call it a wild hunch," he said wryly. "Or just call it a feeling I have that you don't really want to spend the next ten years rotting away behind bars. I've been there, remember, and I can safely say hell looks a lot more appealing."

Aubrey withstood the fierce intensity of his eyes for as long as she could, but in the end was the first to look away. "Why couldn't you just have left me alone?" she asked softly. "Why can't you just leave me alone now and let me finish what I have to do?"

"What *exactly* do you have to do?"

Aubrey bit down on her lip. "That's my business, not yours."

"The hell it isn't."

"The hell it is!" Sparks of anger were back in her eyes as she looked over again. "I haven't come all this way to let some great hulking plainsman tell me what to do. I can and will manage my own life without any help from you!"

"I bloody well wasn't offering any."

"Fine."

"Fine!"

"Then I'll be on my way—*if* you have no further objections."

"Lady, you haven't begun to hear my objections. And if you rattle that damn door latch once more, I swear I really will lay you out flat on your backside."

More to rebel against his tone than to challenge his threat, Aubrey tugged and yanked on the latch, and hammered on the wood until her fist was grabbed from behind and twisted around into the small of her back.

Aubrey spun to try to avoid him, but the hand she swung out to use as a counterbalance struck him on the shoulder, damaging nothing but his already bruised and badly frayed temper. Cursing, Christian swung her up and over the bend of his knee, breaking the stiffness in her legs and causing her to sprawl on the floor at his feet. He was on his knees, straddling her before the shock of her ignominious position replaced the painful impact of the fall.

In a flurry of thrashing limbs and frothed petticoats, she fought to wriggle out from between his knees, and he was forced to catch her wrists again and pin them flat on the floor above her head.

"Let me go!" she shrieked.

"Not until I'm finished with you, and I *will* finish with you, if I have to stake you out hand and foot to the ground!"

She was smart enough not to challenge him a second time, and, after one last struggle, lay still. Her cheeks were flamed with indignation, her eyes were the deepest, darkest blue Christian had ever seen them and he reinforced his grip on her wrists not a moment too soon.

"Now, you were about to tell me exactly what it was you had to finish? I was under the impression you and Bruster worked together as a team."

"We do . . . most of the time."

"*Most* of the time?"

"Most of the time we agree on the mark. We didn't agree this time; Bruster didn't even want to come to Santa Fe, he just—"

"Panicked. Yes, so you already said. And this so-called mark you didn't agree on . . . it doesn't take a great hulking anything to guess it was Maxwell Fleming. Right or wrong?"

"Right."

"And the eighteen thousand dollars Bruster won last night . . . ?"

"A mere drop in the bucket," she said coldly.

Christian exhaled sharply and bent his head forward, counting off a slow, silent ten digits. When he thought he could look at her again without choking her, he still had to strain his words through the grinding barrier of his teeth.

"I have half a mind to hand you over to Pinkerton myself. Do you have any idea what Fleming would do to you if he caught you?"

"You're hurting my wrists."

"I'm this close to breaking your neck," he warned. "Which is mild compared to what Fleming will probably do when he realizes what you're up to. Oh, he'll play with you for a while, and give you just enough rope to hang yourself, but he will kill you, make no mistake about that, and he'll do it in such a way as to teach a lesson to anyone else foolish enough to try to con him. You don't believe me? A week before you arrived, he caught one of his girls doing something he didn't particularly find amusing so he gave her to one of his men to discipline. An animal by the name of Scud Holwell."

Aubrey rolled her head to one side, flinching as much from the name as from the disgust in McBride's voice.

"When he was finished with her, she was so torn up inside, he didn't have to beat her any more to kill her, but he did anyway. Just for pleasure." He reached down and cradled her chin in his hand, forcing her to look back up at him. "That's what you're dealing with, Aubrey. That's the kind of 'mark' you're trying to outfox with your little games and sleight of hand. He isn't as big a fool as I am. He isn't as easy to manipulate with a soft smile and a pair of big blue eyes."

"I never tried to manipulate you," she whispered. "And I never thought of you as a fool."

Christian gave in to the temptation to look at her mouth, then to cover it briefly, fiercely, with his own. "I would have been happy, *querida,* if you had just once thought of me as a man . . . not an enemy."

He pushed to his feet and walked back to the hearth, leaving her to her own devices to stand and smooth the crush of her skirt. He kept his back to her until the rustle of clothes being straightened became the faint shuffle of uncertainty.

"I've arranged to have Sun Shadow take you to a village north of here."

"What?"

"You heard me." His voice was flat, emotionless. "I'm going to make sure one way or another you don't get close enough to Fleming to try lifting the horsehair off his jacket. You'll be able to take Bruster with you, and his wife . . . if she's smart. If not—" He shrugged and dismissed her.

"You can't do this. You can't force me to go anywhere with anyone."

Christian's grin was shaped with pure malice. "I wouldn't test Sun Shadow's patience, if I were you. He doesn't have any where women are concerned. Moreover, he's a mite out of sorts anyway, being given a task he considers far beneath the dignity of a Ute chieftain, and he's just savage enough to sell you to the first buffalo skinner who comes up with an interesting price."

"Why are you doing this?"

His grin faded and his eyes took on a brooding, thoughtful look. "You asked me the same question last night . . . granted, under different circumstances, but I didn't have an answer for you then, and I don't have one now except to maybe tell you that I—"

A single, loud *rap!* hit the door.

Faster than Aubrey could have reacted, she was pushed into the corner behind him and Christian was down on one knee, both Peacemakers drawn and cocked.

It was Sun Shadow.

"Men coming. Five of them."

"Fleming's?"

The Ute's arched brow did not discount the possibility.

Manuelo appeared behind Sun Shadow's shoulder, his face tense and worried. "Why would they come here? Why would they search here?"

"If they knew anything for certain, there would be a hell of a lot more than five. My guess is, there are probably five more groups of five searching elsewhere. Their appearance changes our plans somewhat, but not seriously. Manuelo, my old *amigo*—"

"*Sí, patrón?*"

Christian spun the chambers on his guns, more out of habit than need. "Can you get the señorita away from here without them seeing you?"

"*Sí. Sí,* this I can do."

"Go then. Take her back to the dressmaker's shop and keep her there until you hear otherwise from me. Hold a gun on her if you have to. Knock her senseless if you have to, but keep her there and don't let her out of your sight for a minute—*entiende?*"

Manuelo nodded. "*Sí, patrón.* She will be there when you come for her."

"As for you—" Christian turned to Aubrey. "Get Bruster ready to travel. Do exactly as Manuelo says and for God's sakes, stay out of sight. You'd be hard-pressed to explain what you were doing here with me, in a run-down stable, in the wrong part of town, if Fleming's men find you."

"But what about you? Surely you're not going to stay here and fight them?"

"We'll just keep them occupied for a while until

you're safely away. Don't think you're slipping through my fingers this easily. I'll be by the dress shop in an hour, Miss Blue, and you had better be ready to travel."

"Christian . . . please . . . come with us now."

He touched his fingers to the curve of her cheek. "At least you've got the name right. Now go. Get out of here. Manuelo—!"

The Mexican laid a surprisingly strong hand on Aubrey's arm and started pulling her to the door. Any instinctive resistance she offered was dealt with roughly enough to leave her no doubt that he would follow McBride's orders to the letter if he had to.

At the door, she glanced back one last time, but Christian was busy filling his pockets with extra ammunition.

"Please be careful," she whispered. And, because it was her heart in her throat and not her pride, she added, "I love you!" But so softly, she was not even certain she had said it out loud.

25

Gunfights on the streets of Santa Fe, even on a Sunday night, were not unusual. Cowboys clearing the dust of the herds from their throats couldn't care less which day of the week it was, and often didn't know. Gamblers gambled seven days, seven nights; drunks drank and spoilers brawled, and the local residents learned to keep their doors bolted and their eyes and ears turned away from the windows.

Christian cracked open the smoking breech of his Winchester and fed in another sixteen rounds. He'd hit one man for sure and winged another, but they were dug in well across the road from the smithy, and with the web of clouds tangling up the starlight, it was difficult to spot a clear target.

He could hear more gunplay roaring behind him and knew that as long as he heard it, Sun Shadow was holding his own. With eyes like a hawk, he was probably doing better than just holding his own, which made Christian suspect reinforcements had already begun to arrive. Five men—four, now—were a nuisance; any more and they could be outflanked and cut off from a retreat along the arroyo.

He popped his head over the top of the horse trough and triggered five quick shots at a movement in the shadows across the street. The flare from the rifle muzzle pinpointed his position and he rolled back in the talcum-fine dust, scrambling to the side and under the lowest rail of the small corral to avoid the barrage of handgun and carbine fire that blasted the trough.

Definitely more than four.

Grunting at a sliver of wood that had sliced his cheek, he sprang to his feet and ran in a crouch to the rear of the smithy. He ducked behind two large barrels of iron scraps, and was not there half a second before he realized he was not alone. Someone was diving for the other side of the barrels, frantically reloading. Without a passing nod to any notion of fair play, Christian stood, and because it was awkward to fire the Winchester, dropped it in favor of the two Peacemakers, which he fired simultaneously over the tops of the barrels.

The gunman on the other side was thrown back by the force of both shots striking at such close range. One side of his head exploded in a burst of splintered bone and brains, one arm was nearly sheared off at the shoulder socket. A third shot splattered out the front of his chest and Christian glanced across the yard in time to catch sight of Sun Shadow pivoting away to sight on another target.

Grinning, Christian ducked down behind the barrels again and ran a dry tongue across his lips. So far, he had not seen the grotesquely ugly blot that was Scud Holwell in any of the shadows moving stealthily between the buildings. He would have liked to have gotten one clear shot at the bastard. Just for old times sake.

He held his breath and listened.

The sound came again, a careless scraping of a boot on the earthen floor of the smithy. Someone had made it inside and was creeping up on the rear door.

Let it be Holwell, Christian pleaded maliciously. Let it be his squat, festering face that peeps around the corner.

Christian waited, his breath swelling his chest, his guns rock steady where they aimed at the black slash of the doorway. He saw the gleaming nose of a Colt .45 inch out into the less dense shadows outside the smithy, and was on the verge of squeezing back on his triggers when he recognized Billy Bonney's rumpled blond hair.

"Goddamnit, Billy!" Christian eased back on the gun hammers. "You could have been double-plugged just now."

"It wasn't you I was worried about," Billy hissed in return, grimacing at the sprawled body of the gunman. "I was thinking about that damned redskin all juiced up on firewater or sumpthin'."

"Where's Holwell?"

"I came to tell you he was looking for you, but I guess you figured that out already. In fact, if I ain't mistaken—"

Christian turned to follow Billy's finger and three things happened very quickly. He saw Scud Holwell step out from behind the shelter of a privy house and take aim with his sawed-off shotgun. He saw Sun Shadow make a wildly reckless leap away from the three-tined chaparral that had been shielding him and give a blood-curdling scream, drawing Holwell's fire at the last possible instant. And he saw a flash of blue-black steel swinging down toward his temple and ear from behind.

The explosion from the shotgun, the fatal scream from Sun Shadow, and the blindingly brilliant eruption of agony in his skull stayed imprinted on Christian's senses for the few vivid, slow-moving seconds it took him to turn and gape at Billy in surprise. He saw the Kid's lips moving, but he words were lost as the ground rushed up at him. He fell face down in the blood-splashed mud and there was nothing more to think about but the deep, black void that sucked him into unconsciousness.

•

The promised hour came and went and Aubrey, Dolores, and Manuelo were still seated at the kitchen table, all of them tense and silent and jumping at the least little sound that came from the ominously quiet streets outside. Aubrey was still shaken from the flight from the smithy, shocked at the speed with which everything had happened.

Dolores sat beside her and Manuelo opposite, his rifle deliberately placed on the table in front of him. He was clearly as anxious as Aubrey, desperate to know what had taken place at the smithy during and after the lengthy exchange of gunfire, yet sufficiently respectful of Christian's authority to remain where he was. Of the three, Dolores was the calmest, acting as if it were a common occurrence to have a wounded man in her bedroom, and a wild-eyed moustachioed Mexican holding her hostage at the kitchen table.

She glared at Manuelo, then at the pale, somber features of Aubrey Blue, and with a snort that disturbed the hairs on her upper lip, she slammed her hands on the tabletop, sending the other two jumping clear off their seats.

"Right. We ain't accomplishing nothing setting here like chickens waiting to feel the axe cut across our necks. Manuelo—you get yourself off and see what you can see down by the smithy."

"But the *patrón* . . ."

"You let me worry about the *patrón*. He told you to stay put and keep the señorita out of mischief . . . well, by Jesus Joseph and Mary, do I look loco enough to let her out of my sight longer than it takes to blink? I never took to this damned fool plan of hers in the first place, and I can tell you, it would be my pleasure to rap her one on the brain-box to keep some sense in her head until that rascal McBride comes to fetch her away himself, and more luck to him. Now, *vaya con Dios, adiós,* and all that crap. You vamoose on out of here and do as I say or I'll be tempted to rap you on the ear as well! And you be back here in five minutes flat—*chinquay momentos pronto*—or you'll be wearing that grin out the wrong side of your ass! *Comprende?*"

If he didn't, she helped him by grabbing a fistful of his shirt and lifting him bodily off the chair and herding him through the shop to the outer door. Aubrey heard the faint click of the bolt being slid home again, and was on her feet at once.

"And just where do you think you're going, missy?"

"Out. I have to know what's happened."

"Didn't I just send Manuelo to do that very thing?"

"I can't sit here and do nothing! He could be shot! He could be hurt! He could be—"

"—In the process of being strung up from the nearest tree," Dolores said bluntly. "But I don't see what good you would do him running out to watch. I know it's a hard thing to do, gal, just to sit and do nothing while your man is in trouble, but you have to think about him now, not yourself. You go out there and Fleming's men see you . . . ? Would you feel any better knowing the last thing your man saw was you being pawed by the likes of Clay Wilson, or . . ." She caught herself before she said Holwell's name, but she could see the point striking home in Aubrey's eyes. "Ain't nobody going to take notice of an old Mexican showing some curiosity. You leave the looking to Manuelo; he'll tell us what we need to know."

Aubrey sank back down onto the chair. She laced her

fingers tightly together in her lap and looked helplessly at Dolores.

"Saint's alive, child, you've got it bad, don't you?"

"It's all my fault. He stayed behind to give Manuelo and me a chance to get away. He sacrificed himself and Sun Shadow just to make sure I was safe."

Dolores grimaced. "Don't go eulogizing him just on my say-so. Old Franklin McBride didn't exactly spawn a brood of fools, you know. There's a younger brother lived up north with the Blackfeet for half a dozen years —something no white man has done before. And Ethan McBride . . . well, he might be cut more out of the cloth of a preacher or a lawyer, but he's been holding out against Fleming and his ilk *alone* for nigh on the same five years your young pup was cooling his *cojones* in Leavenworth. Ain't a one of them I'd turn my back on if he was real riled, and ain't a one of them I wouldn't like to see standing at my back if I needed help."

"But who do they turn to when they need help?"

Dolores frowned. She was saved from having to think of a believable answer by a loud and urgent banging on the shop door.

Dolores moved with amazing speed, followed closely by Aubrey, who ignored a previous order for darkness and snatched the oil lamp off the table as she passed.

Could it be Christian? Had enough time lapsed for Manuelo to reach the smithy and return? No. No, it had only been a few minutes since he'd left.

Aubrey held the lamp high, the dimmed wick causing the shadows from the cluttered tables and display shelves to dance eerily across the floor. There were two men being ushered hastily through the door by a pudgy, authoritative arm, and Aubrey gasped as she recognized the pale, waxen features of Sun Shadow. He was supported on the right side by Manuelo; the left front of his shirt and sleeve was soaked in blood.

"Towels," Dolores ordered sharply. "On the sideboard. And fetch some hot water from the stove!"

Aubrey was already retreating to the kitchen, withdrawing the light ahead of them.

"What happened?" Dolores asked as Manuelo eased Sun Shadow gently into a chair.

"I had only gone a few house lengths," the blacksmith said, "when I found him lying by the road."

"Fleming's men," Sun Shadow grunted. "They came from all sides. They were too many and we were too few. We had no chance."

Aubrey froze halfway to the table with the kettle of hot water. "No chance . . . ?"

Sun Shadow looked up at her. "He has been taken."

"Taken?" she gasped.

"Hurry up with that water, gal," Dolores cried. "And fetch those towels before the poor man bleeds to death."

"I am not important," the Ute declared, angrily resisting Dolores's efforts to peel away the remnants of his deerskin shirt. "I came only to warn you. I must go now and see to McBride."

"You ain't going to see nothing but the floor close up if you try to move without me patching you up some," Dolores insisted. She batted his hand away and ended the discussion with a few quick slashes of a butcher knife, slicing away what was left of his shirt.

"Christian is alive?" Aubrey dared to ask, expelling the breath she had been holding. "He's alive?"

"Of course he's alive," Dolores scowled. "Why else would this damn fool redskin come here and scare us half to death? Land sakes, boy . . . what did this to you?"

The wound covered most of his left breast, the flesh

raw and open from the top of his shoulder to just below his nipple. A strip of muscle had been torn from the bone and hung in a bleeding flap, the red streaking in rivulets over the hard, bronzed plane of his belly. Glittering in the midst of the carnage was the regal silver thunderbird, bloodied now, but as defiantly bold as the man who wore it.

"My wound is nothing, woman. McBride's wound is here." He balled a fist and held it over his heart.

Aubrey felt the strength melt out of her knees. "He's been shot."

The fierce, warrior's eyes met hers. "He has been betrayed. By one of the *vaqueros* he trusted."

"Who?" Dolores asked.

"William Bonney."

"Billy?" Aubrey could scarcely believe her ears. He had seemed so young and friendly.

"He will answer for it," the Ute promised, his tone murderous.

"Christian . . . where have they taken him? What will they do with him?"

"Some wanted to kill him there, but others . . . William Bonney among them, said Fleming would enjoy a hanging more. He was dragged away to jail to wait for morning."

"How will they justify a hanging? Even Fleming doesn't have the power to hang a man who is innocent of any crime."

"By morning, the sheriff will see to it that there are charges of murder against him."

"Murder!"

"There are three dead men at the smithy. It will be made to look as if McBride was to blame."

Dolores discarded a blood-soaked towel and reached for another. "Fetch me needles and thread; this cut needs to be closed up some."

"I have no time, woman," Sun Shadow snarled.

"You'll have even less if you bleed to death!" Dolores warned. "And none at all if I have to sit on you to keep you still."

"I should take heed, Mr. Sun Shadow," a very pale and weak Bruster said, leaning on the jamb of the bedroom door. "I assure you, the consequences would be most unpleasant indeed."

Dolores planted her hands on her hips. "Another damn fool voice heard from. What in blazes are you doing on your feet?"

Bruster swayed unsteadily, but pushed away from the support and winced his way into the kitchen. His arm was cradled in a sling and there was a flush of a slight fever across his brow, but he met Dolores's withering stare with a smile.

"I could not help but overhear all the excitement. I am, naturally, come to offer any assistance I can provide."

"Lord, give me wings to fly," Dolores muttered, and rolled her eyes to heaven. "Has the whole blamed world taken leave of its senses? Just what in blazes do you think you can do?"

Bruster glanced at Aubrey before responding. "That all depends, my dearest dove, on what must be done."

"If he's being held in the jail," Aubrey said, "we'll have to get him out."

"And just how are we supposed to do that?" Dolores demanded. "There's you and me, Manuelo, a half bled to death Indian, and a fool. Not exactly what you might call an army."

"I take offense at your attitude," Bruster bristled. "What I did, I did for us, my love. For a new beginning for the two of us."

"Horse droppings," she snorted, but she demurred

somewhat, and a spot of rosy indecision stained each cheek.

"How did you get away?" Aubrey asked Sun Shadow.

"They thought I was already dead and did not trouble themselves to look closer until they had finished with McBride. By then, it was too late."

"Does Christian know you're alive?"

"No." The Ute's jaw was set tautly. "He would only have seen me fall."

"Manuelo—" Aubrey chewed thoughtfully on her lip. "Do you think you could get us some fast horses?"

"*Sí,* señorita."

"And is there somewhere close by the jail where you could hide them until we need them?"

"The mission has a very large, very dark garden," he told her with solemn assurance.

"We will need a diversion of some kind. Something to draw attention away from the jail."

"Nothing short of setting fire to Fleming's britches will do that, honey," Dolores maintained. "And he'd have to be in them."

"What if we burned something else? His precious casino, for instance?"

Dolores threaded her needle in complete silence.

"That might do it," she agreed finally. "That just might do it."

"Bruster—you said there was a wagon of hay out back?"

"It was there last night, yes, but surely it would have been moved by now."

"But it might still be there?"

"It might."

"And with a little luck, a little kerosene, and a match . . ."

"It might work," Dolores muttered. "It might work

too good if the wind fans it across to the hotel next door."

"Fleming's hotel? I don't think I'd shed too many tears, would you?"

"Hmmm. Still and all, it would have to be done right to keep Fleming and most of his hired thugs occupied. Sonny—you want a wooden spool to bite down on or something?"

Dolores said this to Sun Shadow, whose face had gone rigidly pale as her needle started moving in and out of his flesh. He shook his head and continued to stare steadfastly at Aubrey.

"The *calabozo* was built strong and built well," he said through his teeth. "It will take more than a fire to break down the walls."

"All I need is five minutes inside," Aubrey said evenly. "If I can get inside the jail, I can do it."

"*If* you can get inside," Dolores repeated cynically. "Fleming isn't going to pull all his guards off the jail just to douse an itty-bitty fire."

"No, but chances are he'll pull most of them off. The rest . . . we'll have to handle somehow."

"*How?*"

"*I don't know!* But we'll think of something. We have to!"

Aubrey stormed into her room and shut the door, needing to have five minutes alone before she screamed and struck someone. She paced the miserable length and breadth twice before stubbing her toe on the foot-post of the bed and slumping down on the edge of the mattress. When she finished massaging the feeling back into her foot, she was met by her own reflection mocking her from the mirror.

"You're supposed to be so clever," she hissed. "Think of something clever."

When there was no chorus of hallelujah and no bril-

liant burst of fountaining lights, her gaze strayed to the
neat bunches of curls she had tied back earlier behind
her ears. There was a forlorn bit of straw clinging to one
curl and as she tugged it out, the curl unwound and
sprang free of the ribbon and trailed over the modestly
prim collar of the tailored bolero jacket she wore. She
had dressed carefully for her meeting with McBride,
wanting nothing to interfere with their conversation,
nothing to remind either of them of the two passionate
nights they had spent naked in each other's arms.

Aubrey stared a moment longer.

She reached up suddenly and slipped the knots on the
other ribbon that bound her hair, then shook her head,
scattering the black mass wildly around her shoulders. A
quick search through the everyday clothes Dolores had
provided was rewarded with a short, multicolored flared
skirt and a loose-fitting cotton blouse similar to the ones
the peasant girls wore slung off the shoulders.

Aubrey tore off the tailored riding suit and high-
necked blouse, then stripped down to just a thin-
strapped chemise and bloomers. She donned the
patterned skirt and cotton blouse, adjusting the puffed
sleeves and wriggling the edge of the bodice as low as
she could without actually baring her nipples. She
kicked off her shoes and twirled, judging the effect of
the blurred colors against the shapely white length of
her legs.

Almost, she thought. Almost.

She found her brush and stroked it through her hair
until the shiny curls crackled and flew in all directions.
She added a bold, sensuous rim of kohl around her eyes
and brushed soot on her lashes to make them sweep like
raven's wings. A touch of rouge on her cheeks and lips
preceded a generous dollop of cheap perfume . . . and
she stood back, calmly excited by the transformation.

"Saints preserve us," Dolores said when Aubrey stepped back into the kitchen. "You look just like . . ."

"One of Rosita Morales's *putas?*"

Dolores's mouth snapped shut.

"Can you make up a basket for me? A meal of some sort that I can take to the jail?"

Dolores's eyes narrowed and she looked on the verge of arguing again, but it was Bruster who gave her a gentle pat on the backside and urged her toward the pantry.

"You won't be able to hide any weapons in the basket," he said, stating the obvious.

Aubrey raised the hem of her skirt and tapped the secured leather sheath that held her .22 derringer strapped to the back of her thigh. She extended her arm and let the wide silver bracelet she wore slide down to her wrist, and with a flick of her thumb, released the spring that sent a four-inch-long knife blade jutting from the band.

"McBride has chosen well," Sun Shadow murmured in his own language. In English, he added, "We will not be able to make any mistakes. We will only have one chance."

Dolores finished loading a basket with cheese, bread, and a bottle of wine. She wiped her hands on her skirt, clearly displeased that all manner of control had seemed to desert the situation, and rectified it at once by assuming command.

"Lucius and I will take a stroll along the Alameda and see if we can't find something dry and plentiful to burn us up a little confusion. Manuelo—you vamoose on out of here and get them horses over to the jailhouse. Do it one at a time, mind, or you might as well post a sign advising everyone of a jailbreak in progress."

"He knows this already, woman," Sun Shadow growled, pulling himself to his feet. "He is a good man."

"And just where in tarnation do you think you're going?"

"With Blue Eyes. She cannot go alone."

"A strong puff of wind will blow you over if you lean the wrong way."

"Then I will not lean," he said perfunctorily.

Dolores squared for battle, but something in the Ute's eyes won it before any more shots were fired. "Well, you can't go out there looking like a damned patchwork quilt! Hold on until I see what I can rustle up."

She returned from the shop a moment later with a clean shirt (which looked suspiciously like a woman's blouse) and a tentlike serape woven in bands of brown, beige, and russet wool. When the poncho was draped over Sun Shadow's shoulders, it effectively hid the thick bandage over his chest and concealed the fully loaded Henry rifle Dolores fetched from her bedroom. A last addition—a half-empty bottle of spirits—was thrust into his hand without an option for refusal.

"A few swigs of this on your breath and any staggering you do will look natural."

Sun Shadow sniffed suspiciously at the contents and jerked his head away in a backlash of long black hair. "A few swigs of this, woman, and I will feel nothing to stagger about."

"Don't complain, you damned redskin; it's my last crock. And mind you keep a sharp eye on this child's back. If you let so much as a hair on her head fall into harm, I'll pluck you like a chicken and spit you stem to stern."

"Don't worry, Old Witch. If anything happens to Blue Eyes, there will not be much left of me after McBride is finished."

26

The air in the jail was fetid. It stank of old sweat and vomit; the walls were stained, the adobe laced with scratches and crudely written oaths. Christian lay on a pallet in the corner of the single, dark cell. He stared at the ceiling, his tongue idly soothing the gap at the back of his mouth where someone's eager fist had removed a tooth.

His ribs ached as if he'd been kicked for good measure. The taste of blood in his mouth made him think of Sun Shadow, but the loss of his friend was too fresh and too painful and what he needed now was calm, cold logic. He would get Holwell, the bastard. He would revenge the Ute—but first he had to find a way out of this damned cell.

Christian swung his long legs over the side of the cot and tested his sense of balance. The bruised ribs launched a bolt of pain through his chest, and a swirl of hot nausea belched up into his throat, but he fought both reactions and won. He stood up and walked slowly over to the cell door, smiling grimly as he recalled his last visit to one of Santa Fe's oldest buildings. A violent past history of traders, merchants, fur trappers, and cowboys had necessitated the construction of a sturdy jail, and by God, it was as solid now as it had been five years before. The iron bars were mortared top and bottom, the walls two feet thick. There were no windows, only a row of thin ventilation slits high up near the roof.

The outer office was no more than five paces square. No gun case. No stove. No peg of keys temptingly close. There was an old desk against the far wall, and a bulletin board tacked behind it. Someone had left a lamp burning smokily on the top of the desk, but the wick was turned too low to do much more than stink up the air.

He scowled as he returned to his cot. A hefty kick on the wooden frame hurt only his foot, confirming his earlier conclusion that there was nothing remotely threatening to use as either a weapon or a tool.

He was trapped.

So much for well-laid plans. His brother Ethan had tried to talk him out of coming on to Santa Fe, especially after spending only a few days at the Double M. He had hoped the five years behind bars would have burned away some of the impatience, or at least tempered Christian's habit of acting without thinking.

What Ethan didn't understand was that Christian had spent those same five bloody years doing not much more than thinking. He had thought about Fleming and thought about how he would like to repay the gambler for every stroke of the lash he had earned in Leavenworth.

Fleming was paying, all right. Probably with rounds of free drinks all around.

Maxwell Fleming was going to watch him hang in the morning and there didn't appear to be a goddamn thing he could do about it.

•

The wagon of hay had been moved out of the alleyway behind the Golden Eagle, but there was something just as handy and even more ironically suited to the task at hand: firewood. Bruster drenched the tall pile of stacked wood, emptying the bottle of kerosene he had brought from the dress shop, splashing some, for good measure, as high up the whitewashed timber walls of the saloon as he could. While the oil soaked into the wood, Bruster tiptoed from one end of the building to the other, prying the stoppers out of the rain barrels that sat every few feet against the wall. By the time he was finished, he was sweating profusely and the lane was crisscrossed with rivers of muck. The ground was dry enough to soak most of the puddles up the instant the water hissed from the barrels, but as luck would have it, the one puddle that lingered was the one Bruster dropped his small bundle of matches into.

Strike after strike, nothing happened. He began to panic, knowing what Dolores would say, knowing what she would do if he failed at this simple enterprise. But there were lights on in the hotel rooms above his head, and he could not afford to tarry. His shoulders slumped and he was about to admit defeat, when he looked down and saw the lone matchstick that had ricocheted away from the others.

With a muffled prayer, he struck the head against a rough patch of timber and nearly dropped it when the sulfur exploded in a dazzling blue-white flame.

Dedicating the deed to his wounded and throbbing arm, Bruster touched the match to the kerosene-soaked logs and stood back to avoid the *who-o-o-sh* of erupting flames.

Dolores was waiting at the mouth of the alley, and together, they sauntered back out onto the street. They strolled leisurely toward the main plaza and were just rounding the corner of La Fonda when one of the musicians slipped out the rear door of the Golden Eagle, intending to relieve himself, and instead, walked head-on into a two-story pyre of orange and red flame.

•

Aubrey hugged the shadows near the *palacio*, careful to keep her head lowered if any of the late night romantics strolled too close. From where she stood, she had a clear view of the main plaza and of the jail, located directly across the square. She saw Bruster and Dolores round the corner of La Fonda, and a few moments later, heard the alarm and saw the horse-drawn fire wagon race into the Alameda. The plaza emptied quickly, everyone rushing to either discover the source of the fire or help man the bucket brigades. With most of the new construction going on in timber, fire was too serious a threat to take lightly.

There had been eight guards lounging on the boardwalk in front of the jail. Six of them left to follow the fire alarms; the remaining pair paced the length of the boardwalk looking alternately bored and curious as to the activity along the street.

Aubrey tapped impatiently on the handle of the basket. She could not afford to wait much longer. If the fire was a small one and extinguished too quickly, the gunfighters would be returning, doubly on their guard for any more "accidents."

Behind her, a lone figure emerged from the shadows and wove his way unsteadily to the stone lip of the fountain. Aubrey heard the chink of a bottle hitting stone and saw the poncho-draped form slump down as if in a dead drunk, his head lolled forward on his chest.

Praying Sun Shadow was not really unconscious, Aubrey took several deep breaths and started across the plaza. She slung her shawl at a jaunty angle around her hips and swung the basket lazily to and fro, humming to herself as if she hadn't a care in the world.

When she was certain the guards had noticed her, she slowed and swayed her hips provocatively, making a great show of adjusting her blouse flirtatiously lower. With a toss of her wild black hair, she crossed the last few feet and approached the jail.

"Buenos noches, there, señorita," one of the guards called, whistling as he took in the shapely length of bared calf, the narrow waist, the lusciously full swell of breasts straining against the thin cotton. "Now, what's a pretty li'l thing like you doing out all on her own this time of the night?"

Aubrey smiled and fluttered her lashes. "I breeng food for one of your preesoners," she said in broken English. "I breeng bread and cheese and—"

"Food for the prisoner?" The second guard stepped forward. "No one ordered any food for anyone."

"But, señor . . . every day I breeng food. And if there eez no preezoner"—she widened her smile and bowed her head coquettishly—"the sheriff, he eez usually happy to see what Maria breengs."

"Who sent you?" asked the second guard, still suspicious.

"My cousin . . . Rosita Morales. She used to send a deeferent girl every night, but the sheriff, he says he likes me the best."

"Why that randy old bastard," the first gunman murmured. "He gets his cream delivered every night. You think that sounds fair, Charlie?"

"Hell no. Sounds damned smart, though."

Aubrey feigned boredom and twirled a small pirouette in the dust, letting her skirts flare just enough to stop their murmurings cold.

"Well, eef no one wants to share my basket," she sighed, "I will have to return to the cantina and find some other amusement."

"Whoa, now, l'il filly." Charlie leaned over and playfully grasped a handful of black hair. "Who said we don't want to share your basket?"

"Ahh, Charlic . . ."

"Shut up, Hank. You really want to send away something as ripe and sweet as this here morsel of heaven? Besides, what else have we got to do with our time 'tween now and the morning?"

"What if the others come back?"

"If the others come back . . . maybe we'll share"—his arm snaked around Aubrey's waist and he grinned—"or maybe we won't. What did you say your name was, darlin'?"

"Maria Rodriquez," she said, slowly and with much feeling. "And you, my bold gringo?"

"Charlie Boon, honey, and I'd be right pleased to share your basket with you."

He steered her up onto the boardwalk and headed for the jail door.

"You're takin' her in there?" Hank asked, glancing nervously around the plaza.

"Well, where else do you expect me to take her? Out back in the privy?"

"But what about . . . you know . . ."

"The big bastard? He's probably still out cold, and even if he isn't, he ain't gonna put me off none. Now, do you want some of this, or don't you?"

Hank looked down into the deep, soft cleft between her breasts, then at her tongue moving slowly and wetly around her lips.

"Yeah," he muttered. "Yeah, okay. But hurry up and let me have my turn before Wilson gets back. He's so sloppy it's like following after a butter churn."

Charlie laughed and ushered Aubrey through the door. Her breath quickened as she heard the bar drop across the wood, but she barely had time for a glimpse around the dimly lit room before his hands were cupping her breasts and his mouth was suckling her shoulder. Murmuring the appropriate noises, she leaned back against his body, rubbing herself against the growing bulge at his groin.

The desk was the only object of furniture she saw outside of the cell bars. The rest of the room—the floor, the walls, were remarkably clean of clutter. No sign of keys. No weapons of any kind.

The guard was becoming persistent in his gropings and she turned her attention to the cell itself. He was there, on the cot, and she had a moment of genuine panic wondering if he was truly still unconscious, and if he was, how on earth she was going to move him.

"Slow down, my bold one," she laughed, wriggling out of the guard's grasp. "This blouse eez new and I do not weesh to have it torn by clumsy hands."

"Take it off, then," he grunted.

"The sheriff, he always likes to do that heemself."

Charlie Boon reached eagerly for her but Aubrey darted behind the desk, laughing when she heard him curse. She could see movement in the cell now and her heart took a solid leap up into her throat when she recognized Christian's massive shoulders and burnished hair.

"There is wine in my basket, señor," she said hastily, looking back at the guard. "Perhaps you have a thirst?"

He grinned and his hands dropped to the buckle of his gunbelt. "I was just going to ask you the same thing, sweetheart." He set his guns on the desk and reached for the second buckle, the one belting his pants. "You look like the kind of gal who has a real fine thirst and knows just how to quench it."

"*Sí*, señor," she breathed huskily. "I might even know more than one way to do eet."

She raised her skirt to display a length of creamy white thigh and the guard came around the side of the desk, his pants unbuttoned, his pride standing out like a blooded fury, engorged and impatient. He was still grinning, reaching for the silky moons of her breasts when he felt the unexpected bite of cold metal stab into his groin. Startled, he looked down and saw the derringer pressed into the swarm of coarse, dark hairs.

"Stand back," she ordered crisply. "And don't even try to call for your friend."

Charlie Boon's eyes narrowed to mere slits, but he did as he was instructed. The gun, he noted, was held with ease and familiarity, and although each individual charge in each of the four barrels was relatively small, combined, the damage would be excessive at such close range.

"The keys . . . where are they?"

"With one of the others," he sneered. "Shall we wait for them to return?"

Christian was at the bars. "Check the desk drawer, there may be a spare set. Here, give me a gun. I'll watch him while you look."

She passed through one of Charlie Boon's battered Remingtons and ran back to the desk. The hope of a second key was short-lived, but she did find a hunting knife and tucked it into the waist of her skirt.

"Anything?"

"No, but I brought this along just in case." She produced what looked like a long hairpin, thin and bent into a square hook at the end. Christian watched dubiously as she fed it into the lock and began twisting it slowly inside. It was a ridiculous waste of time and he was about to tell her so when the "key" clicked sharply and the cell door swung open.

"Why did I even doubt it?" Christian mused. "I forgot where you went to school."

He stepped out of the cell and signaled the guard to move inside.

"You won't get past Hank with a hairpin," he spat.

"He'd probably say that about you too," Christian said, bringing the butt of the Remington smashing across the back of Charlie's skull. He caught the heavy body as it started to fall and guided it down onto the cot.

"How many more are there outside? It sounded like they had half the town guarding me at one point."

"They did. There's one left on the stoop now, though. The rest are . . . occupied, but I don't know for how much longer."

He looked over at her and there was a gleam of admiration in his eyes. "By God, I didn't believe I was seeing straight when you came waltzing through that door. And I nearly forgot where we were when you went into that little act of yours."

"Kindly remember now," she said, "unless you prefer to stand and chat until others come back?"

"It might surprise you to know exactly what I feel like doing at the moment."

"And you told me *I* had a poor sense of timing?"

"You do, but I'll overlook it this once."

"Sun Shadow won't. Another few minutes and he'll start shooting up the whole street."

"Sun Shadow!" Christian grasped her arm. "He's alive?"

"And *waiting.*" She gave him a little push toward the door. "We were a bit vague about this part of the plan, so if you have any bright ideas—?"

"Just use your charms," he said, tousling her hair, "and lure the poor sod inside."

His hands paused and cradled her face between them and he leaned over, kissing her hard and fast on the mouth.

"What was that for?" she gasped.

"You had to have the proper look on your face. It's there now . . . almost . . ."

He kissed her again, his mouth consuming hers with a warm, hungry passion. He crushed her body urgently to his and was shocked at how quick and deep her response to him was, despite the danger of their situation.

"There," he murmured, his eyes gleaming silver in the dim lamplight. "That's it. That's the look I've been lying here thinking about for the past few hours. You probably don't know it, but a look like that tells a man you're *this* close . . ."

He lifted the bar and opened the door. Aubrey turned, a little dazedly, she had to admit, and frowned when she saw the second guard leap to his feet.

"I . . . need some help," she whispered breathlessly. "Your friend is all used up and I have not even had a fair turn."

Hank sucked in his breath. He pushed eagerly through the door and had a dim memory of two soft breasts filling his hands before he crumpled to the floor as silently as his partner.

Christian tucked the gun into the waist of his pants and dragged the second body into the cell.

"Can you relock this thing the same way?"

"I don't know. There's never been much call to try it."

"I see what you mean." He snuffed the lamp and, strapping on Charlie Boon's gunbelt and slinging Hank's over his shoulder, he cracked the door again and peered out into the deserted plaza. A quick dart across the open square took them to the fountain, where Sun Shadow was crouched and waiting. He fell naturally into step behind them, the three melting back into the shadows, neither man acting as if they had ever been in doubt of the other's survival.

"The horses are this way," Sun Shadow hissed, leading them toward the arched stone gates of the mission. Manuelo was there, along with Bruster and Dolores and six skittish horses.

The gnarled hands of the blacksmith gripped Christian's shoulders, his relief evident in his grin. "I knew they could not keep you behind bars very long, señor."

"Then you knew more than I did, *amigo*. Okay, let's get out of here. I don't think the two we left behind will wake up any too soon, but someone might notice the lack of guards at the jail. Once Fleming knows I'm gone, we'll need every second we can steal to put distance between us. Bruster—can you ride?"

"The arm is somewhat cumbersome, but yes. I can manage."

"Dolores?"

She was looking at the horses as warily as they were looking at her. "Lord o' mercy, I haven't been in a saddle in a dozen years, but I suppose if this fat old buzzard can do it, so can I. Besides, I ain't about to let him out of my sight again. Worthless as he is, he owes me for ten years of wondering where he was at night and wondering which floozies were wearing all the jewels and gewgaws he promised to me on our wedding day. A woman has her pride, you know. She has to have a legacy to pass on to her grandchildren when the time comes, something that tells them who we were and what we lived and died for."

"Ahh, my dove . . . we do not even have children," Bruster pointed out delicately.

"And I suppose you're going to blame that on me?" Dolores demanded, hands on hips. "I wanted children. A woman *ought* to have children, if only to make sure the mistakes she made in life were rectified. Wrongs righted. *Debts paid!*"

Christian frowned. "As much as I hate to interrupt a family quarrel, we are a little pressed for time."

"Well, land sakes, just tell me to shut up and get my fat ass on the horse."

Christian opened his mouth to comply, but thought better of it and turned to Aubrey instead. "Take the paint. It's the smallest and you're the lightest."

Aubrey stood in the chilling shadows, the echo of Dolores's words sinking through her skin like a heavy mist. The man she loved was only an arm's length away. She could not see much of his face, but she knew every chestnut eyelash, every dark stubble of beard, every crease and crinkle around his mouth and eyes, even to the tiny scar that sliced through his eyebrow. She knew him naked and bold, rising from the river like a bronzed Neptune, and she knew him hot, dusty, and reckless enough to steal a kiss in the heat of an Indian attack. She knew his anger and she knew his tenderness; she knew his pride and his sense of frontier justice. He would come back and he would kill Fleming because the man had cheated him out of five years of his life. But he had cheated Aubrey and her family out of much more.

"I'm not going," she said softly.

"What do you mean you're not going? Of course you're going. Get on the horse."

"I can't. Christian . . ." She edged back toward the gate. "I'm sorry. I just can't. I've . . . forgotten something. Something terribly important, and . . . and I can't leave without it."

"Forgotten something? Whatever it is, it can't be more important than your life!"

"Sst! Someone is coming," Sun Shadow warned.

Two long strides brought Christian to Aubrey's side, and an arm snaked around her waist to haul her bodily into the blackness of a niche in the wall. The footsteps passed close by, but they were firm and unhurried, not stealthy or searching. In a moment they had jingled out of earshot.

"That's it," Christian decided. "Get on the damned horse. We can wrangle about this stubborn streak of yours another time."

"I said no!" Aubrey cocked the hammer of the derringer and aimed it at Christian's heart.

Surprise, anger, then a hostile kind of belligerence set his jaw in a hard ridge as he folded his arms across his chest and glared at her. "We're going to have to do something about this penchant you have for drawing guns on me."

Aubrey moistened her lips and steadied her grip on the pistol. "If you make me shoot this, the whole town will be down around our ears."

"Madam, if you shoot that thing, I doubt very much if I'll care one way or another."

Aubrey ignored his sarcasm and kept the gun aimed at his chest. "I said I wasn't going, and I meant it."

"All right. You've made your point. What now?"

"Now . . . you get on your horses and ride out of Santa Fe."

"Leaving you here?" he asked mildly.

"Leaving me here."

Christian moved his hand, just a flicker, and Aubrey saw the edge of Sun Shadow's poncho dip briefly into a beam of stray light. The Ute had been about to come at her from her blind side, but McBride stopped him.

"I can't speak for the others," Christian said, "but I'm curious to know what you are going to be doing while the rest of us are riding out of Santa Fe."

"Don't worry about me, I can take care of myself. Just tell me where to meet you and I will. I swear I will."

Christian bowed his head briefly, and when he lifted it again, there was the slightest hint of a smile tugging at the corner of his mouth.

"And what—if I might ask—makes you think I would want you to meet me?"

Aubrey faltered, her eyes wide and rounded with anguish. "Christian, please," she whispered. "You don't understand."

"No," he said roughly. *"You* don't understand. You either come with me now, or I ride away from here and you don't see me again."

He said it so quietly, with such absolute finality, that she knew he was not just delivering an ultimatum; he was stating a fact.

"I'm sorry," she cried softly. "Christian . . . I'm so sorry . . ."

A hand reached over her shoulder and a finger slid deftly between the trigger and the guard, making it impossible to fire the derringer. A second arm curled around her waist and nearly squeezed the breath right out of her.

"Having a little trouble here?"

Aubrey recognized the voice and gasped, "You!"

"No trouble, Billy," Christian said evenly. "I was just finding out where I stand, once and for all."

"Yeah, well, you better not stand around here too long."

Billy pried the gun from Aubrey's hand and set her back down on her own two feet. She was no sooner clear of him, than she was being shoved aside again, this time by Sun Shadow, who came leaping out of the darkness, the glitter of a scalping knife clutched in his fist. He hurled himself at Billy, the two men going down together in a flurry of tangled limbs and churning dust.

"What the hell—" Christian lunged forward.

"Sun Shadow said it was Billy who betrayed you back at the smithy!" Dolores cried. "He said it was Billy who led Fleming's men to you!"

"Shit! Sun Shadow . . . no!" Christian saw the knife raised to strike and he plunged into the fray. The blade had already begun its lethal descent when he grabbed at

the Ute's wrist and managed to wrench it off target. "No, Sun Shadow! It wasn't Billy! It was not Billy! If anything, Billy was the only thing that kept me from getting a bullet in the head! Do you hear me? Do you hear what I'm saying?"

He said it again, in Shoshonean, to be sure, and slowly, slowly, the Ute's killing posture relaxed and his clawed hand released Billy's throat.

Billy rolled clear and gulped frantically for air. He choked and spat. He coughed and gasped and sucked frantically at the air his lungs needed to fight off the waves of blackness. He could feel his heart pumping in his chest and the dirt clinging to the sweat that popped out across his brow.

"Jesus!" he gasped, and pushed away as Christian tried to help him up. *"Jesus!"*

Sun Shadow was also struggling to steady his breathing but for different reasons. The wound in his shoulder had reopened and there was a fresh flow of blood seeping through the bandage and soaking his shirt. But no one noticed. They were more interested to see how the young gunfighter with the renowned hair-trigger temper would take to coming within a few inches of having his throat slit.

"Billy, are you all right?" Christian asked, kneeling beside him.

Billy massaged his throat and worked his jaw up and down until the joints cracked back into place. "Yeah. Yeah, I'll live. But next time you invite me to share a campfire . . . ? I think I'll just pass, if it's all the same to you." He paused and glared suspiciously up at Sun Shadow. "You sure he's on our side?"

McBride grinned. "As far as I know, he is. Sun Shadow . . . you all right?"

"I will be better when you tell me why I should not have killed this one."

"Billy was there when Fleming ordered his men out to search for us. He knew we'd be at Manuelo's, and cut around the back way to warn us, but the shooting had already started. He knew we were outflanked, and knew I'd never throw down my guns, so . . . he gave me this little love tap"—he rubbed the side of his head—"and told me not to take it too personally; that he'd think of something when things quieted down."

Sun Shadow peered at Billy through the darkness. "I did not know. I thought—"

"I can guess what you thought," Billy said grimly. "Hell, I thought *you* were dead. I thought Holwell plugged you pretty good."

"A scratch," the Ute said scornfully, dismissing the wound and any further questions about it.

Christian stood up and looked around.

"Son of a bitch," he muttered. *"Aubrey?"*

"She was right . . . here . . ." Bruster said, pointing helplessly at an empty space beside him. "She must have taken flight while the three of you were tussling."

"Goddamnit! I'll do more than just tussle with her when I catch her," Christian snarled, and started to head back into the plaza.

"You can't go out there," Billy cried, grabbing for his arm. "The whole town knows you're in jail. They'll shoot on sight."

Christian stopped at the mission wall, banging it with the heel of his hand. "Something important, she said. What the hell could she have forgotten that is so damned important? Bruster!"

Bruster swallowed hard as the plainsman confronted him, but he could not articulate beyond a few squeaks and hand gestures.

"She wouldn't dare go back to Fleming's," McBride said, challenging Bruster to deny it. *"Would she?"*

Bruster sought the safety of darker shadows, but

Christian stalked after him, his fist still knuckled around the skinning knife he had pried from Sun Shadow during the skirmish with Billy.

"Why would she go back to the Eagle? What's there that's so bloody important? *What else is going on here that I don't know about?*"

"Oh my Lord," Dolores gasped. "Oh my sweet Lord."

Christian whirled around. "What? What is it?"

"Well . . . I can't say for sure, but . . . there is one thing she might think is important enough to go back for, and damn it all if I ain't the one who might have reminded her too. Me and my big mouth, going on about grandchildren and legacies and such. Course, then again, I might be wrong . . . but she seemed mighty upset when she told me she saw it last night."

Veins rose and throbbed like blue snakes in Christian's temples and throat. *"Saw . . . what?"*

"Her mama's broach."

"What?"

"Her mama's broach! She saw Fleming give it to that fancy opry singer last night. I asked her how she knew it was the same one, and she said there couldn't have been two like it in the whole blessed world. Emeralds and diamonds, she said. Belonged to her mama and her grandmama, and . . . oh, ten or so grandmamas before her."

"How in Christ's name did Fleming get it?"

"His men took it. Robbed it right out of her dead mama's hands after they orphaned her and burned her home to the ground."

Christian staggered back a pace. He looked from Dolores's tear-filled eyes to Bruster's downcast face and felt his stomach take a sickening twist inside him.

"Which pieces of the puzzle am I still missing here?" he demanded hoarsely.

"You're missing about ten, honey," Dolores sobbed. "But the only one you need to know right now is that, for as much as that girl loves you, she isn't about to leave this town without her mama's broach, and yes, she thinks it's worth the risk of dying for it. Her mama did, and she's been carrying that nightmare around with her for nigh on ten long years."

Ten years?

That must have been quite the nightmare, he had asked.

It always is.

Always? You've had it before?

My parents were murdered when I was thirteen years old. I saw the whole thing.

"Jesus Christ," he whispered. "Why didn't she tell me?"

"I think she wanted to, honey. She just didn't know how."

Christian paced, his anger clipping his strides and keeping his hands bunched into fists by his sides.

"How?" he asked, stopping. "How would she go about getting it back? How would she even know where to find it?"

"The singer ain't got it on her tonight," Billy provided. "Leastwise she didn't when I saw her yodeling on stage an hour or so ago. She had something sparkly around her neck, but not the same thing as she had last night. Fleming probably switched it; he's done that before to impress his women."

"Aubrey doesn't know that, does she? And if she searches Magenta's room and doesn't find it . . . where would she look next?"

Bruster cleared his throat. "I . . . ahh, may inadvertently have provided her with that information."

Christian glared, waiting.

"I, er, seem to recall mentioning that Fleming has a

safe in his office, and that he keeps most of his valuables locked up there."

"A safe?" Christian glowered. "She can open a bloody safe?"

Bruster started to beam proudly and was on the brink of expounding on just how nimble Aubrey Blue was at opening locks and safes of all kinds, but a warning gleam in Christian's eyes amended his intentions to a modest, "Yes. Yes, indeed."

Christian walked to the nearest horse and pulled a rifle out of the saddle boot. "Manuelo!"

The gunsmith stepped hastily forward. *"Sí, patrón?"*

"Do you think you could find your way over the mountains at night?"

"To the Double M? *Sí.* Blindfolded."

"Then get going. Take Bruster and Dolores with you, and if either one of them shows signs of falling behind: shoot them."

The Mexican's eyebrows arched gently. *"Sí, patrón.* How far behind do they have to fall?"

"About as far as you could throw them."

Manuelo considered the answer a good one and nodded.

Sun Shadow collected two more rifles and all the ammunition he could carry. Billy watched and scratched his chin, then stared thoughtfully up at the sliver of a moon creeping over the domed roof of the mission church.

"Whoever started that fire at the Eagle did a good job. Burned up half the back wall before they even put a drop of water to it. Place should be pretty well cleared out, what with the smoke and all, but Fleming . . . he's gonna be madder than a bull with a burr stuck up his nose. Seems to me, though, now that we got most of his guns inside the casino, we got to think of a way to get them *out.*" He craned his neck to see around the mission wall, and smacked his lips together in mock chagrin. "Nope. Sure don't look to me like anyone's thought to check in on the prisoner. Maybe I should mosey on over there and let Mr. Fleming know someone's left the barn door open."

"Can you give Sun Shadow and myself about fifteen minutes to get into position?"

"You got it. Hey . . . ?"

McBride glanced back over his shoulder.

"D'you think she could really do it?"

"Just get Fleming and his men out of there," Christian growled. "What she does or doesn't do in the five minutes before I find her and wring her neck is no concern of mine."

Billy grinned. "Hell, in that case, give her ten minutes inside. I'd surely love to hear the howl he sets up when he finds some of his trinkets missing. And don't you worry none, I'll be right there with her."

"That's supposed to comfort me?"

Billy chuckled and watched the formidable pair dart off in the direction of the Golden Eagle.

27

The fire at the Golden Eagle was extinguished. It had burned hot and bright up the rear wall of the gaming house, but, thanks to the musician's bladder, had not managed to spread to either of the adjoining buildings or the roof. As it was, the whitewashed timbers were scorched black and still hissed smoke. The brigade of men manning the chain of buckets from the horse troughs out front had not stopped splashing water up the sides of the walls. The woodpile had been kicked apart and lay like so many scattered, smoldering lumps in the mud. Men poked and prodded for pockets of heat, and took long iron bars to anything that felt or sounded suspicious.

Fleming was incensed. Great black billowing clouds of smoke had rolled across the stage and moved through the casino like an acrid fog. Magenta Royale, who had been in the middle of a song, sounded the first alarm with a screech that should have shattered every glass and mirror in the saloon. She wasted no time fleeing, fisting one poor fellow in the face when she thought he was not moving out of her way fast enough.

The other girls had added their screams and panic to the cacophony of confusion. The dealers, well rehearsed

in what to do in any kind of an emergency, forgot everything they had been told and had headed for the streets.
The gamblers and hustlers had been half a step behind
—the half step being all they needed to scoop up the
loose coins and abandoned chips before joining the
crowds that stampeded for the exit. Tables had been
pushed over, chairs smashed. One enthusiastic dealer
had started tearing down the swaths of red velvet curtains before being swept up in the general panic.

It would take days to effect repairs, and probably
longer to make up for the losses at the tables.

Fleming no longer resembled the cool, elegant owner
of the biggest and richest casino in Santa Fe. His normally sleek, oiled hair was ragged and falling in greasy
clumps over his forehead. His pleated merino shirt was
smudged with soot and torn open at the throat; he was
jacketless, his sleeves rolled up to the elbow.

He stood in the empty pit of the saloon, surrounded
by the chaos and wary silence of the grim-faced men
who worked for him. They were all soiled and sweaty,
some nursing burned hands and arms, most just nursing
burned tempers.

"I want to know how this happened," Fleming said
quietly, his words very precise, very deliberate. "I want
to know who was in the alley, how he got *in* the alley,
and why it was that no one saw him. Most of all, however, I want him found and I want him brought here to
me. Alive."

He paused and brandished an unlit cigar, making sure
he had the undivided attention of every man present.

"I don't care if you have to tear this town apart and
upside down. Someone had to have seen something;
check with the girls who have rooms out back; check
with the guests in the hotel who overlook the alley.
Someone knows *something* and I want the bastard who

did this caught if you have to tear out a few throats to start people talking."

He stopped and his eyes moved slowly around the room. "Look at this," he hissed. "*Look* at this!"

"Don't worry, boss," said Clay Wilson. "We'll find out who done it. All we gotta do is find out who belongs to that—" A calloused finger pointed to an object on the bar. It was a thin silver chain with a scorched hare's foot hanging from one end. Most gamblers carried charms of one sort or another, even those who professed to have no superstitions or habitual quirks. The hare's foot in itself was not a clue, especially now that it was badly singed and coated in mud, but the chain was. Balancing the other end was a set of silver dice, the dots fitted with tiny chips of colored glass. Worthless to anyone but the owner; unusual enough that it must have been noticed by someone. And it had been found just outside the back door, by the woodpile, near a puddle littered with fallen matches.

Fleming noticed something else for the first time.

"Wilson . . . aren't you supposed to be over at the jail?" He scanned the faces and saw several others stiffen and start to fidget from foot to foot.

"We heard someone shout it was the Eagle on fire and that they needed us to help."

"You left the jail unguarded!"

"No, boss! Hank and Charlie are there. And we ain't been gone but twenty minutes or so."

Fleming opened his mouth to tell the thick-skulled moron exactly what could be accomplished in twenty minutes, but he did not have to. His gaze was drawn instead to the arched entrance, where Billy Bonney was just kicking his way through the swinging doors, his arms full balancing a half-conscious Hank Dunn.

Whatever color remained in Fleming's face drained

away and he looked every one of his forty-four years. He didn't have to ask, but he did anyway.

"What happened?"

"I ain't been able to make too much sense out of it yet, boss," Billy gasped, relieved to hand his burden over to two considerably huskier men. "But I was cuttin' through the square—on my way here—when I looked over and thought the jail seemed kinda deserted. When I checked, the cell was sprung and both Hank and Charlie were face down, out cold."

"McBride?"

"Gone."

"Gone! What the hell do you mean, gone!"

Fleming's fingers squeezed around the unlit cigar, crushing it to a shapeless mass of shredded tobacco. He threw it on the floor and in a cold rage strode through the littered casino and slammed out the swinging doors, his men hastily scraping to their feet and following him along the street to the main square.

With Fleming's angry footsteps pacing them, the sizable mob of gunmen rounded the corner of the Alameda and cut across the plaza to the jail. Scud Holwell and two others followed Fleming inside the adobe building, while a dozen others obeyed a curt order to fan out and scour the surrounding area, even though no one was deluded enough to think Christian McBride might still be in the vicinity.

Fleming emerged a few moments later, his shirt a splash of white against the darkness of the doorway. The gaslights at each end of the boardwalk fronting the jail cast him in a muted yellow glow, throwing a tall, wavering shadow of his outline onto the adobe. Three other shadows joined it as Charlie Boon's half-conscious body was dragged out onto the wooden stoop, propped beside the squat and bulbous shadow that mimicked Scud Holwell's actions.

"How?" Fleming demanded. "How did it happen?"

"It weren't our fault, boss," Boon gasped. "She . . . she took us by surprise."

"She?"

"A woman. A whore. She brought food to the jail. She . . . she pulled a gun and got the drop on me, and then McBride slugged me . . . and that's all I remember."

"That's all?" Fleming asked mildly. His gaze dropped to Boon's opened trousers. "I'm inclined to think we're missing a few details. Scud . . . ?"

Holwell stepped in front of Boon and grasped a fistful of the man's shirt for leverage. He struck a savage blow across Charlie's cheek and jaw, causing his head to snap to one side. A second blow sent a broken tooth flying out in a spray of blood. A third unhinged Boon's jaw with an audible snap and produced an animal-like wail of agony.

Fleming held up his hand.

"You said a whore brought food to the jail. What whore? Who was she? What was her name? Had you ever seen her before?"

"No. Never. She . . . she said her name was Maria."

Fleming curled his fingers in disgust and glanced at Holwell. Two more solidly planted punches into the gunfighter's midsection had him coughing up phlegm and blood, sobbing and wheezing through his broken jaw for air.

"Half the whores in Santa Fe are named Maria," Fleming said tautly. "If you can't do any better than that, I'm going to have to give you to Scud until—"

"Rodriguez," Boon cried hoarsely. "She said . . . her name was Maria Rodriguez and . . . and she worked over at Rosita's. That's all I know. That's all she told me, I swear it."

Fleming drew a breath to steady himself. He beckoned to two of his men, who set out at a run for Rosita Morales's cantina, but Fleming did not put too much hope in their success. McBride hadn't been in town long enough to have won the loyalty of a whore, regardless of his reputation with women. Who did he know? More importantly, who did he know who would risk going up against Fleming's crushing authority? And where would he find a woman clever enough, cool enough, gutsy enough to pose as a whore and break the bastard out of jail, right under his nose?

He paced the length of the stoop and paused beside one of the wooden beams that supported the roof overhang. He stared into the burning core of the gaslight, his eyes reflecting the flame and blazing with an unholy glow. Without forewarning he struck out at the post, smashing it with the heel of his hand, hard enough to rattle glass panes in the lamp.

"That son of a bitch! *He* was the one who set fire to the Eagle! He sent someone to burn me out while his whore was breaking him out of jail! *Son of a bitch!*" He turned and glared back at the sagging, groaning Charlie Boon. "This . . . Maria: What did she look like?"

Boon's head had lolled forward and Holwell grabbed a fistful of hair, yanking him back to attention with a scream of pain.

"Mr. Fleming asked you what she looked like," Holwell growled, his voice sounding like a rusted axle.

"B-black hair." The words came out in a bubble of spit and blood. "Pretty."

Fleming cursed. The *other* half of the sluts in Santa Fe had black hair and were pretty. He was getting nowhere fast, something which probably could not be said for McBride, and Fleming was on the verge of ordering Holwell to remove Boon from his sight—permanently— when another gurgle of sound cut into the silence.

"Blue eyes. Yeah . . . yeah . . . she had . . . real *blue* eyes. And her gun . . ."

Fleming felt something crawl across the nape of his neck. Something cold and icy, and sickeningly unpleasant. "What about her gun?"

"It was a . . . gambler's rig. Four shot .22."

Fleming turned as still as a statue.

Black hair. Blue eyes. A gambler's rig. . . .

It wasn't possible. It couldn't be. And yet . . . even as he tried to discount the notion in his mind, to pass it off as coincidence, he knew the odds were steeply against there being two black-haired, blue-eyed beauties on friendly terms with Christian McBride; beauties who would be calm enough, cunning enough, to mastermind the escape as well as plan a daring diversion; beauties who carried four-barreled .22 derringers.

Aubrey Blue knew Christian McBride. They had ridden halfway from Kansas on the same stage and despite the fact that she had appeared to snub him last night in the casino, there had been something he had seen in both their faces to suggest their animosity was strictly for his, Fleming's, benefit.

Aubrey Blue was cool and cunning. She'd had the guts to fight her way through an Indian attack out in the desert, and she'd had the guts to talk her way into an interview for a job at the casino. Moreover, Fleming had indeed checked on her "references" and found out that there *was* a Pinkerton agent who would be very interested in knowing her whereabouts. It was not difficult to assume she could dupe the likes of two idiots who carried their brains between their legs.

And Aubrey Blue carried a four-barreled .22 derringer. She had shown it to him the same day she had won a job.

Three coincidences?

Three too many.

Fleming heard a shout from across the square and looked over to see one of the searchers returning through the gates of the mission leading three saddled horses behind him. He carried something else in his hand, and it was not until he had come under the influence of the lights that Fleming recognized it as a folded wad of blood-soaked linens.

Scud Holwell stepped down off the boardwalk and snatched at the rags.

"I told you I wounded that Breed! Between this"—he squeezed the cloths until the blood oozed between his fingers and dripped onto the dusty earth—"and what he lost earlier tonight, that Breed ain't goin' nowhere but a grave, they try to move him too fast, too soon."

Fleming stood motionless, his features defined sharply by the guttering lamplight. His rage was at such an exquisite peak, he could feel the effects rippling through him like the shivers of an orgasm.

"Spread out and start searching. Every street, every house if you have to, but I want them found. I want them found and I want them brought back to me . . . dead if necessary, alive if possible."

His eyes narrowed and his teeth gleamed through a feral smile. "Especially the woman. Yes . . . yes . . ." he added with a hiss of unholy anticipation. "I want her so alive, she'll be screaming to die before I'm finished with her."

28

 It had been almost too easy for Aubrey to enter the casino through the back door—or what was left of it. With the number of girls who had run out of the hotel and the casino while the fire was still a threat, no one had spared more than a passing glance to one who walked boldly back inside as if she was simply returning to work.

Hidden by the curtains on stage, she had overheard Fleming's rantings about the fire. She also had a clear view of the staircase Bruster had told her about, but it was twenty feet away, without benefit of any curtains to hide her. Impatience had prompted her to risk a peek out across the main salon and that one peek had nearly cost her the whole game, then and there.

Scud Holwell had been leaning indolently against the bottom rail of the staircase. The sight of him, the sound of his rattling, coarse voice had slammed into her like a fist, knocking her back with the force of a physical blow. She had stood there, shocked beyond comprehension, a swirling collage of memories and senses heightened by the stench of smoke and burned wood.

She was thirteen again, hiding in the arroyo. The sounds of strange men's voices were all around her, hunting, searching, threatening. The flames from her burning house were sending up pillars of twisting black smoke to scorch the night sky.

She had wondered how she would react when and if she came face to face with the living horror of her nightmare. Now she knew.

Tucked into the folds of her skirt, held in a hand that visibly shook with the emotions raging through her, was the slick-oiled weight of the army issue Remington revolver she had snatched from Hank Dunn's holster while McBride had been preoccupied separating Billy and Sun Shadow. The gun weighed over four pounds carrying a full load, and was more than her one hand could manage to raise and aim steadily. She gripped it firmly in her two hands and put both thumbs on the iron hammer, forcing it back until it clicked twice, cocking the gun to fire.

All she had to do was step out from behind the curtain, aim, and pull the trigger. She wouldn't miss, not at this distance, not with the size of the target at hand. The rest of Fleming's men were all seasoned gunfighters, with excellent reflexes and an instinctive response to a threat. They would probably return fire before they had even isolated or identified the source. A quick enough death, she supposed. A fair exchange for the pleasure of seeing Scud Holwell's chest blown apart.

She braced herself and took another peek around the curtain to set the proper distance in her mind. He had not moved, had not detected the threat of impending death.

It struck her as slightly odd that he wasn't nearly as tall as she remembered. He was every bit as ugly—uglier, in fact, with the milk-white film coating the scarred eye. But the massive, towering monster from her nightmares was only a little over average in height and far less imposing in size than the one-eared Goliath, Clay

Wilson. To a frightened girl of thirteen, however, he would have seemed immense and terrifying, more so with his hands pulling at her body and the slimy, sweaty heat of him wedged between her thighs.

Aubrey closed her eyes and willed away the images, but they were already formed and forcing themselves upon her. He had wanted to hurt her, and he had. He had intended to rape her, but she had been too dry and tight and he had managed only to spit on his fingers and shove them deep enough inside her to tear away any other bothersome inconveniences. He had laughed when she had screamed from the pain. He had wiped the pink smear of blood on her breasts just before he had kicked her legs wider apart to complete the act, but the twins had interrupted him. They had gone screaming after the horses, waving sticks and pelting stones, scattering the beasts who were already nervous and wall-eyed from their proximity to the fire.

And Aubrey had escaped. She had escaped and run as far and as fast as her legs could carry her, and—

"Gone! What the hell do you mean, gone!"

Aubrey was jolted back to the present by the sound of Fleming's anger and disbelief. The next instant, he was on his way out of the casino and Scud Holwell was no longer a stationary target, but a rapidly moving one who was already halfway to the exit.

Aubrey raised the Remington, but too late. A sob caught in her throat but that was too late too, because she suspected she would not have been able to kill him in cold blood anyway. She kept the gun raised, however, for there was someone still in the casino and he had seen the flash of her colored skirt as she stepped out from behind the curtain.

Billy, who had not left the casino with others, saw Aubrey, saw the gun . . . and winked.

"Now then," he said, addressing the gunfighter

slumped in a nearby chair. "What say we get you a drink, old man. Might stop all that ringing in your ears. Seems like we got the place to ourselves anyway; *might as well take advantage while we can.*"

Aubrey lowered the gun.

Billy's message was loud and clear: she would not have much time.

With Billy talking to keep Hank Dunn distracted, Aubrey ran barefoot and soundlessly across the width of the stage, forcing herself not to think or even breathe again until she was up the steep flight of stairs and poised on the top landing. There was a sliver of light outlining the shape of the door and she tested the movement of the latch cautiously, not knowing who or what she might find on the other side.

It was Fleming's bedroom. Heavy, dark furniture, including a huge cannonball bed, dominated a room devoid of anything soft or frilly or influenced by a woman's delicate tastes. Yet there was evidence of a woman's presence. Bottles of perfume and cosmetics cluttered a thick oak dressing table. The bedsheets were in shambles and a woman's nightrail was casually flung over the arm of a chair alongside a wrapper of sheer, watery silk.

Aubrey eased the door open wider. The room was deserted. A pair of lamps burned on each of two bedside tables, adding the musty smell of coal oil to the lingering tang of charred wood. She edged farther into the room, careful to close the door behind her, noting as she did so that it had been cleverly disguised as one of the carved mahogany panels that lined the walls. Opposite her, the outer door stood slightly ajar and through it she could see into the luxuriously appointed salon where Fleming had entertained his guests the previous evening. His office would be across the hall.

With a firmer grip on her bearings and her nerve, Aubrey tiptoed across the plush pile carpet and went directly to the dressing table. She had recognized the small ebony box Magenta had guarded so possessively on the stagecoach, but a quick and disappointing search through the tumble of cheap jewelry did not produce the emerald broach.

"You shouldn't even be here, you know," came a husky whisper from the other room. "Fleming could come upstairs at any moment."

Aubrey stiffened and slowly straightened against the rigid chill of tension in her spine. She started to turn, her pulse pounding in her temples, her hand clammy around the butt of the pistol, and it took several taut seconds of staring at the open door before she realized the voice . . . voices . . . were coming from the adjoining room.

"I'm supposed to be comforting you," Greaves chuckled, his words muffled against soft white flesh. "So let me comfort you."

"Darby . . . for heaven's sake, stop it."

"He isn't interested in you right now, Clara dear, regardless of the many charms with which you may have been enticing him recently." Greaves's laugh was accompanied by the sound of whiskey being poured into a glass. "His precious casino came this close to going up in smoke tonight. I'd be surprised if he even remembered you were here."

Aubrey, moving quickly away from the dressing table, pressed herself flat against the wall beside the doorway. She heard Magenta sigh expansively. "Then you might as well pour me a drink too Gawd, I'll never get rid of the taste or stench of all that smoke!"

Darby obliged and passed her a glass of whiskey.

"So . . . apart from the dramatics downstairs, how is it going?"

"Going? How is it *going*?"

"Well, I am assuming, since you appear to have made

yourself quite at home here in his suite, that you've finally managed to get him on his back, bleating."

Through the crack between the door hinges, Aubrey saw Magenta sweep into view. She had changed out of whatever costume she had been wearing and looked as if she had expected Fleming to come and offer his comfort in person. The wrapper she wore was made with an even more scandalous disregard for modesty than the nightgown McBride had purchased earlier at Dolores's shop, and left no doubt that the distraught songstress was nude beneath. But while Darby's eyes had difficulty straying too long or too far from the dark and erect circles of her nipples, Aubrey's attention was focused on Magenta's throat. There, in place of the emerald broach, she wore a diamond necklace comprised of a double string of glittering brilliants dominated by one large, tear-shaped pendant that hovered over the cleft of her breasts.

"It is *going* like we expected it to go, darling," Magenta purred. "He thinks you are a complete fool and me . . . the best thing he's had in his bed since his mammy weaned him."

Darby reached out and ran the backs of his fingers over the fullness of her breasts. "That's probably because you are, sweetheart."

"Better than your little Chinese slut?"

Greaves tossed back his drink and smiled. "She's good. She's damed good, in fact. A regular yellow fever between the sheets."

Magenta's cat eyes glowered. "You're enjoying her, are you?"

"Every day and every night. Every way you can imagine and some I didn't even know about. And not a single whine. Not a single complaint."

"Really." The word was etched in frost. "I'm glad to hear your time hasn't been completely squandered. I should hate to think of you growing bored and lax while I . . . I am forced to endure the depravities of a cruel, coldhearted man."

"You don't look like you're suffering," he said dryly. "And, sweetheart, if bouncing your brains out on top of that mule-handler back at the way station wasn't depraved, I can't imagine anything Fleming could do short of using a pair of broom handles could match it."

Magenta gasped and tossed the contents of her drink into his face. Darby anticipated the reaction and dodged in time to miss most of it, but some of the amber liquid still splashed his shoulder and stained the front of his shirt.

"Get out of here," she commanded, flinging the glass after the whiskey. "Get out of my sight. Go back to your little yellow slut and let her pump you dry for all I care. I don't need you anymore. I *never* needed you. Never!"

"No," Darby mused, the corner of his mouth turning up in a wry smile. "You never needed me. You were doing just fine the night I found you bleeding your guts away outside the back door of that quack doctor's office. And you would have done just fine if I'd taken you back to that nickel-a-night whorehouse, singing a song now and then when your mouth wasn't full of something else." He paused to wipe the whiskey off his lapel and his eyes glittered with promise. "I'll go . . . if you really want me to. But if I walk out that door, baby, it'll be for the last time."

She said nothing and he tucked his handkerchief back inside his breast pocket. He touched his brow in a mocking gesture of farewell and headed for the salon door. He was almost there when Magenta's rigid veneer cracked. She released her breath on a sharp cry, halting him at the threshold.

He retraced his steps slowly, his smile crooked and cocky, his black brows arched with lazy indifference.

"You are a bastard, you know," she hissed.

"And you are a prize bitch. The bitch of all prize bitches."

Magenta reached out, her fingers hooked like bloodied talons, but Darby did not even flinch. He felt her nails dig into his scalp above each ear, poised to rip downward, but he only laughed and grabbed her around the waist, jerking her forward, his mouth crushing possessively over hers.

Magenta responded with a savagery that left his lips bitten and bleeding. She fought him when he lifted her into his arms, and cursed as he carried her, thrashing and kicking into the bedroom. They plunged together onto the tumble of bed sheets and, with the sound of tearing cloth and grunted oaths echoing in her ears, Aubrey darted unseen from behind the door and ran hurriedly into the salon.

Chilled by her narrow escape, she crept out into the hallway and slipped into Fleming's office. She had the Remington clutched tightly in her hand, prepared for any more unexpected surprises, but the office was empty, the silence almost deafening.

Bruster had said Fleming kept his valuables in a safe in the office. It stood to reason that he would have been cautious enough to lock the broach away after Magenta's grand debut, replacing it with the diamond necklace for tonight's performance.

Knowing her time was slipping away, she began with the most obvious places to conceal a safe—the desk, the cabinets, beneath the corners of the rug, behind paintings, shelves . . .

Nothing.

It occurred to her, after ten minutes of growing frustration, that sweet Florinda might have been mistaken, or misleading Bruster intentionally, boasting of knowledge she did not possess, and she leaned on a low cabinet, her fists balled and her eyes burning with the sting of failure.

She blinked and stared at the walls.

The paneling was the same carved mahogany that decorated the bedroom.

With a fresh surge of enthusiasm, she started at one corner of the room and ran her hands over and around each panel, tapping softly now and then, listening for any change in the sound of the wood. She located the false panel on the wall beside the credenza; finding the hidden trigger to release it was child's play, and she allowed herself a small flush of triumph when the door swung open and she saw the dull, metallic surface of the safe.

It was a Wells and Fargo model, one of the newest and most difficult to open, the door twenty-four inches square and three inches thick, the protruding wheel of the locking mechanism capable of an inestimable number of combinations.

Aubrey set the Remington on the credenza and wiped the palms of her hands on her skirt, then spun the cylinder several times to get a feel for its movement and sound.

For a moment she saw Bruster standing beside her, nodding, lecturing, correcting her sharply if he noted an error in her methods. Cracking safes was not a talent either of them fostered beyond the rudimentary knowledge of how the damned things worked, but Aubrey adamantly shook her misgivings aside and leaned forward, pressing her ear against the cold metal.

She gave the lock a series of quick spins to the right, and on the third rotation, began listening for the minute *click* of the tumblers slotting into place. She heard nothing distinguishable through three more revolutions, but on the fourth heard a distinctly irregular rasp of sound at the number 43.

Wasting no time on celebrations, she spun the wheel to the left and began at the 0, creeping counter-clockwise for one full turn without hearing anything.

She backed away from the safe and shook out her hands to ease the tension in her fingers, then attacked it again. Right, 43, left . . . 7 . . . Right again. And again . . .

She gave it several vicious spins and stopped at 43, backtracked to 7, then crept forward again, her fingers steadying on the wheel, urging the numbers gently up and past the small black arrow. She heard the gears click faintly beneath the number 22 and she turned the handle, fully expecting the door of the safe to pop open.

It remained solid.

She smacked the metal face with the heel of her hand and wished with all of her might for a barrel of TNT, but since none was forthcoming, she spun through the first two digits again, and this time, even though the click at 22 went off like a cannon shell against her ear, she gave the handle a dubious twist, fully expecting it to mock her again.

The door swung silently open.

Aubrey stared at the safe for a moment, waiting for her heart to slide back down out of her throat. The interior was divided off in sections, several of them stacked neatly with cash and documents. The largest compartment held a chest made of laquered wood, obviously Oriental in origin and design. It was locked, but an anticlimactic wiggle of her hairpin "key" released the clasp and gave her access to the various shapes and sizes of black leather cases.

Aubrey removed one and slipped the tiny gold hasp. It contained a matched set of rubies—necklace, bracelet, and earrings. A second case contained loose gemstones, all laid out in neat little rows in their nests of plush velvet: pearls, diamonds, sapphires of all shapes and sizes. Her anxious fingers found the empty case that must have recently contained the diamond necklace, and beneath it, the square black box she had seen in Fleming's hands the previous night.

She popped the clasp and there it was, the green fire and incandescent brilliance of diamonds: her mother's broach. Her mother's legacy, and her legacy, if only to the memory of justice and vengeance.

Fearing to be parted from it again, Aubrey removed the broach from the case and settled it snugly in her pocket. She closed the leather box and returned it to the chest, but then the silence and the absolute emptiness of the office struck her again, sending her gaze back to the opened safe and the stacks of paper money. It was there, all of it. Every cent of Maxwell Fleming's worth. His pride and his passion. His destruction and his downfall.

Wasn't that what she had come for?

Aubrey searched behind her for a moment and saw two plump cushions propped on one of the chairs. Using the hunting knife she had taken from the jail, she slashed open the brocade and emptied the stuffing, scattering the feathers like a heavy snowfall over the furniture and floors. She ran back to the safe and emptied it into the pillow slip, adding the leather cases that contained Fleming's prized collection of jewels, but leaving the lacquered chest behind.

Back out in the hallway, Aubrey stopped. She stared at the door to Fleming's salon and cursed Darby and Magenta's sense of timing. She headed for the double doors at the end of the hall—the only other way out—and had to hope that Billy would be able to handle Hank Dunn.

She opened the door and peered cautiously out over the balcony rail. Billy was still sharing drinks with Dunn, but they had been joined by the two gunmen who had apparently just returned from the fruitless quest at Rosita's brothel. Making matters worse, Charlie Boon was slumped at one of the tables, wounded, but, like an injured grizzly, no less of a threat because of it.

Aubrey had heard that Billy was fast, but she had no idea *how* fast, nor could she justify pitting a mere boy of seventeen, eighteen, against four veteran gunfighters.

Retreating back through the double doors, she retraced her steps along the hall. The windows in Fleming's office faced the street, she knew, but the windows in the salon opened onto a narrow balcony that spanned the length of the upper floor. She wasn't sure what was below, or exactly how she would climb down to the street, but she had effectively run out of options.

She closed the salon doors behind her and stood a moment, listening. She would have to pass in front of the bedroom, but there were still whimpers and wet, slapping sounds coming from within and she had to hope they were too busy to pay her any heed.

She went straight for the closest window and pushed the velvet draperies aside. The sash was heavy and would not budge more than an inch or so, and, with a curse, she ran to the next window, managing all of a hand's width of fresh air before the sash jammed fast again.

"He nails them shut so that anyone trying to break in —or out—has to break the glass."

Aubrey froze. It was Magenta's voice, shrill and haughty, coming from the door of the bedroom.

"Darby! Darby, come quickly. I told you I heard someone out here, and I did! A dirty little greaser, from the look of it, although goodness only knows what she's doing in here this time of night. Spying on me, more than likely. Is that it? Is that what you're doing? Turn around, you sneaky little bitch; I'm talking to you. Did Fleming send you in here to spy on me?"

Aubrey turned slowly to meet Magenta's furious accusations. The songstress's mottled, sweaty flesh had been hastily covered by her wrapper, and behind her, Aubrey could see Darby Greaves hopping on one foot, pulling up his trousers.

"Who the hell are you? You aren't my regular maid!" Magenta's blazing amber eyes fell to the bulging pillow slip. "What have you got there? What were you doing in here? *Where is Consuelo?*"

Aubrey's gaze flicked to the window. The glass wasn't very thick; she could smash it with the weight of the pillow slip and hope the glass shattered enough to let her jump through.

Greaves rushed into the salon then, and saw more than just the colored skirt, the cotton blouse, and the cloud of black hair.

"Jesus Christ . . . it's the schoolteacher!"

"It's . . . who?" Magenta shrilled.

"It's the bloody schoolteacher," Greaves exclaimed. "And if this get-up don't beat all! Ah ah!" He saw Aubrey take a step toward the window and he moved swiftly to block her. "Not so fast, Miss Blue. We've got some talking to do."

Aubrey's hand came up clutching the Remington but Greaves blocked that move too, grabbing her wrist and twisting it hard enough that the gun sprang out of her hand and into his.

"Now then," he snarled. "Suppose you stop playing games and let us in on what's going on here."

"Nothing is going on," Aubrey spat. "Nothing that concerns you."

"Nothing?" Greaves eyed the pillow slip. "It looks like you're carrying a hell of a lot of nothing there. Clara—" He wrested the sack from her hands and tossed it behind him. "See what's inside."

Magenta crouched beside the pillow slip and after

only a moment, looked up, her eyes wide and rounded with shock.

"Darby! Darby . . . look!"

"Just tell me, for Christ's sake. If I turn around, she's liable to change herself into a bat and fly away."

"But, Darby . . . it's here," Magenta whispered in awe. "It's all here. The money, the jewels . . ."

Darby was startled enough to look for himself, but took the precaution of slamming Aubrey against the wall first and digging the gun into the underside of her chin. Magenta greeted him with a handful of cash in one fist and a leather jewel case in the other. "It's all here . . . everything I saw in his safe . . . everything I told you about. There are eight, nine cases like this and . . . papers, and . . , and cash. Gawd in heaven, there must be fifty thousand in cash."

They met each other's eyes, then turned to stare at Aubrey.

"I *knew* there was something about you that wasn't quite right," Darby hissed. "I knew it the first minute I laid eyes on you."

"Darby—?"

"Clara, shut up! Let me think!"

"But, Darby—!"

"*Shut up,* goddamn it! This could be our ticket out of here, and a hell of a lot sooner than we planned."

Aubrey looked from one to the other, the gleam of understanding dawning in her eyes. "You were after it too, weren't you? You were planning to rob Fleming yourselves."

Darby glared at her and his mouth pulled down at the corners. "You don't think we came to this hellhole for the sake of our health, do you?"

"Darby," Magenta tried to caution him to silence, but Greaves only laughed.

"What's the harm? She isn't exactly going to rush off and tell him now, is she?"

"By the same token, you aren't going to use this gun on me," Aubrey said evenly, "so why don't you put it down and maybe we can arrive at some sort of a fair compromise?"

"What makes you so sure I won't use it?" He dug the gun deeper into her neck and grinned. "Seems to me it would solve a lot of problems."

"It would also have half the street in here at a dead run."

"She's right, Darby," Magenta hissed, glancing at the door. "Fleming might come back any minute, and then we'd have to give everything back."

Greaves's eyes narrowed. "You're absolutely right, my love. Best I get it out of here now, while the coast is clear."

"You? You mean *we*, don't you?"

"I meant exactly what I said. One of us, moving alone, has a chance to make it." He walked over to where Magenta crouched on the floor and scooped up the pillow slip. "We'll meet in Mexico City . . . just as soon as you can get away from here."

"Get away?" she gasped. "He'll kill me! He'll find out it was you, and he'll kill me!"

Greaves shrugged and, after scanning the street below, used the heavy brass lamp off a nearby table to smash out the pane of glass. He had one leg flung over the casement when he was dragged off balance by a scratching, clawing, screaming Magenta Royale.

"You bastard! You dirty, conniving, yellow-bellied bastard! You're not leaving here without me!"

"Get out of my way!" he snarled, tearing out of her clutches. "It would have happened sooner or later anyway, sweetheart. Your act is old and your body is getting older. I was only sticking around long enough to see if this one paid off at all, and it has, Clara my love. It has."

"No!" She screamed and hurled herself at him as he bent to the window again. He bellowed in rage and pain as her nails ripped deep gouges in his cheeks and throat. He dropped the pillow slip and swung with both fists, catching Magenta on the chin and shoulder, and sending her sprawling painfully to the floor.

"You bitch!" He felt the cuts on his face and stared at the blood smearing his fingers. "I should kill you for that. By God, I should kill you for that!"

"You won't be killing anyone, Greaves."

A familiar, deep baritone cut through the tension, shocking Darby Greaves to inaction and earning gasps from both Magenta and Aubrey as they whirled to face the door.

29

"Maxwell!" Magenta instantly dissolved in a flood of tears. "Oh, Maxwell, thank God you've come! He was going to kill me! They were both going to kill me!"

Maxwell Fleming stood just inside the doorway, his rifle cradled casually under his arm; in the other hand, he held the empty lacquered chest. His eyes glittered as he looked at each occupant of the salon in turn. They widened somewhat when they fastened on Aubrey, but he said nothing.

"Oh . . . Maxwell . . ." Magenta started crawling toward him on all fours. "Darby and the schoolteacher . . . they had it all planned from the beginning. I told you not to trust her. I *warned* you not to take her into your confidence, but you didn't listen. Now look what they've done! They've robbed you and tried to make a fool out of me."

"You lying bitch—" Greaves began.

"That's enough out of you, Greaves," Fleming said quietly. "You'll have your turn."

"She's lying! It was all her idea to come out here, to get herself in good and tight with the boss, then strip him bare the first time he turned his back. If you don't believe me, check the last four or five places she's worked. A few thousand here, a few thousand there . . . all penny-ante stuff; practice for when she found the Big One. You."

Magenta gasped and shook her head. "No, no. He's the one who's lying! He's the one who planned it all, right from the beginning. Oh, Maxwell . . . the things he has made me do! The things he has *forced* me to do! I wanted to warn you. I wanted to tell you what they were planning, but I was afraid. They . . . they threatened to kill me if I said anything!"

Darby made a sound in his throat and started toward her, but Fleming raised the rifle and aimed it at the agent's chest.

"Back off, Greaves. Nice and slow."

Magenta reached the floor by Fleming's feet and plucked at the leg of his trouser. "Maxwell, you have to believe me. I would never do anything to hurt you . . . you know I wouldn't. I . . . I love you, Max."

Fleming smiled blandly. "I'm sure you do, so long as it's convenient and profitable. As for hurting me, don't flatter yourself. You haven't done anything I wasn't expecting you to do. Quite frankly, the only surprise in all of this"—he turned cold, hard eyes on Aubrey—"is you, Miss Blue. Then again, you just seem to be one surprise after another. I take it this"—he held up the empty chest—"was your handiwork?"

"It was *all* her doing," Greaves insisted. "She's the one who broke into your office and took everything out of the safe. It's all there, in that bag—the money, the jewels . . . everything. She was planning to light out for Mexico City with it, she just told us. What's more, she wasn't in it alone, either. She was partners with the plainsman, McBride. Hell, he was more than just her partner too. He was her lover. All the way from Kansas, each and every chance they got, they were groping and pawing at each other, stinking of sweat and—"

"Enough!" Fleming raged. He threw the lacquered chest aside with a loud crash and cocked the rifle in an impressively fluid motion. "One more word out of you, Greaves, and I swear I'll blow the top of your head off!"

Greaves backed away, stumbling to a halt beside the window.

"As for you"—Fleming swung the rifle in Aubrey's direction—"I'd like to hear it from your own lips. Are you in this with McBride?"

"I'm in this by myself," she replied calmly. "McBride doesn't even know I'm here."

"But you *were* the one who helped break him out of jail?"

"I was . . . repaying a debt."

"Where is he now?"

Aubrey shook her head. "I don't know. There were horses waiting outside the jail; he's probably twenty miles away by now. As I said, this was my idea, my plan from the beginning. And despite what these two would like to make you believe . . . I work alone."

Fleming studied the violet-blue eyes for any signs of weakness, but there were none, and under different circumstances, he would have thought her magnificent. His gaze dropped lower, to the gentle swell of her breasts pressing tautly against the thin peasant blouse . . . to her hands hanging loosely by her sides . . . to her feet, bare and delicately shaped. Even dressed like a common whore, she radiated exquisite beauty and elegance.

"I knew you were special from the moment I laid eyes on you," he murmured. "And I had such plans. For you. For us."

"For *us*?"

"You and me, my dear. Together, we would have made an unbeatable combination; your beauty and talents, my wealth and position. We could have owned Santa Fe. We could have ruled it as king and queen." He paused to bring the passion in his voice under control again. "If it . . . had been anybody other than McBride . . . I might have been able to forgive you."

"Forgive *me*?" Aubrey's eyes widened in disbelief. "*You* . . . would have been able to forgive *me*?"

The rifle trembled slightly, betraying the tautness of Fleming's grip. "I was going to make you my *wife!* I would have *given* you all of this"—he jerked his head savagely in the direction of the pillow slip—"and more! So very much more! A home, a family . . . *respectability!*"

"Respectability?" she gasped. "As your *wife?* Why, you stupid, blind, arrogant fool! You still don't know, do you? You haven't been able to see past your own self-importance to figure out who I am and why I've come back."

"Come back?" Fleming's eyes narrowed sharply, his gaze boring into hers. "What do you mean . . . come back?"

The question was asked with the first breathless hint of suspicion in his voice and Aubrey took a small, measured step forward.

"Is that all you thought—that I was special? Didn't you once think that I reminded you of someone?"

Fleming's composure slipped noticeably. "I . . . don't know what you're talking about."

"Don't you? Perhaps this will help."

Aubrey held out her hand. When she uncurled her fingers, the sultry green sparkle from the emerald broach drew Fleming's eyes involuntarily downward.

"You stole it from someone I loved very much," she said softly. "Someone who once made the fatal mistake of thinking you were capable of loving something other than your own greed and ambition."

Fleming's eyes shot back up to Aubrey's face. His could have been carved out of granite for all the emotion he showed, but the granite was suddenly without color, and the shell of his body without heat of any kind.

It *had* disturbed him, right from the outset. Those eyes, that face . . . even the way she smiled raised the fine hairs at the nape of his neck. But . . . Luisa was *dead!* And the child . . .

"No!" he rasped, staggering back a pace. "No! They told me you had died!"

Aubrey shook her head slowly. "No. Your men did not quite finish the job they were sent out to do. They killed my stepfather, they raped and killed my mother, and they drove my brothers out into the desert to die. They did their best to kill me too, but I managed to escape."

"Alicia . . ." The nose of the carbine slanted downward, as if the weight of it had suddenly become too much. *"Alicia?"*

Aubrey smiled tightly. "Hello, Father."

30

"It isn't possible!" Fleming gasped, his face draining to a haggard gray. "You're dead! Holwell swore to me the whole bastard family was dead."

"He obviously lied—*Father*—because I am very much alive."

"Don't call me that! Don't ever call me that!"

"But it's true. I am your daughter. I am your own flesh and blood."

Fleming's jaw clenched into a solid ridge. He staggered to the side table and splashed some brandy into a tumbler, downing the contents in one swallow, shuddering as the liquor burned its way into his belly.

My God . . . Luisa!

He refilled the glass and stared at Aubrey, seeing only the proud and fiery beauty of her mother. Now that the connection had been made, he could admit to what he had been denying since the morning Aubrey had walked so boldly into his casino demanding a job: He had seen Luisa in her. He had seen the same beauty, elegance, and fire in the daughter that he had seen twenty-five years ago in the mother. He had even hoped to recapture it.

Fleming drank again and his knuckles were white on the glass as he went and stood in front of Aubrey, seeing her through new eyes.

My God . . . *Luisa!*

"So you've come back after all these years . . . expecting what? To make some sort of claim on me?"

"Claim you?" Aubrey laughed. "I would sooner claim the devil as my father."

"Your father," he sneered, equally sardonic. "I didn't even believe the lie when she told me. It could have been from the leavings of a dozen men."

"There was only you."

"Is that what she told you? What about Granger? She jumped into his bed so fast there were scuff marks on her heels."

Aubrey shook her head. "You just couldn't accept the fact that she married someone else. *Loved* someone else. Jonathan Granger found her and took her in off the streets. He saved her life. He made her feel like a human being again, not just a piece of property. He loved her and respected her and offered her the happiness and peace she never had with you."

"I intended to give her the world, but she couldn't wait."

"You swept her off her feet with promises, then tried to make her into a high-priced whore."

"I never heard her complain."

"Because she loved you. In the beginning she loved you and she was too blinded to see how you were destroying her, dragging her down to your own level."

Fleming threw back his head and laughed. "The nobleman's daughter. Snatched her fresh out of the convent, I did, and she came willingly enough, even though her family disowned her. After a while, she didn't look too noble, either, with her legs spread and her body sweating for more. But then I'm sure you know all about that, don't you? You have the same look she did. The same pride, the same arrogance that was always there like an open challenge. I hated that look. And I hated her for never losing it."

"Except in Jonathan Granger's arms?"

Fleming lashed out and slapped her viciously with the flat of his hand. She stumbled back from the force of it, but continued staring at him with open contempt.

"You're not my daughter," he grated. "You're *her* daughter, all right, but you're not mine."

"The only father I ever knew is dead," she agreed. "You were just a bad mistake that was made a long time ago."

Fleming struck her again and again she stood her ground, defying him.

"You're Granger's brat, all right," he hissed. "I should pull the trigger on you here and now and finish a job that should have been done ten years ago."

"Then why don't you—Father?"

He bunched his fist to strike her again, but something in her eyes stopped him. He backed away a few steps, fighting to bring himself under control.

"No," he said malevolently. "No, that would be too easy. And you've gone to so much trouble to arrange this little reunion, the least I can do is make our final parting memorable."

He backed up farther and went to the door, barely turning his head as he shouted to someone out in the hallway. "Bonney! Bonney, get in here!"

Billy sauntered through the door a moment later, his eyes flicking once around the room before settling on Aubrey and the wide trickle of blood seeping from the cut on her lip.

"You need a hand, boss?" he inquired.

"Take this . . . woman . . . downstairs. I want her locked in the storeroom and a guard placed on the door.

When the others catch up to McBride and bring him back, we'll see if we can't arrange some interesting entertainment."

"Sure thing, Mr. Fleming," Billy said, and walked toward Aubrey.

"Give her to him and you won't see either of them again," Greaves sneered. "Not if you're trusting a friend of McBride's to lock her up."

"What do you mean, a friend of—"

"I saw them talking in the street today . . . laughing, smiling, joking. I saw them shake hands too, like they were making some sort of deal between them."

Fleming whirled on Billy a split second before Greaves lunged for the Remington he had dropped in his tussle with Magenta. He aimed at Fleming, but the size and feel of the weapon was unfamiliar and he sent the first shot thudding into the paneling behind the gambler's head. Before he could fire the second, Billy's gun was out of the holster and two rounds blazed from the barrel, both landing dead center of Darby's forehead, causing a dark plume of blood to blossom from the adjoining holes and leak sluggishly down between the agent's startled eyes.

Billy fired off two more rounds and shoved Aubrey toward the window. Fleming dove behind a wing chair, but one of the bullets caught the stock of his rifle, jerking it back in his hands and sending the shot blasting over their heads. What was left of the window shattered into a million fragments of glittering powder and Billy shoved Aubrey again, urging her over the sill and throwing the bulging pillow slip after her. He emptied the last two chambers of one gun in Fleming's direction and started firing his second at the lamps behind the chair, forcing Fleming to scramble back from the spray of broken glass and burning oil.

The random volley kicked up smoke and wood

splinters, and sent shards of·glass slicing across the room. In the midst of it all, Magenta stood frozen by terror, surrounded by pandemonium and scalding splashes of flaming oil. She covered her ears with her hands and screamed. She screamed and screamed and kept on screaming, the sound following Billy as he swung himself out of the window and ran after Aubrey to the end of the balcony. There, a shout from below had him lifting her over the rail and dropping her into a pair of waiting arms.

Fleming shook off the particles of glass stuck to his clothes and ran for the window. Magenta, her screams still as piercing as they were deafening, moved to block his path, her hands clawing for his shoulders, her grip deathlike in its refusal to let him pass.

"Get out of my way, you stupid cow!" he shouted. "Get out of my way, or so help me—"

Outside in the alleyway, Billy landed catlike on the ground beside Aubrey, and Christian, wary of the shouts and commotion starting to come from the main floor of the casino, acknowledged Billy's grin with a crude oath.

"You took your damn sweet time getting out of there."

Billy spared a broad wink for Aubrey as he knocked the empty shell casings out of his guns and started to reload. "Told you not to worry. We had everything under control."

A particularly loud blast of gunfire, followed by an abrupt end to Magenta's screams, had Billy and McBride turning to stare up at the second-floor windows. In the next instant, gunfire erupted from the lower level, sending Billy into a dusty roll behind the cover of a nearby horse trough. McBride dropped into a crouch, the booming shots from his rifle driving the dark shapes back from the lighted windows. Billy, reloaded and ready, fired at a movement near the swinging doors, and a moment later, the body of Charlie Boon staggered clumsily outward. He twisted with the impact of another slug and reeled back, spread-eagled, to crash through the Eagle's plate-glass window.

At the first sound of gunshots, the street in front of the Golden Eagle had cleared, the pedestrian traffic scattering like a school of fish startled by a plunging rock. The screams and running townspeople, combined with the gunfire exchanged between the street and the casino, were bound to draw Fleming's men back, and, on a hissed command from Christian, Billy was up and running again, heading for the dark alley across the street. There, a lone figure in an oversized poncho stood cracking off shot after shot at anything that moved behind a door or window in the casino.

Aubrey ran a step behind McBride, her hand firmly grasped in his, her arm nearly wrenched from the socket as he pulled her along the alley. Billy was reloading again, and on his shout, Sun Shadow spun and darted after McBride. A second shout and twelve emptied chambers sent Billy running along the blackness of the alley. He caught up to McBride and Sun Shadow, and, working with deadly efficiency, they ran from building to building, street to street, stopping to fire at their pursuers in leap-frog fashion.

"We're going to need ammunition!" Billy shouted. "I'm almost out."

A shot zinged by his head, snatching off his hat, and the Kid cursed as he stood and calmly pumped a blazing barrage from both guns, firing ten, twelve smoking rounds into the shadowy niche that harbored the shootist. A choked-off scream and the sight of a body crashing facedown in the dirt ended the volley and a grunt of satisfaction sent a hail of spent metal casings into the dust at Billy's feet.

"I'm glad to see you're conserving what you have left," Christian remarked dryly.

Billy frowned. "He shot my hat! And just after I got it good and broke in."

"A major crime by any standards," Christian agreed. "Come on. We can't afford to get pinned down."

Aubrey's hand was swallowed into his again and she was led down another maze of streets. They could hear shouts and gunfire behind them, but fading farther and farther back.

"It won't last," Christian said of their ability to elude their hunters. "They'll be on us like fleas on a dog if we stop. Where the hell is Sun Shadow?"

They had ducked behind a low adobe wall; Billy was reloading, Aubrey was panting to catch her breath, and Christian was standing in full view of anyone with a good sight on his rifle.

Sun Shadow stumbled out of the alleyway a moment later, his arm cradled against his chest, his face drenched in a cold, sour sweat. He crumpled to his knees just as Christian reached his side, and did not protest the plainsman's rough handling as he was half-carried, half-dragged behind the wall.

The light was not very good, shed by a miserly quarter moon and a hazed awning of stars, but there was more than enough to see the wide black stain of blood that soaked the front of the Ute's shirt and halfway down his breeches.

"Christ!" McBride was plainly shocked. "Why didn't you say something?"

Aubrey looked over at him. "You didn't know?"

"He said it was a scratch! Some hell of a scratch, you damned half-breed fool!"

Sun Shadow's eyes had been closed. He opened them at this and smiled tightly. "I recall the scratch you wore down from the mountains, *yanqui.* You were nearer the grave than I."

Christian followed his gaze to the open vee of his shirt, to the faintly visible line of the scar that carved a swath across his chest and belly.

"I was young and stupid and out to prove I was every bit the warrior you were," he said in soft Shoshonean. "You have nothing to prove to me, my brother."

"But much to make up for." Sun Shadow's head sank back against the cool stone. He held Christian's gaze a few moments longer, then gave way to the incredible heaviness of his lashes.

Aubrey removed her single layer of petticoat and began tearing it in strips. "He can't go on much longer or much farther, or he'll bleed to death."

"I've got eyes," Christian snapped. "I can see that."

Aubrey flinched from the contempt in his voice, feeling helpless and useless, and burdened under more guilt than she thought she could possibly bear. Christian was too busy packing the wound on Sun Shadow's shoulder, too angry with himself to notice how very close to tears she was. And neither one of them had noticed that Billy had slipped away until he returned, leaping over the wall with a triumphant grin. In each hand he carried two boxes of .45 ammunition, and in each pocket, as many rifle cartridges as he could fit.

"The way I figure it," he said, matter-of-factly transferring half of his booty into Christian's hands, "if we can make it down to the river, we got us a good chance of catching some horses and tailing out along the arroyo."

"How close are Fleming's men?"

"Close enough to smell through a wad of snot . . . ah . . . beggin' your pardon, ma'am."

"Then we'd better move. Here, take this—" He handed Billy Sun Shadow's rifle, and, after a few seconds of hard debate, thrust one of Charlie Boon's navy Colts into Aubrey's hand. Without another word, he hefted Sun Shadow up onto his shoulders, holding him by an arm and a leg, adjusting the weight and balance as he ran.

They found horses hobbled near the river, and with Christian doubling behind a slumped Sun Shadow, and Billy in the saddle behind Aubrey, they urged the animals into a fast gallop and headed for the bridge, and beyond it, the arroyo leading out of Old Santa Fe.

Fleming's men were waiting. They heard the pounding hoofbeats and started firing, more of them than McBride had anticipated, and he and Billy were forced to rein to a breakneck halt and veer onto another street. Some of Fleming's men were mounted and gave chase. Billy fired from the saddle, one arm around Aubrey's waist, the other stretched out behind, blasting shot after shot into the charging gunfighters.

They found a narrow bend in the river and splashed across, the horses thrashing the water into white fountains of spray. They were on the opposite bank and breaking for the arroyo when Aubrey felt their horse take a terrible lurching step sideways.

"Billy!" she screamed.

He turned and braced his arms around her, flinging them both out of the saddle seconds before the shrieking animal somersaulted end over end in a boiling cloud of dust. Billy was on his feet almost immediately, running and dragging Aubrey toward the deep scar of the arroyo. There was no sign of Christian ahead of them, no sign he had even seen them go down.

"Go!" Billy shouted, and pushed her over the scrublined embankment. "Run! I'll cover you as long as I can!"

Aubrey scrambled down the caked and crumbling incline, her skirt snagging on thornbushes, her bare feet skidding on stones and razor-sharp curls of sun-baked mud. She ran with her hair streaming out behind her and her vision blurred with fright, her heart pounding in her chest and the fear tearing at her lungs.

They were all around her, on both sides of the arroyo, shouting as they searched, cursing as they tried to dodge the lethal fire spewing from Billy's guns. Aubrey felt something bump against her leg, like a kick from an angry child, and she went down in a painful, sliding sprawl, the skin peeled from arms and elbows and knees.

She kept her frantic grip on the navy Colt and scrambled to her feet again, but something was wrong with her leg; it dragged slightly, causing her to stumble into a tangle of spiked scrub.

"There's the bitch!"

"After her!"

"Catch her!"

"Don't let her get away!"

Aubrey tripped again as the terror shot up her spine. It was the voice! The same voice from the Dream! And he was right behind her, plunging through the scrub like a charging bull . . . *laughing!*

Aubrey ran, heedless of the pain to her cut feet, blindly disregarding the stream of hot, slick blood that ran down her leg. Reality melted into the nightmare and she felt herself sliding into the role she had played out so many times in her dreams. The sound of gunfire and shouting faded and there was only the hammering beat of her heart and the sound of her own labored breath echoing in her ears. *He* was out there. *He* was coming for her. *He* was reaching out his hands to catch her and this time there would be no waking up!

Something exploded in the air beside her—a bullet struck a skeletal cottonwood not a foot away—and she veered out into the middle of the arroyo, forsaking the scant protection of the weeds and brush for the extra speed she might gain running along the basin of the dry riverbed.

A man plunged out of the shadows ahead and she changed directions mid-stride, running back the way she had come. A second shadow rose out of the scrub, blocking her retreat, and a third loomed out of the darkness, laughing in a coarse, grating voice that sent the horror pounding into her temples.

His hand came within reach and snatched at the ends of her hair. She reeled away, but he was quicker, despite his size, and a second grab was successful in jerking her off balance and sending her slamming against the sheer face of the embankment. The solid, stinking bulk of his body crushed against her, pinning her arms painfully behind her, and driving the air from her lungs as effectively as if she had been punched.

"Well now, lookee here." Scud Holwell twisted his fist deeper into her hair, angling her face into the stronger light. "Mr. Fleming told me you was back. 'Course, I didn't believe him at first, but now . . ." His one eye glittered menacingly as he reached down and fondled the shape of her breasts and thighs. "Yeah. Yeah, I remember what a sweet little thing you was, girlie, and how much I was lookin' forward to takin' you for a long, long ride. Seems we just got started, though, an' you up and ran away."

His hand stroked her breasts again, rough enough to tear the cotton at the seams, and Aubrey felt the bile rising in her throat, hot and sour.

"Ain't it nice we got us a second chance to get acquainted?"

Aubrey forced herself to meet the single staring eye. A second chance? Yes, she did have that, didn't she?

She numbed her mind to the filthy gropings of his hands and tightened her grip on the navy Colt she held concealed behind her back. She'd had him in her sights in the Golden Eagle, but waited too long and thought about it too much. She was not thinking now. She was only waiting.

"Scud! Hey, Scud! They got the other one. They got the Kid. Fleming wants you to bring the girl over here. Hey? You need a hand?"

"I got me a hand*ful,* boy," Holwell grinned, tearing the cotton lower so that her breast was free to be squeezed and mashed by a calloused palm. "In fact, I got me two hands full of the sweetest-lookin' meat this side of Texas, and I ain't about to let it slip away a second time."

The teeth that showed through his leering grin were broken and uneven, stained black from decay. The rank smell of his breath pressed so hotly against her face acted like a burned feather to keep Aubrey's mind clear and focused on nothing more than forcing back the hammer on the navy Colt. She ignored the pain and the disgust; she refused to give him the satisfaction of seeing her falter as his fingers probed and poked and dug hurtfully at her flesh.

"Holwell!"

It was Fleming's voice, accompanied by the brisk sound of approaching footsteps, and an odd look came over Holwell's face as he stepped back—sprang back, almost, and turned to search out Fleming's shadow, eagerly seeking approval for what he had done.

"I caught her for you, boss. I caught the thieving bitch!"

Aubrey eased forward just enough to bring the Colt out from behind her back. Holwell didn't see it, not until the nickel-plated barrel was planted solidly against the paunch of his belly. She pulled the trigger, sending the pin of the hammer snapping against the fulminate cap of the bullet casing. The shot, launched by forty grains of black powder, plowed horizontally through the fat and gristle of his gut, ripping through muscles and intestines, and deflecting upward to explode through two shattered ribs.

The recoil almost tore Aubrey's arm from the shoulder socket, but she cocked the hammer and fired again, the second bullet blowing a huge, gaping hole out of his groin and sending shreds of bloody flesh and tissue splattering in all directions. She would have fired a third time, but Fleming was by her side, his fist lashing out at the Colt, knocking the barrel sideways so that the shot thudded harmlessly into the ground.

Holwell had spun sideways with the impact of the first bullet; the second doubled him over and sent him sprawling against the embankment. As he slid downward, he clamped his arms over his belly, his face twisted with the brilliant agony of the pain shearing his body in half.

A low, primitive wail choked its way up his throat when he saw the damage Aubrey had wrought. He lifted his hands and stared at the bright, fresh slicks of blood smearing his palms and fingers, then raised his gaze higher and fixed his one good eye on Fleming's torchlit features.

"The little bitch," he gasped. "She shot me!"

"She certainly did," Fleming said, wincing involuntarily at the spreading stain between Holwell's legs. "I suppose someone was bound to do it sooner or later. A pity. You were useful, despite your . . . peccadilloes."

Holwell gulped at a mouthful of air and stretched out an imploring hand. "I'll be okay, boss. If you'll just help me up . . . ?"

Fleming debated the request and the bloodied, outstretched hand with equal indifference. "Of course, Whitey Martin was a good man too, wasn't he? I don't imagine you knew it at the time, but everything Whitey did . . . and I do mean *everything*"—he added with a crooked smile—"he did on my orders. Not like some others who thought they could take unwarranted liberties without my being any the wiser."

"But b-boss, I—"

"I wanted the woman brought back to me alive. I wanted Granger dead, but I wanted the woman brought back alive and *untouched*. And if what I was told tonight was true, you not only disobeyed the one order, you disobeyed both."

Holwell's eye flicked wildly from the master he worshiped so consumately to the pale and trembling figure of the woman who stood beside him. His lips curled back with loathing, and then with a bleated plea as he saw Fleming raise his gun and shoot point blank. Holwell's body jerked once, then crumpled slowly down the dirt wall, leaving a wide, dark smear of gore where the back of his head had been.

"That was for you, my dear," Fleming murmured, turning to Aubrey. "It was the least I could do. But now, unfortunately, we still have our own debt to settle."

Without the slightest change of expression, he pressed the barrel of his gun against her temple. His thumb cocked the hammer . . .

. . . and he fired.

31

Christian had heard Aubrey's shout and had turned in time to glimpse their horse going down and the two of them jumping clear. His own animal, unfamiliar with his commands and balking under the weight of two big men, refused to answer the reins and kept blundering forward, reeling and crashing through a small garden and tearing out a pole that supported the thatched overhang of an adobe house.

Christian cleared the yard and made it down into the belly of the arroyo, but there were several hundred yards of galloped terror put between him and the gunfight they had left behind, before he could saw enough pain into the horse's mouth to convince him to stop. Christian threw himself out of the saddle and smacked the beast on the rump so that it would keep running and carry Sun Shadow out of danger.

Rifle in hand, he started running back, but had barely covered twenty yards when the ground began to shake and tremble beneath him. There were riders in the arroyo—a score of horsemen at least, judging from the sound and fury of the thunderous hoofbeats, and Christian cursed as he dove for cover, knowing this was it.

This was the end. Sun Shadow would have ridden straight into their midst. Billy and Aubrey were trapped . . .

He rolled into the scrub and came up with his rifle cocked and ready. The lead rider came into sight, a tall, lean figure in a caped greatcoat, mounted on a mottled gray stallion. Christian took aim and started to pull the trigger, but something about the stallion looked shockingly familiar, and he pulled up on the nose of the carbine, too late to stop the shot, but narrowly in time to miss the startled rider.

Ethan McBride reined to a halt in a choking swirl of dust. He recognized his brother and shouted for his men to hold their fire.

"Where the hell did you come from?" Christian asked, stunned.

"I figured you would be neck-deep in some kind of shit by now, little brother, so the boys and I thought we'd come into town to have a look. We met Manuelo on the road a few miles back and he suggested we move on up to a gallop."

Christian grinned through the sweat and dust caking his face. "I should have known you couldn't take your own advice to leave well enough alone."

"Runs in the blood, I suppose," Ethan said, grimacing. "Is it Fleming?"

Christian swung himself up into the saddle behind his brother. "He's got Billy and . . . a friend . . . pinned down about half a mile up ahead."

"You should pick your friends more carefully."

Christian's reply was smothered under the rolling echo of three loud gunshots. A fourth, poignant in its isolation, spurred Ethan and his men forward without any further need for conversation.

•

Aubrey heard the explosion and felt the burn of gunpowder sear her temple and cheek. The navy Colt slipped out of her numbed fingers and she felt her legs fold strengthless beneath her. She landed heavily on her knees and raised her hands instinctively to her face, half-expecting most of it to be gone. She knew she was screaming because of the dry pain in her throat, but the only sound was a thin, watery reverberation that seemed to be coming from very far away.

Fleming cocked the gun again. He waited until she stopped screaming, until she realized she was still alive by the grace and mercy of a split-second reprieve, then dug the gun into her temple again.

"You have something of mine," he said evenly. "I want it."

Aubrey heard the murmur of sound and lowered her hands from her ears. The one side was still ringing with the blast of the gunshot and she could feel something wet and sticky trickling down the side of her neck, but she was alive!

Someone had made a makeshift torch out of a branch of deadwood and there were five or six men grouped around them, more walking down the arroyo and dragging a semiconscious, groaning Billy Bonney between them. One side of his face and neck was awash in blood from a graze that had sheared a bright red stripe through the unruly tufts of pale hair. His eyes were rolling with the effort to stay even partially conscious, fighting instinctively to avoid what was surely coming for him at the end of a rope.

"An amazing young man," Fleming remarked, following Aubrey's glance. "I haven't done an accurate count yet, but I would estimate I'm short at least a dozen good men because of you and your"—he stroked the metal gun barrel along her cheek—"misguided sense of vengeance.

"Odd, isn't it?" he continued. "How in the end, it is always the little sentimental things that trip us up. You, for instance. You are obviously brilliant at what you do. You could have gone so much further, achieved so much more, but no. You squander your talents on sentiment. On something so trivial—" He held up the emerald broach and admired it under the torchlight. "I might even have given it to you, had you asked."

He sighed and closed his fist around the broach. "Where are the rest of my beauties? The money and the documents you took from my safe—I want them too. Where are they?"

Aubrey frowned and looked at Billy. She remembered him shoving the pillow slip into her hands and pushing her out the window . . . and she remembered clutching it as she ran through the streets of Santa Fe. She thought she might have had it when he lifted her onto the horse, but after that . . . ?

"Well? I'm waiting."

If she admitted she didn't know, he would have no more use for her or Billy. On the other hand, if she said she did know, he would kill them the instant he uncovered the lie.

And where was Christian? Surely Fleming would have gloated if he had a body to show her.

"Where . . . are . . . they?"

Aubrey returned his stare calmly. "I don't know."

Fleming's expression did not change. He gave no warning for the two swift, cutting blows he dealt her cheek with the flat of his hand, and she cried out involuntarily as the pain crested over existing pain, waves upon waves of it that left her reeling.

Her neck was wrenched cruelly as he grasped a handful of hair and twisted her face up to his. "Don't play games with me; you won't win. Where are my jewels?"

"I don't know," she gasped.

His grip tightened and the muscles in her neck were stretched to the point of tearing away from the bone.

"Tell me, you little whore. Tell me, or so help me, I'll pass you around to each of these men and offer them a hundred dollars bonus for each time they make you scream! Some of them can get pretty damned creative too, especially if the price is right." He jerked her neck again. "Well?"

"Is this what you're looking for, Fleming?"

Fleming whirled around, searching out the source of the wry chuckle. Aubrey's view was obstructed but she searched as well, the voice familiar, yet somehow not familiar at all. She saw Fleming's men reach collectively for their guns, and she heard the corresponding *chic-chock* of twenty or more Winchester carbines being cocked and shouldered as deterrents. They were completely surrounded; there were men braced wide-legged on both sides of the embankment, and more moving forward, even as they watched, out of the shadows of the arroyo itself.

The man who had spoken stood on the bank above them, and Aubrey had to squeeze her eyes tightly shut before taking a second look. He was a leaner, more statesman-like version of Christian McBride, his face cut from the same rakish mold, his hair a shade darker and trimmed into neat, short waves. He wore a long, back-slit greatcoat and carried a scroll-butted Winchester in one hand. In the other, he held the bulging pillow slip.

"Ethan McBride," Fleming snarled. "You're a little late. The party is over."

"It sounded to me like you were just trying to get it started."

"This is none of your affair. You have no business interfering. This is between your brother and me."

"Christian?" Aubrey cried softly. "Where is he?"

"Right here, *querida,*" Christian said, stepping sound-lessly out of the shadows behind them. He had a gun on Fleming and was able to disarm the gambler before there was any time to react. He tucked Fleming's gun into his belt and holstered his own before reaching down to help Aubrey to her feet. The expression on his face, when he saw the bluing bruises on her cheek and the cut, swollen lip, was nothing short of terrifying.

"You just keep adding to your debts, Max," he said, his voice low and chilling.

"My debts? She's the one who broke into my casino and robbed me blind. I'm just trying to get back what's mine."

Christian ran a trembling hand through the slippery softness of Aubrey's hair, holding her gaze for a small, breathless eternity before he finally turned and looked at Fleming. "I heard it was the other way around."

He leaned forward and plucked the emerald broach out of Fleming's hand, turning it into the torchlight so that the stones sparkled with dazzling green refractions of the flame. He admired it a moment, then offered it to Aubrey.

"I believe this belongs to you?"

Aubrey curled her fingers around the broach and felt the warmth in the emerald spread up her arm and flow through her body.

"Thank you," she whispered.

"My pleasure."

"That doesn't change the fact that she is still guilty of robbery," Fleming said tersely. "And of murder I saw hor pull a gun on a man and shoot him, coldly and deliberately—you can see for yourself, his guns are still holstered."

Ethan McBride, who had not moved a muscle since making his presence known, turned his head now, look-ing first at the gory, lifeless body of Scud Holwell, then at Aubrey. "Is that true, ma'am? Did you shoot this man?"

Caught between the considerable power of two pairs of McBride eyes, Aubrey felt herself swaying with a weakness that had nothing to do with her injuries. Even so, she straightened and adamantly tilted her chin upward, her hand tightening around the broach until she felt the facets cutting into her skin.

"Yes," she admitted. "It's true."

"It's also true," Fleming continued, "that she broke a man out of jail tonight—" He glanced maliciously at Christian. "An ex-convict with a violent history of crime, who, I might add, was incarcerated on his own charges of murder."

"You have been busy, haven't you?" Ethan murmured, eyeing his brother.

"It's been a full day," Christian agreed blithely.

"As for Billy—" Fleming hooked a thumb over to where Billy Bonney was just managing to struggle drunkenly onto his knees. "He'll probably be shot on sight once it becomes general knowledge that he shot and killed the beautiful and defenseless Magenta Royale, Jewel of New Orleans."

Billy's head swung up and he tried to focus on one of Fleming's three heads. "Kill't her? I never kill't her! She was hollerin' like a stuck pig last I saw and heard."

"I have witnesses who will testify that they saw you gun down Darby Greaves in cold blood, then turn your jealous rage on Magenta—a rage that triggered a killing spree through the streets of Santa Fe." Fleming smiled slickly. "There isn't a jury in the land would take longer than five minutes to return a verdict."

"She was alive, last I saw," Billy insisted. "And Greaves—"

"Greaves drew first," Aubrey said, laying her hand on Christian's arm. "It was self-defense. Magenta *was* alive when we left. She was alive and screaming and . . . and . . ." She looked at Fleming, mistaken in her belief that she could not suffer any more shocks. "You," she whispered. "You must have killed her."

Fleming arched a brow. "Now who would believe that? She was my star attraction. I paid an exorbitant fee to bring her here all the way from Kansas. Furthermore, it would be my word against yours whether or not she was alive when you shot your way out of my casino. My word . . . against the word of a liar, a thief, and a murderess."

"You're making a damn good case for shooting you here and now," Christian warned.

"You would have to shoot each and every one of my men as well," Fleming pointed out. "Are you prepared to do that?"

"If I have to, yes."

"I . . . ah . . . don't know as we'll have to do anything quite as drastic as all that," Ethan said casually. "Not if we were to, say, offer up the contents of this sack in exchange for their silence?" He raised the stuffed pillow slip and upended it, dumping the contents onto the ground. A couple of the bundles of cash fell over the lip of the embankment, earning hard, speculative stares from the men trapped within the torchlit circle. One of the leather cases split open as well, spilling its glittering collection of loose gemstones onto the dry earth. There was a not-so-subtle stirring of interest in the ranks of Fleming's men—all of them hired gunslingers who would not earn, in their entire lifetime, a fraction of what was spilling on the ground in front of them.

"What do you say, boys?" Ethan asked. "A hundred dollars a month for your loyalty . . . or several tens of thousands to get on your horses and ride on out of here?"

"No!" Fleming roared. "You can't do this! This is my property! It's all mine—you can't just give it away!"

Ethan merely smiled. "Well, boys?"

A few of the men held back a moment or two longer, but the majority rushed forward and started clawing and scrambling in the dirt to pick up the money and jewels Ethan kicked over the embankment.

Fleming screamed again, and in his rage, he lunged for the navy Colt Aubrey had dropped earlier. He twisted and came up firing, but Christian's hand had moved like a blur, drawing and spitting four quick shots before Fleming's first round had cleared the chamber. All four bullets caught him high in the chest and sent him flailing back in the dirt, where he lay stunned and openmouthed, his body slowly curling into a fetal position, rigid with pain and disbelief. The gun wavered in his hand and he tried to fire off another wild shot, but a rifle boomed somewhere out in the darkness and the top of Fleming's head exploded in a mist of red and gray, removing any further threat with a permanence that won absolute silence from everyone in the arroyo.

A faint scuffling of footsteps brought Sun Shadow into the amber circle of torchlight. There was a pencil-thin line of smoke still creaming from the muzzle of his carbine. When he stepped fully into the light, he met Christian's gaze and gave a small nod of satisfaction, his regal warrior's face cracking into a smile even as he pitched forward in a dead faint.

32

Fighting tears and a sudden, aching exhaustion, Aubrey left the confusion and torchlights behind, and walked back to the river. Sun Shadow and Billy were in good hands. Ethan McBride had taken charge at once, dispatching men for a wagon to take the two wounded men to a doctor, and another to collect the bodies and transport them to the undertaker's. Fleming's hired guns had vanished into the night, and Christian, after assuring himself the graze on Aubrey's leg was just a flesh wound, had left her briefly to talk to his brother.

The brief conversation turned into lengthy explanations and Aubrey suspected she would soon be the prime, if not sole topic of their discussions. She did not have to be told what the results of those discussions would be. There was sure to be a furor over the gun battle and the deaths. Fleming's friends and business associates would demand an accounting, not to mention a scapegoat or two to cover their losses when it became known that Maxwell Fleming had cheated them.

She did not have to be told she would have to leave Santa Fe, the sooner the better, nor did she particularly

want to see the look on Christian's face when he told
her.

Slipping away unnoticed, she retraced the mad dash
she had made from the river and found a wide, level
place on the bank where she could sit and gingerly
bathe her leg and cool the skinned and burning soles of
her feet. The water was sweet and cold, having flowed
down out of the mountain ranges, and she drank with
the thirst of a parched desert traveler. She rinsed her
arms and her neck and bathed the cuts on her cheeks
and mouth. Her blouse was torn, stained with blood—
she did not know whose—and not knowing or caring
who could see her, she stripped it off and washed it,
soaking it and wringing it until the stains were diluted
enough to be hardly noticeable.

Before she could shake it out and put it back on,
however, a fringed buckskin shirt was draped around
her bare shoulders.

"It's not much cleaner, but at least it's in one piece."

She hadn't heard Christian walking up behind her;
she certainly hadn't seen him. Feeling awkward and self-
conscious, and more than a little off balance, she
clutched the shirt around her shoulders and stood up
beside him.

"I . . . thought you would have stayed with Sun
Shadow."

"He's all right. He's in good hands." He paused and
blew out a soft, exasperated breath. "I thought you
would have stayed put, like I told you to. Running away
from me twice in one night . . . you're not doing much
for my reputation as a lady's man."

Aubrey smiled faintly, a little tearfully, and simply
looked up at the tall, half-naked plainsman who, with
the breeze ruffling the ends of his hair and swamping
her with the overwhelmingly potent scent of recent violence, reminded her more than ever of a golden-haired

archangel, slightly battered, slightly tarnished, but far more noble a creature than she deserved to have come to her rescue.

"I'm sorry," she said. "It was all my fault. I should have told you . . . everything . . . right from the beginning."

"Well"—he reached out and gently pried her fingers loose from the buckskin—"maybe not everything. And maybe not *right* from the beginning." He slipped her arms into the sleeves, one at a time as if he were helping a small child dress. "Mysteries aren't half so challenging to solve if you know all the answers ahead of time, and you, Miss Aubrey Blue, were both: a mystery and a challenge. One I fear . . . I hope . . . I will never solve completely."

Aubrey raised huge drowning blue eyes to his, her expression as solemn as his was cautious.

"There is . . . one other important thing you have to know," she whispered.

"*Have* to know?"

"Ought to know," she said, amending it. "And you ought to hear it from me, not someone else."

"God love me," he sighed, and hands that were capable of crushing skin and bone to pulp, raked into the silky heaviness of her hair and trembled with the need to prove themselves capable of infinite tenderness. "Does it have to be tonight? Between the three of you— you, Bruster, and Dolores—I don't know how many more revelations I can take."

She lowered her lashes and bit her lip. "I wondered how you knew about the broach."

"They did not volunteer the information easily," he assured her. "And they did warn me there was more to come, but . . ." He waited a moment, and when she still had not looked up of her own accord, he tucked a finger under her chin and gently forced her. "You don't have to tell me anything you don't want to tell me—you never did, despite my obstinance to the contrary. All I ever really wanted—then and now—was for the things you did tell me to be the truth. If you care for someone . . . or if you want that someone to care for you, *you have to trust them.* You don't hide things and you don't lie to them no matter how hard you think they might take the truth. Now, having said all that"—he dropped his hands as if he had already said too much—"can we please just go somewhere—anywhere, I don't give a damn, because frankly, the last thing I want to do with you right now is talk. To be perfectly *truthful,* I want you in a room without any clocks or windows so we can't tell if it's day or night, and I want us both naked enough so that neither one of us will care."

Christian saw a single, bright tear swell at the corner of her eye and he cursed softly in defeat.

"All right," he murmured, bringing her into his arms. "All right, *querida,* tell me. Tell me what it is that's tearing you up inside."

He closed his eyes, expecting the worst, not even beginning to know what the worst could possibly be. He was conscious of her cheek pressed against his bare flesh, and conscious of the threads of her hair snagging on the coarse growth of stubble on his chin. He knew her lips were moving and he heard the words she was saying, and yet when he opened his eyes and stared straight out over the rippling black ribbon of the river, he admittedly, ashamedly, had to fight the urge to push her away.

"What . . . did you say?"

Aubrey felt the shiver of tension course through him, and she heard his heart stumble over a beat before throbbing loudly against her ear. She extricated herself from his arms—not as difficult a task as she might have hoped, and she raised her hands, lost within the buckskin sleeves, and laid them lightly on his chest.

"Maxwell Fleming was my father."

Christian was watching her lips move, thinking a thousand things at once, none of which were reflected accurately in the molten silver of his eyes. What Aubrey did see, however, prompted her to bow her head and simply say what had to be said, in the harsh, plain truths he had demanded.

"My mother was only sixteen when she met Fleming. She had been schooled in a convent and spent most of her life sheltered by family and church. Maxwell Fleming was the total opposite of everything she'd known. Brash, handsome, ambitious . . . an Anglo who cared nothing for tradition and Old World customs. She was naive enough to believe him when he said he loved her and would care for her the rest of her life. She believed him when he promised to marry her and legitimize the child she was carrying.

"She did *not* believe the rumors she heard about him —the rustling, the stealing, the murders. Nor did she believe her family when they told her Fleming had come to see them, and for a price, yes, he would marry her and save the Del Fuegas from further disgrace.

"When my mother confronted him, Fleming laughed and told her she was nothing more than a whore, and that she should be grateful he was willing to keep her at all. They had a terrible argument and in the end, he threw her out onto the streets to fend for herself. Do you know Silver City at all?"

"I know it," Christian said grimly.

"Then you also know what a woman has to do in order to survive on her own. She could have swallowed her pride and gone home, but"—she looked up and Christian could see the traits of the mother etched defiantly on the face of the daughter—"she knew the shame would have destroyed them. By then, she was noticeably pregnant, sick, and starving . . . and too disillusioned to care if she lived or died.

"That was how Jonathan Granger found her. He was in Silver City on a cattle buying trip and when he left, he took her with him. He didn't touch her. Not once. He wanted to give her the chance to heal, to know she was a human being, not just a piece of chattel to be passed from one hand to another. Under his care, she flourished. She was still young and beautiful and he was so proud of her, so loving and gentle that it would have been impossible for her not to have fallen in love with him. They married and he accepted the daughter she bore as his own, and for five wonderful years we lived peacefully and happily, and there was never any reason to believe it would change."

The tears started to collect along Aubrey's lashes again, glittering there like so many precious jewels. "But it did change. It changed the day Fleming showed up in Santa Fe. He had prospered in those same five years. He had more money, more power, more greedy friends in high places willing to turn their backs while he and his kind took over the valley. He found out Luisa was here. He had heard about the beautiful Mrs. Granger. Jonathan was a respected rancher, his wife was a charming and gracious woman whom everyone loved and admired. She was happy and content, and very much in love with her husband, and . . . I don't know . . . perhaps that was what galled Fleming the most. At any rate, he became obsessed with getting her back and destroying Jonathan Granger. He tried everything short of kidnapping to lure her away from her home and family, and when she refused and kept on refusing, his obsession turned to hatred, and one night . . . he sent six of his men to deal with Jonathan Granger."

Christian listened without interruption as she related

the events of that night ten years ago. He remembered
vividly the terror of the dream he'd wakened her from
back at the Cimarron, and he heard it again now in her
voice as she told him of the brutal rape and murder of
her mother, the killing of Jonathan Granger, the loss of
her two small brothers and her fruitless search for them
afterward.

"There was nothing I could do. I was alone and
frightened. The wound on my arm became infected and
I wandered for days in a fever before Bruster found me.
And then . . . I was just grateful to be safe and warm
and moving miles away from the horror I'd left behind. I
didn't care that Bruster was a thief and a petty swindler.
It didn't matter that his sense of values was judged on a
different scale from everyone else's. He made me laugh,
and he made me see how easy it was to use a man's own
greed to destroy him. That's why I came back to Santa
Fe. I knew I couldn't physically kill Fleming, in spite of
how much I hated him, but I knew I was capable of
ruining him, maybe even destroying him."

"Weren't you afraid he would recognize you?"

"I don't think he ever saw me, maybe once or twice
out of morbid curiosity, but never close enough that I
remember seeing him. I was surprised tonight to find
out he'd even bothered to learn my name."

Christian looked up at that.

"It's Alicia," she said with a tight smile. "I haven't
used it for years; it seemed to belong to another life,
another person."

He nodded and bent his head again, his fingers absently picking at a sliver of wood embedded in his palm.
He had all the pieces of the puzzle now, and so much
was explained, so much was clear . . . except, perhaps,
how she could bear to have a man—any man—touch
her. He had never given rape much credence as a crime,
thinking only that it was a stupid, cowardly act commit-

ted by men who had no other way of proving their manhood. But now, knowing that Aubrey had suffered at the
hands of just such an animal, the thought of it made him
sick with anger. It made the blood burn through his
veins like acid and it made him very conscious of the
pain his own crudeness and ignorance must have
caused. At the way station, out in the desert, at the river
crossing . . . all of the times he had mocked her, challenged her, even . . . dear God, even accused her of
whoring for Fleming!

Christian groaned and curled his hands into fists,
wanting to strike out at something—anything! She was
watching him. Waiting. But what could he possibly say
to earn or deserve her forgiveness?

"I'm sorry," she cried softly. "I know I should have
told you before, but . . . I didn't know how. And then
. . . later . . . I was afraid you would hate me because
of Fleming. And I wouldn't have blamed you. I don't
blame you now."

Christian's head jerked up. "You think I'd hate you
. . . because of *him*?"

"D-Don't you?" she asked tremulously.

He unbunched his fists and took hold of her shoulders, afraid of squeezing too tightly and hurting her,
afraid of not squeezing tightly enough and losing her.

"You silly little fool," he whispered raggedly. "You
are no part of Maxwell Fleming. You never were, and
you never will be. You're a part of *me* now, do you
understand? *A part of me!*"

"You . . . still want me?" she stammered.

"Still want you?" His hands slid up into her hair
again, and he didn't know whether to laugh or cry. "You
don't think I've gone to all this trouble just to turn you
loose again, do you?"

"Oh . . ."

"Of course"—he gave as stern an imitation of a frown

as he could under the circumstances—those being the very pressing and urgent need to kiss her until she couldn't stand, and then to find that damned windowless room—"you will have to mend your ways, some. I don't particularly see myself warming to a hearth and home behind iron bars."

"Hearth and home?"

"And I definitely wouldn't take to the notion of having any Pinkerton agents sniffing around after my wife."

"Your . . . wife? You want . . . to marry me?"

Christian smiled and felt another dangerous surge of heat suffuse his belly. "For a clever woman, you can ask some mighty stupid questions. But that's okay, because there is only one question that matters right now and only one answer that is going to affect how long or how hard I'm about to kiss you." He paused for effect and lowered his voice to a husky murmur. "Did you mean what you said at the smithy this afternoon?"

Aubrey's lips parted and her eyes widened in mystification.

"That you loved me," he reminded her gently.

"I . . . didn't think you heard."

"I have ears like a hawk, madam," he said, drawing her body closer. "And I distinctly heard you say you loved me. Was it true, or were you just trying to make amends for calling me a . . . great . . . hulking . . . plainsman?"

"You are a great hulking plainsman," she said breathlessly, "but I love you with all my heart."

Christian angled her mouth higher. "And that . . . wins you the deepest, longest, wettest kiss I can give you while you still have all your clothes on."

"And if I take them off?" she asked in a whisper.

His eyes narrowed. "Can you wait until we get to the hotel before I answer that?"

Aubrey slipped her arms up and around his neck, the

motion causing the loose edges of the buckskin shirt to spread open and reacquaint her bare breasts with his. "No," she breathed. "No, I can't."

He grinned and his lips descended. "Then this is going to be a mighty interesting walk back to town."

Epilogue

It took a week for the uproar from the shoot-out to fade, a week during which Christian McBride and Aubrey seldom strayed from their hotel room. Curious passersby heard a great deal of laughter coming from the other side of the door, as well as other sounds that sent the listeners hurrying away red-faced and a little less comfortable in tight-fitting clothes.

The expected furor over the incident culminating in Maxwell Fleming's death was not as widespread or as profound as it might have been, due mainly to Ethan McBride's curiosity over the small bound ledger he found in the pillow slip. Fleming's desire to protect his own back from his corrupt associates provided Ethan with enough proof of their complicity in a multitude of crimes to silence any potential complaints from the sheriff's office right on up to the governor's seat. There was no telling, however, how far or how fast the news of Fleming's death would spread, or if the involvement of a beautiful lady gambler would capture the attention of any investigative agencies back east. Again, it was Ethan who suggested an "extended honeymoon" trip might be in order; a visit to their younger brother in Montana, for instance, where they would be out of sight and out of mind long enough for Ethan to see if anything could be done to appease the ruffled vanity of the governor of Louisiana.

Dolores and Bruster returned to Santa Fe, where Dolores packed her belongings on a flatbed and made arrangements to have it driven to San Francisco. Bruster followed docile and meek at her side—a curious turn of events that Aubrey later learned had to do with Dolores's taking possession and control of the eighteen thousand dollars Bruster had won at the faro table.

Billy, out of work and in no more serious trouble with the law than he usually was, declared his intention to leave Santa Fe and head south into Lincoln County, where he had heard there was a call going out for gunfighters. A range war was brewing and he thought it might be an interesting way to finish out the summer. He gave halfhearted promises to winter at the Double M, but neither Ethan nor Christian expected to see him there.

Sun Shadow, heavily bandaged but on the mend, insisted on returning to his own village in the mountains, but would, he assured them, appear at the Double M in time for the wedding. True to his word, he arrived a few short hours before the ceremony, the proud leader of a small caravan comprised, among others, of his wife, his newborn daughter, and four strapping sons.

It was a solemn moment and a great honor to meet Sun Shadow's family—indeed, to become a part of it through marriage, and Aubrey very proudly displayed the exquisite silver and turquoise necklace he presented as a wedding gift. With that and her mother's emerald broach pinned to the bodice of a simple white gown, Aubrey stood beside her handsome plainsman and exchanged vows before a select audience of freshly scrubbed cowhands, Utes in formal ceremonial dress, a moustachioed gambler, and a rather rotund dressmaker who sobbed and sniffled quite happily even as she elbowed her recalcitrant husband during each stage of the vows.

It was while the guests were toasting and offering best wishes to the new bride and groom, that Christian leaned over and whispered in Aubrey's ear.

"I have another small present for you."

Aubrey flushed self-consciously to the tips of her toes. She had just finished unwrapping, in front of the entire shocked gathering, the whisper-sheer nightdress he had purchased at Dolores's shop, and she wasn't the least bit sure she wanted to know the reason behind the smoky gray gleam that was in his eyes now.

He turned to Sun Shadow and nodded. The Ute raised his uninjured arm and signaled to two members of his family's party who had, up until then, remained discreetly in the background.

"You see, I have no secrets from Sun Shadow," Christian explained in quiet Shoshonean. "And when things trouble me, I speak of them freely to him." He paused, aware of Aubrey's sudden stillness beside him. "I told him your story, and when I was finished, he gave me the answer to one of the things that had been troubling me most."

Aubrey felt her knees weaken. The two young men had stopped beside Sun Shadow wary of the sudden shift of attention. Up close, they were not as old as they first appeared to be, and it could be seen that their skin was burned bronze by the constant exposure to the sun, rather than by birth. They also had startlingly clear blue eyes set into faces remarkably similar. Their hair was kept long in the manner of the Utes, but it was more auburn than black, and in the profuse sunlight, glinted with rich shades of coppery red.

"Jason?" Aubrey whispered. "Jeremy?"

The two young braves remained suspiciously aloof,

frowning at the woman whose lips moved but who said nothing. They had been surprised when Sun Shadow had ordered them to accompany him to the sprawling *rancho,* and they had been determined not to show confusion or weakness, but . . . who was this woman?

Sun Shadow resolved the dilemma by cuffing both of them soundly on the shoulder. "Can neither of you recognize your own sister?"

The twins lost their fragile hold on manliness and stared at Aubrey with the bewilderment of two thunderstruck children.

"Alicia?"

Aubrey could only nod through the tears brimming in her eyes. For a moment she thought she could not move without the support of Christian's arm around her waist, but that proved false as the two boys hurled themselves into her outstretched arms.

Christian passed a silent word of thanks to his Indian brother. He had remembered Sun Shadow telling him the story about the twin boys who had been found wandering in the foothills near their village ten years ago. They had been half-starved, half-dead from exposure, their stories so jumbled no one could make much sense out of them beyond the fact that their home had been burned out and their family murdered, not an uncommon occurrence at the time. Christian had not made the connection until Aubrey had explained her nightmare in detail and had mentioned that her brothers were twins. Then it all fit.

He watched his wife and his newfound brothers-in-law hugging and laughing and trying to speak all at once, and he felt a strange new feeling of contentment wash through him. He looked at Sun Shadow and Ethan talking together in the corner, and he saw Dolores blush as red as her hair as Bruster gave her a cuddle and a quick kiss on the cheek.

He walked out onto the broad wooden porch and patted his coat pocket for a cigar, crediting the stinging sensation in his eyes to the small sulfur explosion of the matchstick.

"Too much hearth and home for you all at once?"

Christian smiled and tossed the cheroot away without touching it to his lips. He turned and took Aubrey into his arms instead, kissing her long and deep and hard, while behind them, the crimson eye of the sun gave a last glittering wink and slipped down below the rim of the horizon.